M000085281

The book is a work of fiction. Names, characters, places, and incidents are the product of the author's imagination and are used fictitiously. Any resemblance to actual events, locales, or persons, living or dead, is coincidental.

SHADOW BOUND SOULS

Copyright © 2022 by Steven Rudy

Edited by Lydia Renfro

Cover Design by Franziska Stern - www.coverdungeon.com

– Instagram: @coverdungeonrabbit

Map Illustrations by Steven Rudy, using (Wonderdraft and Adobe Suite)

Interior Illustrations by Steven Rudy

except Illustration following Chapter 37 by Ekaterina Vitkovskaya

Published by MysticHawk Press LLC

ISBN- 978-1-7370652-3-4 (paperback)

ISBN- 978-1-7370652-4-1 (ebook)

First Edition: Feb 2022

SHADOW
BOUND
SOULS

BY
STEVEN RUDY

MYSTICHAWK
PRESS

For Lulu

For Cal

For Zuzu

ACKNOWLEDGEMENTS

First, I want to thank my wonderful wife. D, you are a force without equal and this book would not have been possible without your support. Thank you and I love you.

Thank you to my beta readers, Olivia, and Alex, you are both so integral in shaping the final story. When my ideas go wild and rampage the novel, you both spot the missteps and help me find the truth of the story.

Thank you so much to my fantastic editor. Lydia, your enthusiasm, love of books and your entire mindset toward the project, made for a perfect cohort on this journey. I'm so grateful.

Lastly, I must acknowledge my brother Matt. Matt your name is now in my book, and you can stop hounding me about it. Truly you are the best, bro.

A book must be the axe for the frozen sea within us.

— FRANZ KAFKA

A.R.C.

This is an Advanced Reader Copy of Shadow Bound Souls.

This is an uncorrected proof copy of Shadow Bound Souls, specifically issued in order to provide potential reviewers with a timely opportunity to read the novel in advance of publication. The novel has been through beta readers and revised by the author. Additionally, the manuscript received a complete substantial line edit and copy edit.

The expected price ($4.99 eBook, $14.99 paperback) and launch date (February 1, 2022) are all subject to change.

Please enjoy the novel and thank you for your time, and effort.

Happy reading,
   Steven Rudy

Contents

ILLUSTRATIONS

THE NEW WORLD

THE ANAMIC OCEAN

THE ICE PEAKS
Monarch
SEER'S BAY
HAZON

ANDAL
The Citadel

THE GREY SEA

STORMFAST SEA

Suttons Grove

DOMAL

ADALON

MAINSOLIS SEA

AQUAM
Zaro Islands

The United Scholar's Guild

THE FROZEN STRAITS

THE SOARING MOUNTAINS

MARATHAL

TOVILLORE

ELOVEEN

KOTALIA

Pardona

The Howling Forest

The Leaving Forest

ADAVAN

THE FROSTLANDS

THELMARIA

ATAVA

The Shadow Forest

AMERA

AVR NORAY

SKYVIER

POLESTIS

THE IRONLANDS Spires

FAEHATHOR MOUNTAINS

ZAWARIN

XINOR

THE WARHAWK MOUNTAINS

FORTUNES BAY

ZULU SEA

TANTOR

WYCAN

WINGTIP MOUNTAINS

ECHO CANYON

TALON

TRAPPERS BAY

STORMDARK PLATEAUS

RODAIRE VALLEY

LOWTALIA

ONYX BAY

Orvana

Fairy Hill

THE DEADLANDS

RUENOBEE

RODAIRE

RYLABYRE

Reaper's Bay

RAVENVYRE

THE DIRE

THE BROVIC OCEAN

PROLOGUE

Falling water continued to flow in cascades of splatter and spray. The humming had dissipated and the sounds of the water inside the chamber opened his eyes. Across the room, the grand window to the falls filled his vision. He scowled into the void, realizing the rogues all slipped from his grasp.

When Edward sat up, an ache spiked sharply at his side where a bruising to his bones settled into place. Each movement was unforgiving. He found his shoulder stiff at the joint when he reached to wipe clear a dribble of warm blood sliding down his temple to his cheek. Edward tried to lift free of the rock, but his hand on the chalky luminescent surface failed to find purchase. Slowly, the light in the chamber started to eat itself and the room rumbled like the very foundation was collapsing beneath him. The battle below had concluded. He could only assume the Quantum man had survived, again.

"Get up!" a dark voice commanded.

The chilling tone and resonance made Edward's skin tingle. He recognized the source but couldn't find the origin in the shadows. When it didn't speak further, Edward pushed himself to his feet and staggered back to the tomb entrance to study the symbols again. His acolytes made it clear he didn't need to enter the room, but he longed to see inside the resting place of the emperors. He wanted to claim his crystal bed for the afterlife. Outside of the copper doors, a lone object lay on the stone step: a polished black scepter resting at the entrance landing. Edward picked it up, confused, and studied the inlaid sigil lines that wrapped the object until the light shifted over the surfaces nearby. Shadows seemed to pull free from every crevasse like a living smoke moving by command.

Edward turned to find the darkness of the room gathering on the partially submerged stone steps, where it came to form a being that rendered most of the chamber's light vanquished by its presence. A moving black mist over the water collected into a hulking form with evaporating wisps of smoke lifting free. Edward watched with the same revulsion he always did, until the sinister orange eyes came alive, and Edward lowered his head in servitude.

"Leave here," the voice said, "You cannot gain access without Qudin, and he has escaped."

"Without the stone, I can't read the testament. How can I complete the task you have asked of me?" Edward inquired.

"There are other ways. I have retrieved the Scepter of Adar for you. Take it," the Wrythen ordered.

Edward didn't know who Adar was. He knew the object by another name: the Scepter of Corinsura, the Sagean Empress. The shadows swirled about him, and he placed the scepter inside his cloak.

"This is all that I require of you, here. Qudin Lightweaver has opened the tomb and in doing so, he has unlocked the Temple of Ama. Leave here and gather your Court of Dragons. Journey to the temple. There you will swell your numbers and with your acolytes risen, I shall return."

"It will be done as you say, Master," Edward said, bowing his head.

"Go, but beware. Qudin has gathered powerful allies. Do not under-estimate him again."

"I won't, but my resources are stretched."

"Ha," the entity grunted a dead laugh that made Edward cringe, "Fear not. Our numbers swell and I have many agents besides you at my disposal. Some are making discoveries even now. Be warned, your Court of Dragon's have their own goals."

The news of his acolytes was no surprise. They controlled him and he despised them for it, but he would play their game for now, because he had no other choice.

"Yes, Master."

Footsteps of soldiers rumbled into the chamber and the Wrythen's eyes tightened in a predatory glare that pierced Edward's soul before it disappeared in a powerful swirl of tangible shadow that funneled to the ceiling. The form unraveled and scattered back into the surroundings.

With his men approaching, Edward realized he was cowering against the door and adjusted his posture appropriately.

"Your Eminence, are you hurt?" the first soldier said.

Edward reached his open hand out and toward the man and ripped free the energy to heal himself. The soldier crumpled off the steps and into the pool. The Bonemen behind him halted in place with bowed heads.

"Check on the wounded and clear this place of all that dishonors it. This is the resting place of my ancestors. The site must be cleansed, immediately," Edward demanded, and strode back toward the Honor Guard Hall, the forum of bronze soldiers on the side walls.

"Your Holiness?" a soldier called out to Edward from the back cavern wall. Edward reeled on him in anger and found men dragging two limp bodies up out of the depths. "The Prime Commander is dead."

"And the general?" Edward said.

"He lives, but he is gravely injured."

"So be it. Get them out of here. Their fates are with the Light, as are all of ours."

Emerging from the shrine and into the bright courtyard, the many ranks of Bonemen filed to attention at the sight of the Sagean. The movement and noise dispelled into silent regard. Edward surveyed the ranks and pointed to the nearest lieutenant in charge. The soldier rushed over, his red cape flowing out behind him, and bowed his head, awaiting a blessing and his orders.

"The Light sees you lieutenant."

"And I see the Light. What do you require, my lord?"

Edward knew his court would be anxious for an update, "I need to send your best warbird to my acolytes with a message."

"Yes, your Holiness. It is this way," the soldier said, leading Edward to a tent with a table full of gadgets splayed out and waiting use.

"The scientist, Mordal, assures me these are his best work, your Holiness," the soldier said, holding a small shimmering bird the size of a large hummingbird in his palm for Edward to inspect.

"Fine," Edward agreed, and a messenger approached, handed the lieutenant a rolled note, and left. The lieutenant inspected the note and exhaled; his hesitation obvious to Edward.

"I already know that the rogues have escaped. Does it say how?" Edward grilled him.

"It does not, my lord. Just that there was a temple hidden underneath the falls."

"Was?"

"Everything but the front façade was destroyed. There is no sign of the rebels, my lord."

"What do we know about their arrival or their movements last night in the city?"

"Scouts have reported seeing them arrive from the west. We are looking into it, my lord."

"And what of the Whisper Chain?"

"The overseer there claims that the Whisper Chain's melodicure machine is broken. They have their best gadgeteers working on it now."

Even though the Wrythen told him as much, it irritated Edward to be reminded of his failure. His fists clenched and small sparks of electricity crackled. The lieutenant stepped back but froze when Edward seized the mechanical bird from him. Edward spoke into his palm while streaming in a binding of energy. His words burned into the scroll inside. He thrust the warbird back to the lieutenant to send, vexed. *Emperor Mayock Kovall wouldn't have suffered under this Court of Dragon's; Sagean Kovall would have slit their throats and found new advisors he could trust.*

"The rebels can't hide forever," Edward said.

The warbird fluttered to life. Its shimmering wings beat in a blur, and it took off into flight out over the shrine, disappearing from his eyes.

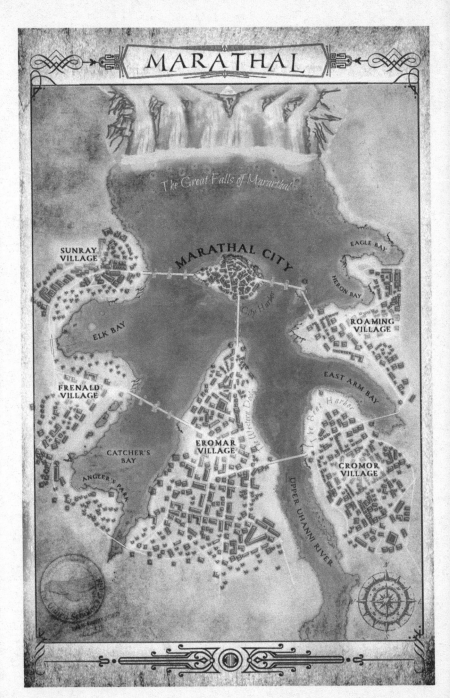

ONE

Y*ou can regard the dawn with disdain, but dawn comes anyway,* she thought as the sunlight on the water flashed in her eyes. In the aftermath of the battle with the Sagean and his automatons, Ellaria was struggling not to drown. The rolling deluge of lake water continually coated her face, threatening to claim her.

There was an old adage she knew: *the wisdom of dawn comes from the revelation of awakening from a dream.* For Ellaria, the nightmare had persisted into the morning and the only thing she discovered in the new day's light was her own desperation and with it, a tunnel to despair.

Drifting in the cold waters, she told herself to *focus*, but with the chill penetrating her bones, the shore loomed like an unreachable horizon. *Focus on what you can control,* she repeated to herself.

As mantras go, it was a simple meditation to believe in but in practice, not an easy one to live by, not with water relentlessly charging up her nose.

By the time the eastern shore came within reach, her old legs felt numb. The cold water had settled in and compromised her senses. When her feet found the rocky bottom, it was hard to gain any advantage over the drifting. The proximity to shore gave her hope and that hope won out over panic. With the rock below her, she hoisted the body she pulled alongside her, more easily now, steering them both toward their exit. The slope brought her out of the lake in trudging steps and she arrived at the shore, breathing in large heaves. Still holding on to Elias, she rested only a moment before she dragged his listless form ashore.

Ellaria pulled him from the water's edge, through the rock congested shoreline, up the gravel slope, and into the cover and canopy of the forest foliage. She groaned and dropped in a heap to her butt with a last gasp of effort. Sitting in her shivering skin, she gazed back at the sunlight glinting on the rippling surface of the lake beyond. A set of muddled lines in the gravel stretched from her to the lake's edge. Drawn by Elias's boot heels, they recorded both the distance and Ellaria's effort.

Transporting a water-sodden body forty feet up the uneven ground after everything that occurred the previous night tapped resources she didn't know she possessed. Ellaria looked at the roaring falls beyond and checked the shoreline for movement. There were no soldiers patrolling and no boats in the water that she could see. With nothing stirring, she began inspecting Elias and leaned in to confirm his breathing. He had lost consciousness after they cleared the curtain of falling water. Given the amount of unbelievable energy he put into destroying the Sagean's Automatons and then the temple, it was amazing he endured that far before collapsing.

After Tali, Learon, and Wade had gone through the wave gate, Elias cut through the rest of the rendered Automatons with that fascinating sword of energy and light. When the last one fell, the sword evaporated, and he pulled Ellaria to the steps. From there, he cast blaring bright bolts of white lightning into the temple ceiling and columns. The structure buckled and came crashing down. Elias's entire body glowed with energy, and they jumped into the lake to escape. Once they began their swim, his glow faded rapidly, and with it, a ghosted expression masked his face. She kept her eyes fixed on him the entire time through the falls, which is why she saw the instant he stopped moving, his eyes rolling back in his head. She reached for him in a panic. She still didn't know what had happened to Kovan. They never did see him. And she could only hope the others arrived through the wave gate. All things beyond her control, but she dwelled on them anyway. Love it would seem can be as distracting as desperation.

With her ear to Elias's open mouth, she heard wet strained breaths cycling forth. When it turned to a choking sound, Ellaria rolled him to his side and slapped his back repeatedly. Elias heaved and coughed out a cupful of water. Confident he was through, Ellaria rolled him back over. His breathing was stronger, but he was still unconscious.

Satisfied that he wasn't dead, she set her jaw against chattering teeth and grabbed a fallen branch. She scrambled back to the shore to cover the drag marks, sweeping the gravel trenches from Elias's feet and her own deeper dug depressions. It was the best she could do to hide their presence. Nothing that would pass close inspection, but from a distance, the coast blended unceremoniously.

She returned to the trees and observed the shoreline; her head throbbed, and her arms hung inert. She took in the crisp air and scanned across the lake, back towards the waterfall. She wanted to look for Kovan, but part of her was sure he was gone. They were each lucky to survive the falls. She would have drowned if not for Learon helping her find the surface. If Kovan had taken as many tungsten rounds as Tali suggested, there was very little chance a wounded man in his fifties had survived. It was a realization that, minute by minute was crushing her insides, and the prospect of giving up was easier than forging ahead.

The heart is like a pane of stained glass we carry on our chest, everyone can see when it's broken, Ellaria thought. She couldn't help but dwell on the mangled shape of her own heart. It didn't matter how she picked up the pieces, once repaired there would be no hiding the fractures; hers felt shattered this time. She put her fingers to the bridge of her nose and massaged the ache below her old eyes. She wished she could wash her hands of the world and let the perils it faced fade with the dust of ages gone by. Her old skin and wrinkled hands had lived as fists to fight for too long. She didn't know how to relax; she had never learned that skill.

From the pouring water and distant shores, her eyes gaped up at the vast mountain above where the water tumbled down. Her sight lingered on the dominant peak, where the shining crystal pyramid rose above. The sun sparkled and threw colored rays off at the edges of the brilliant pyramid. The entrance pavilion was beyond her sight, but she imagined it was overtaken with the army of the Sagean's Bonemen soldiers. With her breathing returned to normal, Ellaria's composure returned with determination, and she decided it was time for action.

She came back to Elias, who was slouched over himself in what looked like a failed attempt to sit up.

"Elias," she called out to him and dashed to his side, "Elias?"

With exertion, he lifted his head to see her; or more accurately, he tilted his head to her voice. When she reached his side, he spoke in a muted whisper, "Ellaria . . . poisoned. . . I . . . need a healer," he slurred.

"Poisoned, what poison? If you need medicine, I will go into the city?" she proposed, while helping him keep his head up. His eyes drooped open and closed; the color in them paled and faded away. Where a regular human's eyes might have been bloodshot, Elias's Luminary blood was pooling vivid silver vessels. But it was the lack of focus in the irises that worried her most.

"Not medicine . . . I need to see the tree . . ." he said, his words trailing off.

"Trees?" she repeated back to him, perplexed. With the slightest twitch, she felt him trying to shake his head, no.

"Tregorean . . . Only their healer can help me now," he said, and he sunk into her hands. Ellaria's nerves spiked from the sudden dispatch. As the last of his energy gave way, Elias crumbled into the ground. She touched his face and tried to open his eyes, fearing he had died.

His pulse was faint, but it existed.

Ellaria momentarily took measure of the situation and formed a plan of action. Everyone always thought she enjoyed making all the decisions, forming the strategies. She hated it, but she hated wasting time on indecision even more. She only happened to possess a quicker resolve than most.

The majority of the situations she faced in the war were strategic maneuvering of troops, and her knowledge of Tovillore gave her an edge over her enemies. Born to a high order, she had the privilege to travel extensively, which gave her an uncommon familiarity with the Mainland that served her well. Once Kovan explained the finer points of battle—attacking positions, high ground, flanking, diversion, protection, and all the rest—she became a formidable general. Ellaria learned early on to rely on the input from anyone with more expertise than her. She witnessed other commanders fail because of ego and she didn't want to be that kind of leader. Ego clouds judgement and presents an inability to recognize deficiencies. Artists take inspiration for source material, science builds on the trial and error, and a formidable general takes advantage of the knowledge of others. Every bit of information is vital to synthesize a perfect plan. Though, in truth, no plan is ever perfect.

What was her plan now? There was much she didn't know. *Where were the rest of the Bonemen soldiers? Had Elias cut through all the rendered machines or were more lurking out there? Were they being searched for?* So far, she had seen nothing stirring on the lake, but that meant little. What she couldn't know was how close Elias was to death, and *why would he need a Tregorean healer?* They were two thousand leagues or more from the Tregorean lands: a half a world away. Which meant she had to figure out how to get them across Tovillore, then across the Zulu Sea, and hope to find the Tregorean Province without being killed, captured, or losing her patience. Ellaria swallowed hard and sighed.

She had to assume that Elias could make the journey. Still, they needed horses, food, money, and she desperately wanted a change of clothes. An idea formed in Ellaria's head, to return to their hotel on the main island and retrieve their horses. Securing what they needed in the short term was paramount.

Ellaria dragged Elias close to a tree, disguising his position with a makeshift blanket of branches and brush. Before she left for the long hike to Marathal City, she bent down over Elias,

"I'm going into the city. We need horses and supplies, but I will return for you," she said to his closed eyes, unsure if he could hear her or not but telling him because it felt like the right thing to do.

She moved to get up and paused to say more, "Don't you dare die on me Elias Qudin. The world needs you. I'll be back soon."

ELLARIA ENTERED THE ROOM AND MOVED FAST. BASED ON THE LACK OF soldiers around the inn, she figured the Bonemen never tracked them to the hotel. Unconvinced, she focused on moving and thinking quickly, in case her assumption proved false and she found she had willingly placed her head in the noose. She prioritized what they could use to travel and discarded the rest. It would be both impossible and comical to haul two rolls all the way to the stables, so she over-packed her own roll and took off. Before passing through the revolving doors of gilded metal, Ellaria slapped payment on the counter and left.

The streets were in turmoil. Their fight with the Automatons in the fog-filled island the night before had not gone unnoticed. The Rendered had been seen by the locals, and to see tall lumbering beings of metal and breathing steam was frightening. Eventually an explanation would be issued to calm the public, but until that happened, the sidewalks and roads would continue to fill up with like-minded people trying to flee the city.

Ellaria made her way to the stabling depot near the pier in the south of the island, careful to avoid any of the alleyways where greencoats were investigating the night's destruction. There probably should have been a larger presence of troops around, considering the unrest on every block, but this wasn't the case. The only reasonable explanation was that the Sagean Lord was now concentrating his troops' effort on the Tomb and digging through the rubble Elias had left.

Ellaria bartered with the stable master to sell four of the horses, but she kept her own and Elias's nyrogen horse, Ghost. Given the mass of people trying to leave the city, she received far more than they were worth, too. With the two horses packed, she traveled across the east bridge back toward the Roaming Village and out to the shoreline on which she had left Elias. Once she cleared the village and the tip of Eagle Bay, she was able to gallop on an old trail north to his position. The spirited white mare would not be slowed. It charged through the forest directly to Elias like it already knew the way. Without Ghost, Ellaria wasn't positive she would have remembered the way so easily.

She dismounted and advanced to Elias's side. She wiped sweat from his forehead and placed her hand there. His temperature was unexpectedly cold. Ellaria's eyebrows scrunched, and she felt for his pulse. His heart still beat, but his breathing was shallow and his color even more washed out than before. She grabbed some crystals from the supplies, wrapped them together, and placed them directly over Elias's heart. Ellaria drew all the sigils she knew for healing and spirit cleansing on the wrappings. There was more she would do once they were settled somewhere safe, but this had to suffice for now.

Looking around, she couldn't fathom how to get him up and on the horse. She just didn't have any strength left for such a feat, but she led Elias's horse close enough to try. The horse, through its own volition, started to kneel next to Elias. It gently lay down beside him and looked back at Ellaria. She smiled and understood, and with a heave, pulled Elias over the mare's back. The horse huffed and found its feet, with Elias on its back. It was one of the most miraculous sights Ellaria had ever seen.

With everything secured for the ride ahead, she walked the horses back to the trail, mounted her warm-blooded horse and kicked to a trot. It was a long ride to Fairville, and she expected the road would be dangerous. The exodus would result in packed roadways and long caravans united in their desertion. If the Bonemen were watching the east pass, the crowd would be fortuitous for their escape.

As a general in the war, anticipating the enemy's every move was essential. The line between success and failure was often simply the difference between time spent worrying versus preparing. In the end, control was an illusion.

Ellaria took heart in her own ability to survive.

TWO

THE DAWNING GALE (LEARON)

E ach of them regarded the flames in silence. The drifting embers rose into the still wind and dispersed amongst the stars above. The crackling and unpredictable pops of the blue flames overtook the sounds of the night and wilderness around them.

Their unanimous decision to light a fire and go to sleep had been the only thing they could collectively agree on that day. The stress of the battle and fleeing through the gate had manifested in each of them in unkind ways. Learon tried to keep them moving, but sometimes the arguments would throw them off track and slow them down. Wade was frustrated that they were stranded on a mountain and Tali was infuriated by seemingly everything Learon or Wade said.

He suspected that her real anger was at Elias and Ellaria for staying behind. However, Learon had been the one to lead them back to the gate, and Tali was mad at him for agreeing to do so. He could understand that. With a little time and distance from the moment, he was surprised how easily he had chosen to protect Tali and Wade and abandon Elias. Ultimately, he believed Elias could survive anything, but he also understood Elias's need to conceal the gates' existence from the Sagean and that superseded their need to be together. No matter how they calculated it, none of them saw the night as a win. A crystal in exchange for Kovan's life was not a deal any of them would have chosen.

They made it to the cabin by nightfall, with each of them weary and agitated. Learon made a protection fire near the lake's shore. They spread out around it and laid down. Learon, waiting for his exhaustion to overcome his senses, heard Tali shift to her side. He observed her trying to communicate with her watch again. It must not have been working, because her face held a scowl of frustration. Learon reached into his own pack and grabbed Elias's watch.

"Tali, try this one," he said, reaching over and handing her the watch.

"Where did you get this, whose is it?" Tali examined.

"Elias gave it to me when we were searching Marathal City for you. Before the giant rendered machines started attacking."

Tali examined Elias's watch and a similar frustrated glower masked her face.

"It's no good. This one's broken too. It could be the pen is broken. I'm not sure."

"Perfect," Wade retorted from his spot against a boulder.

"You're not going to find the solution tonight. But maybe we can go to Atava if we need to fix them," Learon offered.

"What should we do next?" She asked them.

"I think I'm going to go to Adalon," Wade said.

"So, there is no *we*, right Wade?" Tali said.

"I didn't say that. What do you think we should do?" Wade pressed.

"I don't know but going back to Adalon is probably last on my list of places to go."

"Well, let's just live in the mountains then. We have Mr. Woodsman himself, we'll be fine," Wade said sarcastically.

"Would you two stop?" Learon said. He watched Tali bite her tongue. "We aren't going to get very far with what we have. I know that much. We need to go to West Meadow first. It's the easiest route out of here. We need supplies and we need help."

"That sounds good. From there, I think I want to head back to Elias's hideout in Polestis," Tali proposed.

"Why? So, we can wait to see if the others are all dead? Besides, isn't Polestis like six hundred leagues to the north?" Wade said dismissively, still unable or unwilling to hide his frustration.

"Isn't Adalon a thousand leagues to the east?" Tali spat.

"What do you want from me, Tali? I can't do anything to help Elias and Ellaria. Even if they survived. I can, however, get back to Stasia and see if I can get a beat on whatever ship Tara was sailing on in the Mainsolis Sea. That's what the Whisper Chain's ancient machine said, right? That my sister Tara was on the Mainsolis Sea?" Wade questioned her.

"Yes," Tali conceded. She had told them about the events at the Whisper Chain as they had hiked. How Ellaria, Kovan, and she found the ancient machine and how it told them that Danehin, the Peace King of the Free Cities, was in Andal and that Wade's sister Tara was somewhere on the Mainsolis Sea.

"But Wade, it also said that Tara and Danehin were both alive and dead." She added.

"I don't get that. Was it malfunctioning or simply an answer the machine isn't equipped to provide?" Wade wondered.

"I asked, *is Tara Duval alive?* It said, *yes and no.* It could be like you say. The machine can't decipher the difference," Tali said.

"They're both a long way from here. If we did go to Polestis, at least we can hide the Tempest Stone in Elias's vault," Learon offered.

"You're probably right. Kovan died trying to get that stupid stone so we probably should protect it." Wade said.

"He might be alive," Tali said.

"Oh Tali," Wade said sadly, "The way you explained it, he took multiple charged pulsator rounds to the back and fell out into the lake. I don't think anyone could have survived. We barely survived the jumps ourselves."

"I know but, remember how the chamber was making things go crazy? The Bonemen tried shooting at us before and the rounds fell flat in midair."

"Right, but that was before the Sagean Dark Lord turned off whatever was happening."

"I know, but . . ."

Learon watched Tali get more upset as she faltered for excuses to explain why Kovan might be alive, so he broke in, "We don't know if Kovan survived or not. We never saw his body. We don't know if Ellaria or Elias are alive either. Tali, you said you injured everyone in the chamber with your powers. Is it possible you killed the Sagean?"

"I don't think so. I definitely injured him and his Prime Commander and the Adalon ambassador too, but whether I killed them or not, I don't know," Tali said.

A new silence lingered and Learon sensed they were all content to listen to the fire. They each lay back down to stare at the sky.

"So, you used to come here all the time with your father, Learon?" Tali remarked, staring up at the stars.

"Not really. Honestly, my father traveled a lot for the Scholar's Guild.

All over the Mainland, to the New World for a few years, and even to Merinde once. But every time he came back, we would make a trip up here."

"I like it here," Wade said.

"I like it, too. At least when there's not wolverack beasts trying to hunt you, I like it," Learon said, and closed his eyes.

When he awoke, he felt re-energized in a way he hadn't in weeks. He found Tali sitting with her legs crossed at the edge of the lake and walked over to her. Learon was used to being the first person to wake up in the morning, but with Tali or Elias around, he couldn't measure up.

The sun really wasn't up yet, but the meadow was gaining a soft light, enough by which to see. The surface of the lake appeared soft and inviting and the fish were jumping at the morning insects.

He sat down next to Tali without a word and shared her view. He hoped he wasn't intruding, but the day would bring new stress and he wanted a moment to talk to her. Wade and he could see the loss of Kovan had shaken her badly.

Tali moved the free strands of dark hair from her eyes and quickly glanced at him with a welcoming smile. One that Learon felt held a small amount of loneliness to it.

"Hi Learon."

"Good morning."

"It's peaceful," Tali observed.

"It is," he agreed. "Did you sleep well?"

"I did. Maybe the first time in a long time. How about you?"

"Same. I haven't had a restful sleep in a while."

"Nightmares?" Tali asked.

"Yes. Sometimes."

"Me too."

"Listen, I wanted to say, I'm sorry," Learon said.

"For what?"

"I'm sorry how everything turned out; I'm sorry Kovan didn't make it."

Her eyes began to tear up, and a drop rolled down her cheek before she could wipe it.

Learon continued, "And . . ."

"There's more?" she breathed.

"Well, I'm sorry about the arguments last night. I just want you to know I'll follow your lead. Whatever you want to do, I'll stick with you. I told you I would before, and I will."

"You will? Why?"

"You have good instincts, and you're smart."

"Neither of those things is true," she contested.

"Smarter than Wade or I."

"Well . . ." Tali said, and she put her empty hand out in a gesture to say that didn't mean much.

"And . . ."

"And what?"

"I can't explain it. I just have a feeling like I'm meant to follow you. Does that sound dumb?"

She took her eyes off the water to look at him, her head tilted, and smiled again.

"No," she said, and rested her head on his shoulder, her attention back on the still surface. "I liked your idea about Atava. I think fixing the communicators should be our first move."

"What if Ellaria's is broken, too?" Learon said.

"It's possible all three of them were broken. But at least we can get the two we have working, and then if Wade wants to go, he can," Tali said.

"I don't want to go. I'm just worried," Wade said from behind them. They both turned to his voice. "Let's go to Atava. Do you still want to go to West Meadow?"

"I think we have to," Learon said.

"Well let's get going," Wade said, standing up and brushing his clothes clean. He was starting to say something else when a rustling in the overhead trees diverted their attention.

A bird launched out of the limbs, the leaves shaking from the depar-ture. At first, the bird emerging above was unseen. Only the beat of its wings gave it away. When it soared over the water, an image on the surface mirrored the changing colors of the bird. The underside turning white and then the entire body and wings shimmered into being.

"Is that what I think it is?" Tali said, following the bird's flight.

"I—I think it's a Dawning Gale," Learon said.

"Have you ever seen one before?" She asked, astonished.

"No. Not with their camouflage abilities, and I've never known anyone who has either."

"Me neither," Wade said, "I mean, I've heard their whistling before."

"Right, me too," Learon said.

"Aren't they supposed to be a bad omen if you see one?" Tali said.

"The worst," Wade said, "I heard a tale that two brothers saw one in the Wing Shadow Mountains and when they returned to their village, they found everyone there had been hanged from the rafters of the town's church, and all their eyes had been pecked out," Wade said.

"I've heard a similar tale, but it was bodies on spikes, I think. Also, with their eyes pecked out," Learon said.

"And the brothers, what happened to them?" Tali asked.

"They went crazy. They buried the dead, and sailed into the Brovic Ocean," Wade said.

"That's right. They sailed the Brovic never to be seen again," Learon agreed, and a puzzled frown creased Tali's forehead.

"Well, the Brovic can't be crossed. In Ravenvyre there are many stories about that," Tali said.

"Why can't people sail the Brovic? Is it just the waters that are too dangerous?" Learon said, unsure. As a mountain kid, he knew the saying that *no one sails the Brovic*, but he didn't know why.

"It's the water, the wind, and the air. The weather itself is wrong," Tali said.

"You've been out there, past the Dire?" Learon replied. The Dire was supposed to be the point of no return; a group of islands off the coast of Rodaire.

"I would go on fishing trips sometimes for my mom's restaurant. The Amatori market was right off the pier. We had close relationships with our suppliers. As soon as the ship ventured too far into the Brovic, the air would start to feel… off. I'm not sure how to describe it. We got off course once, about a league past the Dire and I've never been so scared. It was like the ocean was alive. The saltwater began to evaporate into the air. It became so thick, none of us could breathe. We couldn't pass further if we tried, but the currents had the ship, and we realized it wasn't up to us where we went—it was up to the water. That day the water chose to throw us back toward the coast. I've heard stories about the ships sturdy enough to go deeper. Eventually, the waves get higher than the ship. Wild swells crest and attack the hull. Those that don't pull out in time are crushed. Some of the old sea dogs call it *the dark currents*. They say the ocean beyond the Dire is cursed and if it takes you in its grasp, you're lucky if it throws you back out. Most are never seen again. The sea just swallows them."

They packed up in silence, but Learon felt the tension had returned. He took the fishing pole from the cabin and they hiked toward West Meadow. It took most of the morning to get down. The sun was heading into the blue when they found Garner's cabin. Learon checked for a

moment but found no signs of anyone having been there since he and
Elias left it last month.

They proceeded on to West Meadow, stopping at the river crossing at
the edge of town. They had decided Wade would go into town first to see
what kind of presence the Bonemen had there before all three showed
themselves. While he was gone, Learon took Tali to a bend in the river to
fish.

Learon led her around the brush of fallen trees. He searched the
water a moment to help select the fly, and then cast his line out into the
tumbling surface, letting the red bodied zip roll through the whitewater.

"You're really in your element in the wilderness, aren't you?" Tali
observed.

He smiled, unsure how to respond. On his third cast, a spotted river
trout took the line. He brought it in to the bank where Tali sat smiling. It
was a good size, and he laid it on a wet rag, bundling the fish up and
setting it in the water to keep cool. Learon caught another one after the
second cast, performing the same routine. He tried a few more casts and
proceeded down the river with Tali following.

A short distance down the river, he caught another. This one fought
and jumped high out of the water. It was larger by far than the previous
two and Tali laughed at the sight of it. Another fish caught; every cast
brought more. Learon couldn't help himself, he began to laugh with Tali.
He was good at fishing, but never this good.

He was bringing in his sixth one when they heard someone running
their way.

"Learon! Tali?" Wade called out.

"Over here," Tali shouted back.

Wade came sprinting through the wild grass. His face was downcast
and his eyes wide, obviously shaken by something. Learon turned in the
water to get out and the fish fell from the line as he moved.

"Thorns," Learon muttered.

Wade stopped at the bank and put his hands to his knees, gasping.
Something was really wrong.

"What's going on, what did you find?" Tali said.

"You two need to come with me. There's something strange going on
in that town," Wade said waving them to follow.

"What? Are they all dead?" Learon teased, "Did you find Rose . . ."

"No. Seriously. You need to come now. It's hard to explain,"
Wade said

Learon nodded his understanding and stepped out of the river. He found a fallen branch with a sharp edge and slammed it into the riverbed. He pounded the stick down until he was satisfied it would stay and tied the rag full of fish to it, then they left.

THE THREE OF THEM WALKED INTO TOWN ON FOOT AND FOR THE LONGEST time, Learon didn't see anyone around. It was beginning to feel like a ghost town. A few shapes were seen inside houses, but Learon didn't stop until they reached the town center.

In the open green space, about fifty townspeople lingered aimlessly. Learon almost went past them to the Inn until the truth of what they were doing hit him, *they're not moving.* The sight of them standing still chilled him to his bones.

"What's wrong with them?" Tali whispered.

"I don't know. I tried talking to a few of them and none responded. Sometimes they'll look at you, but that's it," Wade said.

Learon surveyed the area and waved for the others to follow, "Come on, I need to find Rose."

He ran over to the Inn and up the porch steps. There were others inside all in the same static state, and a foul smell of mildew and excrement made it hard to breathe. In the kitchen, the smell was worse. There he found Jema, the cook. She was standing in the darkened room with a butchers knife in her hand. The ghosted look in her eyes was frightening. They were glossy and yellowing.

"Jema. Jema, where's Rose?" Learon said, but there was no response. Jema blinked and seemed to be breathing, but she didn't answer. He stepped closer to her.

"Be careful, Learon," Tali cautioned.

Learon tried again, this time touching Jema on the arm, "Jema, are you . . ."

At his touch, she took a step forward. The sudden movement startled Tali, and she backed into some empty egg crates. Learon moved away to give Jema space. Jema slowly strode to the counter and began to chop some rotten meat on the board. Her movements were almost mechanical and she did it all without registering their presence in the room.

Learon didn't know if he should stop her or not. His pulse raced and his breath felt uncontrollable. He needed fresh air, and retreated back outside. Tali was happy to follow. Wade was waiting with his gauntlet sword shining in the light. He turned at their appearance.

"Anything?" Wade asked.

"No," Tali said, "We got one to move, but it wasn't natural."

"Yeah, they move sometimes," Wade concurred.

Learon stood on the porch trying to think. He ran his hand through his hair and examined the many faces he knew. Mark and his son Ben were sitting on the porch. In the alley, he could see the town's peace-keeper Dan Raylee standing in the shadows. Learon dashed off the steps to him.

"Mr. Raylee," Learon called out, to no answer. Behind him, Rose was standing alone. Learon ran to her and shook her.

"Rose. Rose!" he yelled, but she did nothing except blink at him.

"What's the matter with you!" Learon screamed in terror.

Wade came and pulled him away. Learon was breathing hard and beginning to panic. His crystal necklace started itching, so he pulled it free from beneath his shirt. Rose's eyes darted to it and Learon's heart stopped. The hair on his arms lifted.

"Rose," Learon said again. This time when Learon spoke, Rose looked at him.

"What do I do guys?" Learon mouthed with trepidation.

"I don't know. Ask her something," Wade said.

"Rose, how can I help you?" Learon said trying to watch her eyes. She gazed at him a moment and then, as though a fly were buzzing around, her focus disappeared.

"Ask her to do something?"

"Like what?"

"Something simple," Wade said.

Learon nodded, "Rose, walk to the fence."

Rose twitched her head intently at her name, and with the slightest hesitation, she started out toward the fence line behind the inn.

"Rose, stop," Learon called out, and she halted in place.

Learon's breathing became rushed and disordered. He was close to hyperventilating. Wade stepped closer to him and pulled him back to the porch where Tali stood staring at what they all just witnessed. Learon met her eyes with his own look of horror.

"What kind of horrible magic is this?" Wade spat.

"It's not me," Learon insisted.

"I know, I saw. Rose lit up when you pulled that crystal out," Wade replied.

"So, what do we do? We can't leave them like this, just meandering around the town. I'm shocked the wolveracks didn't come," Tali said.

"Maybe the wolveracks are smarter than us," Wade said.

"You're right, I can't leave them like this," Learon said.

"What if you round them all up?" Tali said, but her suggestion obviously lacked confidence.

"Sure. Maybe I can lead them all into the Town Hall," Learon said.

"At least until whatever happened, or is happening, passes," Tali said.

"I can do that. But I don't want to be here any longer than we have to," Learon said.

"Agreed," Wade said.

"You two start gathering supplies and horses while I shepherd," Learon said.

They nodded and got to work. The sunlight was fading and Learon's stomach had weakened the longer they were around these things. These shells made his shoulders shrink into his body. He led every person he could find into the Town Hall. It was the largest building in town, but it filled up quickly, and each person he shepherded inside made him nauseous.

West Meadow was a modestly sized town and Learon knew most of the people; if not by name, by their face. By the time the hall was nearly full, Learon had grown cold inside himself.

He stepped from the oversized gray wood doors and walked toward another shell. His mind flooded with dark ideas. *When an animal is dying and suffering, it should be put out of its misery.*

He walked past Wade and Tali, who stared at him dumbfounded. Tali's face was washed with worry and she tried to grab his shirt, but Learon continued past.

"Learon? Learon, are you all right?" Tali asked.

But he ignored her. *All right? These things are closer to white slugs than humans, no I'm not all right,* he mumbled to himself as he rounded up the next slug. His eyes fixed on the warding basin and stacked blue pine. Learon began to consider a way to end this misery once he had them all inside the wooden building.

"Wade, help," Tali cried.

"What?" Wade said.

"Something is wrong with Learon," Tali said.

Learon retrieved the old merchant and walked her back toward the church. His eyes lingering on the torch and flint near the basin, he looked up to see Wade in his path.

"Move," Learon said, and he pressed forward.

Wade put his hand to Learon's chest to stop him—tilting his head to look Learon in his downcast eyes. The crystal at Learon's necklace pulsed with a dim glow between them and with a startling swipe Wade tore the necklace free.

Learon fell to his knees and gasped for breath.

"Are you all, right?" Wade asked.

"Better now," Learon rasped.

"What happened?" Tali came to his side and helped him to his feet.

"I don't know. The longer I was at it, manipulating these people the more my thoughts became clouded and . . ." Learon trailed off.

"And what?" Tali asked.

"Evil. I can't even tell you what I was contemplating."

"How about we take turns rounding these people up then?" Wade said.

"Not Tali," Learon said.

"Why not?" Tali protested.

"Because I shuddered to think what a Luminary could do controlling these things with the crystal and worse what they might do to you."

With everyone in agreement Wade and Learon finished rounding up the townspeople together. Wade's eyes went wide the first time the sleepwalkers responded to his call.

While they walked around looking for anyone they might have missed, Tali lit all the protection fires around the square and gathered supplies for their trip. When everyone was gathered and safely inside, they prepared to leave, but Learon stood transfixed by the sight of the building now full of shadowed silhouettes.

"Maybe they're just sick, Learon?" Wade said handing the necklace back.

"We both know that's not true Wade. They were made this way for a reason."

"What reason?" Wade said.

"I don't know, it's like they're an army in waiting though."

"But how? What happened to them?" Wade said.

"I don't know," Learon said.

"Tali, what do you think? Can they be cured?" Wade asked.

"I don't have any answers. But what can be taken, could be returned. Maybe there is a way to put things, right?"

"How?" Learon said.

"I don't know, Learon. But if there is a way, then we will find it. Together," Tali said.

Learon turned to his friends and said, "Let's go. Hopefully someone knows something in Atava."

They climbed atop their horses and as they rode away the dreadfulness of manipulating the husks around lingered like the foul taste of spoiled eggs in his mouth, but Learon never looked back.

THREE
CROWDED RETREAT (ELLARIA)

Crowded roads produce anonymity, but also slow travel. Amongst the carriages and single riders, there was a contingent of the people on foot. Ellaria assumed passage through the Uhanni river had been shut down. There was no way this number of people were all going to a nowhere city like Fairville. Especially not from such an affluent city as Marathal.

Fairville was fifty leagues from Marathal and even at a good gallop, the trip took a little over two days. The first night on the road, Ellaria got Elias dismounted and comfortable on the ground. The massive congregation of people on the open road provided certain protections and dangers. The night's camp was sprawling, and the various blue protection fires loomed and cast enough light to keep the beasts from approaching. The atmosphere was oddly joyous, possibly out of relief or from some shared sense of adventure. Certainly, the whispers she heard all concerned the rendered machines and their rampage around the city.

Ellaria learned that the battle in the alleyways was not the lone attack that night. The Sagean's Automatons were not so well-trained as they appeared. By the sounds of it, there were seven people killed on Marathal island, some in Spray Village, and a group on the South pier were injured. Like the genetically mutated beasts, there was no taming the wild creations. The Sagean himself probably controlled them.

In the moment of respite, Ellaria unpacked all her things and took stock of what she grabbed from the room. It was then that she checked her watch and realized it wasn't working properly. The top face clock didn't function at all, and though the hidden script dial below would light up, no message would send. She didn't fully understand the construction of the devices, but she thought it was out of balance somehow from being underwater for so long. After that, she tried to rest, but the campers kept going long into the night. By morning, they were through all their tins of alcohol and the general cheer turned to snores.

Ellaria got out as early as possible to try and put distance between her and the caravan, but she charged headlong into a second band of travelers. By the second night, Elias's condition was not improved. An alchemist spell she knew, which syphoned strength from her and imparted to him, came with risks. The most dangerous of which would leave them both vulnerable for a night, and there were far too many strangers around for that.

This second group didn't have as much spirit as the first one she encountered. That, or they exhausted it all the first night in a similar fashion. The quieter camp was oddly less comforting. That night, she heard Elias talking in his sleep.

"I told you, you couldn't hold me . . . You can't be . . . You're nothing, your crusade is for nothing . . . You can't be . . . You'll never protect them all . . ."

None of it made sense, and the ranting soon turned louder.

"Nobody is safe from me! No one!" Elias called out.

She forced him to drink some water and talked softly to him until she was sure whatever sickness was agitating him had subsided. Another restless night filled with nightmares and again she was up at dawn, riding with a small band into Fairville.

Fairville was a dying city, one that reached its pinnacle long ago. Before the canal was built that connected the Frayne River to the Uhanni River at Anchor's Point, it was a major stop on the way to the north. But when the economic lifeblood of a nowhere city is removed, the city dies. Once the Frayne came in use to transport goods from Adalon through the more efficient river system, the city lost its reason for existence.

Over the years, Fairville found its geographical equilibrium and the local farming replaced the lost revenues of transported goods. But it was a rough evolution over many years. This was well before the Great War, but Ellaria knew the history well and had seen similar things happen to other frontier settlements. The Empire had no interest in the sustainability of wayward cities like Fairville. Unless there was something inherently important about the land, the Sagean Empire was content to let these places disappear. The people had no value to the Empire.

Ellaria remembered how the Resistance had struggled to take smaller cities like Fairville during the war. While the Empire didn't care about them, they tended to be more ardently faithful. Being ignored, they had also escaped the tyranny and cruelty of the Empire's righteousness and wrath. If this new Sagean understood the power of these small towns, and Ellaria suspected Edward did, then it explained why the Bonemen soldiers were not crawling around. They wouldn't need to be, not with all the fanatics among the population. Ellaria's weariness and fear of the zealotry was as strong as her fear of the Bonemen. The Legion of Light or the Lionized, or whatever they wanted to call themselves, could be more vicious than soldiers. Soldiers were capable of hurting strangers and other soldiers with impunity, zealots could do it to their neighbor.

Ellaria followed the buildup of the city and found an extensive market among some of the more prominent buildings. She went to the nearest stabling house first and paid for a quiet spot in the back. To the stable master, she explained that Elias was sleeping off a night of drinking and paid extra for the understood discretion. Leaving Elias alone in the stables weighed on her and she rushed to the market.

It was midday and the sacred sun shone its blue-hued rays, but she found the center bustling with shoppers. The heat of the day brought sweat to her forehead; the summer swelter was settling in and soon the rainy season would be back. The older Ellaria got, the more she found she lost her ability to stay in the sun without burning. It didn't help that the olive-toned skin of her youth had faded to the lighter skin tone of her mother's people.

The center market had an organized setup easy to navigate. She procured food before moving on to find any of the more obscure oddities for which she was searching. The likelihood of finding an alchemist merchant here was low, but she must be careful if she did. Sometimes other merchants would be reluctant to deal with a person should they observe one patronizing an alchemist.

To her surprise, she found a small cluster of alchemy shops in an offshoot alley. She was only looking for a few ingredients: some blood stones and thistle vine or nightshade would help Elias. Her plan was to get the supplies and then try to find a coach ride to the south.

Scanning the alley, a particular alchemy and apothecary shop looked promising with its inviting dark-colored brick and stained wood store-front, as well as a window display suggesting the best selection. The shop was empty when she walked in. The selection of crystals and stones was still limited, but she found some substitutes and some efferial-rock salt. At the counter, a man had come inside and struck up a conversation with the proprietor. He had a top hat and a finely made vest. Ellaria tried to listen in as she browsed the teas and herbs.

"You rode all the way out here for that?" the store owner said.

"They don't have your selection in Harden," the man said

"I suppose they don't. Well, you're in luck. I got a delivery of the powder you 're looking for, two days ago."

"Perfect. We go through almost half a barrel a night," the man said.

The merchant went to the back a wheeled a pair of two-foot-tall barrels up to the front, "That's all I got."

"That will do until we reach Nearwin. Thank you," the man said.

The conversation had piqued Ellaria's curiosity, and she lined up at the counter to pay. She tried to comprehend who would be going through a half barrel of barium star-powder every night. Ellaria noticed the patron held a roll of advertising banners under his arm. The stars along the edge made her realize who he was and an idea popped inside her head—a possible way to escape Tovillore with an injured man, while hiding from the Bonemen soldiers. The man paid and left. Ellaria needed to talk with him. She paid for her selections in a hurry and rushed out to catch up with the man.

Outside, she found the central thoroughfare twice as crowded as when she had walked into the shop. Most of the people were new arrivals from Marathal, but some of the groups were obviously the local Lionized radicals out to scrutinize the influx of travelers. They all wore yellow and black striped bands around their upper arms, the same as the Legion of Light. Proof that the hatred and zealotry born of ignorance and fear never truly dies, it only changes its face and name.

The man from the shop was nailing up his advertisements at the center posts, and Ellaria choose to wait until he was done before speaking with him. She found her reflection in a shop window and tried to fix her appearance before she spoke. It was the first time she had seen at herself since scrambling around the room in Marathal. In just two days of traveling, she looked like a worn old shoe and her hair was an insurmountable mess.

In the reflecting glass, she spotted a small group of Lionized watching her. One man had long dirty blonde hair and seemed to command the others. His eyes were deadly. *Why had they already taken an interest in her?* In other circumstances she probably would have confronted them, but at the moment she didn't have the luxury of escalating animosity amongst the locals. Ellaria fixed her hair up and pulled it away from her face. When the man she was looking for passed by, she approached him.

"Excuse me, sir," Ellaria spoke up. The man turned around, tipped his hat, and smiled at her. He was probably in his thirties and had a manicured beard. His smile and demeanor spoke of a general politeness. When she considered her current condition, she hoped he was very nice.

"Hello, miss."

"I saw your advertisements. Is the showman's troupe coming to Fairville?" Ellaria said, pointing back toward the nailing post. She suspected they weren't, based on what she overheard.

"No, the show is working the Imperial Road. We will be in Harden tonight and then Nearwin after that."

The trope was heading the right direction. Now she needed to find a way in. "That's even better. I'm heading to Harden now with my friend. My name's Aria, and you are?" Ellaria asked.

"Will. Will Brandon. It's a pleasure to meet you, Aria. You and your friend should both come see the show. We have all the curiosities you can imagine and ones you can't. We have acrobats, alchemists, and an exceptional Talesman."

"How extensive is your menagerie these days?"

"Our exhibit is renowned and one of our biggest draws," Will said.

"Any of the beasts? I would love to see those up close." Ellaria said. She figured there were two routes to pursue to gain a position. Depending on the disposition of the master of ceremonies, it could require both.

"We do. We have two wolveracks and a bonelark. Our master trainer, Alexero, handles them. They are for show only of course and in highly secure cages."

"Oh, how wonderfully dangerous. No ravinor though?"

"No. I'm afraid not," Will said.

"Interesting. I actually traveled with master showman Manus Zabel, when I was younger," Ellaria said, hoping to further pique his interest.

"Really?"

"Oh yes. Does your Talesman still perform *The Echo of Silence*?"

"It's actually a full production now."

"Well, then that settles it. I'll be there. I think you might have a packed house, too. I came in on the old road from Marathal and a mass of people have abandoned the city and are heading south," she said.

"All of Tovillore is on edge because of the Prime Commander's death. There's talk of a New Sagean Lord, too. I think the upheaval has people going crazy."

"Um . . ." Ellaria stammered. She didn't know the Prime was dead, and the revelation rattled her momentarily out of her friendly manner, "Yes. It was a shock," she said finally.

"Were you in Marathal when it happened? The paper said Qudin Lightweaver murdered the Prime and the New Sagean Lord saved the city," Will said.

"That's ridiculous. I was in Eromar Village when it happened. I saw these giant machines attack the Western Harbor there. We left immediately," Ellaria lied, trusting that Will knew about that incident, too.

"I heard about those machines. Scary times."

"Indeed," she said, and pointed to the barrels he was wheeling, "All that star-powder, are you the fire-master?"

"No, I'm just an assistant. We have a skilled pyrotechnician. Master Showman Archibald likes his fireworks," Will said.

"Well, I'll let you be on your way. I need to get on the road before more people flood into town," Ellaria said.

"Me too. I'll see you out there. If I don't, please stop by the show and ask for me. I would like to introduce you to Archibald. Mr. Zabel was a mentor to him. I'm sure he would love to speak with you," Will said.

"That would be lovely. Safe travels," Ellaria said, and she walked swiftly away. Tracking movements as she traversed the city back to Elias, Ellaria was starting to see Lionized at every corner and alleyway. The longer it took to get back, the more her pulse raced. Alone in an unfriendly city, surrounded by strangers, was suffocating. Her quickened pace turned into a sprint. For some reason, the look of some of the Lionized spooked her and her hands shook by the time she reached the stables. She already lost Kovan. She wouldn't lose Elias.

Back at the stables, a long line of people stood waiting to barter for a horse. Ellaria edged past them. There weren't many horses left inside. Ghost huffed and neighed loudly at her when she was outside the stall. A warning stomp proceeded, but the horse eased when Ellaria let her hair down and it fully recognized her.

Elias slept in the hay behind both horses. The stable was pungent, and the thought occurred to her that eventually she would have to figure out how to clean Elias if he didn't get up soon. Even in the low light, she ascertained his color had improved. She retrieved her waterskin and lifted his head to drink. The water touched his lips and his eyes fluttered open.

Elias squinted at her, and a slight curl crested his lips. The recognition in his eyes made Ellaria shudder and cry. She hadn't realized how much she needed him to be all right. He drank it in gulps and lifted himself to sitting up. Then he slumped into the back wall.

"Where are we?" he moaned.

"In Fairville."

"How long was I out?"

"Almost three days. Can you stand?" Ellaria asked.

Elias paused as though thinking about it and shook his head *no*.

"It's good to see you awake," Ellaria said

"I'm sorry."

"Don't be sorry. You scared me but . . ."

"Ellaria, listen," Elias interrupted her.

"Yes?"

"I don't know how long I'll be conscious. I have an energy sickness. I need to get to a Tregorean healer."

"Is there nothing I can do for you?" Ellaria asked.

"No. It's an imbalance. It's hard to explain but essentially my energy-well and my own spirt are untethered inside me. I don't know how to heal it. I can feel a fog in my mind has cleared temporarily, but it will return."

"But you believe the Tregoreans can heal you?" she reiterated.

"Yes. They did it before."

She wondered what he meant by before, but she didn't ask. Instead, she said, "Fine, but I'm still going to try treating you."

"Thank you," he said.

"How long do we have? I'm trying to figure out a way to get us all the way to Nahadon. But to get all the way south, we must travel through some of the most heavily guarded cities in Tovillore. I have one idea but I'm not sure it's fast," Ellaria said.

"I don't know how long I have. I think I can maintain my strength for two or three weeks. Is the Uhanni River closed?"

"Yes, apparently Tali killed the Prime Commander in the tomb. Closing the Uhanni was the first thing they did."

"Good for her," Elias said.

"I share your sentiment, but the chaos that had just begun is now exploding."

"So, what's your idea?" Elias asked.

"I think we could hideout with a showman's traveling fair. At least until Midway, and from there we can catch a winddrifter. It's risky, but they only stop for the night and move on. With the state you're in we would be stopping anyway. and with the Uhanni shut down I don't know any other way to get us out of the Mainland. We could go north, but airships are scarce up there and traveling by sea will triple our time. An airship is our only chance."

"Don't worry. I'm not dying today. But the energy imbalance wipes me out. I'm not—myself."

"I've seen. I'm sorry Elias I just don't know what else to do."

"Considering our options—it's a good idea. If we can conceal our identity from the traveling trope members, then their grand caravan should work to hide us from the Bonemen and the Sagean. Now, help me up," Elias said, grabbing the wall for support. Ellaria helped him rise and clutch to Ghost's reins. The horse huffed, and its tail swooshed widely. Once Elias was atop Ghost, Ellaria waited until she was sure he could ride and not slide off before she stepped away. She packed what needed packing, grabbed the reins from her horse, and started to walk them out. Their presence had elicited some notice when they emerged, but they quickly became an afterthought. Elias sitting atop his horse, instead of draped over it, helped. Ellaria paid the stable master, then checked Elias's bootstraps again.

Elias grabbed her hand, "It will work. I have faith in you, Ellaria."

"I will do what I can, but Elias. If you die on me. I will never forgive you."

FOUR
DEAD ENDS (TALI)

The gates of Atava were heavily guarded, and everyone who entered the city was being screened. On the ramparts above, Atava security monitored all the traffic in and out of the city. Tali didn't see many of the Prime Commander's Bonemen around. Instead, it was only Atava greencoats running the security check.

"What's going on?" she asked Learon.

"I don't know, let's find out," Learon said.

The south gate acted like a bottleneck, clustering all the travelers from the road into an ever-growing knot as they tried to enter the city. The inspection guard at the gate scrutinized the three of them, but ultimately let them inside, taking down a few notes to his questions—who they were, how many in the party, their business in the city, and where were they coming from. Learon answered the questions, and they were allowed to pass. The crowded sidewalks and city streets neared capacity, and everyone seemed to be carrying bulky packs.

"Have you ever seen it like this?" Wade said.

"This crowded? No, never," Learon replied.

"Do you think there was an attack?" Tali asked.

"Maybe West Meadow isn't the only place being affected by this. . ." Learon paused, "Disease," he concluded.

"Do you believe that's what it is, a disease?" Wade said.

"No," Learon said.

"Me neither."

"Somehow it's tied up with whatever the Sagean and the Prime Commander have been planning," Tali said.

"And the missing people over the last two months?" Wade quipped.

"I didn't say that," Tali said.

"You didn't have to. It's obvious, isn't it? The Sagean Lord returns, and people start to go missing and his beasts are more active all over. Meroha had a name for them, what did she call them?" Wade said.

Tali could remember the girl's story well. A refugee from Kotalla, Meroha had seen this happen in her own country before she escaped.

"The Scree," Tali said.

"Right, the Scree. What a horrible word for such a horrible thing," Learon said.

"But what's wrong with them?" Wade said.

"It could be an alchemist's spell," Tali suggested.

"Whatever it is, we'll figure it out and set it right," Learon said, his eyes tight.

Wade nodded his agreement and Tali decided it best to let the conversation die. She didn't want to tell them it was worse than they knew. She appreciated Learon's mindset. By the sounds of it, Learon had come to the same conclusion she had: that anyone who had gone missing, if they were still alive, were probably turned into these husks of humans. She hadn't told Learon or Wade, but back in the Town Square when Learon was leading them into the building, she tried searching for Rose's energy—but found nothing. Only an empty place where a spark should have been. Sensing that absence made her shiver and queasy.

It made what the Whisper Chain's Melodicure Machine said more understandable. When the mysterious machine told her *yes and no*, she assumed the machine didn't understand the question. But it had understood perfectly, it just had no simple answer. There was no sense in expressing her misgivings about a cure, so she changed the subject.

"So, where are we meeting you?" she asked Learon since he knew the city best. Tali and Wade were going off to retrieve the parts for the communicator devices and Learon wanted to find out if anyone knew anything about West Meadow.

"The Shiner's Den. It's a tavern around the corner here. The shops you're looking for are a few blocks up. If you reach the park, you've gone too far."

They parted in the road, with intentions to meet back in a few hours. Tali and Wade found the Tinker's Row Learon described, and Tali began to filter through every shop until she found the right gears she needed and the tools to fix their communicators. They purchased a small bag full of parts and returned to find Learon in the tavern.

He was waiting near the front at a small table with drinks ready. The marksmen bow that he took from the West Meadow peacekeeper stood propped up against the tableside. They sat down and Learon immediately handed her the paper.

She read the headline and her eyes opened wide. The Prime was dead, and some cities were moving toward a complete lockdown, with a mandatory curfew being instituted in the major cities. All in preparation for the return of the Sagean.

Tali read it again and handed it to Wade. Learon was looking at her, awaiting her reaction.

"I guess that explains some of the craziness happening here. What else did you find out?" Tali delved.

"I talked to—"

"Wait, the Prime's dead? You killed him?" Wade blurted out.

"Shhh," both Learon and Tali said in unison, and she shot him a look to be quiet.

"Sorry. Go on Learon, what did you find?" Wade said.

"I came here to talk to the owner, Frank, who I met through Rose. He said nobody has been seen from West Meadow in eight days. Which means whatever happened to all those people, happened about the same time we were all in Adalon. Probably a week after the riot at Anchor's Point."

"I'm sorry, Learon," Wade said.

"I can't help feeling like it is my fault," Learon said.

"Don't say that. You know it's not your fault," Tali said sternly.

"I know, but that doesn't mean it's not my duty to fix," Learon said.

"Why does it have to be up to us to fix any of this?" Wade said, and he put his empty tank down. "Where are all the old rebels? The Resistance?"

"We're seeing a little of that here, actually," Learon said. "Look around. You notice anything odd?"

Tali and Wade scanned the room but did not immediately identify what Learon was talking about. Certainly, the disheveled interior of the bar resembled the crowded streets. Tali observed the entrance and realized what he was getting at.

"Where are the Bonemen? Where are all the Sagean's soldiers?" she said.

"Right. There's no Bonemen in this city. Frank was telling me that the city threw some of them out. A lot of the citizens here are not thrilled with the decision, but the mayor of Atava, Jori Haywell, said she wants her city shut down to outsiders. She has decreed that her city can defend itself. If you read more in that paper, you'll see that the Coalition is completely gone. Jori was an ambassador on the Coalition and her only concern now is Atava."

"Can't say I'm full of sympathy here, Learon. Atava voted for the Prime if memory serves," Wade said.

"Atava has the walls to keep out whoever they want," Tali said.

"I think we were lucky to get in when we did. The gates are only open for a short amount of time each day," Learon said.

"All these drastic measures, because of the Prime's death?" Wade said.

"I asked the same thing. The word is that West Meadow is not the only place where something odd is going on. Reports from the North and East suggest the same thing has happened to a handful of the smaller cities. Especially ones near the forests where beasts have attacked. To your point Wade, about where are all the rebels—apparently a group of renegades rode out two nights ago, their band of fighters intent on hunting down all the beasts."

"That's good, but wasn't that already tried like thirty years ago and failed?" Wade said.

"That's true. Also, it's not all good news; it sounds like they're after the beasts because they assume Qudin controls them," Learon said.

"So, everything that's happening is being blamed on Qudin?" Tali said.

"Correct. Until the Sagean appears in public, Qudin is the lone Luminary for the people to throw all their fears onto. It's easier to blame the sudden turmoil on something they already fear. It's harder to come to terms with something new to fear. It takes courage to admit when you're afraid," Learon sighed.

"To your question Wade, the Resistance is old. I mean Ellaria is what, fifty-seven years old? And she was one of the youngest in the Resistance at the time. Most of the leaders are gone. They died in their homes. And the ones still alive have gone into hiding," Tali said.

"Right, it's up to us. Not just us three, but our generation. It sounds like these Renegades, are all young, and they may blame Qudin, but I understand they despise the Legion of Light and the Lionized," Learon said.

"You're probably right, our generation has never really understood the faith, but my parents, they're big believers in the Sagelight Faith. How about yours?" Wade said.

"In the Sagean religion? My mom was a believer. I don't think my father was, though. How about you, Tali?" Learon said.

"Rodaire is pretty diverse. There are some old beliefs that still permeate the cities, most are Sagelight Faithful, but there are a lot of Followers of the Fates, too. However, since the war, Rodaire probably has diverged more quickly than other places. The Warhawk Mountains have always been a dividing line of cultures. Rodaire was always ruled by the Sagean Emperor's highest-ranking acolyte, and they were allowed to rule with little oversight. The last one, Heradon, was killed by Kovan," Tali explained.

"When you live in Tovillore, Rodaire feels like another world away. I wonder if the distance led the Empire to give them more anonymity than the rest of the world?," Wade said.

"Could be. It's always been heavily protected, with military support along the coastline. The Empire even built giant towers on the Dire." Tali said.

"I thought the Dire was a group of islands in the Brovic Ocean that people saw as a sign to turn around. There are structures there?" Wade said.

"Just the towers. It's mostly jagged rock," Tali said.

"Is that to keep people from sailing west, or to guard against something from coming from the Brovic?" Learon said. Tali shrugged.

"So, what are we going to do?" Wade said, rolling up his sleeves.

All the talk of Rodaire had Tali missing her mother and she was happy for the change of subject. She peered around the room before she said, "Let's finish our drinks and continue this conversation outside, before the wrong person overhears us."

Agreeing that was best, they ate and talked of simpler things. They laughed at stories of Ellaria and her sway over Kovan and Elias. When they ran out of shared stories, they told ones of their own. For the briefest of moments, they forgot the things that haunted them. Their youth and energy infused a fortitude between them, like an electric charge imparted and absorbed from one another. When they finished a second round of dinks, they left the tavern and headed to the airfield east of the city. Tali was hoping to find the aeronaut Bazlyn Adara and his winddrifter stationed there. But so far, their luck had been going from bad to worse. Simply pondering about bad tidings made her recall the Dawning Gale.

"What are you thinking, Tali?" Learon said, while avoiding a street haggler.

"We're going to the airfield. I think we need to split up," Tali said, slowing her pace to speak in a lowered tone.

"I don't want to do that. Split up, I mean," Wade said.

"I know, but things being the way they are, it's important you get Stasia out of Adalon and we get the Stone somewhere safe," Tali said.

"Is Elias's hideout safe?" Wade said with cocked eyebrows.

"I'm not sure," Tali said, "No one is getting into that vault, I can tell you that. Even if you could get past the door's intricate locking system, it's warded by magic."

"Can we get an airship to go north to Polestis?" Learon said.

"I'm doubtful, but I'm no expert. I've only flown once on Bazlyn's winddrifter. But if they can't, Wade can take a ship to Adalon and get Stasia, then come back," Tali said.

"Or we all go to Adalon," Wade countered.

"No. I'm not taking the Stone to Adalon," Tali said decisively.

"Should we be looking for a way to get to the New World and the Free Cities?" Learon pondered.

"That would mean protecting the Stone for a much longer journey. Ultimately, we probably have to, but I'm not leaving Tovillore until . . ." Tali stopped.

"Until what?" Wade said, looking at her.

"Until she's searched for Kovan," Learon said wistfully.

There was a moment of silence where Tali stared them down, daring either to challenge her. She watched as Learon debated suggesting an alternative, but his shoulders slumped, and he remained silent.

"Does anyone know we have it? The Stone, I mean?" Wade said, changing the subject.

"We have to assume the Sagean Lord does and is looking for us. Because of the ancient cloaking spell, it's probable he's unaware of the traveling gates. Which buys us some time," Learon reasoned.

"Because they think we are all still in Marathal?" Wade said.

"Right," Learon said.

"Which means if Ellaria and Elias survived, they are in greater danger than us," Wade said.

"True," Learon said.

"Let's find out if Bazlyn is even here in Atava and where he's willing to fly. If he's not here, he told me of another aeronaut. A woman named Margo," Tali said.

"This all felt much easier with three war heroes to follow. We don't know what we're doing, do we?" Learon said.

Tali and Wade shook their heads *no* in agreement.

THEY SEARCHED THE AIRFIELDS FOR BAZLYN'S WINDDRIFTER BUT CAME UP empty. There were more ships at the station than the last time she was here, but the Ragallia Savona was not one of them. When Tali spotted a purple sail drawn high on the last ship in the corner, she wondered if it belonged to the aeronaut Bazlyn told her about. Her short-cuff boots tramped over the beaten grass, her pace quickening with each step. If it was Margo's ship, then it was possible she would know where Bazlyn was.

The ship was as beautiful as Bazlyn described, with the name *Skybreaker* written proudly at the bow. The purple sails were all tied off, and two people were moving around the deck. One of the figures was a man—his attention was focused on a piece of machinery he was manipulating with his hands. The grease and dirt decorating his skin was obvious even from a distance. Two ship mechanics, Tali decided.

"Excuse me, sir," she called out.

"Excuse me," Tali said again, louder this time.

"He'll never hear you, he's deaf in one ear and selective in the other," a woman responded back to her. The short, slender woman walked atop the boom. The cuff of her pants tight above her calves, she proceeded out over the open grass and away from Tali.

Tali pursued her around to the back and found the young woman sitting precariously on the boom. With her legs tightly wrapped around the pole, she had a tool in her hand fixing the slide line. Her dark skin glistened with sweat, and her hair was pulled back.

In the grass below, Learon and Wade arrived, and the young woman swung upside down, while still holding on with her thighs to look at them. Tali could see her friend's mouths were open, and each had their necks angled to gawk at the sight of the woman above them and her neckline.

"Hello, gentlemen," the young woman greeted them, "My name is Nyra."

"Hi Nyra, I'm Wade and this is Learon. And Tali," Wade said with a grin, adding Tali's name on the list almost as an afterthought.

"Is this Margo Adree's ship?" Tali asked.

"That it is," Nyra said.

"Is she here?" Tali asked.

"Nope."

"Thorns, we were hoping to talk with her. Do you know when she'll be back?" Tali asked.

"I don't," Nyra said, and she shifted her weight to fix a bolt. "Margo likes to go into the city to drink and gamble. If you know Atava well enough, I bet you could find her."

"If I leave a note, will you see that she gets it?" Tali asked.

"Once I've fixed this last sail line, I'm leaving. But if you drop it on the deck, she'll find it, I'm sure."

Tali flipped the top flap of her bag over and reached inside for a piece of paper. For the briefest moment, the glimmer of the Tempest Stone could be seen. The cloth wrapping around the crystal had slid away. Tali noticed the glint and told herself to remember to re-wrap the stone later. She wrote out a quick note and started to walk the ladder to climb aboard.

"Wait," Nyra said. She grabbed a loose line nearby that hung down and swung on it. She glided down to them on the ground and held her hand out for the note. Standing in the grass next to Tali, she could see Nyra was slightly shorter than she first estimated. Tali smiled.

"I'll give it to her," Nyra said.

"It's no trouble. I'll leave it aboard as you suggested," Tali said and she found the ladder and climbed up. Nyra watched her a moment before turning to talk with Wade and Learon. The Skybreaker was a much larger ship than Bazlyn's. The deck was like two ships fused together. There were rigs for six sails rising high to the tubular balloon above and another four smaller angled sails at the sides like wings. Tali appraised the construction and marveled at the wheels and tie-back controls that wound the outside to a forward wheel.

The head of the man she saw from before appeared from below and he climbed up from the interior lower cabin bay. There was a stubble to his cheeks, and dirt and black residue covered his shirt and skin in splotches.

"What are you doing up here, we don't take off till just after sunrise?" he said.

"I'm not a passenger," Tali said.

"What's that miss? You have to speak up."

"I was looking for Margo. Nyra said I could leave her a note on board," Tali said loudly.

The man eyed her crookedly, but nodded his head that he understood, "Why don't you leave it with me. I have to give her a run-down of everything we've worked on."

Tali hesitated but decided there was no harm in it. "Thank you, sir. I'm looking for another aeronaut I know. A friend of Margo's named Bazlyn Idara. He pilots a winddrifter called the—"

"I know Baz," the man cut her off.

"You do? Have you seen him recently?"

"He was in Amera last time we crossed paths. That was about a week ago. If I see him, I'll let him know you're looking for him. Miss...?"

"Tali."

"Tali, I'll let him know. I'm sure if Margo sees him in Adavan, she'll tell him for you, too."

"That would be helpful, thank you. Is that where *The Skybreaker* sails tomorrow?"

"Yes."

Tali turned to go back to the ground. "Do you know if anyone around here sails to Polestis?"

"Not many do, miss. The only one I know that does is Baz."

"Thank you," she said again and climbed back down.

When she got back to solid ground, she found Nyra laughing with Learon and Wade.

Something about the woman's manner annoyed Tali. She kept touching Wade's arm and shaking her head. It made Tali have to hold her eyes in place so they wouldn't roll right out of her head. She loved those two idiots, but neither were that charming.

"Tali, Nyra was telling us that most all the roads out of Atava are too treacherous to travel," Wade said.

"It's true, everything north of Jenovee is crawling with beasts," Nyra said flatly.

"Soon the summer rains will wash out those roads not crawling with beasts. I'm guessing the south roads will be closed soon, too," Learon said shifting in his stance.

"What about the pass?" Tali said.

"I haven't heard any trouble going west. You three should be able to travel it if that's what you're planning. It stays dry most of the summer. Probably worth paying for a coach if you can afford though, given the way things currently are. There's no trouble on the pass yet, but you know what the old-timers say: *the last place to see the shadow becomes the darkest point.*"

"Nyra's a mechanic for airships around here," Wade said.

"Yes, my hands are always busy," Nyra said.

"How long have you been working around here?" Tali said. She couldn't remember seeing her the last time she came through.

"Not long. I was working in Amera before this," Nyra said.

"How are things there?" Learon said.

"Amera? Amera is a cesspool of lawlessness. I was happy to get away, and I don't ever want to go back," Nyra said, and she rubbed the back of her left shoulder. It sounded like the sincerest thing she had said yet.

They thanked Nyra for her time and started back to Atava. Tali explained that they could wait for Bazlyn, but Wade and Learon thought it was better to head to Polestis, than wait for an airship that could never arrive. She wanted to argue to wait, but she felt too anxious to hole up in the city. They proceeded to the stables, mounted up, and departed out of the south gate. The long ride to the east was ahead of them. On the west road, still in the shadow of the city walls, they found a rider in a short shawl cloak waiting for them.

The figure waved at them and pulled the hood away. It was Nyra. Wade redirected and trotted over to her.

"If you three are intending to cross over the Thorn, then I wondered if I might come with? If you'll have me. Things being the way they are, traveling in groups makes a lot of sense. If you want to get anywhere safely, that is, and I don't like the idea of traveling by myself," Nyra said.

From his raised eyebrows and far off blue eyes, Tali could tell Learon was wary to agree, but Wade more than made up for Learon's dismissal with his own enthusiasm.

"It's a good idea, Tali. Four is better than three on the open road," Wade said.

"I'm a terrible cook, but I can fix anything, and I know the pass well," Nyra added.

Learon remained silent and acquiesced to Tali for the final say. Tali wanted to say *no*. Nyra seemed harmless enough but adding a stranger to their group wasn't a good idea. Of course, it was a free world and having her follow at their heels felt uncomfortable. *Why couldn't Wade just have kept moving?*

"I promise I won't slow you down. Margo can vouch for me, if you want to go find her first," Nyra said sensing Tali's hesitation.

"Where exactly are you going?" Tali said squeezing the leather of her reins.

"I'm trying to get to Rahmil in Rodaire. It's just in the foothills, on the eastern slope."

"I know where it is," Tali said. Rahmil was a tiny town east of Rashan. It probably didn't show up on many maps.

"Oh, right, I suppose you would," Nyra said, placing Tali's appearance as a Rodairean native. Her tan skin color, dark hair, and big brown eyes were a giveaway here.

The concern on Nyra's face suggested she was running from something, but from what Tali knew of aeronauts, they loved their ships more than people. If Margo trusted Nyra to work on her ship, then they probably could trust her company for a day. Tali ground her teeth in frustration that the boys had left the decision to her and sighed.

"You're welcome to ride with us to Thorn Pass, but from there, I'm afraid we will part ways and you'll be on your own to Rahmil," Tali said.

"Thank you," Nyra said, and they kicked off together.

WHILE THEY TRAVELED ON THE WEST ROAD, NYRA TOLD THEM ABOUT HER time working on ships in Atava and Amera. She had stories about other aeronauts and ones about passengers fighting amongst the clouds. Tali's impression of the young woman had softened over the course of the day. Nyra, was nice enough, and while Tali found her to be overtly flirtatious with Learon and Wade, it wasn't an indictment on her character. Tali came to see it as a sort of fun banter, that kept the guys' mind off worse matters.

They rode until just before nightfall, when Learon made them stop with enough light remaining to see what they were doing. He chose a spot nestled against some boulders, believing their camp was about ten leagues short of the town of Last Ride. While Learon and Wade set up camp and scouted the surrounding area, Tali settled the horses and placed their bedrolls around the fire. She grabbed her own tinker's tools and one of the watches to fiddle with before she slept. The light wasn't good for detailed work, but her mind needed the distraction.

The blue flames of the anthracite came alive, and the first thing Tali worked on was a necklace for the obsidian coin Elias had given her long ago. She found herself rubbing her thumb over the amethyst stone inlay, an unconscious habit she developed while traveling. The crystal was set in a ring around the edge and at the center was a large alchemist sigil Tali had never seen anywhere else. Something about the coin made her feel closer to the others that were missing, and she didn't want to risk losing it. When she was done, she tucked it inside her shirt and slowly disassembled a watch to inspect the housing. Learon rested with his arms behind his head, staring at the stars. The fire crackled and from the far side of it, Wade and Nyra glanced at her.

"How can you see what you are doing?" Wade said.

"I put them together, so I sort of know where everything goes without looking," Tali said.

"Tali, are you a gadget maker?" Nyra asked. Intrigued, she was angling her head for a better view.

"Not really, but I have some skill with gears and moving parts."

"More than just some, by the looks of it," Nyra said.

Tali smiled. Having a fourth person with them was more intrusive than she anticipated. Normally they would be planning their next moves or discussing the Sagean. A night without it would probably serve them well, but Tali didn't like the feeling of being alienated from the truth. They were a few hours outside of Atava when Tali realized that Nyra didn't know Tali was a Luminary. There was no way to tell someone you were an ancient being with the power to control energy. Tali was starting to understand that she needed to get used to hiding who she was; both her identity and her abilities. She didn't consciously think about it in Atava, but the fact was a rise in energy inside her would be visible to others. The scars at her eyes and temples might glow if she didn't control the flows of energy inside herself.

Eventually, she put the watches away and lay down. Wade and Nyra had talked for a long time before each of them had fallen asleep, but Learon was still awake. Their fire pulsed and light flickered and threw shadows in the trees. The howls of an animal were heard far in the distance.

"Learon, is this safe?" she whispered.

"Our campsite? Yes," Learon replied.

"No. I meant traveling the Thorn and you know, all the rest of it?" she said, trying not to say what she really meant in case Nyra was still awake.

"If we stick together, we'll make it," Learon said.

Somehow, Tali was always calmed by Learon, then she heard him say something else, but it was faint and with a peculiar intonation, *'No matter the path you choose, I'll protect you.'*.

"What did you say?" Tali asked.

"Me?" Learon said, confused.

"Yes, just now."

"Nothing," he told her, *'Nothing aloud, I think'*.

"Are you doing that?" She said, hearing the voice again, but somehow muted.

"What?"

"Umm, nothing. It's nothing. I'm just hearing things in the trees," Tali complained, pulling her blanket tight around her shoulders and covering her head slightly. She fell asleep thinking about how much she missed the quilted blanket Kovan got her for their flight on the airship, and she missed her friend.

FIVE

SEPARATE WAYS (TALI)

A rustling amongst their campground brought her eyes open. Tali sat up abruptly and her movement stirred Learon to do the same.

"What's happening, did you hear something?" Learon lifted himself to look around for intruders.

Tali tilted her head trying to figure out what had awoken her. A loud snore croaked from the opposite side of the fire and they both turned their attention to Wade. The spot where Nyra had slept was empty. She had snuck away in the night, *but why*?

Tali pointed to the empty spot next to Wade, "Where did Nyra go?"

Learon was about to say something but jumped to his feet. He bounded over to the horses and tore through Tali's things.

"No," Tali said. Dread washed over her in a single, devastating wave, "No, no, no."

Her cries awakened Wade, too.

"It's gone," Learon said. He dropped Tali's bag and climbed the boulders to look out over toward the road.

"What's gone?" Wade got to his feet.

"No!" Tali said again shaking head to foot. Wade picked the bag off the dirt.

"The Stone. Nyra stole the Stone?" Wade said dumbfounded, "How did she even know about it?" Wade wandered the camp and walked back.

The flames of fire flickered and withdrew. Tali had drawn the heat into her well without meaning to. Her eyes burned with rage. Wade spotted her and rushed over.

"We'll get it back, Tali. She can't have gone far," he said putting his hands gently on her arms.

Tali could only stare at him, tears welling up in her eyes. They let their guard down for one night and lost the stone Kovan gave his life for. She shrugged his hands off, snatched her things off the ground, and marched over to her horse.

"Pack up, we're getting out of here. We have to go after her," she reeled.

Wade jumped to do as she asked. She realized her tone was harsh, but she couldn't calm herself. Learon skipped down from the rocks and grabbed his bow.

"Someone's coming," he said.

"If it's Nyra, I'm going to kill her," Tali spat.

A fluttering overhead rattled and something small landed on a tree limb above them. It squeaked and flapped its wings. High in the branches, it was too dark to see.

"It's a bat," Learon said.

Tali appraised him, surprised he could even see a shape, let alone tell what it was. The firelight only reached so far, and the tree foliage quickly swallowed the light.

Out of the underbrush, a small black cat came sprinting to her.

"Remi!" Tali said. She knelt, and it jumped into her arms. Remi had grown bigger in the short time they had been apart. Relief flooded over her: relief that it wasn't an intruder, relief to be reunited with Remi. Clarity came and the rage pulsing through her washed away. Moments before, she was lost in the throes of aimless anxiety. She still understood the stakes of having the Stone stolen, but the path seemed clearer.

Another white mystcat pranced into their camp and Meroha, the young refugee from Kotalla, followed it onto trampled ground. Ducking under a low tree branch, Meroha lurched forward into a tight hug when her eyes found Tali,.

"It's so good to see you all," Meroha said.

"Meroha, what are you doing here!" Wade said rushing over.

Tali pulled back from Meroha's tight grip, her eyebrows raised. She was almost lost for words, and could only think to say, "Explain while we pack, we have to get out of here."

Meroha spoke while they hastily gathered everything.

"About a week ago, Elias's cat Merphi was going wild trying to leave.

I realized I needed to follow her. I grabbed some things, and we left. We reached Polestis, and the cat stopped. That's when we changed directions, and Remi started leading us south. I purchased a coach ride south along the mountain roads to Thorn's Pass. We arrived there yesterday morning, but Remi kept moving. So, I got a lift on a carriage going east to Atava. At some point, Remi cried and jumped out of the window. I had the driver stop. I told a quick lie and ran after that determined little cat. We crossed over some wilderness, in a straight line for you. I saw a woman leading a horse out of this grove. She mounted and kicked off toward the road. I thought it was Tali and called out, but the woman didn't hear me or didn't care. She rode out hot, like the burning sun was beneath her."

"Not beneath, but it's on its way," Tali said coldly.

"Why would the mystcats do such a thing, Tali?" Wade said.

"Maybe Merphi sensed Elias was in trouble, but for some reason lost her connection to him," Tali said, equally curious.

"But why?" Wade said.

"I don't know, but it's best we don't think the worse," Tali slammed down the last strap to her bags and started for the road.

"I think maybe they saved me, too," Meroha said following her.

"How's that?" Learon asked, as he led the horses out of the trees. Once out, Wade pulled Meroha up on with him on his horse.

"When I got into the coach at Polestis, I heard an explosion. I could be wrong, but I'd swear it came from deep in the mountains. The same direction back to Elias's house," Meroha said.

"Where are we riding to, Tali? Nyra's got at least an hour on us now," Learon asked.

"I'd bet all the amber in the world Nyra is heading back to the airfield in Atava. The mechanic said it was flying out at dawn to Adavan. That's where were going," Tali said, and she kicked off through the wild grass to the road.

THEY CROSSED THE GRASSLAND AND PASTURES THAT BORDERED THE surrounding area of Atava in a blur. In a thundering gallop, they flew along the fringes of the long shadows, stretching off the massive city walls. The early rays of sunlight glinted upon the tall structures protected within. A few hundred feet from the gate and the adjacent air station,

Tali saw the purple-sailed winddrifter clearing the tree line toward the distant sunrise.

They slowed their strides slightly to crest over the mounded road and back down to the fence line outside the airfield.

Learon pointing to the sky, "That's it, isn't it?" he shouted in disgust.

"Thorns," Tali cursed into the wind

Coming to a brisk halt outside the ship-teller's post, Learon dismounted in one smooth motion. His feet caught the ground in a run with his horse and continued in stride for the last twenty feet. Tali's ability on a horse had advanced significantly since riding her first one out of Atava a month ago with Kovan, but she would never be able to do that. Instead, she tugged back on her horse with all her strength to stop. Learon was already speaking with the teller on duty by the time she got down and over to him.

"Was she on it?" Tali said breathlessly.

"Sounds like it," Learon said. "The teller saw a young woman fitting Nyra's description arrive. She left her horse and ran to catch the Skybreaker."

Learon's words fell on her like a stack of bricks. She hung her head, contemplating what to do. They were too late. When Wade came riding up with Meroha holding tightly from behind, he stopped next to Tali and pointed behind her.

"Isn't that. . ."

"Yes, she's gone. We're torqued."

"No. Not that one: the one on the ground. I didn't see that ship yesterday. Didn't you say your friend's airship had maroon sails?" Wade said.

Tali spun around hopefully. The Ragallia Savona sat off in the corner of the airfield. Bazlyn was here, and that meant there was still a chance to catch Nyra.

In a trot, they approached the ship. Tali dismounted and called out for Bazlyn. It took a moment, but she spotted his crossed feet sticking out just beyond the edge of the high lofted ballast mast. The ears of a small terrier dog popped up to the edge, and the feet shifted.

"Miss Tali, is that you down there?" Bazlyn called back, and Tali waved energetically.

Bazlyn climbed down the tall ladder from the ballast and the sidewall door to the hull swung free. He pulled a lever and steps imbedded in the shell popped free. That was new. Tali walked around the side to meet him.

Bazlyn's last foot found the grass, and he put Zephyr down. The small dog scampered over to Tali and bounced between her legs excitedly.

"Do you like the new ladder? I just installed it," Bazlyn said. There was something about seeing the warm and gracious old man again that made her smile, and she hugged him like they were dear old friends.

"Oh, hello," he said, absorbing her crashing into him. "Is everything all right?" His eyes studied her.

"Not exactly. Let me introduce you to my friends," Tali said, and brought him over to the others.

After the introductions, Bazlyn scanned around and back to her. "Where's Kovan?" he said. Tali should have expected the question, but she hadn't, and the sudden look of grief on her face told Bazlyn all he needed to know. He hugged her again.

"I'm sorry, kid. Trouble's been brewing all over Tovillore. Where did it happen up at Anchor's Point?" Bazlyn asked.

"No, in Marathal," she said.

"Yep, heard about that one, too. Well, everyone heard about that. I suppose it makes sense if it's as they say and Qudin was there, then old Kovan Rainer would be by his side," Bazlyn said.

"Wait, you knew who Kovan was? When you flew us to Atava just before summer, you knew that whole time?" Tali said.

"Of course. Well, not the whole time. But I'm no slug. I know when a hero of the Great War is on my ship. So what's happened, where are you headed now?" Bazlyn said.

"A woman stole something of ours last night and we think she's on Margo's ship," Learon said.

"How do you know she's on the Skybreaker?" Bazlyn said.

"We met her yesterday working on Margo's ship and we thought we could trust her," Tali said.

"Was her name Nyra?" Bazlyn asked.

"Yes," Tali said.

"Ratspit. She's a mechanic, yes, but she's also a purloiner for one of the southern syndicates," Bazlyn cursed.

"A purloiner?" Learon asked.

"An indentured thief. In Nyra's case, she has a talent for fixing things, so she works off her debt that way. But I heard she's been marked by someone dangerous," Bazlyn said.

Tali didn't know what holding a mark was, and she didn't care, "Bazlyn, we have to go after her."

"What did she steal? No, don't tell me, I don't want to know."

"You don't, but I'll tell you Kovan risked his life for it," Tali said.

"I understand and I'll help. The Savona can be airworthy in an hour. But I have to tell you, there's no catching the Skybreaker. It will take us a day and a half to get to Amera."

"Not Amera. They were flying to Adavan," Tali corrected him.

"Adavan is a three-day flight, but I feel better about it," Bazlyn said.

"Why is Adavan better than Amera?" Tali asked.

"Amera has always been a lawless land, but this last month, since the Prime took over, the syndicates have all moved in to stake their claim over the best gem mines. It's gotten extremely cutthroat. Once word reached them of the Prime's death, the place sank further into disarray. The Bounty Hunter's Guild is headquartered there, the Moonstalkers, and they're in control of everything. Every man or woman still there are on someone's payroll or multiple payrolls. It's so bad, the Bonemen have pulled out."

"Why don't the regular folk leave, too?" Wade said.

"Many of the locals have left, but there's a lot of money down there. Amber exchanging hands, amber to be made; crystals and gems are big business."

"Change of plans. I'll fly with Bazlyn to Adavan and chase after Nyra. Wade, you should get passage on another winddrifter to Adalon and get Stasia," Tali said definitively. She reached into her pocket and produced a communicator watch. "I was able to fix one of them last night. Once I fix mine, I'll send a message, but I only have the one enchanted pen to send a message."

"There's one problem," Bazlyn chimed in.

"What?" Tali said.

"Only cloudparters are allowed to land in Adalon anymore, and all of those are manned with those damned Bonemen. Not sure when the next is scheduled to stop here. Also, you should know the larger cities like Adalon and Eloveen, Adavan too, are all instituting curfews," Bazlyn told her.

"Besides, Tali, I'm not sure I should be showing my face anywhere near the Arcana. I think I should go with you to Adavan. I grew up not far from there. I know the city. My parent's farm is just north of the Eye and if Nyra escapes the city, I know the outlying country well," Wade offered.

"But what about Stasia?" Tali said.

"I don't mean to tell you your business, but you don't have to pick her up in Adalon, Tali." Bazlyn said, "Send a message for her to travel to Midway. All the aeronauts are re-routing through there now. I can drop you both in the south, refill, and run up to Midway for her."

"How long would that take?" Wade asked.

"Probably five or six days, with good weather," Bazlyn said.

Wade's frown revealed his unsaid misgivings. Tali shared his sentiment, the prospect of their friend, a young woman traveling by herself was hard to accept, given the state of things.

"I'll meet her in Midway," Learon put forth.

"Learon, no. There has to be another way," Tali said. There was merit to the idea, but Tali hated the sound of it.

"It's fine. I know the country from here to the Uhanni River well, or fairly well. I'll send a message to meet Stasia in Midway. Then I can ride east. I think it's a four-day ride, so I should arrive a day before Bazlyn gets there."

"Are you sure? Nyra said the east roads were dangerous," Wade put in.

"The thief? The thief said not to take the east roads and you believe her," Learon said.

"You think she was lying?"

"She could have been telling the truth. I guess I'll find out."

"We." Meroha said.

"You want to ride with me?" Learon said.

"No, but I'm not getting in that thing," Meroha pointed to the wind-drifter above.

Tali quietly watched the two cats roaming the field of trampled dirt, contemplating the reality of going in two directions, neither of which they had discussed before. She had a strong connection to Learon that she couldn't explain and was not eager to part from him, but it was the best plan they had, and so she reluctantly agreed.

The hour went by fast, while Bazlyn readied his ship, they began dividing supplies between them for two different journeys. Remi was too big now to ride in her cloak pocket, but he still fit in her satchel. She handed it to Wade who took it aboard, along with his own pack.

"You should take the elum blade, Learon," Tali offered, handing it to him, strappings and all.

"Are you sure? How will you defend yourself?" he said.

Tali put her palm out face up. They both expecting something to happen, but nothing did.

"Were you trying to produce lightning?" Learon said, with a small upturn of a smile.

"Yes, but . . ." Tali bit her lip, "Torque it. How does Elias do it so easily?"

"Practice, I suspect," Learon said.

"You sure you'll be safe, Learon?"

"We'll be fine."

"Wade should be going. Stasia is his friend," Tali said. She knew it was an insensitive thought, but she had to say it.

"If Nyra proved anything, it's that we need all the friends we can get. It's not that long a trip and sooner or later, you'll have the second watch working. Maybe we'll hear from Ellaria."

"What if we can't get the stone back?" Tali said.

"You will. Approach it like one of your mentors," Learon said.

"What, kill everyone with lightning?"

"No. I meant your other mentor, Kovan. When in doubt, improvise, and don't be afraid of Plan B."

Tali smiled and hugged her friend. When she finally pulled away, she turned abruptly for the ladder, sure if she lingered any longer, she would change her mind. Whatever the bond between them was, it was a sense of *you go, I go*, and they were breaking that today.

Wade helped her get into the hull at the top rung and leaned out over the sidereal, "Tell Stasia I'm sorry, and I'll see her soon," he called down to Learon.

"I will."

From the back bench, Tali looked down at him and Meroha. Learon twirled his horse around and led the others a short distance away. There he stopped and gazed up at her, waving. The ship slowly started to rise and before she knew it, she couldn't see the details of his face anymore. When she finally turned her eyes away, she found Wade sitting off to the side with a death grip locked on the railing, and she laughed.

In Bazlyn's supplies, she spotted a deck of Reckoner cards. Tali retrieved them and approached Wade. As the air cooled around them rapidly, she pried him off the rail to sit with her.

"You teach me Reckoner and I'll teach you some of my card tricks," she said.

SIX

THE DRAGONS PLOT (BATAK)

There was a time when Batak had thought about murdering all the remaining members of the Court of Dragons—six years after the death of the Emperor Sagean Mayock Kovall, when they emerged from hiding. That's what he had planned, but not what happened. They had come together at a banquet at his estate in Anvil to form the Court, and Batak was going to poison them all. However, smart men take advantage of opportunity, and the death of an Empire was an extraordinary opportunity. He decided they had a use.

The Sagean Empire was like immense machine that suddenly no one knew how to operate. How were people fed and controlled? The Coalition of Nations had taken over, but they had their hands full and the Court realized they could control it all. With delicacy, they placed the whole of it on strings for them to pull and puppeteer. The opportunity from the upheaval was filled by entrepreneurs charging toward an advancing age. Money was the new emperor, and the acolytes of the old emperor took advantage. The destruction of the Orders left but two classes: employers and employees. When industries reached their hands out to the Coalition for aid, it was the Court of Dragons that shook it. True, wide commerce was born, and the Court-branded products and banks become monuments to power. The one weakness in their plan, the one cog stuck in the gears, was Qudin and their own limited humanity.

Without the Atlas Tablet, they could no longer track Luminaries. Qudin, to their surprise, didn't show the slightest interest to rule; but if another Luminary came, it could easily unravel all they had worked for. The Illumination Surge took most Luminaries in their early teens and the ones it didn't, they tracked down and eliminated. One of their own, Helena Knox, a cousin to the line of emperors, had given birth to a son. Edward's powers appeared six years after the end of the war and the court came back together to discuss what to do.

It would have been so easy then, Batak thought as he walked the steps up from the Dragon's Well to the surface. The Well was a subsurface complex of rooms that housed many of the acolytes' prized possessions, powerful objects that once lived—as they did—in the Sagean's Palace. None of them had been back to the Palace in Adalon since it was raided at the end of the war. There had been some discussion of returning with the new Sagean, but the Court had a new base of operations here in Denmee.

It had cost them each a small fortune to renovate the old ruin, but it was more heavily guarded than the Palace ever was. The island was a good headquarters and positioned well enough that their defenses were strong. When the Traitor, whose name was never spoken, escaped the palace all those years ago with a few magical items and rare books, the alarms were raised, but he escaped before palace guards could find him. Here on the island of Denmee, a similar event was nearly impossible, cut off as they were from the Mainland.

The Court had many structures built over the years, including massive stone watchtowers positioned along the coast from the northern tip of the island to the south. Batak had received a report from the north tower that riders were approaching from the airfield. The new Sagean Lord was approaching with his guardsmen, and Batak wanted to speak with the Sagean before the meeting with the full court.

Every move against the other Court members had to be done with delicacy, including simple words to their Sagean Lord as they walked; maneuvers he could have avoided if he had gone through with his scheme to eliminate them. Batak was a much younger man then, after the war. A lot of them he didn't know, and the other half he had never trusted.

The War had decimated their collective power and influence, but not entirely, and certainly not their wealth. He told himself at the time that he needed them, if they were to have any chance of reclaiming the world. After the actions of the Traitor amongst their numbers, it was hard to trust any of them ever again. It took a few years to realize that unlike life under the Emperor, in the Coalition, wealth was power.

After forty years of growing their wealth, the prospects of disposing of any of his rivals was daunting. Batak almost felt bad he left these decisions to Delvar. His son would soon be raised up by the Sintering Fountain and his rebirth as a Luminary would solidify his standing amongst the court. Batak trusted Edward's friendship with Delvar would help his son rise to a trusted Number Two position, which the others could not hope to achieve. He was dumbfounded how some of his colleagues remained oblivious to Edward's contempt of them. Batak was not under any such delusion. Once Edward had the ability to strike out against them, he would. Their only real hope was to convince the new Sagean the Court could be trusted—they were his council and not his equal or rival.

Still, I should have killed them, Batak thought. Not Herod, of course. He was too amenable, and useful. But it had been thirty-four years ago and a lot of them were so young, Batak falsely believed he could control them. That was his real failing: his inability to predict who the most formidable ones would become. They were all hungry to reclaim the world, but someone like Verro Mancovi was hard to foresee.

The son of the late Emperor's treasurer, Eron Mancovi, who himself had been a complete pushover, and killed in the War. Verro was smart and calculating, quickly figuring out how to leverage others' wealth to build his own. Theomar Kyana hated him for it, but they all owed Verro for his shrewd investments. Still, Theomar called Verro *fresh* behind his back, as though Mancovi's money was somehow less valuable.

Batak had passed all of his knowledge and foresight onto his son. A natural fatherly instinct, but also a strategic one. Navigating the treachery of the Court was like walking atop a thawing lake of ice; every step could be the last.

At the top of the Well was a single ring of marble columns and a small portico where the stairs began. The small town that existed here before they moved in was meager. Between the Well, the estate, the towers and the new port, the town blossomed into a small city, but the Court's control over the entire island was absolute. The meeting was set for inside the Estate and Batak had to divert Edward outside, ideally beyond the sight of any of the other six Court members.

He made his way to the cascade of steps at the north fields to intercept the Sagean. At the top of the steps, he saw the riders pulling up and stationing their horses. He cut across to the middle landing and waited.

"It is good to see you, my Lord. It's good you have come," Batak greeted the Sagean.

"Did I have a choice?"

Batak ignored the question born of frustration, "They await you in the pavilion,"

"Even that damned Queen, Rotha Durrone?"

"No, my lord, she has returned to Andal, temporarily."

"Good, I despise that woman."

"She has considerable wealth and influence."

The Sagean shook his head and unconsciously rubbed his hand as they walked. The pain Batak knew was a result of the dragon ring Edward wore and could never take off.

"When will I be rid of this ring, Batak? I know the Court believes it necessary, but it's a collar."

"Some do," Batak said. Though in truth the Court saw the ring and the attached spell as protection, and the smart ones worried for the day it was removed.

"You must know that as my powers grow, its hold over me diminishes."

"I understand, my Lord. The ring is a safeguard devised long ago for your protection as well as ours."

"Spare me the speech, Batak. It should have come off after my Illumination Surge. That was twenty-eight years ago. Since I was fourteen, I have done as my Court would ask of me. But you did not come out to meet me to talk about the ring. So, what's on your mind Batak?"

"I wanted to inform you that I have decided Delvar shall take my place under the Fountain at the Temple of Ama."

"I will appreciate a friend by my side. I assume the others know; did they question the move?"

Edward had always possessed a perceptive intuition. It was his best skill, outside of masking his appearance. It was possible he possessed other talents, but this Court of Dragons lacked the knowledge of the acolytes of the past who had guided the Sagean Lords before him to fully develop any talents. He was apparently keenly aware of the Court's constant bickering over the seats at the Sintering Fountain, and their Casts.

"Among the Court, my wisdom is often overshadowed by my strength and seniority. If they were surprised by the move, they quickly adjusted."

They arrived at the arches and proceeded through the arcade in silence, past an ornate set of doors to an interior courtyard of open archways that overlooked the Mainsolis Sea. Most of the Court was seated around the long table or out on the cliff-side terrace. At his entrance, they all turned, expecting the Sagean. Batak strolled to his seat with his hands clasped at his back. He found his spot next to Herod and silently observed his fellow Court members. As the oldest man on the court, Herod Mimnark was always a good person to sit next to at things like this. His natural temperament lacked some of the venom the others had seeping from their pores. Herod kept Batak calm amongst the snakes. Opposite of him was Theomar Kyana, the train baron of Rodaire and shipping tycoon along the Zulu.

Theomar Kyana was crafty and deceiving. All the Court was made up of capitalists, but besides Batak's own family, the Kyana's were the oldest generation. Theomar's parents had saved him from fighting in the war. They were smart enough to see that Emperor Sagean Mayock Kovall, the twelfth Sage, was being out-maneuvered all over the Mainland, and they hid Theomar away. They themselves were killed in the raid on the Sagean Palace on the night of *The Weeping*.

When word of The Resistance's victory over the Empire came, it was met with disbelief at first. The world could not accept it until the Emperor's war banner was taken to Adalon and the tattered remains placed over the Reverence Bell at the heart of the city. The bell was a thousand years old and rang for the observance of the blue sun: six rings for the start of the blue sun and three for the end. The banner of the Resistance and the Hawk of Freedom were raised and draped from windows and over horses and carriages. The Resistance had made a point to show this exchange of power to the Mainland cities all the way from the Valley of Thorns beneath the Dragon's Spine to Adalon. That very night, as though a rage had erupted in the newly freed citizens, there were terrible riots. The remaining Bonemen in the city were killed, as were sympathizers. People previously too afraid and witless to choose a side in the war were made into mad men overnight. It culminated with the raid and attempted destruction of the Sagean Palace. If not for Ellaria's squadron, the Palace would have burned to the ground. The day became known as *the Weeping*.

"So, where is he?" Shirova asked, "I saw you run to meet with him on his way here." Her eyes glowered and arms crossed.

"He will be here shortly," Batak said, and the doors opened as guards entered. The Sagean walked in with a squad of his red caped guards, each with the gold metallic faceplates that covered their mouths like a hard, shining veil. Everyone stood from their seat and put their hands in front of their eyes.

"By the Light of the Blue, we are enlightened," they said, as was customary.

"The Light sees you all," the Sagean replied.

They lowered their hands and waited for the Sagean to sit before finding their own chairs.

"Lord of Illumination, we are grateful to receive your presence. Your communications were received, but they didn't say much. Please tell us of the battle inside the tomb," Verro bowed and took his seat.

"We heard the Prime was killed and the ambassador of Adalon," Theomar Kyana said, a tinge of displeasure in his question.

"They're both dead," Edward said, "But we shot and killed Kovan Rainer in the battle."

That was a rumor they had heard and the Sagean's confirmation sparked some low murmurs between Shirova and Aylanna. All had unfortunate dealings with Kovan in the past, but Aylanna had been particularly aggravated when Kovan escaped capture in Ravenvyre. Shirova had delighted in emphasizing the blunder.

"We have word that Ellaria Moonstone and Qudin Lightweaver are on the run. Did you see them get away?" Verro asked Edward with his calm defusing nature. His manner was always agreeable. It was one of his strengths.

"I didn't and I'm unsure of their whereabouts," Edward said with empty hands.

"We know they were spotted in Fairville," Theomar taunted. Theomar was not nearly as tactful.

"I did not receive such a report, but you did, Theomar?" Edward said, his temper flaring.

"Of course, we did, Edward. We--"

Whatever Theomar was going to say, he didn't get to finish. He crumpled to the floor, writhing in pain. Screaming, he kicked his chair over.

"Don't forget yourself. I am your Lord!" the Sagean declared through gritted teeth.

Batak was unsure what the Sagean was doing to Theomar, but a wave of heat radiated from him. It was not a surprising outburst but Harrimon, sitting next to him, shivered. The cowardly man was easily intimidated by every other member of the Court, his obedience born of a weaker wealth and position.

"Sagean, please desist now," Verro said, and he held his thumb and finger over the ruby ring in his hand. Verro applied pressure to the ring and the Sagean's hold on Theomar stopped as he fell to one knee. Aylanna's face held a smirk; she had always despised Theomar for swooping in to build the trainline in her homeland.

"Let us move on. Did you recover the Scepter?" Verro asked.

"I did," the Sagean said, reclaiming his seat.

"You did?" Verro said.

Edward narrowed his eyes, "Yes, Verro," he said, and he withdrew the black scepter from his cloak.

Something about it swallowed more of the light than it reflected. Batak almost couldn't look at it. It was a combination of charred black wood and some sort of inscribed metal. A dragon wrapped around near the shaft and the blue crystal top was intoxicating. But a darkness gathered about it and made him wince to look at it.

"Please put it away, my Lord," Aylanna said, shrunk back in her seat.

"As you wish."

"That is wonderful. It is the key we need to activate the Sintering Fountain," Verro said.

"It will be useless if we can't deliver the Gem of Souls there to power the Fountain. What are we doing about that?" Theomar asked, his eyes fixed on Verro.

"We have a group of soldiers transporting the Gem and our Casts from the Andal train to Adalon. Once there, we are loading it abord a barge for Aquom."

"Why not just set sail from Andal? And why have the Casts been moved from the Red Spear?" Herod said. He had a studious way of speaking that suited his age.

"The situation in Amera has become untenable. We moved the notable prisoners from the Red Spear to Adalon. Half the prisoners were already in Andal. As for the Gem, we have discovered that the closer the Gem stays to the land, the better. Its energy gathers the sea currents to it otherwise. We don't want to risk losing it in the ocean," Verro said.

"And the Scree, have they a use, or are they just dead weight?" Shirova Edana said, unable to hide an audible grumble of her displeasure.

It was a common expression for her. She was an unlikable and unhappy woman. Too hungry for her own good, but in an odd way, her open hostility and ambition made her more trustworthy. More than the rest of them, Batak always knew where Shirova stood on an issue. Her son, Nathan, had been a fast riser in the Cloaked Knife at the Citadel, and Delvar's friend during training. Batak considered him a colder, less cunning version of his mother.

"Yes, they will follow the direction of the Sagean. All he has to do is direct his influence through the Scepter and they will follow his command," Verro assured her. Edward simply glanced between the two, following the exchange and did not betray his own feelings on the subject.

"And we're not worried about releasing them back into the world?" Aylanna said.

"It has created some turmoil in the west of Tovillore and in Rodaire, but that's it. I'm unconcerned about the effect of their presence among the people and more interested in having them in position to fight," Verro said.

"Are you still on that? We delayed the completion of the train lines in the south because of your concern for the people of Tovillore," Aylanna said.

"I have no doubt they will revolt. It has already begun. Atava has shut us out," Verro said.

"Enough," the Sagean spat angrily. "You said Qudin and Ellaria were seen in Fairville. Tell me more about that."

"Yes, they were spotted there, amongst the many other citizens fleeing Marathal," Verro revealed.

"Well then, I shall leave immediately to finish the Quantum Man once and for all."

"There is no need, my Lord. We have someone we trust tracking them, and we can't risk you. Our man will follow them and, if necessary, divert them as needed."

"But they're exposed. We can take Qudin now and eliminate him," the Sagean argued.

"We need you to help ensure the Gem makes it to the Temple of Ama."

"You would seem to suggest that I do your bidding?"

"No, my Lord, but we are your Court and our oath is to advise you and protect you. That has been the sacred duty of the Sagean's acolytes for centuries."

"Ah, but no Sagean's Court in history has had as much wealth and power as this one. Of course, even with all your power and knowledge— not to mention having the Whisper Chain at your disposal—none of you knew that Qudin had found an apprentice!" the Sagean scorned.

"So that report was true?" Aylanna said.

"Yes. Who is she?" the Sagean asked.

"A girl?" Theomar said. His face cringed, aghast.

"Yes. A young woman. You know nothing about her?"

"We don't and since she is a Luminary, the Whisper Chain's melodi-cure machine can't find her," Verro declared.

"Well, she was powerful, I can tell you that. She was the one to kill the Prime Commander."

"All the more reason we need your help securing the passage of the Soul Gem. We have Queen Rotha Durrone overseeing its preparation as we speak, but we would like you there to ensure its safety."

"The Queen? Have you lost your mind, Verro?" the Sagean snapped, slamming his fist to the wood table, "Is she part of my Court now?"

Batak knew what he was really asking was if she had a ring.

"No. But she is willing to prove herself, which makes her a useful ally," Verro said.

"I would say it makes her a liability," the Sagean rebutted.

"My son, Nathan, and Batak's son, Delvar, are on their way there, as well. They oversaw escorting the prisoners from the Red Spear to Adalon. You will meet them and Queen Rotha there. Once the Soul Gem reaches Adalon, you will all escort the Tributes to the Genesis Chamber," Shirova advised.

"Tributes. That's funny," the Sagean mused.

"What would you have us call them?" Verro said.

"I don't care what you call them. They're your Casts, your transistors to survive the Fountain. Call them what you will."

"Once you are in Adalon, we will announce your return," Batak told him, something he knew Edward was eager to see happen.

"Very well. Will we be reinstituting the Orders again?"

"Whatever it takes to bring the people under control," Verro said.

"Good. I don't mean to rule over ruins, but I will be the Emperor. If that takes terror and fear to achieve, so be it. I expect you will have my stock of Automatons remade and by my side?"

"We are seeing to that now. How many do you have left?" Theomar asked.

"Only a handful. Qudin cut down the rest with a sagelight gauntlet," the Sagean said.

"The one that was stolen?" Aylanna said.

"The very same one, I believe."

"We did as you suggested and raided the entire town to look for it," Verro said.

"I heard."

"Will the gauntlet be a problem?" Aylanna said.

"Not with the Scepter. From what I read. . . No," the Sagean paused mid-sentence as though thinking of something, but finished quickly to cover it up.

"What of the Old One, did it show itself to you at the fight?" Verro said.

"No."

"We have not heard Its voice or felt Its presence in sometime," Herod reflected.

"Doesn't this worry anyone else; It obviously has Its own motives?" Harrimon said. It was the cowardly question to ask, but Batak doubted it wasn't on everyone's mind.

"The Old One has helped us find the Tomb and Scepter, I believe It awaits our rise at the Sintering Fountain inside the Genesis Chamber," Verro said confidently.

Aylanna shifted uneasily in her seat and Batak could tell she wanted to argue but decided to hold her peace.

The Sagean filled the silence, "As do we all. I shall leave you now, and be on my way to Adalon."

They all stood until he left before breaking into smaller conversations. Batak walked over to sit by Verro and talk.

"Let us walk," Verro suggested, gesturing to the terrace. The warm breeze blew lightly at their backs, the drape of Batak's cloak rolling a little with the wind. Verro, on the other hand, always wore a suit. In his right hand, he held a short stem glass of wine.

"What do you make of all this, Batak?" Verro said, sipping his drink.

"I think Theomar is going to find himself dead at the end of this adventure," Batak said.

"That may be so. He is unhappy with Edward's lack of talent."

"I'm surprised Edward didn't ask about why Qudin could access the tomb while he couldn't," Batak observed.

"Does anyone besides us know the truth?" Verro said.

"I suspect Aylanna knows."

"I'm sure you're right. She's too smart by half. I believe our best recourse is to avoid the topic. At least until we can't," Verro said.

"Before long, it will be an issue, but I don't see any other recourse. With this transport, I sense some trepidation in you?" Batak asked.

"Obviously the Viper Lords will support us. Made up of former Sagean Supremacy soldiers as they are, they will easily heed the Sagean's call. It's the Tregoreans I'm worried about," Verro said.

"I thought you said the Temple was found outside of their province?" Batak asked.

"It was. It is. It's in an area of the jungle that they consider forbidden. But Polaris is their port city to the south and our best access. Funneling a mass of troops through it will cause a war we aren't yet equipped to fight. With the blockade in the Anamic Ocean and the civil unrest throughout Tovillore, we are spread thin as it is. However, even anchoring in the bay may be seen as too aggressive," Verro explained.

"They trade with Merinde through that port, correct?"

"And Rodaire, but both rarely. It is mostly a fishing import for the province, "why?" Verro said.

"Then we should use Merinde Ships to conceal our own," Batak suggested.

"Yes. I think we must. I will contact the councilor of Merinde and work out an agreement."

"I found it interesting you told Edward that Qudin had been seen. Our report said that only Ellaria Moonstone was seen. Is the man who is tracking Miss Moonstone Theomar's son?"

"It is."

"Ellaria is a formidable opponent that we have continually underestimated. Is Aramus up for the task?" Batak asked.

"He is a weasel it's true, but a sneaky one and very resourceful."

"He's a fanatic and a cold-blooded killer," Batak protested.

"He has an aptitude for many things," Verro said. He tossed the dregs of his glass over the cliffside and walked back to the others.

SEVEN

THE SHOWMAN (ELLARIA)

On the ride to the city of Harden, Ellaria had to stay close to Elias to keep him on his horse. Any change in pace or the terrain jostled him close to falling. The city of Harden was spread on rolling hills, but it was not expansive enough that the circus grounds would be difficult to find. It was known as *The Traveling Show of Wonders*, but the name of the circus was always changing; new names to suit new acts and spectacles. When Ellaria was a kid, she remembered it was simply called *The Showman's Traveling Circus*. The years that Ellaria spent traveling with it, in her teens, it was called *Manus Zabel's Show of the Magnificent*.

Her time with the fair was not well known, nor was it ever officially documented by anyone. All the times she answered questions for historians, she had never spoken of it, beyond her general fondness for spectacle and theatre in general. Her opportunity came when the show turned up in Rovana, the small village on the western edge of Eloveen which her parents governed. Manus Zabel came to their estates and performed for them personally. He was an accomplished illusionist and actor and Ellaria fell in love with his talent and charm. To a fourteen-year-old, Manus was handsome, dark, with clean hair and fancy clothes. He was also smart and worldly unlike anyone she had ever met.

After that, Ellaria began to follow where the show traveled and found news clippings about every performance she could, typically months after the fact. When she realized the show always followed a pattern across Tovillore and Rodaire, she asked her parents if she could ride with the show on her way to Adalon, where she stayed every summer with her aunt since she was seven years old. To Ellaria's surprise, her parents agreed and arranged for her to travel with the show on her way back home. That following summer, Ellaria was taken on as an apprentice of sorts.

It was a drastically more eclectic education than most High Order children received. It allowed her to learn the customs of every region, at least the ones that survived under two thousand years of oppression, and to see the world for what it was. Ellaria was introduced to many things and met many people, but alchemy was her greatest discovery. The craft and its practitioners were outlawed under the Empire, but Manus knew strange people in every city and he was always looking for ways to expand the show; new acts to bring on or new tricks to mesmerize a crowd, and his search brought him to the fringes of society. Whatever underground cultures existed, he delved into them for the good of the show. Ellaria found her crush and admiration for Manus the Showman transformed into an obsession with the mystical. She felt like she had discovered an art that no one else knew about.

The bell towers of Harden dotted the horizon. The evening air was finally cooling, and with the last hill crested, the jumble of short, white stone buildings spread out on the soft hills. Ellaria spotted the Showman's grounds from a distance, arranged in an open field just off the Imperial Road.

The road from Fairview merged with the stone-laid Imperial Road, and Ellaria fell in beside a carriage. Sweeping farmland took up most of the area outside of the city. Monolithic stone pillars flanked the road as markers at the border. Each pillar had copper fire-basins attached to them, one on each side, held by wood brackets angled out of stone pockets. A cart was positioned below one of them and a two-man crew was igniting the protection fires when she passed.

Outside the circus was a set of simple stables adjacent to the entrance gate. Ellaria stationed the horses there. Elias slumped off the saddle, more than dismounting under his own power. He mumbled indecipherable words when she helped him down into the hay bed. There were stacks of hay at the head of the stalls against which she propped Elias. The look of such a powerful man sagging weakly into bale of hay was a startling sight. The image of her friend only further impressed upon her how much they needed help if they were to cross the entirety of Tovillore without being caught. Ellaria was lost in her thoughts when a man spoke her name.

"Aria?"

"Hello, Will," Ellaria answered, wiping her eyes.

"I'm glad you came. If you follow me, I can take you back to see Archibald. I told him about you when I arrived and he was very interested to meet you," Will said.

They passed the entrance teller and a pair of guards walking the open grounds outside. The circus was arranged with huge canvas tents colored in stripes of dark blue and yellow. A quick survey of the entire setup had Ellaria both in awe and feeling nostalgic. It was easily five times larger than *Manus's Show of the Magnificent*.

In the largest cities, Manus's show played in the Empire's beautifully built amphitheaters, but they stopped anywhere they could and often, the troupe performed for meals and supplies before moving along. Amongst the traveling troupe, they saw themselves as the only free folk of the Empire, and the people they played to saw them as their only refuge from the monotony of their lives. Looking over the spectacle before her, she doubted such an operation could find enough value in the smaller villages.

While they walked, Will saw her gawking at every feature. "Have you not been to the *Show of Wonders* before?"

"Not in many years. I've taken in some theatre in the cities, but those are only worthwhile if they are one of the Lore Tales or a story penned by one of the Three Bards of Renown," she explained.

On their way to the back lot, they passed all sorts of attractions; jugglers, fire-eaters, showoffs, and a contortionist, among the passing throng of the open ground between tents. Each performed to a pocket audience gathered in close to watch. In the eight-pole tent to her left, the entrance curtain flaps opened to reveal an interior space full of animals. Before the flap closed, Ellaria saw two large, longneck cawacons, a caged pair of yellow-maned lions, a spotted shadow cat, and a lone wolverack caged off to the side.

"As you can see, that was the Menagerie tent. Those two tents over there are both the Mystics tents. The Elustri Sisters cycle through shows there. Fortune telling, elixir exhibitions, seance rituals, you name it. I don't know if you saw, but the first tent is the Joybirds tent, the tavern and open stage for local performers. And this," Will stopped before the largest tent of them all; it had twelve points to the tent top and two entrances manned by ushers and security guards. "This is the Grand Spectacles tent. All the larger stage shows, acrobats, and more play in here."

Near as they were to the entrance, Ellaria could hear the crowd within moan with a collective gasp, followed by a mass of cheers and clapping.

"What's playing now, the illusionist show?" Ellaria said.

"Umm," Will paused to answer and checked his pocket watch. "Yes, I believe it just ended."

"Is Archibald the performer?" she asked.

"No, Archibald is the Master of Ceremonies. Though he does take the stage for a few roles. He is backstage now getting makeup for tonight's feature show," Will said, and he opened the entrance flap high for her, "After you."

Ellaria entered, but to her surprise, it opened to a concourse around the main space, a perimeter walkway behind the seating was brightly lit by lanterns strung on crisscrossing lines. Three incredibly small women passed them in skintight outfits and hair tied tight to their heads. Each had a rushed expression to their eyes and sweat on the brows, but they also wore wide smiles and jubilant energy radiated off them. It was a spirit born only from someone doing what they were meant to do. She recalled seeing that before, but it was the smells all around the fair that made her the most nostalgic. The smells had never changed.

When the Empire's mandatory schooling took precedent, Ellaria had to stop traveling and had to stay indefinitely in Adalon for her education. She followed the show from afar, but never saw Manus again. Manus had no love for the brutality of the Empire and when the Great War started, he secretly began transporting goods and rebels around the Mainland. When the Bonemen found out, he was brought to Andal where he was killed. The remembrance of him brought tears to her eyes when they reached the back of the tent and a skinny set of stairs up to a short wooden door.

Will knocked three times and called for Archibald. Then he peered down at her, and his eyebrows came together in curiosity as she wiped her eyes for a second time since he had met her this evening.

Ellaria averted her attention to the stage and the back of the enormous set they stood beneath. The constructed backdrop contained connected catwalks and props awaiting at the various openings.

A man roared from inside, "Come in, I said."

Ellaria had the sense Archibald had been calling a few times before being heard. Will opened the door and stepped inside. Briefly disappearing, he popped back out and waved her in.

Archibald was sitting before a long desk with a small rectangular mirror that stretched from the desktop almost to the ceiling. He was a short, burly man with a stylized mustache and chin hair that ended in points, the reddish-brown color fading to gray. Archibald wiped his face clear of makeup and greeted her.

"Welcome to my circus of curiosities, Miss?"

"Please call me Aria. I'm sorry if we interrupted you," Ellaria said.

He looked at the stained rag in his hand and tossed it aside, "Nonsense, I had to start over. Without the popper base, it would have been running by Act Two. So, Will here said you knew Manus Zabel?" Archibald said.

"I did. Manus was a complicated person, but he was a supreme inspiration to me in my life."

"So, you saw him perform his magic show?"

"No," Ellaria answered flatly, wary of the question. *Was it a trap or a test?*

"But I thought you said you knew him?" Archibald's smile widened and lifted his fat cheeks.

"I knew him well enough to know he never called his act magic. He believed true magic was not something to show off or to trick people with. He always called his art *illusion* and himself an *illusionist*," Ellaria said.

"Very good. I speak with many people who claim to have known Manus you understand, but they are really after something from me. They know my affinity for my uncle and use it against me."

"I see."

"Since you did know my uncle, please let us have a drink in his honor," Archibald said, and he opened a drawer next to him, withdrawing a dark green bottle of Emerald Spell, a very strong liquor used only for sipping. He handed her a sipping tin and poured what was at least a double for each of them. When he finished, he replaced the latching stopper and raised his cup,

"To Manus," he said, watching her.

"To Manus, the first free man of the Empire," she said, lowered her eyes and sipped. The liquid was buttery and tart and burned after swallowing. She looked back at Archibald and found him smiling.

"I must tell you, I am impressed by the scale of the *Show of Wonders*. How many does it employ?" Ellaria asked.

"Including the techs, hands, and performers, there are fifty-nine people traveling with us at any time. Sometimes more when we need extra help in the big cities. In that case, we hire locals to help us set up and take down. I am the Master of Ceremonies for this menagerie. The

Show of Wonders is an ageless delight. No Empire denies us, no republic can brand us. People come from near, and far, from the mountains, from the stars, with money in their hand and hope in their hearts to experience the majestic, the wild, the magnificent wonders of our world," he said confidently.

Ellaria could tell he had slipped into his typical sales speech, but when he spoke the words, she could see he believed every word. His eyebrows had a slight shaping to them and would flare in points every so often. There was no denying he had the magnetism required of a master showman.

"Will told me you perform *Echo of Silence*?" she said.

"Penned by Lamdryn himself, one of the Bards of Renown. The best one, if you ask me. Of course, we do. Didn't you see the set?"

"That's for the show?"

"Yes. How else to show the madness of the True Being, than through the many doors of his soul?"

"And what part do you play?" Ellaria asked.

"I play Time, and I'm also," he adjusted his voice to a high-pitched cackle, "the beggar and," he changed his voice a third time, "the thief."

Each voice distinct in timber, tone, and syntax, Ellaria couldn't help but smile. She was impressed. Archibald was nothing like his uncle except for their flare for the dramatic.

"Tell me Aria, how could a High Order kid like you come to travel with the showmen?" Archibald said.

She wanted to ask how he knew she was a High Order born but didn't. "My father's family was originally a lower order. As such, he was raised differently, with different values, and he passed those on to me. From his childhood, he had traveled throughout Rodaire and he valued experience over obedience."

"You don't look like a Rodairean?"

"No, I don't, I look more like my mother."

"A lower order raised up to the High Order. There were very few who received such favor. If I recall, the Order Adjustment was to reward distinguished citizens and punish the louts."

"It was."

"So, what did your father do to deserve such a raise."

"It was my grandfather, and he discovered something valuable to the Empire."

"Interesting, and were you hidden like most High Order children during the Great War, or. . ."

"Of course not. I fought and served for the Resistance," Ellaria said with fire. She regretted it though. She didn't know where Archibald's allegiance rested.

"That's interesting, but not a surprise. You don't seem like one who could sit ideally by, and you knew Manus. Don't get me wrong, the Fall was a glorious thing, but the cleanup was an unmitigated disaster. I can't complain, the crowds of free people are larger, but rowdier and many poor have to be turned away."

"You sound as though you preferred the old Orders that segmented everyone?" Ellaria said.

"Oh, those Orders still exist. Only the terms have disappeared, and even those remain in some parts. Now the Orders are purely based on wealth. It's true those old Orders eliminated any chance to advance one's station, but no more than the current system of have and have-nots does now. The Empire was cruel and tyrannical, but it cared for all the Orders of people under its rule. Don't get me wrong here, I am no supporter of the Sagean Empire but nor am I a believer in the Coalition either. The poverty of this new republic is never spoken about, but it's prevalent throughout the Mainland. Triple, or more, than what I recall as a child. And the unrest and hatred among this loosely held-together society is but a strand thick. A fuse, and one that's burning home."

"I will not argue the value of the former Coalition, Archibald. Not anymore," Ellaria said.

"You are a very interesting person indeed, Aria. Now tell me, what is it you want from me?"

"It's true I need your help, but I can repay you."

"Ha, ha, ha." He laughed in chest heaving bellows, "I told you, Will," he barked and turned his attention back Ellaria, "Aria, I hate to disappoint you, but I have an established and clever means of making my amber, and favors are not part of my business."

"I don't mean to repay you in amber, but I did see you had a wolverack in your menagerie tent," Ellaria said.

"And a bonelark," Archibald said proudly.

"But do you have a ravinor?" Ellaria watched his eyes lit up like gleaming gems.

"Impossible. They live in the jungles of Nahadon and are a communal breed; most have evolved beyond their bestial origins."

"Wild ones can still be found in the swamps south of Aquom."

"Very interesting indeed, and what help do you need?" Archibald inquired.

"My friend and I need safe passage to Midway. I wouldn't resort to such a cover, but my friend is very sick and neither of us are friends to the new powers that be."

"You cannot bring a sick man amongst my troupe, dear lady. Not for a hundred ravinors and twenty dancing bogdrins," Archibald said.

"He is not contagious. He was wounded in Marathal and he has Wanderer's Mind," she lied, but while most folk didn't understand Wanderer's Mind, they also didn't fear it. "He won't let himself be treated by anyone and we can't afford to stop in a city."

"So, you would like to hide out amongst my troupe until we reach Midway? What's in Midway?"

"An airfield," she said simply.

"I see," he put his fingers to his mustache as though he was contemplating his decision, but Ellaria knew she had him.

"You have yourself a deal, Aria," Archibald said.

Relief flooded her, and she stood to clasp arms.

"You and your friend can ride with us, but I can't have two free riders in my caravan. Everyone works. It's a bad precedent and given you have a sick man with you, you will need your own traveling carriage house. So, what kind of skills do you have? You travelled with Manus; can you do illusions, or are you an actor, a singer perhaps?"

Ellaria bit her lip, but said, "I am a trained alchemist."

"Perfect. Will, can introduce you to the Sisters and a show of sorts will be arranged. Now if you would excuse me, I have a show to do. And Aria, be wary: the world is growing dangerous and chaotic, especially where we're traveling."

"I'm comfortable with chaos, I accept it."

"Yes, yes, chaos accepts us all; the trick is surviving it."

"I'm not worried," Ellaria said, and she slammed back the rest of her drink. "I was born for chaos."

She bowed her head slightly, thanked him again, and followed Will back into the fairgrounds.

THE CARAVAN CIRCLE OF CARRIAGE HOUSES WAS ARRANGED AROUND AN expansive field. A broad firepit sat off to one side and lantern poles were staked every thirty feet around the perimeter. Each massive carriage also had a lantern hung near the doorway. After helping Ellaria get Elias inside, Will stood out in the dirt while she peeked inside.

The carriage was impossibly big, with eight wheels that reached above her head, two at the front and six at the back. It resembled three stacked wood shacks built into one moving craft for the road, but with carefully constructed lumber, all stained, smoothly finished and stylistically fastened. A short set of stairs to the entry door, pulled up to the wall when in motion, led to a tiny sitting room. Inside, there was a narrow stairway to a lofted sleeping spot with a horizontal band of windows at the headrest. There were only a few windows in total, but each one was uniquely shaped to fit the spot in the wall into which it was set. A round port window at the head was aligned to speak with the driver, a tall band in the sitting room was integrated into the shelving, and an elongated skylight came equipped with a lifting pole. It was an enchanting cottage on wheels, but a peculiar one.

"Is your friend all right? Does he need a doctor?" Will asked from the door.

"He'll be fine in a few days," she said. She hoped it was the truth but knew it wasn't, but there was no reason to worry the troupe. Ideally, they would be gone before any paranoia set in.

"Would you like to meet the Elustri Sisters then?"

"Please."

Wandering the circus backlot of carriages had a neighborhood feel of a community space. Ellaria had been to nearly every major city in the world, seen scientific inventions still on the drawing table, and seen a Luminary cast waves of heat and claim the lightning, yet this caravan of troupers was a delight for her eyes.

"These carriage houses. I had heard of them, but I confess, I've never been in one before," she said.

"They're from the New World. Archibald had them shipped over two years ago. They have steam engines in the under-rack that help propel the weight and allows for a limited number of pull horses needed to drive them."

"Really?"

"How long has it been since you've been to the Free Cities?" Will asked.

"It has been a long time. Maybe ten years," she said, and her mind drifted. How could it be so long, she thought, but it had been at least ten. Kovan had left only four years after the death of their daughter, and she did not stay much longer herself.

"You should return. Ten years there is like twenty-five here."

"I heard that they had surpassed the Mainland inventors over there."

"Surpassed and lapped. Their trains run all through the coast. The last I heard, they are starting to supply electrical lights beyond the cities and to the countryside. None of the gas-charged lanterns either. Electric coils and filaments. They glow a gentler yellow orange. It's a relief from all the bright krypton-filled spheres you find in the Mainland cities," he concluded and knocked on the door to a house.

No two carriages were exactly the same, either in terms of size or adornments. The one before her was the most colorful and had three pronounced cabins, with roofs popping off the top like a loaf of bread that had risen in thirds.

A commotion behind the door was faint, until finally a lovely woman with tan skin and a colored scarf in her long brown hair answered.

"Yes?" She said sweetly. "Oh, it's Will, come in Will," she turned to someone inside, "It's just Will."

Ellaria stepped inside and the aroma of clover weed was strong, but it was masked by juniper and teal thistle. The Sister's carriage was even larger than Ellaria's. Three padded, round, short stools were in the first room. Something steamed on the counter and a floor-to-ceiling apothecary credenza took up the entire back wall. Another woman sat on the stairs up a bed. She looked similar to the first, but her hair was darker, and she had a slightly rounder face; there was no doubt they were sisters.

"Ladies, this is Aria. She signed on with the troupe for a short run until Midway. She needs to come up with a show for the next stop in Orwin and she'll need a costume."

The one on the stairs waved Will off like he wasn't there, but the first woman came up and hugged Ellaria.

"Aria, I'm Desee and that dark haired gal is Ronee. Jolee will be back soon. We are the Elustri sisters, the mystics of the troupe."

"And . . ." Ronee said.

"And what? What did I forget?" Desee said.

"That we're amazing, and way better to hang out with than those twiggies," Ronee said with a smile.

"Right we are."

"Twiggies?" Ellaria asked.

"She means the acrobats," Desee said.

Will sat down awkwardly on one of the short stools.

"You can go, Will," Ronee said, excusing him with a shooing motion of her hand.

Will promptly got up and exited. He was only a step outside when another woman stopped him to talk.

"Will, I'm glad I ran into you. Did you get the ingredients on our list?" a woman said.

"I did. I'll have them delivered," Will said.

"Even the branch-spider eyes?"

"No. He didn't have those."

"We can't possess Harvey without them, you know?"

"I know. I know, don't worry, I already told Archibald. I'll look in Orwin, but it might not be until Nearwin. It's possible the Mayfair trader's post at the Frayne crossing will have them."

A third sister then entered the room. She was shorter than the other two but had an equally kind face.

"No spider eyes, girls," Jolee said entering and upon seeing Ellaria, she squinted, "Desee, Who's this?"

"This is Aria, she's part of the show."

"Hello, Aria. I'm Jolee. Welcome to the circus," Jolee said and went about her business.

"Who's Harvey?" Ellaria asked

"Our ferret," Desee said.

Ellaria turned, "You can possess your ferret?"

"No, don't be ridiculous. He is exceptionally well-trained and when he eats spider eyes, his eyes get bloodshot and he looks possessed," Ronee explained.

"Ah I see," Ellaria said, turning again. Each of the ladies was moving about the cabin changing and getting ready for something and Ellaria got the feeling she was in the way.

"Do you have any ideas what to do for your show?" Desee asked, adorning her wrist with bands of jewels and pewter symbols.

"No, not really."

"Don't worry about it, you'll figure it out," Ronee said, patting her on the back and opening the door to leave.

Desee followed and Jolee was about to leave to before stopping to wave Ellaria on.

"Are you coming, or what? You can hang around here, but don't smoke Ronee's stash of clover weed. It's the only thing that keeps her calm."

"Where are you all going?" Ellaria said.

"Just to the Joybird's tent before they take it down. Ronee likes to hit on all the available guys and some of the unavailable ones, too. Desee, on the other hand, is waiting for a poet or prince to sweep her off her feet," Jolee said, with a grimace.

"You don't approve?" Ellaria appraised her eye roll.

"No, I don't care."

"You're the oldest?" Ellaria guessed, more from her demeanor than any appearance of age.

"I am, but I don't care what they do. They're big girls. They can make as many mistakes as they want, as long as they don't bring them home. Our carriage may look big, but it's a tight living," Jolee said.

Ellaria spent the night drinking at the tavern and attempting to fit in. A momentary lapse of despair over deepening darkness on the horizon, she set those things aside like a gunfighter hangs his weapon on a hook next to his dirty coat. It called to her, but she ignored it for the chance to recharge. She was introduced to most of the performers and techs, including Owen, who was going to be her stage manager. He was close friends with Marley, another stage manager; Tyron, a performer; and Alexero, the animal trainer. Alexero struck up a conversation with her about the ravinor she had promised Archibald. It seemed rumors and secrets spread fast among the showrunners.

Returning to the carriage house in the early morning darkness, she found Elias standing outside their door. A sudden drop to her stomach made her sick, and she rushed to him. He was looking at his hands and mumbling to himself.

"You're weak," Elias growled.

"Elias, what are you doing?" Ellaria asked.

"You can't keep me inside forever," he said spitefully.

"I wasn't, I didn't think. . ."

"You can't keep me locked up, anymore!" Elias shouted.

"I'm sorry, Elias," she said urgently. His voice had risen to a level anyone around could hear. He still wouldn't look at her, so she gently touched his face to apologize. He jerked back at her touch and scowled at her. She could have been a stranger for all the recognition he gave her. His swirling irises didn't focus on her at all.

"Elias?"

He blinked hard and shook his head. "Ellaria?" he said weakly.

There were beads of sweat on his forehead, but he felt cold to the touch. She had the impression he was very confused and led him back inside to bed. After making him drink water, she warmed a set of crystals in a linwood fire for him. With the crystals wrapped in silk, she placed them under the covers with him. He stirred but fell into a deep sleep.

Restless, she waited up to watch the sunrise. In the early morning the next day, the fair was packing up and moving on before first light. The

Show of Wonders and all its components were immense, yet the crew deconstructed everything and were ready for the road faster than Ellaria would have ever believed. With the efficiency of a machine, teams of hands disassembled the poles and tents and strapped them to the beds of long flatbed wagon pulled by six horses. Some of the trollies had contraptions of wheels and a crank to manipulate a long, empty spool that ran the length of the flatbed. The lever released and it spooled the canvas in tight for traveling.

The front door to her carriage house was of a two-piece construction and she opened the top half of the door to see out. She placed a pot of tea on the heating stone and sat down to watch the proceedings with admiration. It was all done with the discipline of a military squad. Everyone with a job to do and all on task.

In no time, they were off and when her view from the door became the passing countryside, she couldn't help but mourn Kovan. She was coming to accept that the love of her life was really gone. Thoughts flooded her mind: memories with Kovan and her life's experiences, from the big events to the minute choices. All her life, like a boundless splintered path beneath the stars, was within her and a new truth came to her.

The mind and soul are curious things; one shapes the other, but she was coming to realize her soul would always retain more. Age had no equivalent in compelling someone to contemplate their own mind, and the subsequent toll which time took. Sometimes it felt like pieces were paid in whole to the house of death, like a yearly tax; parts syphoned before a person knew to miss them.

Ellaria now knew for a certainty that her soul would always bear the marks of what she knew, and what she thought she knew, with what she remembered and even that which she had forgotten. She settled into place and felt the fringe of contentment.

EIGHT
NEW MORNING (CALEB)

H e awoke in a room he didn't know to muscles that refused to work. His eyelids felt locked, and he strained to lift them. Once open, his sight was foggy, but he couldn't raise his arms to his face to wipe them clear. They were numb and heavy, foreign at his side.

In the haze, a shape moved around the room and disappeared. He heard footsteps on wood, shuffling away, returning a moment later. The form in his vision was slender and came right up to his side. A hand gently touched his forehead before a wet cloth pressed against his eyes. The figure wiped his eyes clean, and his vision cleared to find a blonde-haired woman he didn't recognize staring sympathetically down at him.

"Good morning," she said with a kind smile.

He swallowed hard trying to find his voice, but his throat was raw.

"Hello," he managed to say, but he stumbled to project much louder than a whisper. Even that much hurt, but amongst the many pains, it was nothing compared to the throbbing tightness at his chest or the piercing headache. If not for the drawn curtain over the sun-blazed window, he didn't think he could stand to have his eyes open at all.

"Do you remember me?" The young woman asked. The question confused him. While her face was pleasant, he was sure he didn't know her.

"Should I?"

"You opened your eyes two days ago, and we talked. But you were weak. How are you feeling?"

"Awful. Who are you and where am I?"

"My name is Raina, and you're at the Wrenwa farm outside of Kindaru," she said. *Kindaru?* He tried to place the point in his mind. He was in the north.

"How long have I been in your care, Raina?"

"You've been here six days," she said.

He supposed the time felt right considering how horrible he felt, but he couldn't reconcile the passing. A door closed somewhere far off, and he tried to sit up. Raina helped him and called out to the newcomer.

"Father, he's awakened."

A slight scuff on the floor signaled her walking away, followed by a creak to the door he couldn't see beyond a corner. Then nothing. He closed his eyes to the weight of eyelids impossibly heavy.

When he opened them again, it was to the sound of an older man near his bed.

"You sure?" a second voice said, "Good, he goes then."

"Father, he has barely lifted his head and you 're going to kick him out?"

"I shouldn't have dragged him out as it was. Someone could be looking for him. I may have put us in danger, Raina. He should go as soon as he can walk," the old man said, "So, do you have a name?"

His mouth moved but it was like his mind had locked down his throat, no sound came out. He knew it.

"Umm. . ." His eyebrows dipped, and he licked his lips, "I can't seem to. . ." what was wrong with him? A name popped in his mind, "Caleb. My name is Caleb Ray. . . Reaver."

"Caleb Reaver? Like from the children's tale?"

"I think so, yes," Caleb said, unsure. He struggled to recall the children's story at the moment.

"You were named after the Guardian of the Gates of the Beyond?"

"Yes?"

"Did your parents think you might one day ride a red dragon, too?"

"I'm sorry?" Caleb said confused.

"Like the story. Caleb Reaver rode a Red Dragon and welded the Midnight Sword against the army of the dead? You have some years on you but you're not that old," he smirked, "Although, in one version of that ancient tale, I think Reaver found the Elder Stone and couldn't be killed, so maybe you are him. My name's Lowell. You're on my farm. I'm glad you're alive, Caleb, whoever was watching over you, but I need you out of here as soon as you can go. You understand?"

"Yes."

"What were you doing in Marathal anyway? Did those machines attack you?"

"Machines? No, I was sailing the Frozen Straits, and I . . ." Caleb began and paused. He knew it wasn't right, but he remembered being so cold and the words came out.

"Excuse me. You were where?" Lowell said.

"No wait, I was chasing someone around the Watchman's Tower and the tide was monstrous and it crashed into both of us," Caleb said, and he could clearly see the giant wave reflecting the moonlight before slamming into him with a force that drove the light from his eyes. But he couldn't recall who he had been chasing. By the suspicious look on Lowell's face, he knew something he had said didn't make sense.

"The Watchman's Tower? Off the tip of the Zuvo Islands? Caleb, I found you downstream in a small creek off Eagle Bay in Marathal Lake. Something dreadful had happened to you. You're lucky I found you at all. If I had known there was trouble in the city, I would never have gone. I try to avoid the Bonemen when I can. I've had enough of them for a lifetime. In the last six days, my Raina here has brought you back to life, but I can see you still need some more time."

"I'm sorry. It's just that everything is fuzzy."

Lowell nodded his understanding and turned back to his daughter, "Remember what I told you?"

"Yes, Father."

"Good. I'll be out fixing the roof on the shed if you need me."

"Father, just hire someone. You shouldn't be up there with your bad leg."

"I'm fine. I haven't even needed my cane in days," Lowell said, and he left the room muttering under his breath.

"Sorry to be a burden. I don't mean you or your father harm," Caleb assured her.

"I know. I think he's still angry with you for all the vomiting you did the first day."

Caleb couldn't recall that either, but it explained the sore throat. He flexed his fingers and tried to move his arm. A sudden sting and stiffness flared. The spike of pain led to another twice as excruciating in his chest. He moved his hand there in a natural reaction. He stopped short of touching the tender wrapping around his torso. His fingers crossed over a finger-length scar. While the action of passing his fingers over the scar felt like habit, the scar itself felt foreign to him.

"I didn't mend that one, that's an old wound," Raina said, "Actually, you have a lot of old wounds. Did you fight in the Great War?"

"I... I don't remember. I know that's something I should remember, but I don't," he said, and he winced. An anxious breath filled his lungs, "I'm not sure of anything," he whispered more to himself then her.

His mind seemed unable to focus on anything but his own breathing. Thoughts strayed before synchronizing like they were slipping away. When he tried to delve deeper, he only found confusion. Raina came to him. She gently took his hand and placed it back at his side.

"You'll be fine. I can see in your eyes. It's all still there. A whole life lived. Just give it time. My father wasn't exaggerating. You've come back from the dead. As your body needs time to heal, so does your mind," she said reassuringly. Her eyes were wondrous, and the irises swirled with silver light. He wondered if he should be afraid of such an oddity, but instead there was something familiar about them that comforted him. She smiled and began cleaning up the bedside table.

"They weren't always that way," Raina said.

"What wasn't?"

"My eyes. They were blue when I was a child. When I was fourteen, I got very sick. A friend helped heal me. I survived but my eyes were never the same."

"No, they're lovely. It's just that they reminded me of someone but..." he tried to explain but trailed off. "How many bullets did you pull from me?"

"In total, fourteen. Most were not very deep. As though they were shot through something else first. The worst injury was your head wound. We didn't know if you would ever wake up," she said. When she had collected everything, she headed for the door,

"Get some rest Caleb. I will return to check on you in the evening."

"Thank you, Raina."

She smiled and backed the rest of the way out of the room.

Caleb closed his eyes and thought about what Lowell had said. But he could see himself flying atop a dragon. He remembered being above the clouds and the sun rising as he soared. He could feel the warmth of the sun and the wind in his hair, and he wondered who would shoot such a man in the chest. But he didn't worry over it because he knew no such people and so he slept.

THE NEXT TWO DAYS, HE WAS ABLE TO GET UP AND MOVE AROUND THE room. Raina would bring him meals and change his bandages. Only the head wound still bled, but the pains in his chest and arms reacted to tentative movements, especially lifting out of bed or dressing.

While Raina helped him, she would ask, "What do you remember today, Caleb?"

"I made a chair for the Peace King once. I crafted it out of monarch heartwood. It had black nine-branch wood at the armrests and an artisan crafted copper emblem, I inset into the back. The side rails were finger jointed," Caleb replied.

"Wow, you were a carpenter for the Peace King?" she said.

"I think so. I also keep seeing all these sculptures in my mind, too. Maybe I am an artisan?"

"Would you like some drawing materials? I can bring you some. It could help with your memories?"

Caleb was reluctant to ask for anything or expect anything, but he agreed anyway. The prospect of anything helping his state of mind sounded worthwhile. Nothing substantial seemed to be coming back to him, and some memories he was starting to realize weren't true.

Later, when Raina gave him the drawing materials, he was excited to discover something about himself. It didn't take long for him to see that he had no artistic ability. Unless stick figures had more significant value then he remembered.

He lay in bed that night with his thoughts consumed by the sculptures he had vividly envisioned. Finally, he concluded he had no memory of crafting them. No memory of the material in his hands or working on details. Instead, he could see them clearly and with distinction, but his viewpoint was always from below, like frozen people in stone had stood over him for a long time. He could see the smoothness of the white stone and even recall the way the marbling veins mimicked real veins. A vast collection of beautiful strangers personified and captured in monuments of stone. Some he pictured with green vines snaking around them and others he started to recall had been grimy and dirt-covered, water dripping off them.

Caleb placed more confidence in his memories of carpentry and woodworking, but he wanted to find out if that skill was real or another imagined ability. He had a vivid image of sanding the legs of a table and carving ornate rafter tails for a building.

At dinner that night, the father, and daughter invited him to eat at their table and he asked Lowell if he could help him with some of his chores around the farm. It had not slipped past Caleb that Lowell was constantly on his feet, fixing this or that, mending a door hinge, digging a trench, repairing a roof. All while limping around on a bad leg, though he tried to disguise in view of Raina. Lowell grimaced constantly and used everything for leverage to relieve the weight on the leg. Caleb could slowly work off his debt to the man for saving his life, which for some unknown reason felt not only right but essential.

Lowell took some convincing but the following morning, there came a knock on the door to Caleb's room. "I could use your help today if you're up for it?" Lowell said.

"I'm happy to help," he said, and it wasn't a lie. The prospect of working outside and being of use excited him.

Stepping out of the house to the dirt path, Caleb gazed out at their surroundings and for the first time, he could fully appreciate the land around them. A deep breath of fresh air filled his lungs, and he realized his muscles didn't hurt. Lowell handed him a hammer and waved him forward to follow.

For the rest of the day, they worked on the shed roof Lowell had been trying to fix for the past week, replacing some of the interior trusses. A spring storm had lifted the roof off the small building and ruined some of the supplies. Lowell had been trying to repair what was left, but Caleb quickly realized what was needed. He found lumber around the farm and built the broken trusses. Together, they set them in place and fastened a new roof system of thatch and wood shingles.

In the evening, after they had finished, they sat on the porch and drank cold water from a pitcher full of ice that Raina brought them.

"That ice is precious you know, Caleb? Though it's not from the Frozen Straits," Lowell said.

It took a moment for Caleb to realize Lowell was teasing him. A slight grin of embarrassment crested his face and he stared off toward the hills in the distance, too new in his own skin to feel wary. His only anxiety was wrapped up in a growing sense of dread, not that he would never remember, but that when his memories came, he wouldn't like what they brought. Or worse, that he had abandoned something or someone that needed him.

NINE
RENEGADES (LEARON)

From Atava, Learon and Meroha headed east to Fort March. There, they took a ferry down the Valor River to the town of Eve. Learon expected to run into this band of Renegades he heard about, but instead they found the town deserted.

The journey from Eve to Pardona was considered by many to be one of the most treacherous roads in all Tovillore. Nestled between the two forests as it was, they wouldn't be able to stop until they reached Fort Mare. Both the Leaving Forest and The Howling Forest were crawling with beasts, and the road had earned the nickname, *the Jaws*. The prospect of riding into the mouth of the monsters had Learon worried, but he didn't want to stay the night in Eve. The town had the feel of being abandoned. The few people still there didn't want to talk to strangers and appeared exhausted, a mix of dark and baggy eyes and slumped shoulders. He knew the feeling, but he didn't want to stick around to find out what had happened to the other townspeople, and no one was talking.

He returned from his quick look around and found Meroha holding Elias's cat, Merphi. She wore a purple shawl that covered her shoulders. Meroha was always wrapping herself up in an extra layer, and Learon supposed it was because her island home of Kotalla was on the equator.

"What do you think?" Learon asked.

"There's no one here, Learon. This place gives me the creeps," Meroha said.

"Agreed. We should move on. I know I said we might stay here, but I think we should ride for Fort Mare tonight."

"I'm fine with that. Better to sleep anywhere than here," Meroha said.

"We may find it in the same state, but it's supposed be one of the most heavily fortified cities west of the Uhanni river. It would have to be, to survive trapped between the forests."

Learon appraised the sunset and approaching clouds. The only thing worse than traveling *the Jaws* at night was if they were caught out there in a storm. The clouds were gathering, sweeping in from the Warhawk Mountains, but rain looked to be a day off.

"We will have to keep moving, no stopping. We can't get caught out there, or we'll be in terrible danger," Learon said.

"What's the phrase you Mainlanders say, *torque it*?" Meroha asked.

"Yes, that's the one."

"Well, torque it. I don't want to stay another minute here. The emptiness gives me the creeps," Meroha said.

"Me neither," Learon agreed. He mounted and began a light trot through the edge of town. The road slowly transformed, and soon they were riding in amongst the solitude of tall trees. Both sides of the path were lined with trees pressing in like walls of a tunnel, the forest's interior cloaked in shadow thirty feet beyond the gravel surface. Learon picked up the pace, but they had to avoid galloping. In the case that something did attack, the horses needed sufficient energy to run. Meroha closely watched both sides of woods while they went.

"Why are some of your cities called forts?" Meroha asked. They had been riding in silence for a while and Learon suspected it was a question born of nervousness.

"All the fort towns were major headquarters for the Resistance Army in the Great War. In most cases, there were already small towns in that location and the army encampments became big; requirements to feed an army of that size leaves a mark. The Resistance generals maintained their positions even as they advanced to fight the Emperor's forces on other battlefields. You'll find a lot of them outside major cities. It was part of a strategy to liberate cities and provide a haven for traitors against the Empire," Learon explained.

"We don't learn about the War in Kotalla. I wish I knew more."

"You don't?"

"Not really."

"What were you told happened?"

"As faithful servants of the Sagelight, we believe the Sagean Emperor is or was the manifestation of God or the Great One."

"Then how is his defeat to Qudin explained?" Learon asked.

"We are told that the Sagean's spirit was corrupted by Qudin, because Qudin was a messenger of Ovardyn."

"You think Qudin is a demon?"

"No. I mean, I am meant to, but after the culling started and I witnessed my people being sacrificed for the faith, I started to see everything they spouted as lies."

Learon remembered something Elias had told him about how the destruction of truth begins with the lies we tell ourselves, the ones we live with, blinding the world in imperceptible degrees. At the time, he thought Elias was trying to tell him about his pursuit of his father's killer, but as with most things Elias said to him, there was a personal meaning and a greater one, too.

It wasn't until late in the evening as they neared Fort Mare that they spotted the trailing scouts. Two riders came in from the trees to either side to escort them the rest of the way.

"What's your business on this road, kid?" The scout spoke with an odd confidence considering Learon was more heavily armed then he.

"We're on our way to Midway. I need to meet my wife there in two days."

"Your wife? Then who's this you're riding with?"

"My friend," Learon said. For a moment, Learon contemplated what it would take to get rid of both men. Simple shoves could knock them out of their saddles, but they would probably be stranded out on *the Jaws*, which meant certain death.

"Is that right? Well, you'll be staying in Fort Mare tonight. We'll have to see what Ronick says about you two."

"Ronick?"

"Yeah. You heard of him?"

"No. But maybe I was mistaken. I thought you were with the band of Renegades, one led by a man named Darringer?"

"We are. You know Darringer?"

"No, I've heard of you is all."

"Well, Ronick is Darringer's second, and no one sees Darringer unless they've talked with Ronick first."

"What about you, miss? You don't talk," the other rider said to Meroha.

"Leave her alone," Learon said coldly.

The rider appraised Learon's tone and look. Learon knew he wanted to challenge him, but he didn't.

"All right, it doesn't matter, Ronick will decide your fate."

Learon quickly determined that he was not going to gain any valuable information from the two riders, and he held his tongue until they reached the fort. He wanted to meet Darringer and see if this band was a new rebellion that could help stop the Sagean, or another organization of zealots. Part of him hoped Darringer was another old war hero; someone to trust. According to Frank, the band had been scouting some of the larger towns and cities in the west of Tovillore, trying to increase their numbers to go reclaim some of the cities that had been attacked. Frank had mentioned Anchor's Point and the Fork, specifically, but other cities had also seen some skirmishes. By the sounds of it, the entire renegade party was made up of young men the same age as Learon. Learon just wanted to get to the truth of them. The more people fighting to set right what the new Sagean had wrought upon them, the better. Learon was hopeful they could get to Stasia quickly and without incident, but the guards reception gave him misgivings.

It was not long before the fort gate could be seen. From what Learon had been taught about the Great War, Fort Mare was established to protect their line from the Sagean's troops coming from the Uhanni River. It was half a day's ride from the river city of Perdona, positioned ideally to ambush any arriving soldiers and to strategically sabotage supply lines.

The Fort was larger than a simple village and some of the interior buildings had grown to six or seven stories in height. To Learon's eye, it was like a miniature version of Atava, but the perimeter walls were enormous. There was a three-foot-tall stone rubble foundation, but the walls were constructed of tied timber, stacked as high as the surrounding treetops, with archer's windows below the spiked pediment. Some of the weathered spots showed signs of age, but most of it had been modified and strengthened over time with metal bracing and steel straps.

Outside the walls, and along the entire boundary, was an endless basin of glowing blue flame, a trench of blue fire that circled the town. During the Great War, the fort had become known for supplying horses and Learon had wondered how they maintained protection from the surrounding forests. While its meager beginnings were as an army encampment, Fort Mare maintained its livelihood as a refuge within *the Jaws*.

There was a clearing in front of the gate, a raised fire basin, and a lone, slender stone lookout tower. Once beyond the gate, the scouts led Learon and Meroha down the widest street for a short time before asking them to dismount and go further on foot. Learon tied off the reins and hid the mystcat and artificer's bat Jules the best he could. He also left Elias's Shadowyn sword bundled inside his bedroll and, more reluctantly, left his bow. The scout waved them to follow with an impatience in his stance. Apprehensive about leaving their things, Learon realized there was nothing to be done and so the two travelers followed the scout.

The city wasn't deserted like the small river town of Eve had been. There were lights in most of the windows, the street lanterns were all lit, and some locals sat on the steps outside their homes, staring from their porches. If they were put out by the Renegades, they didn't show it, but it was night and things always looked different in the day.

For their part, the Renegades had seized the principal roads of the city. Various fires burned at makeshift camps spread out along the streets. If the Renegades had liberated the Fort, there were no signs of it, and if they were claiming the city, they had done so without resistance. The people had simply let them in, and they had swamped over and set up camp. Now this Darringer character was holding court like he was the King of Fort Mare. First, they had to impress Ronick to even have a chance at meeting Darringer. Learon was starting to see this diversion from reaching Midway for what it was, a huge obstacle, a road of mud, and if they weren't careful, they would get struck.

They reached a town square of sorts, where an opening between buildings was crowded with people looking at a small stage as a man stood speaking to the congestion of makeshift soldiers and locals alike. A huge supply building with a sign reading *Stockade* was behind him. Learon assumed the orator was Darringer but couldn't know for sure. He certainly had the crowd's attention. The soldiers gathered around had handmade armor and most carried cobbled-together weapons, tools not meant to be weapons at all but now modified to a new purpose; a field hoe made into a spear, three-pronged rakes with the ends broken to sharp points. This band of Renegades were farmers, Learon realized. Regular people that had no business being soldiers. Learon supposed he didn't either and wondered if this was what it had been like during the Great War. He didn't know, and he didn't really care to find out, but his generation's fight seemed to be upon them.

The whole scene gave Learon a queasy feeling as he recalled a similar gathering at Anchor's Point, one held by zealots of the Sagean faith: servants of the Lords of the Sacred Blue Sun, calling themselves *the Lionized*. Their rally had quickly ignited into a riot and in turn, had destroyed the city. In his mind, Learon could still see the pier exploding as they sat helplessly on the river barge. The crowd that day had also been driven by a charismatic leader, shouting lies to stir his followers into action; *was Darringer no different?*

The scouts stopped outside a dark green tent and when they were waved through, they entered to find a tall young man studying a map of Tovillore. He had dark hair and a full beard that was interrupted on his right cheek by a scar in the shape of an upside-down check mark. It stretched from his chin to his cheek bone and back to his ear. He looked up at the intrusion.

"Sir, we found these two on our patrol. Twenty minutes outside of the West Gate," the scout said.

"Thank you, Billy, you may leave," Ronick said.

"Sir, he carried a marksmen bow," the scout said.

"Is that so? Thank you. Please go find some food," Ronick dismissed the scout.

The scout slipped out, and they found themselves alone with Ronick.

"What are you two doing riding *the Jaws* this late at night? The road is dangerous in the daylight, and at night, it might be suicide. This says to me that either you are both naive idiots running from something, or as I suspect, you are allies of the Shadow. Which one is it?" Ronick questioned them. Learon started to reply but was interrupted,

"If you are allies of the Shadow, I will behead both of you on that stage. So, go on, convince me you're not who I say you are," Ronick said through gritted teeth.

"We're neither of those. We are simply trying to get to Midway. We don't want any trouble with you," Learon expressed, a heat rising inside him from being threatened.

"We are no mere group of Renegades. We call ourselves the Band of the Redeemers. We have purpose. Can you say as much? You're a sticks kid by the look of you. A local mountain boy by the sound of your accent. Born on the eastern slope of the Warhawk, and you probably haven't been but a hundred leagues from your hometown before. Which marks you as puppets of the Shadow," Ronick removed a knife on a plain silver handle and came closer to them; too close to Meroha for Learon's liking,

"And you," Ronick continued, pointing the tip of his knife at Meroha. "Who are you? You don't look like anyone I've ever met from Tovillore. Mainlander women rarely have short-cropped hair and you're not Rodairean?"

"Leave her alone," Learon warned. Ronick tilted his head and stared at him.

"Do you have a gauge for the wicked, kid? Because the wickedness of man, beast, and self-proclaimed gods are upon us once again," Ronick said.

"We're just passing through," Learon said.

"Passing through. No one gets to pass through anymore, or did you go blindfolded through the towns before reaching us?"

"We're not blind, and I've seen these beasts and much worse. That's why we travel. We are trying to reach my wife on the other side of the Uhanni. She was attending the University, the Arcana, and we are to meet in Midway in two days' time," Learon replied

"Aren't you a little young to be joined?" Ronick said.

Maybe I should have said sister, Learon thought, but he pressed on, "Love doesn't know age. When you meet the right person, someone you inexplicably know you are bound to, that's not something you walk away from," he said, and Meroha appraised him oddly, smiling.

"I applaud the ideal. The Light of the Blue knows we need that in the dark times ahead, but we are falling under a Shadow, kid. We all must fight to survive. You can either fight by our side or you can run," Ronick said, pacing now. "But if you run, you won't get far. We saw the beasts destroy Fort Seal, zealots burned down Anchor's Point, and machines destroyed Marathal. Did you hear about those nightmares, kid? Unnaturally alive, they say, and twice as tall as any man."

Not twice as tall, Learon thought, but more terrifying than Ronick could imagine or than could be explained without seeing them.

A soldier came in. His handmade leather shoulder armor was comical but stitched with care.

"What is it?" Ronick barked.

"Wolveracks at the West Gate. Hundreds of them," he said with a nervous stutter.

"Watch them," Ronick ordered, and left the tent.

Outside, Learon could hear speaker still addressing the crowd. The voice stopped a moment as though he had been interrupted and when he spoke again, it was to warn the audience of the beasts.

"They're here. The beasts gather at the West Gate as we speak. This is why we have come to Fort Mare, into *the Jaws* of the deadly forests. We will protect this city. If the fires go out, they will be inside the walls. I am going out there to fight them, to kill them, and take back our land. I will not come back inside the walls until every last one has been killed. Who among you is going to fight by my side?" the speaker called out and a roar of cheers and yells from the crowd echoed into the night.

Ronick popped back into the tent and made direct eye contact with Learon, "You want to prove you're not of the Shadow? Fight. Help us protect this city."

"I'll fight, but I need to get my bow," Learon said.

"Do you know what you're doing out there?" Ronick asked.

"I've killed wolveracks before. I can handle myself."

"Get what you need and go to the West Gate," Ronick said, and he turned abruptly and left.

Learon and Meroha rushed back to their horses. Learon found Elias's sword and strapped it to his side. He still didn't have much skill with it, but the weight of it had always felt good in his hand, so he took it just in case.

"Learon, I don't think we should get involved," Meroha said, as he prepared.

"I'll be fine. Besides, we don't have a choice. If something happens though, I left the communicator watch and all our amber in my saddlebag. It's not a lot, but it will get you to Midway and purchase fare on an airship. Leave in the morning and find Stasia and keep the artificer bat hidden or you'll draw more attention to yourself. You both should regroup with Tali and Wade and get out of Tovillore," Learon said, noting the worry on her face from all his instructions. The fear of being left alone again had her trembling. Learon gave her a hug. The top of her brown hair barely reached his shoulders.

"I'll be fine, I can keep my distance with my bow," he assured her, ruffling her hair and sprinting away before she could convince him otherwise.

At the gate, men crowded in, preparing to battle a swarm of beasts in the night. They stood abreast with their collection of weapons-that-weren't-weapons. The heat of so many was making Learon sweat and the feeling like everyone was breathing on him sickened him further. A man Learon guessed was in his thirties stood at the front, directing people and trying to prepare them. When he spotted Learon and his bow, he yelled,

"You! Archer! Are you any good with that thing?" the older man asked.

"I'm a fair shot," Learon replied.

"Fair is better than most. I have a job for you then," the older man said, and Learon started to push forward in a squeeze to the front.

"What do you need?" Learon said when they were face to face.

"Our best archers are manning the fort wall in the battlement windows. But I want three archers on the stone tower outside," he gestured to the bowmen next to him. Each was younger than Learon and one had recently thrown up by the look of him, his pale face suggesting more was coming.

"I need one more, you up for it?" the man asked.

"I can do that." Learon said.

"When we get out there, the tower is about a hundred feet from the gate. Do you know the one I'm talking about?"

"Yes. I saw it coming in."

"Good," the older man said.

Waiting at the front, Learon could see the faces of every man behind him. Most were too scared to even stand in their own boots. Solders with real weapons, quality swords, had more confidence than the others, but from what Learon could see, there was no one who carried a pulsator gun.

The older man tapped him on the shoulder, "I'm glad to have you out there. I'm Gerald."

"Learon," he replied. He would have clasped forearms with the man but squeezed in as they were, there was no room.

"We'll protect you three all the way to the foot of the tower. Once you're on top, open fire on those things. Unleash death and do not come down until your arrows are spent."

"Got it."

A small group of horses came in with mounted riders more heavily armed than the rest, Darringer at the front and two others behind him. Ronick brought up the rear. He had painted his eyes with some odd dark marks, each with a black tee intersecting at the eye. He glanced at Learon with psychotic, unregistering eyes. Ronick had two blades strapped crisscross behind his back. With a quick estimation, Learon was glad to have him on the field against the beasts. Looking at the rest of them, he suspected Ronick might be the only one crazy enough to survive the night.

FORT MARE

The Leaving Forest

To Pardona

Tower

Tower

North Gate

Harvest Fields

Tattered Village

Protection basin

The Wells

River Gate

To Riverride

3

Smiths Village

Rider's Villages

Breeders Feilds

West Gate

2

2

Tower

To Eye

1

The Howling Forest

1. The Jaws Road
2. Protection Fire Trenches
3. Stockade

TEN

BATTLE FOR FORT MARE (LEARON)

T he clearing outside the gate was deserted and there were no natural sounds of the forest to be heard. Learon sprinted to the tower with the other two archers behind him, holding a nocked arrow as he ran. Learon's entire focus was on reaching the tower alive and he set a pace the two behind him struggled to match. He'd seen wolveracks chase down escaping prey, and his eyes darted around scrutinizing the forest for one that may be waited to pounce. He reached the tower's heavy wooden door, but it resisted his initial pull. The door was wedged tight in the stone opening, most likely moisture in the wood had swollen the door in place. Learon stored his bow and arrow and wrenched at the handle with both hands. It gave way with a loud scratch as the other two arrived. Once they were through, Learon tugged it closed and latched the inside bar, then he ambled up the narrow spiral stairway to the top.

Learon perched his aim off the battlement, scanned the area and waited. A hanging fog had settled among the trees, and the wind seemed uninterested in pushing it out. The road was slightly clearer, with the fog choosing to stick to the pine needles. Wrapped in among the trees, it concealed the beast's movements within.

The wolveracks came first. When the beasts prowled in close, their eyes emerged in the darkness, snarls awakening amongst the brush and tree trunks and exposed roots. Yellow eyes began glowing deadly all around. Learon heard shouts and nervous chatter from the men below, as countless sets of menacing eyes ignited in the dark.

"I see them," someone said from the ground.

"How many are there?" another soldier said.

"Under the Blessed Blue, they're everywhere," A man below cried.

The last sentiment wasn't wrong. From Learon's position above the fray, the wolveracks lurked everywhere. He hoped they weren't skilled climbers, as he didn't want to waste arrows to defend the tower.

"Be quiet and wait for them." Darringer said, pulling his horse back in amongst the men. He dismounted and found a trembling young soldier. The kid took the three horses away, on Darringer's order, and headed for the gate. Learon watched the kid gallop back and when the gate closed behind them, the horror began.

The wolveracks drone screamed to a high pitch, and they attacked. The beasts collided with the mass of soldiers and a chaos of screams erupted. Learon felt like it had taken him too long to settle on a target. He finally unleashed an arrow at the largest wolverack attacking the right side. Still, he was the first archer to let an arrow loose and his arrow began a downpour. The two archers next to him shook with indecision and fired into the underbrush randomly.

"Don't waste your arrows on areas. Find targets to shoot," Learon told them.

The sound of the battle was turning Learon's stomach more than the sights. From his perspective, the splattered blood painted the grass everywhere and bodies of men were tossed around by monstrous teeth, but the chorus of moans, screams, and crunching was hard to block out and maintain his focus. After the initial attack, the beasts were knocked back. Most of the time, Learon could block out the terror of the blur, find a target, and strike. But the sounds, the sounds he couldn't un-hear.

Out of the sky, a cry pierced the night and huge winged monsters descended. Five bonelarks swooped in and dropped into the crowd of men. Four came away with someone in their clutches. Some dropped their catch and bodies flew into the walls of the Fort. A shadow came overhead and Learon, sensing the beating wings, ducked. A sixth bonelark snatched an archer right next to Learon and dropped him in a heap below.

"Take out the bonelarks!" Learon called out to the man left next to him.

They proved harder to hit than the wolveracks, but more easily injured. Every clipped wing or leg they found with an arrow threw the beasts off their flight and men caught them and cut them down. Though they fought alongside one another, the wolveracks were no friends to the flying monstrosities. Learon saw two wolveracks attack and drag a bonelark away into the forest.

When all the bonelarks were gone, Learon scanned the area until he found Darringer and his three officers. They were pushing back the left flank, tearing through the beasts. A big man whom Darringer called Harlon swung a doubleheader mace with forged spiked ends like he was swatting flies. Ronick was a whirling, ever-moving bringer of death with his double blades. Maybe the best swordsman Learon had seen, other than Elias.

Derringer was quick and shouted orders while he moved around the field, killing the beasts. When he would pause, Learon could see steam drifting off Darringer's shoulders. A contraption on his right wrist fired bolts into the wolveracks. The spinning rig launched short arrows on a revolving steam-powered gantlet. In his left hand, he spun a sharp axe with a long arching crescent blade.

On the far side, Learon spotted wolveracks climbing the trees. He panicked that some could already be positioned aloft to strike. Scanning, he found two ready to ambush Darringer and his team. Learon reached into his quiver, but it was empty; the man next to him had released his last, as well.

Learon shouted, "Darringer the trees! They're above you!" but over the distance and the sounds of the battle, there was no way to hear his call.

On the ground twenty feet from the tower, he spotted two arrows belonging to the other archer that was taken by the bonelark. But an immediate threat suddenly took precedence. A snarling wolverack was clawing up the side of the tower toward him.

Learon drew the Shadowyn sword and jumped. He slammed the sword into the scaling wolverack and together they went in a heap to the grass below. At impact, Learon sprang off and toward the arrows. Coming up on a roll, he snatched the two arrows off the ground, his entire focus on the ambushing beasts preparing to spring out of the boughs. He nocked both arrows together and fired. The arrows split directions in the air, and both found their marks. The pair of wolveracks fell at Darringer's feet in thuds, each with a heart kill. Darringer and Ronick looked around and up into the trees for more, than back across the field to the source of the arrows.

Learon got to his feet and took a few deep breaths, as if he hadn't breathed through the whole incident. He searched for the sword, but found it already sheathed to his side, another thing he didn't recall doing.

The truth of what he had done stunned him a moment. He had never seen a shot like that and knew with certainty he couldn't repeat the feat if he tried a thousand times.

The wolveracks fought until the last one was dead. Their rage and bloodlust never left their glowing eyes until the life was extinguished. When it was over, Learon didn't bother to count the dead. Neither how many men nor how many beasts had perished interested him. He helped the nearest wounded and returned inside the town to find Meroha, and to make sure no beasts had breached the wall, vigilant in case word came from the East Gate of another attack.

A stranger stopped him in the street, and she wrapped his arm where a gash which he'd taken during his vault to the ground bled down his sleeve. As he waited for her to finish, he watched Darringer return. The man they all followed waved off aid for himself and drifted between his soldiers, checking on their health. Darringer said a prayer over the ones who had died, and he delivered orders to the men he knew needed the distraction. He somehow was able to understand what each man under his charge required, and not as a group dynamic, but down to the individual. When Darringer finally stopped to rest, he placed his hands together under his chin to support his head and looked around uneasily. Glossy eyes appraised the outcome, a vacant look of both exhaustion and mourning.

Learon approached Darringer to speak with him. A guard stopped him short and Ronick was there, talking to a group of men. He eyed Learon more suspiciously now than he had before if that was possible. Darringer spotted him, too.

"Let him pass," Darringer said, and the guard finally lowered his arm at Learon's chest, allowing him to proceed. Learon slowly came forward, hesitant to interrupt the moment of peace, but intent on finding out more. Darringer was not a young man, nor was he old, but his red eyes suggested he hadn't slept in weeks.

"How long has it been since you slept?" Learon asked, unprompted.

"A full night? I forget," Darringer said. He wiped his forehead and motioned for Learon to sit. Learon sat and appraised the tired eyes before him. Darringer had a look Learon was becoming accustomed to. But beneath the apparent strain was a weariness; something deep was destroying this man. He had seen this haunted gloom before in Elias and Kovan.

From up close, Learon could fully appreciate the mechanical weapon on Darringer's arm. It rested atop a tree stump where Darringer was reloading it with custom arrows, cut to size and notched for the propulsion ejector. Darringer opened one chamber at a time, placed an arrow inside and spun to the next slot. An entire system of tubes extended past his elbow and to his back shoulder, where a compact steam compressor was strapped to power the bolting rig.

Darringer caught him studying it intently. "Are you a gadgeteer, Learon?"

"No sir."

"Don't call me *sir*, call me Darringer or Darrin. As I was saying, do you know anything about machines?"

"A little," Learon admitted.

"If I let you study this," he positioned the last bolt and spun the chamber. A clicking in the gears prattled until it came to rest, "Could you make another?"

"Probably. I know someone who could look at it once and remake it. Matter of fact, I could probably explain to her how I thought it worked and she could make one," Learon said.

"But you're not so skilled?"

"No."

"None of these country blades would know where to start. I admit, I could use a man like you," Darringer said.

"I don't think Ronick likes me much," Learon said.

"Don't pay him any mind. He hates everyone. It's probably why he's the best fighter I have."

"I'm not sure who you even are?" Learon said.

"We are a band of men trying to reclaim the land. Trying to redeem what the Resistance fought for."

"To be honest, I'm not sure I buy into your dogma," Learon said.

"And what would that be?" Darringer said.

"I thought I heard you saying something about Luminaries. You seem to blame Qudin for the ills of the world?"

"I don't blame him, though I know some of the men do, but I don't trust the Luminaries. Everything we know about them is shrouded in war and tyranny. I'm unsure our world can survive their kind any longer," Darringer said.

"Do you think they're evil?"

"Evil is learned. Good can be killed inside a man. Power breeds evil and those that have it will do anything to keep it. They are morally compromised. Luminaries are handed power from birth. How can humans stand to survive against their like? Do you know what they are capable of? Have you seen the plague they have begun again? At least it was the beasts this time, and not those other things." The last part, Darringer said, more to himself than to Learon.

"You've seen them, haven't you?" Learon said.

Darringer looked up finally. "The sick ones?"

"We call them the Scree," Learon said.

"We?"

"My friends and I came across an entire town of them."

"Where?"

He didn't want to tell Darringer the truth for some reason and instead said, "Fort Murk."

"That makes all the smaller cities and towns between Atava and Thelmaria."

"Wait, all of them?" Learon said.

"Yes. We never made it to Murk. I chose to come east to the river instead. Why the Scree?"

"It means *the cry before death* in the old language," Learon said.

"That sounds appropriate to what they are or what's left of them. Where are you headed, Learon?"

"I need to meet a friend in Midway. She's trying to get out of Adalon. After that, we've talked about crossing over to the Free Cities."

"Ronick said it was your wife? It doesn't matter though; you'll never get to the Free Cities."

"Why not?"

"No Airship can make that flight. A cloudparter maybe, but certainly no winddrifter is making that jump. And with the blockade against the New World, the Anamic Ocean is at a standstill, unless you can navigate the icy north or go south and try to cross over the tip of Merinde. But I hear Merinde has fallen mad, too. Stay with us as we ride to Pardona on the way to Midway. I could use you. Most of my men are greener than the hills of Rodaire. If there is no fight to be had in Pardona, you can cross the Uhanni freely and I will wish you luck. However, if there is a fight to be had in Pardona, you will be glad to be in our company and we will be better off to have you."

"Deal," Learon said. He planned on crossing at Pardona anyway and he liked Darringer. Even if he was misguided in his views on Luminaries, the man was trying to hold the country together and protect people.

Learon came back to Meroha with Ronick eyeing him the whole way. Unsure if his fighting had earned trust with Ronick or frayed it further. Meroha lunged at him and embraced him tightly when he arrived. She was young, but Learon was discovering she was strong and fiercely loyal. He laid down in the spot she made for him, and Elias's cat Merphi came over to curl up in his lap. The cat licked his forearm where a bruise was starting to form around the cut. His mind was somewhere else, otherwise he would have stopped it, but to his surprise, the pain subsided, and the cut sealed up. The magic of it left him speechless.

"How bad was it?" Meroha asked.

"Bad. . . Any trouble while I was gone?" he asked her.

"No. I met and talked with some of the women. There aren't many, but some of the men are married. This woman named Gretta told me they had been with Darringer since the beginning. The Renegades have traveled most of the west the last few weeks since Darringer's home was attacked. He was a peacekeeper in Fort Seal, and it was overrun by the beasts. She said some of the towns folk there had gone missing in the spring and they began returning two weeks ago, but they were different," Meroha said.

"The Scree?"

"Yes. When the beasts attacked, the ones in the town that were changed, they fought with the wolveracks, murdering their neighbors and kin. Darringer has been rounding people up anywhere he can ever since. What are we going to do, Learon?" Meroha asked.

"We will ride with them to Pardona tomorrow and then move on to meet Stasia in Midway."

"What if Pardona is overrun?"

"Then we will fight to eradicate the beasts."

"What of the Bonemen in Pardona? Won't they cause trouble?"

"We'll see," Learon said, and he laid back on the bedroll. Merphi moved from his lap and sprawled atop his torso, and he slept.

ELEVEN
BEAR VILLAGE (CALEB)

emories are tethered to the self, like pathways through the
dimensions of a life; but without memories, with those pathways gone, *who was he?* He desperately wanted to know who
he had been, but not to inform the future. He had no interest in who he
was as a means to tell him where to go, but he had begun to crave an
explanation for why he was.

In the days after he had first awoken, his health and strength
returned quickly and as it did, he helped around the farm wherever the
extra hand was needed. Lowell recognized his skill and put him to work
fixing, building, and rebuilding. Caleb surprised himself that he had the
skill, and he was happy to help.

Lowell's leg had caught a bullet in the War fighting as a Bonemen
and it had never been right since. In his first battle, he was shot by Flynn
Dryden himself, and now he had a story for a lifetime. The story stirred
something in Caleb, but when he tried to find the moment, it slipped
from his mind before taking hold, leaving vague images that had him
seeing visions of himself pulling lighting from the sky. Caleb wasn't
disturbed by his missing past, as much as his own mind's inability to regu-
late fact from fiction. Sleep had been erratic. If he didn't dream, he slept
well, but on the nights, he did dream, he found he couldn't breathe.
There was an agonizing awareness that there was an importance to his
memories beyond the sentimental.

Once the day began, the feeling dissipated like morning dew, and he
found solace in the work. In rapid succession, his fresh experiences were
reshaping him. People change through time and experience, and he

could feel himself finding more comfort in the simple life of keeping the farm running. He grew to like Lowell's dry humor, and the kindness of sweet Raina was healing. When he wasn't helping Lowell fix something or another, he was helping Raina prepare meals.

In the evening, after the sun had gone down, he would ignite the protection fires. With the blue flames illuminating the grounds in the cool mountain air, he would chop wood. He did this late into the night. It helped him rebuild his strength, but there was also something about the repetition that calmed him. Where he should have felt empty, there was a sense of gratitude that filled the vacancy. He felt both unconnected from everything and appreciative of everything in a way that was satisfying. Though Lowell had mentioned his time at the farm was coming to an end, Caleb paid it no mind. Not because he thought it might not come to pass or that he had a plan, rather his sense of anticipation for future events was absent. He couldn't remember much, but he knew he would struggle to find any moment in his life he felt this truly happy to be alive. It was a happiness only those unburdened can know, an outlook he realized that meant the previous version of himself had been a cynic.

A few days went by, and then one evening on the porch where Caleb and Lowell liked to retreat after dinner, Lowell told him of the man named Warren Poe. Poe had helped heal Raina. He was a man of many talents and not one easily found or called upon, but Lowell knew he owned the White Horse Tavern on the Island of Nima in the Grey Sea. As it happened, Lowell would be traveling to the east coast where he traded once every season and he was overdue for his summer run. If Caleb came with, there was a possibility Poe could help him. Caleb took the offer to travel with them and they left the next day.

They traveled at the foot of the Soaring Mountains and with every day that passed, Caleb grew more frustrated with his mind. Not for the longing over something lost, but the confusion was difficult to manage. One thing he was sure of now, was that his name wasn't Caleb.

The memories that had returned to him felt more like he was peeking into the open window of someone else's home rather than recalling his own experiences. He could picture things but knowing what was real and what was not, haunted him.

Two days from the farm, they reached Bear Village just after the sun had shifted out of the Blue. The northern mountain city was one of the larger cities along the Sunwake Cove. Caleb recalled that the cove was known for its whaling industry. While the city proper was a few leagues from the cove, Lowell drove the coach directly to the rocky shore, where he preferred to trade directly with the many fishing outposts. Finally pulling to a stop, they got out and stretched their legs.

"I'm going to go talk to the man inside."

"Do you want me to start unloading the crates?" Caleb asked.

"No, let me barter the best price first and then I'll return with a wheeled lever to help."

Caleb nodded his understanding and started to stroll along the rock-filled shoreline. The smell of the sea was intoxicating. Nothing yet had stirred such a response from him, and suddenly an image and memory struck him. Like the morning he had awoken, he saw himself scrambling up a lighthouse tower. The Watchman's Tower on the tip of the Zuvo islands. A sword in his hand and a storm out on the sea. The sounds of his memory and the shoreline at his feet melted away and were inter-rupted by boot heels clacking loudly on the nearby wood pier.

A group of men were walking down the dock. All three were easily half Caleb's age, and they each walked upright with a sense of owner-ship. The lead man stepped from the wood planks and jumped down to the rocky embankment where they left the cart. Raina still sat there, reviewing her father's supply sheet.

"Raina Wrenwa, have you finally come to marry me, sweetheart?" the man said. He wore a finely embroidered jacket, too nice for a fisher-man. Caleb could see instantly that the guy made Raina uncomfortable, and he came over to help her. The man's friends followed and they all three ignored Caleb completely until he was standing next to the cart.

"Raina, do you know these men?" Caleb asked.

"She knows us, old man. Go back to your ale and leave us," the leader said.

"Yes, Caleb. It's alright," she said, but her eyes told him a different story.

Caleb observed all three, trying to gauge what kind of men they were. All had clean hair and boots, and none of their hands showed any signs of labor. Two of them wore swords, and the leader also concealed something beneath his black coat.

"Come on Raina, come over to the Highmark with us. We can have some fun. I'll show you a good time and you can ride home with your father tomorrow."

"No thank you, Arden."

"What do you mean, no thank you? I'll pay for everything. There's no reason not to go," Arden said.

"She said *no* kid, leave her alone," Caleb said.

"Listen Grandpa, I don't know who you are, but you obviously don't know who I am," Arden said, and he pulled his coat back only slightly to reveal a pulsator gun strapped to his side. "I'm talking with my friend. Be gone," Arden said.

With the warning hanging in the air, Arden put his hand on Raina's wrist, and something snapped inside Caleb. He knew instinctively how to hurt the man, but his action was quelled at the sound of Lowell's voice,

"Arden? Can I help you?" Lowell said from the rampart. His voice was cautious, but cold. Arden released Raina's arm and turned to talk with Lowell.

"Nope, I was just saying hello to Raina."

"It's fine, father," Raina said.

"Well, of course it's fine. You don't even have to tell him. Lowell, Wrenwa knows everything is on the up and up. I see you hired yourself an extra hand. That's good Lowell, you need the help. Did you get a good price inside?" Arden asked.

"I got a fair price," Lowell said.

"Fair. Now if it was only fair, I can go talk with Huen, or my father can. We know you need all the help you can get so far out west," Arden said.

"We do just fine, thank you, Arden," Lowell said.

"My pleasure," Arden said, and he turned back to Raina. "Raina, I'll see you later."

Caleb felt the heat that had risen inside him still lingered and he leered at the three men as they walked away, never taking his eyes off them until they had disappeared far down the road.

"Help me unload everything and then we are going down the way to the Warehouses at the Whaling Marina," Lowell said.

While they unloaded everything, Caleb remained quiet about the encounter, but it weighed on his mind the entire time. Pulling the last load of crates up the ramp, Lowell looked him over,

"Let it go Caleb. It's just the local mayor's son and his lackeys."

"I see," Caleb said.

"I do have good news for you, Caleb. I talked with Huan inside, and he told me that Poe's ship came through the cove not long ago. At the southern point of the pier, there's a ferry that will take you across the cove to Nima."

"Thank you, Lowell."

After everything was unloaded, Caleb and Raina drove the cart further along the shore to another traders' warehouse. Here, the whalers' crews were coming in, their ships filled the bay. The entire complex of jetties and docs was lined with storehouses, supplies, bait, and tackle shops, with a few taverns mixed in for good measure. The docks were wide enough to allow for stacks of crates coming in from some shipping vessels and still provide room for the whaling crews to move freely with their equipment and catch.

Lowell showed them the places they were trading with and what materials needed to be loaded on the cart for the return trip. Bells rang out in the distance, and he scanned for the sound. At the southern tip of the docks, a ferry boat was making a last call before setting out over the cold water.

"Don't worry, there's another one. The last of the night leaves in an hour," Lowell said. "The White Horse Tavern is on the east end of the city. There are sheer white limestone cliffs there and a winding stone path up to the tavern. Just ask anyone and they can point you where to go if you get lost."

They went back and started to collect the things Lowell and Raina were going to take back home with them. When they were done, Lowell offered to buy Caleb a drink before the next ferry came and they would part ways.

They split up to gather everything faster. Lowell didn't want to stay in the city if he could avoid it. Caleb helped get a new well pump lifted and onto the cart then set off to find Raina and that drink before catching the boat. Raina was supposed to have been picking up one last basket of frozen fish for their ride home but had lingered or was perhaps held up by something. Caleb wandered around the docks to find the store she was supposed to have gone to. He found the shop and the owner but was told she had picked up the catch and left. With the daylight waning, a slight panic set in and Caleb found his steps had hastened to a jog as he searched for her along the docks. The pink of the sky reflected in the sparkling sea where open spots along the piers left pockets of water and small fish visible. Periodically he began calling out her name, but no reply came back. He looped his way to the tavern where they planned to get that final drink. Outside, he found Lowell leaning against the grey-slated wall.

"Lowell, is Raina with you?" Caleb said winded, his breath trailing his feet.

"No, I thought she was with you?" Lowell shook his head.

"I can't find her," Caleb said.

"What do you mean you can't find her?" Lowell said.

"She never came back to the cart and horses, so I went looking for her."

"All right, I'll look up and down the docks, you backtrack to the cart. Maybe she went to go get something for herself."

Caleb agreed, and he ran back to the cart. Turning the last corner, he saw her sitting in the cart. At first, he only saw her and the tears on her cheeks, then he saw she was surrounded by the same men from before. This time, a fourth had joined them. The man named Arden was talking to her while his friends' dumped things off the back.

Caleb ran to reach her. The four men appraised his arrival but disregarded him.

"Oh look, your grandpa's back," Arden sneered.

Caleb ignored the jab and unconsciously calculated everything he was seeing. As though he were an animal in his previous life, he attentively defined minute details about the men and the situation. He knew which ones were left-handed, who had stamina versus strength, which one would run, who would strike him first, and who would follow that lead. He knew that two of them would move to hold him so the leader could hit him. With the quick information overload, he also weighed the ways to defeat the lot of them. The squad began constricting around him, but he instinctually knew what to do: who to strike first, how the scene was to evolve with each clash... he couldn't help himself; a grin came to his face.

"What are you smiling at?" Arden said.

"Four ugly halfwits," Caleb replied.

An obvious tension in the man's stance, a muscle in his jaw clinched, and the attack began.

The first man swung at him, and Caleb dodged the punch. Then Arden stuck him across the shoulder, but he shouldn't have. Caleb had anticipated that strike, but his muscles and instinct weren't in tune to coordinate the block.

Caleb side-stepped the next man charging in with his sword drawn, grabbing his arm as he passed. With a twist, the man's sword fell to ground, and Caleb flung him back into the next attacker sending both men tumbling into a small boat. The boat fell from its stanchion and a clattering of whaling instruments toppled out, a lance, flensing knife, net, harpoon, and hooks all scattered about their feet.

Arden rankled his nose in hatred, and directed the fourth man to attack. This one came in with his sword high. Caleb bounced on his feet and kicked a low strike into the man's knee buckling him to the deck. He cried out holding his kneecap.

Arden swung his own blade in, a swift slash that made Caleb withdraw on his heels. Arden's training was obvious by his grip and form, but his anger had him swinging wildly and in longer, undisciplined sweeps.

The two men that crashed with the boat, scrambled to their feet and rejoined the attack. Caleb retrieved the long whaling lance from the dock planks and turned back to face them. He smacked Arden's sword aside and followed with a sweeping blow that tripped Arden off his feet.

The two others came in swinging and Caleb smacked one with the blunt end across the temple, and disarmed the other with the spearpoint. Holding the lance with both hands, he crashed the middle of the shaft into the disarmed man's face.

With all four men moaning on the wood dock, Caleb threw the lance aside and began to walk back to Raina, assuming the miscreants were through with the fight. A loud grumbling from the defeated men was rage-filled and Arden barked at his men to get up.

From down the docks, Lowell came running toward them, hobbling slightly on his bad foot. Caleb saw him and heard the unmistakable tone of an amp hum from a pulsator powering on.

Raina screamed out, "No!"

Caleb kicked the flensing knife from where it settled, up and into his hand. He spun on the attackers as a charged blast fired. But Arden's gun misfired on the first attempt. He glared at Caleb and back to his gun, confused. Caleb closed the distance in a flash and stepped through the four men in a sort of dance of five slashing steps that ended with them screaming on the ground. He had lacerated through them with single slices that left them all wounded and had severed a hand from the leader.

The gun hit the deck, and Caleb slammed his foot into the crystal. A small electric discharge popped, and the light went out. He removed his foot away to make sure the gun was out of service. The crystal was broken, and the power surge had burnt out the oscillator, but he couldn't help but notice the gun was in pristine condition besides what his stomp had done. *How had such a pristine gun misfired?*

"Caleb, what's happened?" Lowell said. When he saw the blood and men on the dock, his face paled, "What have you done?"

"Lowell, they were terrorizing Raina. I just reacted," Caleb said.

Lowell grimaced and rushed over to Raina. Her eyes and face were blotchy and red.

"I tried, father. I tried to hold back," she said, her voice rising with panic. Caleb looked where her hands gripped the seat and burn marks were imprinted into the leathered cushion. Lowell saw it too, and he hugged his daughter.

"It's all right. You did well, Raina," Lowell said, and he turned back to Caleb.

"You need to go, Caleb," Lowell said, still holding Raina, "Green-coats will be here soon, and you should be gone by the time they arrive. The ferry is leaving. If you run, you can catch it." Lowell handed Caleb a small leather pouch.

Caleb took it quizzically and looked inside. It was full of amber coins, he thrust it back, "I can't take your money, Lowell."

"Take it, you earned it. But Caleb, don't come back through Bear Village. There will be people looking for you."

"Thank you, Lowell, and you Raina. Thank you for nursing me back to life."

"Go," Lowell said, "And please don't tell anyone," He gestured to the cushion.

"I won't," Caleb said.

"Then by the Mercy of the Light, my friend, go, and may you remain under the Blue."

Caleb nodded and heard the bell of the ferry ringing. He shook Lowell's hand and ran to the southern end of the pier.

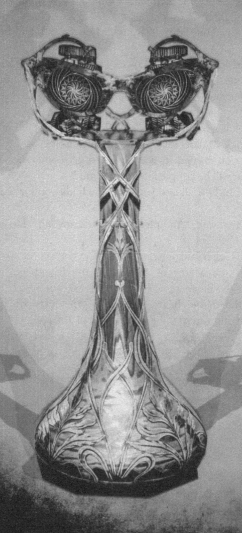

THE ANAMNESIS VASE

TWELVE
THE WHITE HORSE TAVERN (CALEB)

When he arrived on Nima island, the marina was decorated with hanging lanterns. Strung from all the water posts, they glowed in red and orange. The ferry was less than half full. Caleb stepped off the boat and walked with a quickened pace that reflected his nerves. His blood still pumped furiously from the fight. He asked for directions and set off to find the White Horse Tavern and the man named Poe.

A few roads away from the water, the darkness of the night became apparent. Lights in the hills and trees spoke of a vast sprawling city of small villages. Everything was spread out amongst the island hills and trees, but the directions he had been given were clear and the path took him away from the heart of the city. With every step, Caleb was positive he had never been here before. But with every step, he asked himself if this was what he wanted.

He couldn't remember who he was, but he could remember other things—mundane things—but the derived meaning was gone. He feared when or if his memories came back, that they wouldn't be the same; that the time out of mind would have an altering effect on the significance of them. Would they feel alien, *how will I reconcile them?* How would memory returning from the mist change him again and which him was real: the one slowly remembered, or the one unburdened and unconnected?

What he had done on the docks to those men had been real, but how he had done it confounded him. Now more than ever, he was torn to discover himself.

One thing they never talked about at the farm with Lowell was why he came to be in their care. Lowell explained how he had found Caleb washed up on the east banks of Marathal lake. At first Lowell had confused him for a fish, because of the blood. It was not unheard of for dead fish to wash up and Lowell was curious. There were tales of giant fish in Marathal, like every lake.

Whoever had shot him never came looking for him, and neither had anyone else. Whoever he was, he had not been worth looking for. That was the mystery that ate at him. How could no one miss someone worth shooting fourteen times?

The White Horse Tavern on the island of Nima overlooked white cliffs, as Lowell had said, less than a league south of the marina where the ferry had dropped him. He walked a good hour before finding it. The outside stone foundation tapered in at angles from the rocks, high on all sides. Elaborately-crafted wood posts and beams made up a front facade where a large circular wood moon gate arched over the entrance, concealing a courtyard of stacked stone walls amongst a garden.

There was something familiar, but not intimately recognizable, about the place. He passed beneath the moon gate, the arching wood stained dark brown, and entered the garden. Lanterns floating in a still pool of water lined the path to the main doors.

At the doors, he never had the chance to knock. They parted free as he stepped close, and the noise of the interior boomed. The volume of the interior was exposed, and he heard music above the throng of talking, laughter, glasses, and tins. A doorman in a black suit held the door. He wore a wool hat and gold pocket watch tucked into his vest. Caleb passed by him into the darkened hall. The first fifteen feet inside were cave-like, but beyond it lay the lively and bright tavern.

Six-foot-tall hearths at the sides flanked the main bar. Glowing passageways to the sides suggested smaller private rooms toward the back. A very large man was moving around in one of them. The shadows passed, and the light wavered and returned. The room was a mix of low tables and chairs and smaller intimate sitting areas with thick cushioned chairs amongst wafting clouds of smoke. For the late hour, Caleb was surprised to find so many people within.

He was halfway to the bar when a someone voiced their displeasure at seeing him.

"What are you doing here, Kovan?" a man in a long black coat sneered.

Caleb continued a few steps before realizing he was the one being called Kovan. Still, he ignored the man and approached the bar. The tender stood attentive, wiping the counter clean of condensation left from a previous patron.

"Can I help you, friend?" she asked.

"I was told by Lowell Wrenwa that I could find a man here named Warren Poe."

"Just who might . . ." The tender was interrupted before she could finish the question.

"Kovan Rainer, I'm talking to you," a man behind him shouted.

Caleb turned to find three men stepping up to him. He looked at them with a squint. Trying to search for recognition. None came.

"I heard you were dead?"

"We'll, I'm alive. Who are you?"

"I'm John Dodge. I've been looking for you."

Caleb gave him a confused look as he searched for recognition, "Should I know you?"

"No. But you should remember my brother, Jake. You killed him in Amera two springs back."

The news of having killed someone, even falsely accused or not, should have had a bigger impact on him, but he took it without a reaction. *Seems about right.*

"Look at him boys, this is the great Kovan Rainer. The best dueler in the south. Why you look past your prime, Kovan."

"I don't know what to tell you. I'm not the man you say I am," he said dismissively. *Or was he?*

"Once a killer, always a killer."

"Well, I have no sword, no gun, and I'm not interested in dueling you even if I did."

"That's too bad," John said.

The man's henchman moved to grab Caleb, and a waitress came charging in.

"Boys, leave this establishment now," she ordered.

Caleb searched but saw no bouncer or security to help.

"Mr. Poe understands retribution, darling," the man said.

"That may be so, but this man," she pointed to Caleb, "Has already asked to speak with Poe. You know the rules."

"I don't care about your rules, girl," the man snarled and pushed her aside. She stumbled easily into a nearby table. The crash drew the attention of everyone inside. Another patron helped the woman to her feet and she ran to the back.

Either his hatred for Caleb couldn't be contained any longer or he knew what he had done had escalated things beyond turning back; but the man's eyes went wild.

"Well, let's get on with it," Caleb said with a shrug.

One of the henchmen rushed Caleb and swung his fist into him. He dodged it and took the man's hand, quickly twisted his arm over and back. Caleb plunged his compacted right fist across and through the man's face. John reached for his pulsator, and Caleb jumped into him. Together, they tumbled backwards to the floor. The third man unsheathed a short sword and swung toward Caleb's head. He moved in time to see the blade gash across the hardwood. The roll freed John to draw his weapon. The pulsator pointed at Caleb for a split second, but he was able to grab the gun and deflect the shot. The sound blared and the muzzle flash singed his hand. Caleb's hand on the main converter box spun the adjustment gears, and he scrambled back. John fired again and the pulsator's tethers overcharged, causing a sparking fire and blast back from the chamber. John's hand caught fire.

The third man was now creeping toward Caleb and as he tried to pick himself off the floor, two more attackers entered the fight. They grabbed Caleb and held him. Caleb struggled, but they held him tight. John got off the ground, picked up his pulsator and smashed it across Caleb's face. A spray of blood hit the floor from an instant gash to his cheek. The split went deep, and blood flowed freely. His head was woozy, and blood dripped to his neck when he lifted his chin. His vison blurred, the old headache returned, and he could barely keep his eyes open. John adjusted his pulsator to fire.

A huge form loomed behind him, and he heard a voice growl a warning. The large man hit John so hard Caleb heard a crack and saw John flying lifelessly. The men holding Caleb let him go and he slumped to the floor, grabbing his head. He closed his eyes and heard more fighting but passed out. The big man's voice calling to him was the last thing he heard before everything went dark; it sounded vaguely familiar.

AGAIN, HE DREAMED OF FIGURES OF STONE LOOKING OVER HIM AND THIS time, there was a young woman with red hair, but *who was she?* Pain in his chest blazed and a silver spear spade was piercing his breast. It cut right through him. Everything stopped and he died. From the fading blackness he heard a friend scream his name. He lurched and convulsed awake.

When he came to and lifted his head, he found himself lying atop a bar. Caleb looked around, his eyes found lights above him, and he recoiled. The brightness brought the intensity of pain in his head to peak. He rolled off the bar to his feet and found a stool nearby to steady himself. He wasn't prepared to walk yet.

"Sit," a voice said.

Caleb looked up and found a cloaked man with a flat-brimmed hat sitting nearby, his face placidly starring into the warm drink in his hands. His features were familiar, but his voice even more so.

"I know you, don't I?" Caleb asked.

"We are not friends nor enemies, but yes I know you, Kovan."

He didn't respond to being called Kovan again: instead, he inquired about the man who had helped him, "Where's the big guy? I would like to thank him."

"Mayzanna Buroga. He is cleaning up and closing the place down for me. I was told you asked for me?"

"You're Poe?" Caleb said. *Maybe he was this Kovan.*

"Sometimes. I am many people. Sometimes I am him, sometimes I am someone else," Poe said.

"I was injured a few weeks back and when I awoke, I was in the care of Raina Wrenwa"

"Lucky you."

"She said you helped heal her once, and that you might be able to help me."

"I did help her, but something tells me you are not suffering from the same thing as she. So, what ails you still?" Poe asked.

"When I awoke in her care, I had no memories. Neither of my past or of myself."

"And you want this remedied."

"If it can be, yes."

"Why?" Poe asked.

"Because I want to know who I am."

"No, that's not it. Tell me the truth."

"I . . . I am haunted by something. Something I need to do or someone I need to help."

"I can help you, but you won't like it."

"What's the payment?" Kovan asked. Looking around the room, he could see Poe had expensive taste. The walls were full of paintings, there were shiny instruments all over, and a shelving casement to the side was full of all sorts of odds and ends that looked ancient and valuable.

"No payment, maybe a favor one day," Poe answered, "but it is an unpleasant procedure to have your memories returned. I first have to extract them."

"That doesn't sound fun," Kovan said, and he eyed the big carving knifes.

Poe caught his glaring. "No, nothing so barbaric. I have another way,"

Poe walked to a side table. The piece of furniture there was very old, with a set of doors, a golden plate encircling the front keyhole. On top lay a towel covering something. He removed a towel from the console table. A metal head brace lay next to a long needle. Poe smiled,

"Don't worry, that's for something else."

Then Poe picked the key up from the towel. He knelt to unlock the doors to the console and removed an antique vase, beyond compare. Poe closed and locked the cabinet and returned to his chair near the window. Placing the vase on a small table, he waved Kovan to come forward and take the opposite chair.

Kovan sat down inspecting the vase, but he didn't touch it. It was a medium size and made of some sort of mercurial glass, an integrated metal filigree entwined the whole thing. From the gold base to the top lip, lines wrapped and formed a symbol of sorts. At the top, the lines grew from the opening and formed a set of tilted eyes. The eyes had a structure and a depth with a mirroring that reflected on its concaved spiral. It was both beautiful and haunting.

"Not sure what I expected. But I guess when you play in a game with the morally grey, you must be willing to bend the rules?" Kovan said.

"The morally grey rapidly become morally bankrupt. But as you'll soon find out, morality is but a pathway in your mind."

"Does it hurt? This vase?" Kovan asked.

"It's not without pain, but the extraction is not the worst part. The worst part is when you take the memories in again. The method of extraction looks elegant, but I promise you, it is painful." He rotated the vase so Kovan could see the back. There was a cluster of purple crystals connected behind the eyes. Deep and dark in its luster, but brilliant and mesmerizing.

"It has been called the Eyes of Deja Maru by some and the Anamnesis Vase by others. The magic of the vase is old. It was used during the Luminary Wars two thousand years ago," Poe explained.

"How do you know about it? Where did you get it?"

"The Scholar's Guild is not the only group interested in the past. There are others, collectors, archeologists, and curators of unique antiquities. Myself, I have traveled all over this world and sometimes when I hear of especially unique items, I dig a little deeper. And I've found that the deeper you dig into the past, the more you discover that this world is plagued by poisoned minds. The manipulation of the mind by Luminaries and alchemists of old. I've heard stories that you wouldn't believe," Poe said.

"I see, and you're confident this will work?" Kovan said. He thought fear should be rising in him, but it wasn't. He couldn't know if that was due to his own nature, from which he was estranged, or the lack of nature where what was missing from him should be properly regulating his sense of dread.

After a long silence Kovan said, "I trust you."

"Why? You have no reason to."

"True, but I have no reason not to. Let's fire this thing up and see what happens."

"Very well. The process goes like this."

He pulled a small silver bladed knife from his coat pocket and laid it softly on the smooth surface of the table.

"You must draw fresh blood. Don't ask me how much, I don't know. Everyone is different. Since we are going deep to recover as much as we can, I believe it will be several vials worth. The blood is poured into the small reservoir behind the crystal. You will then stare into the eyes. The magic of the vase once connected to you will not free you from its gaze until it has completed the extraction."

"That's it? I mean, the blood part sounds unpleasant, but I just stare into the eyes?"

"Yes. Afterward you will need to rest. The vase extracts the essence of your mind and the memories pool into the base where it solidifies."

"Solidifies?"

"Yes, into a small cube," Poe said. He tilted the vase so Kovan could see down to the bottom. The interior of the glass had a different pattern than the outside and various grooved lines funneled to three square pockets at the bottom. "When they are ready, you can either swallow the cube or place them in hot water and drink your memories back."

"Wait, could someone else take them?" Kovan asked.

"Yes, ultimately, it's up to you when you take the memories, but while the vase will leave you exhausted, taking your memories can have untold effects."

"Have you ever done this, what's it like?"

"I have. Though it was not my own memories I sought, but another's.

I slept for half a day and dreamt of things I had never known. When I awoke, the memories were not mine exactly but a more intimate knowledge of another," Poe said.

Kovan didn't want to ask why he had taken another person's memories. The man's business was his own to reconcile, but he did want an answer to the time frame, "Half a day?"

"It's impossible to tell, but while you recover, I will have Buroga take you to North Ride."

"What's in North Ride?"

"Like I said. I know you and I know that's where you'll want to be when your memories return," Poe said.

"I'm ready."

"I have to ask again. Are you sure? You realize what you're giving up?"

"What?" Kovan asked.

"A cleansed consciousness. Right now, you are a man outside of time. There can be no one wealthier than the unburdened mind."

"I may not know who I am or who I was, but I know one thing true about my spirit. I'm loyal, and I can't turn my back on my friends. Deep down I have a sense of duty that I can't shake, and it haunts me," Kovan said, and he reached across the table and grabbed the knife.

Poe understood it was time to begin. He retrieved some vials and placed them in front of Kovan, along with a wrapping of cloth. Kovan took a deep breath and cut a gash into his left arm. The blade was cold and sharp and sliced through on an easy, searing drag. He collected two vials' worth and wrapped his arm with the cloth, tied it off, and handed the vials to Poe. He could feel his heart pounding in his chest.

Putting his hands to his chin, he moved closer to the table and got comfortable to stare into the eyes. He took a deep breath and when he was ready, he pulled it forward and nodded for Poe to pour the blood in.

The eyes were mesmerizing. The glass inside was not unreflective as he had first thought. They mirrored an endless fracture of light in an infinite tunnel. His breathing steadied and a light from the crystal sparkled in his peripheral vision, but he paid it no attention. He couldn't. The eyes consumed his thoughts. Soon, even the vase was glowing, and Kovan was pulled through a vortex of time to a place without knowing. He stood in darkness and every surface shined like liquid and reflected more blackness. There was light, but not from any source he could find. He walked in the great void alone and he called out, "Poe."

His voice traveled in an echo without reverberation. But no call came back. He was alone and then he wasn't. Voices called to him, but everywhere he looked was the same blackness, the same shine of nothing. If he stared at a surface for too long, he found himself standing atop it, as though the space folded on itself.

More voices called his name, and he focused on the one that mattered.

"Kovan!" A woman's voice called.

Again, it had no direction or form and she called out again, "Kovan!"

The voice needed him.

Tiny spots of light winked into existence and went away. White light burst into pinpricks and fluttered out of sight. It started with only a few, but soon there were thousands of points, and each fluttered beyond his reach, his eyes unable to focus on any single one point. It was everywhere. The sound and light died, and the blackness swallowed him. Until something new burst forth and suddenly he was staring at cliffs above the ocean and the cold water crashed violently. He shuddered with dread and closed his eyes, but they wouldn't shut. Then he was in the water and drowning, but he had to keep looking. She had slipped below, *but she was here.* Her dark hair, *she was just here. Where did she go?* Frantically he twisted in the current, the tide jostling him wildly and he touched her fingers.

Aleah!

Aleah! His heart and mind screamed, he kicked and convulsed. He desperately needed to breathe, but he would not surface; not until he had her. He breathed the water and choked, but he clutched to something. Then he heard two people talking.

"He's had enough. You've taken everything from him," a man pleaded. The voice belonged to a friend.

"I must make sure they never remember," a woman said unflinchingly. It was the voice of someone he knew long ago.

"But you're killing them!" the man yelled.

"She destroys the world! Together, they break the world. I can't let it happen."

"Together, with who?"

"It doesn't matter. I won't let him come to be, either."

"Maybe you're wrong?"

"I'm not. You don't understand his reach, breaches the void. It corrupts everything, and when they fail everything is lost," The woman's voice cried.

"You're killing them, Stop! . . ." someone screamed and a loud thump of a body hitting the floor, crashed.

"KOVAN!" A NEW VOICE SAID AND SUDDENLY HE WAS BACK, AND POE WAS pouring water into his mouth. He instinctively jerked away. The water spilled, but he drank what he had already and found he was so parched he couldn't speak.

"Drink," Poe said, and he sat back and exhaled. They were both lying on the floor, Poe with his back against the wall and Kovan flat on the floor. He sat up and grabbed the cup of water. He threw the remaining contents back and placed the cup to the floor.

"More?" a deep voice asked.

Kovan didn't look at who had asked, he just nodded his desire for more, and lifted the cup.

The man took the cup and brought it back and again Kovan drained it entirely without stopping. When he had caught his breath, he found both his arms now had wrappings, and both dressings needed to be changed. *When was I cut a second time?*

"What happened, did it work?" Kovan rubbed his eyes, they ached in a way he had never felt.

"It worked," Poe sighed.

Kovan noticed for the first time the sunlight streaming through the windows, "How long was I at it?"

"You've been under for nearly thirteen hours. When the first two vials of blood ran dry, I tried to disconnect you from the device, but I couldn't. I took more blood from you. In the end, it took five vials. When it was finished, you fell off the chair and started choking. I've never seen it last so long. I can't be sure, but I think someone in your past blocked your mind."

"What?"

"I think that's why it took so long and," he paused and reached up to the table. He grabbed something silver and metal that fit in his palm and slid it on the floor to Kovan. "Here."

It was a small metal case; the kind in which a High Order gentleman might carry his cigarettes. It was a dull silver and locked with a sliding pin at the side. Kovan held it up and gave Poe a quizzical look.

"Open it," Poe said.

Kovan opened it. The top rotated back on interior hinges. There was a thin black cloth inside and beneath the cloth sat three cubes of swirling colors. There were numbers and other symbols marking each one where the liquid had pooled inside the vase. To Kovan, they looked like vibrant dice.

"I thought you said *a* cube. There are three cubes in here?"

"I have never seen it produce all three. Even two is rare. You take the cube marked with the number one first, and each dose after will add more memories."

"Chronologically?"

"No. And I wouldn't advise you to take them all at once. You don't even have to take all of them, that's up to you, but the spell is not complete until you do. You should burn the cubes you don't take. But I should warn you: the second dose is harder to commit to. It would be a great mistake not to take it. You will never feel like you."

"I don't feel like me now."

"True, but the small itch you have to discover your past will be much stronger once you've taken the first dose."

When his head stopped spinning, Kovan got up off the floor but stumbled. His legs were squishy and couldn't sustain his weight. A large man caught him before he fell. Kovan looked up at him. It was a Hazon man.

"I know you?"

"Yes," the Hazon man said.

"Kovan, this is Mayzanna Buroga. He will take you back to the mainland while you recover from the first dose. I suggest you take it now."

Kovan nodded his understanding. Buroga deposited him in a chair and brought him a steaming cup of water. Kovan opened the steel case, removed the cube numbered one and hovered over the cup. He hesitated, admiring the colors and the branded symbols, and dropped it in with a definitive plop of sound. The water immediately swirled. The liquid rotated rapidly as though he had used a spoon and it didn't seem like it was going to slow. He drank it.

The liquid was sweet and bitter and tart and buttery. It was all things. He couldn't explain the taste if he tried. It tasted like everything and nothing else. Once he got past the oddity of it, he loved it. He finished every drop.

Poe and Buroga studied him and when he was done Poe said, "The first things to come back will be the thoughts and worries you had before you were injured. For the next few days, your mind will begin recalling more. It will be disorienting to manage who you've become with who you were."

Kovan thanked the man and got up to leave.

"I have one last gift for you, Kovan Rainer," Poe said, and he grabbed a bundle on the bar top and handed it over. It had some weight to it and he started to open it, but Poe rested his hand over top to halt him, "Wait a few days and open it in North Ride."

"Thank you for everything, Poe. I really do owe you one."

"Don't forget it." Poe said. "Be Careful out there, Kovan Rainer. There's a madness to this world. And it's not the good kind that drives ability, turning energy to art, to create, to invent, to live. It's a madness for denial and a madness for self-preservation, a madness of ignorance. The people are plagued with an unwillingness to allow anything to change their world."

"I'm not afraid of change," Kovan said confidently.

"Good. If you stand against change, you will perish in the wind with but a whimper."

The tavern was closed at midday. The light inside was bright, and the smell of hardwood and leather hit his senses. Something prickled in his head. He closed his eyes tight, like a headache was coming on. Kovan stepped past the entry doors and into the blue shining sun. The waves of blue light were stronger than he had ever seen, and it splintered the sky. Suddenly, the wispy clouds in the sky started to swirl like his drink. An image of endless falling water and a firing squad hit his mind. His vision blurring his mind spellbound. He made it through the courtyard and the moon-gate before he collapsed. The Hazon man lifted him from the ground and Kovan smiled with recognition before succumbing to his racing mind,

"Thanks, Gigantore."

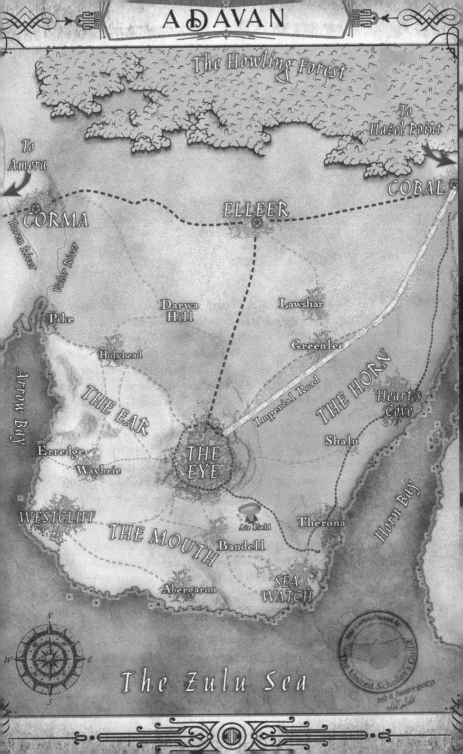

THIRTEEN
VISITORS (TALI)

T he winddrifter glided through the clouds on its decent to Adavan. From the cold mists, they came out shivering from head to toe, but the bright sun coerced the chill away, and warmth enveloped the ship. The heat of Adavan was humid and the air thick, Tali uncomfortable in her cloak. Bazlyn spun gages at the midship engine console and pulled a lever to raise his sails and steer them with the wind.

"Getting the wind here is like catching a Dawning Gale at dusk," he spat angrily to himself.

When Bazlyn achieved what he was looking for, he locked the wheel and returned to helping Wade. Together they had been trying to repair some of the wood on the ship deck and siderails over the course of the trip. The drastic changes in weather, over time, had produced expansion cracks in the hull. Some gaps were wide enough to see the blue sky through.

"No wind?" Wade gestured to the sagging sails.

"It just comes from every direction out here, is all," Bazlyn said.

The trip had been uneventful except for the knowledge that Wade had a fear of heights which amused Tali. It had come as a surprise to Wade himself, who swore he had never had a problem with heights before. When his nervousness turned to nausea and, in turn, to vomiting, he simply blamed the fish. In truth, it wasn't debilitating, beyond the initial shock of being in the clouds, but to avoid thinking about it, he had asked Bazlyn what he could do around the ship. Bazlyn mistook the offer as if that was Wade's nature to be handy. Having never met Wade, he didn't know better, but Bazlyn put him to work all the same.

For Tali, the flight so close to the stars and sun re-energized her, but with the rejuvenation, a sullenness set in. She tried to shake it off, but she couldn't help but feel they should have done more to find Kovan, Ellaria, and Elias. If they had decided early enough, maybe they wouldn't have lost the Tempest Stone. Being reunited with her mystcat, Remi, brought her the comforting companionship she needed. Remi and Bazlyn's dog Zephyr got along like old friends, except when they fought over who was sitting with her. Remi typically won out and Zephyr would bounce away and back to Bazlyn with it's tiny goggles shaking as it went.

While the flight was reminiscent of her first one when she crossed the Warhawk Mountains with Kovan, there was something very different this time. She realized the first night that what had changed was her. Her Luminary powers were alive, and the energies pulsed around her in ways she wasn't cognizant of the last time. Soaring in the sky had drastically affected what she could sense. The light waves and radiated heat of the sun were so easy to breathe in that she had to be cautious.

Elias had taught her about the well of energy within her. Every Luminary had a well or limit to how much energy they could hold. Based on her age when the Illumination Surge came to her, Elias suspected that Tali had a greater capacity than usual. However, it wasn't wise to hold energy at the maximum or even at all if one didn't need to. It could alter her mood and senses and eventually, a desire came to use that energy. This high up, Tali was unsure what work to put the energy into. She was not as skilled in kinetic transference as Elias, nor in electrical charge. Light and heat seemed to be where her talents resided. Elias, in one of their training sessions, had told her that every Luminary had energies they favored; ones that they could sense easier than others and transform easier too, but beyond those, sometimes they also had a talent.

Tali was unsure if light was her talent or just the energy she favored, but up here above the world, it flooded her. The only outlet she found was using it to subtly heat the air around them, so they didn't get as cold in the night.

The thing she couldn't shake was the feeling of being alone. Her powers, her Luminary blood, made her feel different. It was never a big deal when Elias, as another Luminary, was around. Elias had told her they weren't their own race of beings, alien of the human race, but a variation in the species. But sometimes she didn't want to be a variation. She had all these things happening inside her and she couldn't confide in anyone. Worse, she had to hide herself.

Maybe you don't feel like you because Learon is gone. Her own thought surprised her, and she walked to the sidewall near the stern of the ship, staring out at the city coming up fast and the Zulu sea beyond. A haze draped over the horizon, even from this vantage point. The more she examined the city, the more details become discernible and somewhere while she was lost in her thoughts, they were already near to landing.

"Bazlyn?" she called out, surprised he hadn't made adjustment to land yet.

"What is it, miss?"

"We're here," Tali said.

"We're here? Impossible," Bazlyn said, still concentrating on filling a gap with putty.

"No, we're *here*," she said urgently.

Bazlyn pressed his eye to the opening he was working on and then jumped to his feet. His eyes bulged at seeing the city rising around them. He sprinted to the heat valve and rotated it fully open. The craft suddenly halted its fall, and they all slammed into the deck.

"Sorry! I don't know how this is possible. We should have been an hour out. It's almost like something is pulling us in," he proclaimed while wiping dirt and a putty stain from his right eye.

"I guess you found the wind," Wade said.

A few minutes later, they touched down gently in the Adavan airfield. It was three times the size of the airfield in Atava and held a cluster of winddrifters, each unique in size and design. Tali searched for Margo's ship and found it before they landed. It was parked on the far side of the field, purple sails tied down already.

"We can't thank you enough," Tali said to her friend, and she hugged him.

Bazlyn stood with an *aww shucks* sort of look and he smiled at her.

"And you'll go to Midway to get Learon?" she said.

"Of course. I have to get some more fuel for the balloon and supplies for the trip, but I'll be back in the sky by nightfall."

"We really can't thank you enough, Baz," Wade said, handing him some amber coins.

"Your money is no good. You did a lot of work for me, fixing the Savona. Plus, you're going to need it, like I explained the first night. From what I know about the girl, I suspect Nyra will be headed to the local syndicate and probably to Amera after that. The people she owes are in Amera, of that I'm certain."

"It was a pleasure, and safe travels," Wade said, exiting the craft.

With her green cloak on, Tali slung her bag over her shoulder.

Holding the flap open for Remi, the cat came running, jumped in smoothly, and sunk into place. She hugged Bazlyn again before climbing down the short ladder to the ground.

"Miss Tali, where am I taking Learon when I pick him up?" Bazlyn called from above.

"He'll know where. I'll send word to him in Midway," she replied.

"Tali," Bazlyn called out again, and she looked back at him, "Take care and don't make any sort of deal with the syndicate. They will as soon kill you than make good on a wager they've lost."

"Got it," Tali said.

"Also, avoid the Bonemen. They're everywhere now," Bazlyn said.

"Got it, thank you," she said. She waved goodbye and hurried to catch up to Wade to begin their search.

ADAVAN WAS THE CITY OF THE RHUSKERO BULL. THE SOUTHERN COUNTRY was divided into regions named for the bull. The most congested and the heart of Adavan was in the Eye of the Bull, but the city stretched along the entirety of the coast, from the Ear in the west to the Horn's Tip in the east, a span close to two hundred leagues. If there had never been an Empire to temper the birth of new cities, large nations like Adavan would have sprouted many within its borders. The spread was such that most of the regions had their own character and commerce, but the whole of the country was Adavan. Having never been here, Tali was worried that tracking down Nyra could be impossible. She had at least a two-hour head start on them, though probably more like four hours.

The Adavan airfield was in the far south, in the Mouth. Straight away, they found the first travel office they could and secured a coach to take them to the Eye, hoping that was where Nyra was headed. Wade, as Wade tended to do, got lucky. The coach-finder inside the travel office happened to have procured a carriage for a young woman fitting Nyra's description. She was traveling by herself and headed for the city of Elleer in the north. Trusting that the man was talking about Nyra, they did the same.

From her coach seat, Tali admired the great city she had never seen: a mixture of white sandy buildings and gray stone roofs, sometimes burnt orange buildings and red stone roofs. There were tall trees the likes of which she had never seen either, with sprouted feather-like leaves that fanned out at the top. The trunks looked like a hard-thatched shells.

They were everywhere and Wade called them *thatch ferns* when she asked. From a distance, the richest buildings in the Eye looked like coiled honeycomb towers. Their gleaming stone and presence produced stark and frightening shapes.

Most of the day was spent traveling through Adavan and past the Eye. Never once did they seem to have closed the distance on Nyra. On the open road north of the city, there was no coach in sight of them. *We're pursuing a ghost,* Tali thought. When the heat of the afternoon began sweltering inside the cabin, Wade turned to her with an idea.

"What if we head her off?" he said.

"How are we going to do that?" Tali asked. She wasn't sure they were even on her tail any longer as it was, but she was amenable to any idea that freed them from the confines of the small cabin.

"Follow me on this. If she's headed to Elleer, Nyra won't arrive until later tonight."

"Right."

"From there we know she's going to head back west to Amera."

"We know that for certain."

"The best we have to go on suggests she's headed there. Bazlyn said she had debts to the syndicates in Amera."

"But which one?"

"Probably the Reckers or the Bounty Hunters' Guild, the Moonstalkers. They operate out of Amera, and I know that the Reckers run Adavan. There are certain cities my father will travel to trade with and ones he avoids because of their influence."

"So, what are you thinking?" Tali said.

"In the morning, Nyra will leave Elleer for Corma on her way to Amera. The journey is too long to make without stopping in Corma for the night. My family's farm is thirty leagues west of the road we're on now. If we head to my family's farm, it would be like taking a short cut to Corma. In the morning, we can leave the farm before the sun rises. We will be hours ahead of Nyra, no matter how early she leaves. We set up somewhere in the city and wait for her to arrive," Wade said.

"That's a pretty big gamble, Wade?"

"It's not. Right now, the best we can do is arrive a few hours after her in Elleer and then try to search the entire city in the night for her. Maybe we get lucky and find the inn where she's staying. Most likely she slips though our fingers once again and we're racing to Corma, anyway. My way puts us ahead of her and waiting."

"What if she stays in Elleer or goes east?" Tali said.

"She's not going to. If she was going east, she would have traveled the Imperial Road through the Horn of Adavan."

"Wade, if you're wrong, I'll kill you."

"I'm not wrong, trust me. We can get a home cooked meal out of the deal, too."

With a very reluctant nod, Tali agreed to his plan and Wade informed the driver where to turn off. It was risky, but they were never going to catch Nyra traveling in her shadow.

The carriage dropped them off on the hardened gravel road in what looked like the middle of nowhere. Tali looked around, her feet crunching on the dirt. There was nothing to see but hills and hills of tall grass and wheat fields. Wade took them through the fields, along a trail with tall oaks and sprawling willows. The house sat on the second hill, above undulating rows of farmed outcroppings. The neatly-cut lanes of vegetation blanketed the land. With the sunlight fading behind the large windmill, Tali thought it was about as pleasant a sight as she had ever seen.

A cascade of bugs chirping droned around them on the path. Two hundred feet from the house, a young boy met them on the way. His white shirt was loose at his pants and the sleeves rolled up in a manner similar to Wade's.

"Zeke. Is that you, little brother? Man, you're getting tall," Wade said.

"Why does everyone say that? Do they expect me to stay the same size?" Zeke said.

"I suppose not."

"So, brother, who's this?" he asked, and he removed his hat and bowed.

"This is Tali. She's, my friend."

"Hello, Miss Tali. I'm Zeke," he said, and he kissed her hand.

"He's ten," Wade explained.

"I'm twelve now. Get it right."

"Oh, that's right. Twelve, nearly twenty-six. I trust Mom and Dad are home?"

"Mom's cooking. Dad is in the lower north fixing that cursed fence again."

"Great. Do me a favor, Zeke. Run ahead and tell Mom she has two extra guests for dinner. Go on."

Zeke closed one eye at Wade like he was annoyed, but he then he broke out in a run for the house. Tali felt extremely odd about showing up unannounced and continually asked Wade if it was going to be all right. At the door, a young girl, no more than four, stood at the screen in a green jumper, with her blonde hair frazzled and wild. Her eyes grew big at seeing Wade on the porch.

"Delia!" Wade said, and he beamed.

Wade opened the door, and the girl jumped into his arms. She said a bunch of words Tali didn't understand. They all sounded jumbled and squished together. The only ones she understood were *Wade, mom,* and *cooking.*

Holding his baby sister, Wade called out for his mother, "Mom?"

"Back here," a sweet voice answered from through the house.

A tall strapping boy came trampling down a set of stairs. Each step pounded and, in a flash, he passed them and was through the door.

"Hi, brother," the kid said, jumping from the porch and racing into the fields.

"That was Mark," Wade told her.

She smiled and followed Wade through a dining room to the back.

In the kitchen, Zeke was stealing something to eat from the spread Wade's mother had on the counter. Zeke had almost gotten away with it but went back for another one when his mom slammed the wooden spoon she held with a smack on the counter near his hand.

"Boy, I told you to stop putting your grubby fingers all over my kitchen. Now out with you until I call you for dinner."

Wade's mother caught sight of them at that moment, and her stern expression turned to a warm, inviting smile.

"Wade dear, what are you doing here, and who is this you 're with? She is much too pretty to be with you?" *This can't be Stasia, didn't he say she had blonde hair?*

Tali blinked at hearing the last sentiment from Wade's mother. The words came to Tali's mind and in a tone true to the source. She was aware of them as though they had been spoken aloud, only for no one's hearing. Something similar had occurred the other night with Learon; *what was happening to her?*

"Hi Mom, sorry to stop in on you. This is my friend, Tali. We're just passing through."

"Passing through on your way to where? Thorns, son! You don't write, you don't send magnotype messages. We're not living on the moon out here. The last time we heard from you, you were going off to find Tara. Then we heard about all the trouble in Adalon during the New Year celebration. You're not mixed up in any of that right?"

"No, mom."

"Wade?"

"Promise. We are just meeting a friend tomorrow in Corma," Wade said.

"Corma? You can't go to Corma."

"Why not?"

"I don't know, ask your father. He said some such thing about the Reckers taking over the town."

"I'll ask him about it," Wade said. He paused and took a deep breath, "Mom, I never did track down Tara. I'm sorry, I know the last message I sent said that I was getting help to find her. But we just never did," Wade said sorrowfully. His eyes studying the wood floor.

"Well, I can't say I'm surprised," she said and paused like she wanted to say something more. "You're a good son, Wade, and a good brother. Now go find your father for dinner."

Wade carried his little sister out the back door and into the field. An uncomfortable silence come over Tali as she glanced around the kitchen.

"Can I help somehow, Ms. Duval?" Tali asked.

"No dear, but you can keep me company. I would love to hear more about how you and Wade became friends."

Tali started toward the small table off to the side, and Wade's mother looked at her with her eyebrows raised. Tali knew the look was meant to tell her to wash up. She feigned like she was looking out the window,

"Ms. Duval, where can I wash up?"

"Did that cloud-headed son of mine not show you around? There's a bathroom around the corner, dear."

When Tali came back to the kitchen, Wade's mother had placed a glass of tea on the table and a small sweetbread.

"Is this for me?" Tali said.

"Yes, dear. You're from the Rodaire, right? I don't mean any offense, but I have heard Rodaireans drink tea, and I thought you might like some. I know my son. Even if I haven't seen him in a year. I know he waits to eat until his stomach barks like a dog to remind him. Then he eats like an animal."

"No offense taken. I would love some tea," Tali said and took the open chair to sit. She devoured the sweet bread so fast she had to keep a hand in front of her mouth to keep the crumb shrapnel from flying.

"I must say Tali, I thought if Wade would ever bring a girl home, the first one would be Stasia."

Tali was unsure it had been a question or a statement. She chose not to be offended.

"I know Stasia. She's lovely," Tali answered.

"And smart as a Menodarin too, I hear."

"She is."

"So, you're at the Arcana, too?"

Very quickly Tali felt like the conversation was going to ruin the night if she didn't start lying to this woman.

"Umm. Yes. I'm studying mechanics and tinkering."

"Is that right? Well, that's the wave of the world, isn't it?"

"It seems to be," Tali said.

Wade's father came in the side door, rubbing his hands. He looked every bit the older version of Wade. He also had blonde hair, but his was messy, and he sported a sharp chin with stubble. And the same blue eyes. He noticed Tali straight away, and his eyes didn't show even the faintest bit of surprise. He put his finger to his lip for Tali to be quiet and he went to his wife and put his arms around her. Wade's Mom sighed with annoyance.

"Wife. My great Beacon of Light. How are you getting on this evening?" The timber of his voice was pleasant, and he wore a wide smile.

"We have guests, dear," Wade's mother said.

"I know, Wade told me. Hello dear, you must be—"

"This is Tali," Wade's mother advised.

"Well, of course it is. Hello Tali, I'm Aaron, Wade's father."

Tali's mouth was full, and she waved and smiled back. Aaron's eyes brightened at seeing the sweet bread and he came over to sit with Tali.

"Don't you dare sit down Aaron; I'll never get you up," Wade's mother said.

"But what about a before-dinner snack or a private tasting?" Aaron said.

"We have guests; we're eating at the table. Get washed up."

Aaron pretended to be shot in the heart, smiled, and walked away to do as he was told.

"Tali, could you set the table, please dear?" Wade's mother asked.

There was a sudden pit in her stomach every time Wade's mother said her name. In just a short time, Tali realized she was the woman who ran the ship.

"I would be happy to," Tali said.

Zeke came in and tried to sneak through, but not before his mother was asking him to do something too,

"Zeke, please help Tali with setting the table, thank you."

"Right Mom, come on Tali. I'll show you how mom likes it," Zeke showed her where the plates and utensils were, and they retreated to the dining room to set the table, Zeke continuing to talk.

"Mom's picky about things. Where everyone sits and placemats and everything. Whatever you do, eat everything she serves you and don't spill anything. I know what you're thinking, it's a wood table, wood floor, what's the big deal? Well, I don't get it either and mom doesn't explain herself. If you do spill something, best to pretend it didn't happen or blame whoever's sitting next to you. That's what I do. Best day of my life was when Delia started sitting at the big table with us. Now, I blame everything on her. Sometimes I pass her my spinach when mom's not looking, but mom's always looking."

Tali smiled and tried not to laugh.

Wade finally reappeared with Delia still in his arms, and two more boys at his heels. His brother Mark looked like he was in his teens and the second boy, Julian, was not much bigger than Delia. Of all the bunch, Julian was the quiet one. Wade introduced Julian and Mark again and they gathered around the table to eat.

For Tali, being around the pleasant sounds of a large family eating together was new. The conversation consisted mostly of simple laments of mundane things. They bickered back and forth, but no matter the tone or language, there was an unspoken sense they all loved each other dearly. Most of Wade's siblings seemed to take after their father, Aaron, a warm, fun, and easy-going man. Wade did too, but he was also like his mother in many ways. Her name was Lorea, which Tali picked up on from Aaron, as she had never introduced herself as anything other than Wade's mother. She was protective, loyal, and strong, though some of her children thought she was strict. Tali thought they wouldn't last a minute with her mother.

As the evening went late, Wade's younger siblings left the dining room to go to bed. During dinner, Tali had noticed Lorea had excused herself a few times to go upstairs. The last time, Tali noticed, Aaron had shared a look with her. Something curious was going on, but Wade hadn't noticed so he didn't ask about it, but he did wait until after dinner to discuss their trip to Corma in the morning.

"Can we take Berry?" Wade asked his father.

"That horse is old, Wade. She can't carry the both of you to

Corma," Aaron said.

"How about Flint or Frill?" Wade asked.

"Those are my best horses, Wade. I keep telling you Corma is dangerous, you should stay away. Amera even more so," Aaron said.

"We rode through Adavan from the mouth through the Eye, and everything seemed all right," Wade said.

"It only seemed that way. The Bonemen have taken over the main cities pushing out the Reckers. They then reorganized in Corma, where they can hire more guns from the Moonstalkers. The Bonemen won't even go into Amera."

"We have to go, Dad"

"What's this all about, Wade?"

Wade looked at Tali as though asking for permission to tell his parents the truth, but she just shrugged. What else could she do? These weren't her parents, she couldn't know how they would react, nor did their reaction hold sway over her actions.

"We're following someone who stole something valuable," Wade said.

"Yours, what is it?"

"Not ours exactly," Wade said.

"Then whose was it?"

"Ellaria Moonstone's."

"Moonstone the General? That Ellaria Moonstone?" Aaron said incredulously.

"That's the one," Wade said.

"It's my fault, Mr. Duval. Ellaria gave me the Stone to protect, and this woman stole it," Tali chimed in, hoping to take some pressure off Wade.

"It's not your fault, I convinced you to let Nyra ride with us," Wade disagreed.

"Wait, what is it that was stolen?" Aaron asked.

"It's an old stone. An Eckwyn Age artifact, actually," Wade said.

"Eckwyn Age? Great Light of the Creator, Wade! You had a stone of the ancients and you lost it?"

"We didn't lose it. It was stolen."

"Valuable? How valuable?"

Wade looked to Tali for the answer. "Honestly, sir, it's immeasurably valuable. Ellaria feared the Bonemen might get it and if the New Sagean gained control of it, they would be, unstoppable," Wade cringed.

Aaron rose from his chair and paced around the room. He stopped to look out the window and stared a long time at the tumbling water wheel.

When he turned around, his smile had returned. It was somber and slight, and it matched his eyes.

"Take Flint and Frill. Leave early. There's an—"

"Aaron?" Lorea interrupted him, shaking her head.

Aaron ignored her and continued, "There's an inn, just off the east bridge called the Proud Star. Ask for a man named Red. He can get you a room overlooking the road."

"Aaron, no," Lorea said sternly.

"Mom, I promise you we can take care of ourselves," Wade said and he looked at Tali, as though she might show them her abilities. She shook her head no and cast him a stern look. Wade grabbed his pack and withdrew the pulsator gun.

Tali could almost feel Lorea's heart seizing up at seeing the gun, but Aaron appraised it and moved on.

"Put it away, Wade. Does Tali have one as well? Or do you need something, dear?" Aaron said.

"Umm. No, that's the only gun we have," Tali said.

"I'll get you Wade's grandpa's silver six, you can take that."

"That's too much! Aaron, No!" Lorea cried. She was irate now and shouting.

"I want to do what's right for them, Lor."

"Do you want him to end up like Tara? She doesn't eat, she doesn't sleep. She—"

Wade sprang to his feet. His chair sliding back with a loud groan against the wood, "Wait, have you seen Tara?" Wade said.

"She…" Lorea couldn't finish her sentence. It was as though the air had completely come out of her. Her whole body sagged with defeat and sadness. Aaron turned back to look out the window.

Tali realized what was going on. "Wade," she said, and his piercing gaze settled on her. Tali pointed up, and Wade put it together and scrambled to the stairs.

There were only two rooms upstairs, most of the bedrooms arranged on the sprawling main level. Wade approached through the skinny dark hall to the door, a sliver ajar.

"Tara?" Wade called quietly, pushing the door open and entering.

A single lantern was lit on a side table beneath the window, where the night's breeze blew white curtains in subtle waves. Tara stood in a corner of the room, staring at the wall.

Tali immediately felt the odd, empty feeling she sensed in the people of West Meadow. She pulled on Wade's sleeve, but he shrugged her off.

Casting a glance back at her, Tali could see tears streaming from his eyes. He knew. He probably had known since West Meadow, but he had held out hope until now. She tugged at his sleeve again,

"Come back downstairs, Wade," she said softly.

"Just give me a minute," he whispered.

"Tara. Tara, it's your brother, Wade."

Tali didn't want to watch, and it made her skin crawl to be next to a Scree. She removed herself from the room. When she reached the stairs, she heard Tara say *Wade* in a voice that sent a cold chill down Tali's spine.

Tali walked back and waited for him at the bottom of the stairs. Wade's parents sat at the table, not speaking. Wade emerged a short time later, his eyes red. Tali met his hand on the banister with her own and squeezed. Wade walked directly to his mother and hugged her. They embraced for a long moment before all four were sitting again.

"I'm going to fix her, Mom," Wade said.

"I hope you do, son. I hope you fix them all," Aaron said.

"All?" Tali said, "How many came back?"

Aaron was drinking a glass of ember-broth liquor now. He poured more in his glass and spoke, "A week ago, a ship showed up in the night at the harbor in Sea Watch. People were unloaded like cattle and the ship left. The dock's men that saw the ship said it was a larger galley ship like the ones out of Andal, but it was all metal. The next day, the people, all like Tara, had barely moved from the pier. A few, I was told, drowned. I was down in Sea Watch the day after when I heard a commotion that the people who disappeared in the spring had come back. Not everyone, but most, but there was something wrong with them. I found Tara muttering to herself and brought her home."

"We've seen them before. The new Sagean has done this. Our friend's entire town was turned into these things," Wade said.

"It also happened in Kotalla," Tali said. "They had a word for them. They called them the Scree."

"Has she said anything, or does she do anything?" Wade said.

"No, she just sits in her room or stands in the corner. She knows us. I know that. And she started saying words. She said *Dad* and *Mom*, but her voice isn't right. It's—cold," Aaron said.

"I heard it. She said my name. Does she eat?" Wade said.

Lorea nodded but kept her eyes staring at the table. Instead, Aaron answered,

"It's the oddest thing, but she eats eggs. Only raw eggs."

FOURTEEN
CARNIVAL OF ILLUSIONS (ELLARIA)

"Come one, come all. See the amazing and the wondrous. Let your eyes see the truth of energy and light!" the peddler's voice called out from the fairgrounds.

Ellaria had been listening from her bed to the commotion of the lumbering crowd arriving that afternoon, but the announcement effectively startled her awake. Their collective shuffling and murmurs chattered above the calls of the peddler but sometimes, his voice boomed above the horde. She sat up from her bed and realized the evening had arrived in a hurry, and the time for her performance with it. Ellaria had not gained the rest she sought from the nap, but it was the best she could hope for. Every night was filled with nightmares, and they left her drained; a frustrating development which made her appear her age when the bags under her eyes looked like bruised fruit.

The calls continued, so she climbed out of her bed and down the tiny staircase to the main cabin. There she found the troupe's props master had left her an outfit while she slept. Even though she couldn't recall reaching a deep sleep, the proof was before her that she had. A neatly scripted note lay atop the folded costume.

The outfit was utterly ridiculous: a hooded purple dress overlaid with thin silken robes of multiple colored lace, all cut to fall at various lengths. The fabric shone and sparkled with specks of glitter that lined the stitching. And, as though all that wasn't enough, there was a black undertaker hat, the straight elongated brim of which finished with a veil. She put all of it on and looked at herself in the mirror. Looking like an insane elder

with festival decorations turned into a gown, she exhaled her annoyance
and read the note.

> *Master Showman, Archibald Zabel, requests that you wear this. Don't forget to treat*
> *your eyes, to accentuate them for the patrons at the back. Also, Will left the knifes you*
> *requested, the fanciest he could find, and the mask you asked to be painted will be*
> *ready in the prop car before your show.*
>
> *May your tongue flatter and your curtain be made of strong wool. – Marcus*

The ending was the classic good wishes for all performers on a showman's stage. It was thought that the Emperor had taken the tongues of
those minstrels that didn't flatter him or who spoke ill of the Sagean
faith. The curtain referred to the famous bard massacre of Greelee in the
city of Luveka, now called Pardona, when the audience's anger erupted
into much more than lettuce thrown at the stage.

Under the costume were the two knives. One had a long blade and a
gleaming purple handle with a red gem on the bottom. The other had a
silver handle that held gems of three colors and a double-edged blade
that shone brightly. An engraved line down the center of the blade
somehow emphasized the sharpness. She liked the second one. While the
blades were real enough, the silver handle and gems were fake, but the
look was what mattered. The knife needed only to be memorable, but
since she now had two, she could swap which one she used if needed.

Ellaria had always felt comfortable with knifes, even when Kovan had
tried to train her to use a sword. It was knives that she could control with
greater ease. Kovan had said she had fast hands. The weight mattered
most to her. Which was the reason she preferred the silver-handled one.
She could spin it or flip it with nimble dexterity.

With her things collected and costume fixed, she threw on some
makeup to draw out her eyes and left for the prop car. The mask was
needed for her final trick. She was amazed Will had already acquired
everything she had requested. It turned out Will had many jobs. He rode
ahead of the show to promote their imminent arrival, gathered supplies
and support from local authorities, and verified the site was ready for set
up. It was an important job and made him Archibald's unofficial
manager of the entire extravaganza, though Ellaria noticed most in the
troupe were oblivious to this. Some of the performers treated him as a
tech and the techs looked at him as the site warden, while the acrobats
treated him like a pull horse. Will took it all without complaint and the
show functioned through his leadership, not Archibald's.

At the prop car, she found her mask waiting for her. It was a terrifying thing and expertly carved. So much so, she wondered if it wasn't a relic from Merinde, a country known to wear masks in public, though usually ones without expression as this one contained. Ellaria reminded herself to ask Archibald or the props master where they had acquired it. There were a series of pronounced lines from the nose and wrapping the cheeks to the eyes, a spread grin with top and bottom fangs, and more carved lines from the chin forming the cheek. The lines swirled together at the chin. The carved flare of the nostrils was the smaller reverse of the larger curling eyebrows. She knew it was perfect the instant she saw it, with the mask painted black and blueish grey to offset the features. Tentatively, she lifted it to admire the painting, but it was dry. Her reflection in full costume was a sight not soon forgotten.

The sounds beyond the prop tent were growing tense. Curious, Ellaria stashed the mask up her sleeve and emerged to discover a loud and energized crowd in the common grounds. The circus had brought in a much larger crowd than she expected and the bulk of them were heading to a four-pole tent where the peddler, Conner Marteen, was still shouting,

"Come see the Quantum Man, before the Bonemen find him!"

Ellaria's breath caught, and she ran to get inside the tent. *Had Archibald double crossed her somehow?* She had mistaken his suspicion of her motives as a general distrust, but now she knew he had recognized her. Or maybe Will had recognized Qudin when he helped her bring him to the carriage house.

Gaining access through the front was going to be impossible. The crowd flooded in at a slow pour. She tried to push through before abandoning it to go around to the backside.

Ellaria reached the rear flap, slipped through, and charged inside. The sound of electrical blasts was unmistakable. She dashed around the backstage framing and found a route to the stage. Marley was holding the circular curtain-line, the back portion set in place as a backdrop with the front half open to the audience arrayed around the oval shaped tent with wide gawking eyes.

Beyond Marley, to the stage, was a man in a metal cage surrounded by copper coiled electric pillars, flashes of electricity surging to the cage. Ellaria was ready to rush the stage when she realized the man inside was Tyron and not Elias.

The crowd looked mesmerized. The strikes of electricity continued. From her vantage point, she could see a black cloth fixed to the top of the cage above Tyron's head. The strikes of white blasts concluded as the charged coils ran empty. Final blasts zapped out and plunged the stage and room into darkness. The crowd murmured and gasped in the darkness. Marley lit a lantern and proceeded on stage. As she got close, a glowing hand appeared. Marley screamed and dropped the lantern and a portion of the stage caught fire. Woman in the audience screamed. Tyron completely removed the blanket and revealed himself. His entire form was glowing. With his hand out toward the fire, it was abruptly extinguished by unseen means and, with the momentary light gone, all that remained was the glowing man. Marley pulled the curtain and the tent's gas lanterns came on to signal the end of the show.

Tyron hurried off the stage. "Marley, help. This damned algae itches something awful."

Marley was ready and waiting with towels and Tyron gave Ellaria an odd look.

"Aria, what are you doing here? Doesn't your show start soon?" Tyron said.

Ellaria stared a moment, while her breathing returned to normal, before comprehending what Tyron had said to her.

"My show," Ellaria said with alarm. Jolted back she hurried away through the back and toward her own stage.

THICK MAROON DRAPES AND GOLD CORDS BEGAN TO PART AND LIFT AWAY. A sea of faces and dark eyes stared at her, the globe lights of the stage reflecting in their faces, anticipation, and expectation apparent. Her breathing, still unsteady from her running late, had yet to settle. Any belief she held that this would simply be like a speech washed away, and her mind went cold. For a moment, she forgot everything in the presence of so many awaiting her performance. From off stage, Owen, her stage manager, was waving his hands for her to say something. Ellaria looked to her surroundings and her ridiculous clothes and felt the comfort of the insane masquerade envelope her.

First, she introduced the furies with a mix of unseen tricks and simple alchemy potions aligned to the elements. She threw firespark dust in the air with enough territh ash to make it float a second and then with some ignition flints in her glove, she snapped her fingers and the air fractured into flames. The ball of fire was much larger than she anticipated, and her heart raced from the explosion at her fingertips. The first trick was the easiest and designed to arrest the audience's attention. Her next tricks required all the knowledge of alchemy she knew of, a combination of sigils, potions, spells and enchantments.

Following the fireball, she did displays of water, territh, spirit, wind, and transformation. First, she used sigils to turn a cylinder of ice into water. Placing the block of ice on the prepared table, it instantly collapsed into a pool of water.

"Water," she said, and it drew some applause, but not as much as she thought it would.

Next, she spread enchanted strunic powder on the water to turn it into a mound of dust. Hovering her hand over the pool, she dropped the strunic in a circular motion and the water pulled and condensed into a mound of dust that reached her fingers by the time she was done.

"Territh."

Again, applause but the appreciative kind, not the enthusiastic sort. Not yet.

With an incantation and the stage lights projecting on a sigil above her, she made the dust burst from the table and float all around the room.

"Wind," she said. This one got their attention. She drew the last sigil into the floating dust.

"Spirit," she said, allowing the sigil to stay in the dust before she spun the air with her finger.

"And finally, transformation," she said and quietly Ellaria whispered, "Quae in lucem prodeat."

The dust ruptured into tiny fragments of light and became butterflies in midair. The eyes of the crowd looked stunned, before clapping and applause began. Shouts that called for more were amongst murmurs of *how?* and Ellaria even heard a *what is she?* from somewhere.

For her grand finale, she ended the show with a transportation spell she had learned a long time ago. Ellaria had never tried it herself but had seen it done. She knew the symbol well, having never forgotten it once she had seen its power. The spell required two versions of the same sigil made in exact opposite alignment. Both symbols were required to be drawn in the same medium. There were many factors to making it work. The order mattered in which the symbols were drawn, the order of the blood used, and from which hand imparted it. She also needed an amethyst stone and obsidian and finally, two magnets. Will had provided everything for her and she had fashioned the symbols simply into two pieces of thick parchment. The better the medium the symbols were drawn in, the farther something or someone could be transported.

With everything in place, she unrolled the parchment on the stage, placing a candle at one corner and stones at the other three to keep it in place.

She looked back at the crowd and continued her show.

"There is an old saying," she announced and circled to the back, grabbing the ornately detailed silver knife, "Bring a weapon into the underworld and you make a friend of Death."

She lifted the knife high and twirled it in a fashion Kovan had taught her and then stepped atop the sheet of parchment.

"Death himself wears many masks, but to defeat Death, you must hide in plain sight from him, like a mirror among his palace of shadow."

She looked down and hid her face. From inside her sleeve, she removed the mask. Small explosions to her left and right of the stage erupted, and she put on the mask. The small explosions startled the crowd and the smell of star-powder settled in the tent. Ellaria lifted her head adorned in the mask to the crowd. The ones that hadn't noticed her put it on during the distraction inhaled sharply at the sight of her.

"If you travel as a friend of Death, you can kill Death." Ellaria said loudly, and she dragged the knife across her palm, the shadow dust concealed within. A black smoke bloomed and enveloped her, and she whispered, "Ut me ad meliora dies."

The symbol at her feet surged with light and she disappeared off the stage and back beside her carriage house.

The transportation made her stomach turn and she stumbled on the grass, the sensation akin to seasickness. Even from the two hundred feet of distance that separated her from the tent, she could hear the pandemonium of applause. The remaining cloud of shadow dust that traveled with her blew away in the breeze, and she picked herself up to go inside her house. The Elustri sisters came running toward her excitedly.

"How did you do that!" Desee said.

"Which part?" Ellaria replied.

"All of it," they said together.

Ellaria smiled at them, "A great magician never tells her secrets."

She excused herself and retreated inside to change and clean up. Inside, she was surprised to find Elias sitting up in his bed, drinking water. He looked more lucid today than the night before, color having returned to his increasingly gaunt face.

"Are you hungry?" she asked. It was a stupid question—he had done nothing but sleep and drink water for days now, and his already sickly appearance was looking worse for it.

"I'm starving."

"Good, I'll find you something to eat."

She rummaged through her small pantry cabinets for food and prepared some bread, cheese, and fruit. She handed it to him straight away.

"This is what we have in here, but I can get some meat for you or stew from the food tents," she said.

"Thank you, Ellaria, I'll start with this," he said. Then he handed her the crystals she had placed with him last night. "Here."

She took them without looking at them and studied his eyes. The swirl of color in his irises was gone. Depositing the crystals back in a drawer, she passed Elias's boots piled at the front. He hadn't been wearing boots the night before.

"Were you able to get up and walk around?" she pointed toward his boots.

"I did."

"Where did you go?"

"I walked around the main camp," Elias said.

"I'm glad to hear you were walking, but Elias, you have to be careful. I don't trust everyone here."

"I simply stretched my legs and returned. What did you do to the crystals for them to work so well last night?" Elias asked.

"I heated them over a linwood fire."

"Ah, I'll have to remember that."

While Elias ate, she got changed, but their conversation continued.

"I think someone came into our carriage while you were gone," he said.

She pulled her clothes on and peaked around the opening to the stairway. "Why do you say that?"

"The door slammed and woke me up," Elias said.

"Maybe it was me when I ran out," she said, unsure if what he had heard was real or not. But she knew the door hadn't slammed when she left.

"Maybe," he said.

She sat at the small table and began clearing her makeup off when a loud knocking pounded on the door. The sound and aggression of it startled her.

"Come in—" She didn't even get the words out as Desee charged in.

"Aria, come quick. It's Tyron," she said, panicked and trembling.

"What's wrong, dear?" Ellaria asked, grabbing Desee's hand to calm her.

"He's dead," Desee cried.

Ellaria motioned Desee to lead the way, "Stay here Elias," she said, one foot out of the door.

They scrambled around to the far side of the carriages where the transport carts were all staged. A small group huddled around a body on the ground. Tyron's lifeless figure was crumpled face first into the dirt and sunburnt, yellow grass. A knife with a purple hilt stuck out of his back. Ellaria's heart sunk at the sight of the knife. It was a match for the one she had chosen not to use. *A match or the same one?* She wanted to run back to her carriage house to check but needed to wait with everyone around.

Archibald came rushing toward them with two security guards. His shorter, stocky stature was tense, and his face held concern, but to Ellaria's surprise, also anger. When Archibald reached the circle, he began shouting.

"Everyone needs to go back to work. Bruno and Edman will take care of this. No one says a thing. I don't want wild rumors running through this place. Go." Archibald said, dismissing everyone with haste.

Ellaria headed back to the carriage house, accompanied by Desee and Ronee. Walking next to them, she could hear Alexero talking with Marley, "I was just with him."

Alexero was in tears. Even in her short time with the troupe, she had already picked up on the subgroups among the show and Tyron and Alexero were inseparable. Both were close with Marley and her own stage manager Owen, as well.

Back in the carriage house, Elias was already asleep again when she came in. Wasting little time, she began to tear the place apart looking for the purple handled knife, but it wasn't anywhere to be found.

FIFTEEN
THE CAGED MAN (KOVAN)

A spear punctured into his heart again—Kovan jumped and grabbed his chest. He was lying in a bed, in the dark, in a foreign city. The onslaught of memory had flooded him continually over the course of a previous day, generating a deep exhaustion. The continuity of his life was returning, but there were so many memories at once that his comprehension of his own timeline sometimes seemed jumbled. His first waking thoughts were on Tali and Ellaria. He didn't know where they were or if any of them were safe. Other memories came too, older ones, flooding his head unbidden. Fresh and new, as though they happened yesterday. Exhaustion overcame him and he closed his eyes.

When he opened his eyes again, the morning light filled the room where the Hazon man had brought them. There was a loud commotion outside in the streets, but he was too disoriented to get to the window yet to see what was happening. He had been exhausted when they arrived, and his brain still throbbed from the influx of conscious weight. Buroga sat near the window, his large form imposing and watchful.

"Are we in North Ride, now?" Kovan said.

"We are."

Kovan sat up and breathed deeply. His hands found a bulky package next to him that Poe had given him. Buroga had set it there for him to find. The loud disturbance continued outside, and Kovan opened the wrappings. There was a nice, wide-brimmed hat and inside it lay an elegant pulsator gun, complete with a gleaming heart crystal to power it.

Poe had told him the best place to start would be North Ride. It was a curious suggestion from a curious person.

Buroga stepped to the bed and leaned over to look at Kovan in the face.

"Can I help you, big guy?"

"I can see in your eyes; God has returned your mind to you. You look good, and strong again," Buroga said.

"God has? Please tell me you don't mean Poe?" Kovan said.

"Ha, no. I mean God. The Great Creator. For the Hazon it is *Amazuie*; for the Sagelight faith, it is the *Great One* or the *Light*; for the Faith of the Fates, it is the *Entwiner*, I believe. But everyone has a God."

"I don't," Kovan got up and strapped the gun to his hip.

"I am sure you do. Maybe you need to figure out who or what they are. I am told, even in the Karnika Waste in the New World, the Harrinari follow the Great Diviner. The old races have theirs too, though I don't know them."

"That's great for them and you. For me, faith is a bog of mud. You walk in it too long; you will get stuck. Gods creating worlds for men to make myths of God and themselves: it's all very self-serving and I am no one's puppet," Kovan said. He wasn't sure where the words came from or the sentiment, but he knew they were true to who he was.

"Kovan Rainer, my friend, we are all part of the same great painting, drawn by the same hand, but with many brushes and a pallet of endless color," Buroga said.

Kovan looked at his new friend and shook his head in a pleasant but sarcastic nod of agreement.

"I have a standard rule to not believe in man. We are but a speck of dust amongst the colossal. Since the dawn of time, someone has stood on a tall rock and shouted about what they know. Hear me little people, I know where to find food. How to grow crops. Which bug bites. Trust me, they say. I know what leaf to use to best wipe our asses with. Eventually this expands to bigger rocks and bigger ideas. Someone shouts they know there's a God. They know the meaning of life. We know nothing and every time we learn, we prove we knew nothing."

Buroga looked at him with an odd smirk, "I hope the next dose of memories makes you a more agreeable person, Kovan Rainer."

"I wouldn't count on it." Kovan said, and he changed the subject to the noise in the street, "Poe said I should go to North Ride. I need to find out why. What's happening in the streets?"

"The Bonemen are escorting a prisoner through the city. He is in a cage. The Inn Master said they captured this man two nights ago and were taking him back to Andal."

Kovan went to the window to see the spectacle for himself, but their view of the street only showed the angry crowd and no caravan. Back to Andal?

"Did the innkeeper know why? What did the guy do to be shackled and treated like an animal?"

"Apparently he attacked a squadron of Bonemen at the train station in Andal."

That was no flight of madness, nor would they capture such a man and keep him alive for transport. Kovan had an inkling of who it might be.

"We need to get down there," Kovan said.

"Why, do you know this person?"

"That's what I want to find out."

"Are you sure you're ready, you don't need more rest?"

"I've rested long enough."

Advancing to the front of the line was much easier with a Hazon man. Buroga cleared a path by his presence. Kovan settled on a spot to watch the carts come through, around a long bend that provided enough time to see who the Bonemen were escorting.

Two greencoats rode at the head of the caravan that stopped nearby. Their main job was to keep the public contained as the prisoner came through. Shortly after they had taken their positions, the large cage teetered on a wagon cart hauled around the bend.

Kovan could hear conversations around him and had pieced together the story. After attacking and killing a group of soldiers at the train station, this man had escaped into the Omen Woods where they ultimately caught him. Poe must have heard the story and thought that this man could help Kovan somehow.

An onlooker called to the greencoats on horseback, "How did they catch him?"

The greencoat waved off the question. The cage rumbled into view and lying motionless in a bed of hay in the corner was Semo, the Dark-hawk warrior who was supposed to be in the New World by now.

"They say he killed ten Bonemen with his bare hands before they captured him," the sidewalk spectator was saying amongst his friends. "He killed twenty at the train station. And they say he's a Darkhawk."

Kovan edged his way over to two big mouths. "Did you hear where they're talking to him for the execution?"

"He's going to be hanged in Andal. Queen Rotha of Andal wants to make an example of him," the stranger said.

"Serves him right. Filthy New Worlder should have stayed over there with his kind," his friend spat.

Kovan started to take a swing at the man, but Buroga caught his arm.

"It does you no good to punch out every idiot we come across, Kovan Rainer."

Kovan eyed him but shrugged his resigned agreement.

They took off from the street to follow the squad but kept a pace that wouldn't have them noticed. While in pursuit, Kovan tried to untangle how to free Semo and not have to attack twenty soldiers.

"You know the man they take in the cage?" Buroga asked.

"I do."

"What do you want to do?"

"Free him."

"I have horses ready at the Inn. If they are heading back east, they will be riding all day. How are we to catch them?"

"Right, but they'll stop to observe the Blue. They're Bonemen and faithful. Wait, you don't have to pray during the Blue, do you Buroga?"

"No Kovan Rainer. Amazuie has made the sun blue and we are grateful for the beauty, but if he wishes the Hazon to do anything during it, he has not told us, so we do not. All times are good times to be grateful of God."

"Sure," Kovan said, and he hoped that Buroga's God didn't keep him from fighting when the time came.

On the road, Buroga made for good company. He was a much happier man than Kovan would have believed based on their first encounter. Buroga was not a simple brute; he was calm, intuitive, and thoughtful.

Kovan's first memories to return all concerned Tali and their journey across the mainland to meet Ellaria. He remembered perfectly well breaking free from the prison in Ravenvyre. Kovan had called Buroga *Gigantore*, and it was fitting for the man which Kovan met in that prison was a beastly version of the man he rode next to now. The change probably spoke more about Kovan's expectation than Buroga's true nature. The trials of captivity had brought out anger in a man Kovan was finding out was naturally peaceful.

With the first dose of memories taken, Kovan's personification reoriented to align with who he had been. However, most of his strongest memories were only the last few years' worth and some of the moments of his life that had left the greatest impressions. Even then, he consciously struggled, as no detail felt fixed. It was not much better than believing he had been Caleb, the guardian. At least those self-created memories had felt *real*. Most of the memory of himself was a passing recollection of how others saw him. He knew he was a war hero but could not recall the war. The confusion had deepened, not withdrawn.

The Hazon people were known to keep to themselves. Mainlanders knew very little about the Hazons and when very little is known about a subject, people fill in the gaps to fit their own needs. Some believed the Hazons were the descendants of giants, and some believed them great oafs. Others thought them a threat that should be eradicated like the other old races had been. If one spent any time in the north, Hazons were known as excellent workers, doubling a man's strength and energy, and complaining half as much. While they were more commonly seen in the north, very few lived among the Mainlanders. If a person lived dock-side along the eastern coast, then they had met at least one. Hazons were great sailors, and famous builders of ships. A Hazon ship was considered one of the finest vessels on the sea, the sturdiest of ships to voyage the ocean.

Kovan vaguely recalled their land, but as with a lot of things, there were gaps and he had forgotten the details. He wondered how long he should wait until taking the second cube of memories. The tin box pressed into his leg through his pocket, as a reminder. The things were simply colorful dice, but Kovan would almost swear he felt connected to them. With the return of his first batch of memories came a great sense of duty that was completely gone when he was at the Wrenwa farm. Even though they called to him, he needed to free Semo. Poe had said that each dose would be harder to take, but Kovan would have to cross that bridge when he found time to take the next one.

In the waning hour of the Blue Sun, Kovan and Buroga came upon the armed escort. The group of soldiers were resting off the Imperial Road at the banks of the Foam River outside of Anesta. Kovan steered them off the road to approach from the woods.

HIDING WITH A HAZON MAN WAS NOT EASY. FROM THE TREES ACROSS THE road, they assessed the Bonemen camp. For faithful servants of the Sage-light, they looked to be drinking and sleeping instead of praying during their sacred Blue Hours. He counted twenty soldiers. Seven asleep, five drinking and playing cards, four in prayer, and four still on their guard patrolling, albeit lazily. Semo was stirring in his cage. The heat of the sun must have made the metal bars burn because Semo made sure to lean against the hay pile and avoid the cage. The wagon was closest to the river, and Kovan had an idea.

"How strong are you, Buroga?"

"I have average strength for a Hazon."

"Let me rephrase, could you push the prisoner cart into river?" Kovan asked.

"Yes, I believe I could do that."

"Wait here until I wave you over. I'll free Semo from the cage and you push the cart into the river. With luck, these idiots will think it happened accidentally."

Crouching low, Kovan crossed below the stone bridge and into the camp. His hand guided along the moist mortar joints as he slowly lifted his feet from the grassy river's edge. None of the soldiers were watching the stream or they would have noticed the disturbance to the ripples. He snuck around the one empty wagon and to the cart with Semo aboard. He crawled below the flat wagon cart to detach the hitch. A large snake slithered in the grass near him and Kovan felt a tremor through his body, he hated snakes. He found the instinct to recoil from them, came as a surprise. *I hate snakes.* He watched it glide in short lurching jolts and he cringed. Returning his focus to the latching he found the pin wouldn't budge. The position on the slope put too much weight on the hitch.

Kovan cursed under his breath and crawled to the back. It was time to change the plan. He peeked up at the cage's lock. It was typical iron lock with a key held by one of the guards. He pulled his pulsator gun out and detached the tether cables at the back. He rose slowly and placed the wires into the keyhole and pulled the trigger. The guns charge produced a tiny blast into the lock. It was louder than he wanted. Kovan ducked and hid at the wheel.

The Bonemen had yet to see him, but they were searching for the odd sound. Kovan replaced the tethers on his gun, as the snake slithered by. He slowly pulled up beside Semo's head and poked him with a stick until he awoke. It took only two jabs and Semo's eyes popped open with a deadly gaze that faded at seeing Kovan. He motioned to the gate. Then Kovan turned back to the snake. *Most horses hate snakes crawling in the grass around their feet,* he thought. His skin crawled with each movement. *Torque it,* he said to himself, and he grabbed the snake, launching it into the Bonemen's horses.

The group of horses neighed and huffed. The camp went momentarily crazy and the Bonemen tried to calm the animals. Some ran wild and galloped away. Kovan spun up and pulled the latch off, Semo limped out the door and they ran, Buroga meeting them on the far side.

"Take him to the horses, we have to ride," Kovan said.

"The prisoner!" a soldier cried out at their backs.

Buroga could run faster than Kovan, even carrying Semo on his back. He placed Semo on Kovan's saddle and Kovan reached them at a dead sprint. Half the squad of Bonemen were running for them and Kovan blasted bolts wildly into the throng and kicked off south into Omen Woods.

THEY EMERGED FROM THE WOODS TO SEE THE TOWERING HANG-WAY frames of the train line. Each massive steel frame was anchored into the rocky coastline with the rail lines of the elevated train connecting each along the coast. They followed the train line for most of the evening without stopping. The night fell over the forest and still they kept moving. The lights of the city of Searest bloomed in the distance like a glimmer of hope. The horses were beat and Kovan struggled to keep Semo upright. He was strong, but he had been beaten when they caught him and hadn't eaten in days.

When they reached the city, Buroga went ahead of them and found a room at the Harbor Rest, a small inn connected to the city harbor. They met Buroga at the stables where he led them in through a back door. They moved fast through the hall and up the service stairs to their rooms. Semo's relief at seeing a real bed was palpable.

"I shall see what food I can bring back for you both," Buroga said.

"Will that be a problem?" Kovan sat down and settled atop the second bed. A soreness spread in leg muscles where bruising was settling in.

"No. I'm Hazon. People never question how much food I can eat."

Buroga left and Kovan rested his head against the wall. He closed his eyes and opened them when his Hazon friend came back with two bowls of soup underneath plates with roasted pies steaming heat into the air. Kovan shook Semo's leg, and he awoke with a start. The smell of food hit his nose, and he sat up. Kovan let him eat before launching into his questions. He started with the simplest one.

"What happened after you left Polestis?" Kovan asked.

"I went to Domal as Ellaria instructed me. There, I sent a message back to Dalliana in the New World. I sailed to Anvil to await word from the New World. I was in Anvil when I heard about the sighting of King Danehin. He was said to be in Queen Rotha Durrone's company at the Andal palace. I did not believe these reports true, but I sent word to The New World of my intentions to investigate the matter. I intended to infiltrate the Palace, but when I arrived, I found Danehin getting into a carriage with the Queen Durrone. He looked like he was in a daze. He didn't talk, and he moved slowly and only to her call.

"I followed them to the train station where the strangeness grew deeper. The station was closed down and a legion of Bonemen troops were loading a glowing object on the train. It was encased in a large crate, but a vibrant light escaped through the cracks. Even the splinter of light I saw was eerie and hard to look away from. Amongst the soldiers were three men in elegant attire. They looked like wealthy merchants observing a great investment, each with top hats, pocket watches, and shaded spectacles. As I spied from the shadows, a procession of prisoners came through. Two men and two women in chains, and at the back walked Danehin. They all looked sickly, but only Danehin had a blank and lost expression in his eyes.

"When they tried boarding the train, I attempted to free my King. I do not know how many men I fought and killed. They kept coming. Finally, I had him and tried to escape, but Danehin would not move. He mumbled under his breath. His eyes were glossed over. At the very last moment, when Bonemen had returned with triple their number, I ran. He mumbled one clear sentence just before I left. He said, *the Red Spear*. So, what is the Red Spear?" Semo said.

"I'm not sure. There's a place called the Red Dune. It was a prison in the eastern reaches of Echo Canyon. The Empire used it before the Resistance found it and shut it down. It's possible the Sagean has reopened it," Kovan said.

"Can this prison be breached?" Semo asked.

"Not easily. It is a column of red sandstone in the canyons. There is only one way in, a steep stone stairway that has no rail. It was shaped out of the territh long ago and crafted into a prison. There must be two hundred stairs or more and the entire structure is at least three hundred feet tall, probably more. It looks unnatural, like it grew from the ground, and the surface has gouged lines from the base to the tip. The entire thing looks like a spear tip."

"Have you been inside it?" Semo asked.

"I can't remember. The image of it is vivid to me, but nothing else," Kovan said.

"What is wrong with my King? Is it like the girl Meroha told us? Is he a Scree?" Semo starred at him unblinking.

"I'm afraid he might be. Did you receive any other communication from the King's daughter, Dalliana?"

"The last message said that a small regiment of the Free Cities ships were idling in the Barruse islands, mostly a collection of ships on this side of the blockade when it was formed. Among the ships, only a few are capable of battle. The rest are merchants, eager to return to the New World," Semo said.

"What are we to do now, Kovan Rainer?" Buroga asked.

Kovan smiled at Buroga's insistence to say his full name, "Buroga, is there a way through the blockade in the Anamic Ocean?"

"In the North, ships can pass. The Prime had left it open for Whalers' ships. Though the Prime was killed, I believe those waters are still open. It's a long trip from the Grey Sea to the Ioka and the capitol of the Free Cities. What are you thinking, Kovan Rainer?" Buroga said.

"I've never been the best strategist—that was always Ellaria—but I want to track whatever this object was that they were protecting and transporting to Adalon. I can't say they were taking it or the prisoners to the Red Spear from there. I find it very odd they wouldn't sail out directly from the Citadel, wherever they were going. I'm afraid we make a motley crew traveling together, one that will raise too much suspicion if we go sneaking around. But I mean to travel to Adalon to find out more," Kovan said.

"I believe Mr. Poe can help us get to Adalon," Buroga offered.

"How?"

"Mr. Poe has many friends in many parts of this world. Most owe him a favor, same as you. A smuggler's coach can take Semo and me where you need us."

"We need a good ship, one with a trustworthy crew, to get us to Adalon and find out what happened to the train. From there, we can follow the trail and if needed, head for the Barruse Islands. But if this object is as peculiar and important as you say, Semo, then someone was bound to see it and remember it. If the Red Spear is back in operation, The Bounty Hunters' Guild in Amera will know of it," Kovan said.

"I saved you, Kovan Rainer, from bounty hunters at the tavern. Should I plan on doing it again?" Buroga asked.

"That's why you're coming with, big guy. Besides, that was just a misunderstanding… I think."

"I will find us that boat and return," Buroga said, and stood to leave. His head edging close to the ceiling, he ducked through the door header and left. Kovan leaned back in the bed against the headboard. He tilted the hat Poe had given him over his eyes and tried to rest. Every moment that passed, he felt more like himself, and he was reminded of the truth: that loyalty and duty were heavy burdens.

ADALON

1. Ascendancy Spier
2. Arcana Spier
3. Craftcore Spier
4. Rooftop Walkways
5. Twine Knot Bar
6. Frog Leg Tavern
7. Lilaria's Quarters
8. Fisherman's Market
9. Whisper Chain
10. Sagean's Palace
11. The Watchmen's Port
12. The Merchants Belt

MAINSOLIS SEA

SAGEAN'S PALACE

TOWER RIVER

NORTH BRIDGE

ARENA

GREENBELT

WATERFRONT BRIDGE

THE CRESCENT PIER

DEAD RIVER

Sixteen
Leaving Adalon (Stasia)

The red magnotype letter rested on the counter while she gathered her things to leave. Stasia had received the letter the night before and was still unsure how she felt about it, but she packed anyway. Learon's words had been short and to the point, which she thought made sense for the man she remembered though she had only met him once. And there was the source of her aggravation. She wasn't mad at Learon, but whatever Wade had gotten into, he was too deep to see straight, or too busy to meet her himself. Aggravation in this instance was her convenient mask for her uneasiness.

She supposed she was happy to find out that her best friend was still alive. With the way things were going around Adalon, she was eager to get out of the city. Since the night of the New Year celebration and the explosion on the pier the next morning on the Day of Light, the amount of Bonemen in the city was suffocating. They marched through the streets and had almost completely overtaken the Crescent Pier. But it was the news of the death of the Prime Commander and the ambassador of Adalon that had rocked the foundations of the great city.

The wealthy were frantic about their investments. As it went, their care for their money superseded their care for humanity, but Adalon was the modern city of Tovillore and one that thrived on borrowed funds. The Spires, the three great buildings at the heart of the city, were affected the most. The Ascendancy Tower, home of the Coalition of Nations, was in disarray. Then the news of the return of the Sagean came. What was still under control faltered and what little resemblance the great city had to its magnificent old self was plunged into riots and rage.

Armed soldiers now stood guard in the Core District, aligned with the giant automatons: nine-foot-tall metal beings, crafted machinery rendered alive by a complex system of wires and gears, powered by puffing steam and a mysterious orange liquid.

The Craftcore, the epicenter of inventors, was shut down. The smoke from their pipe stacks had ceased in the night and the doors found locked. The Arcana University would logically be next. Stasia had seen a lot of professors leaving the city over the last few days, and now she looked to be another person fleeing the broken city.

With the university gone, and without her friend, she had no reason to stay. Meeting Learon in Midway sounded like a fine idea, especially if it allowed her the opportunity to see Wade again and punch him in the face.

She triple-checked her bag to make sure she wasn't forgetting anything, cross checking it against the list she had made to be quadropoly sure. Hefting it behind her back, she snatched the red letter and stuffed it into her pocket.

The roads were full of carriages and estate coaches among the tiny dollop steam cars. Finding a coach ride was hard in the mass of moving vehicles and horses. She began her walk to a coach caller at the corner when a black carriage pulled up to the sidewalk in front of her, the curtains drawn in the cabin. The door came ajar on a release from the driver. Headmaster Edward Knox was stepping from the park path toward it when he caught sight of her.

"Miss Mimnark, how are you?" he asked politely, his eyes hidden behind colored spectacles.

"I am well, thank you, Headmaster."

He looked at her bag and his eyebrows lifted. "Are you going somewhere? Can I give you a lift?"

"I'm headed to the Crescent Pier."

"How fortuitous. I am also headed to the Crescent Pier. Please, join me?" he said, offering the coach door for her.

Something about it did not seem like an offer as much as an insistence. But Edward had always been nice to her, and she knew he and Ellaria were friendly, so she got in, even as something in her screamed to run away. Whether it was the perfected suit or his odd ring, something about him reminded her too much of someone her family would have over for dinner. The ring, she was sure, was a twin of her grandfather's.

"You are leaving the Arcana?" he pulled the door closed, as she settled into the plush red upholstered seat.

"Only for a short time. Hopefully."

"You are one of the best students at the Arcana. I would hate to lose you."

"I will be back for sessions when they start up again. If there are sessions."

"Yes, I know. Nasty business, the things that have been happening. You know if there aren't sessions, there are many places that would love to have you. I know many people who are looking to hire the brightest minds."

She was one of the best students at the Arcana; that was no secret, but the offer sounded ominous.

"It's a nice suggestion and I will remember it," she said, pulling the curtain aside to look out the windows while they traveled the beltways through the city, the giant edifices passing in slow despair.

"Did I ever tell you I know your grandfather?" Edward said.

Her grandfather was a very wealthy man, and she was accustomed to the name dropping that always seemed to happen with the wealthy.

"How unlucky for you," Stasia said.

"You are not close to your family?"

"You could say that."

"It's a shame. Your family is one of the great families in Tovillore."

If by great, he meant blood-sucking, then sure, "If you say so."

"Have you seen or heard from Ellaria?" he asked. The question threw her off.

"Um. No, I haven't. I thought she left after her seminar," Stasia admitted.

"She did, but she said she would be back. I remembered you knew her."

"No."

"Didn't you stay after her seminar to speak with her?"

"No. I mean I did, but only because my friend was her test subject."

"I see."

They reached the Crescent Pier and crossed the Waterfront bridge into mayhem. The chaos of travelers and transports was a throng of shouts and disorder like she had never seen.

"I can get out here," Stasia said.

The headmaster tapped the outside of the coach and the driver stopped. Stasia nearly leapt out. She found her manners at the last moment and politely smiled and thanked the headmaster for the ride.

"Safe passage, and Stasia, remember what I said. You could be on the ground floor of making the next great inventions."

"I will, Headmaster. Thank you again for the ride."

The pier was twice as wild as the center of the city, and she did her best to slip in to the crowd as quickly as possible. Something had changed about Edward. He had been more congenial and even-tempered during their previous encounters. That person in the coach was venomous and cold.

At the lower south docks, she hired a vessel to take her upstream on the Frayne River to the Imperial Road. She had the amber to get on the next one that was leaving. She paid and came aboard. By the looks of him, the captain was a veteran of the Great War. He was an old man, and his frayed brown hat was pulled low to his eyes. He barked at the crew to cast off. His left arm sleeve was rolled up and tied off short, where he had lost his arm.

With a longing gaze, she watched the great city move away, all the while casting glances back to the dock to see if she was being watched. The city could sometimes make her skin crawl and with the pier in shambles as it was, her nerves were restless beneath her skin.

THE NEXT DAY, SHE AWOKE TO THE HORN BLASTS OF TWO LARGE STEAM ships passing swiftly in the water. She climbed the stairs to the captain's deck and stood near to watch their last hours before reaching the trader's port.

The captain scrutinized her a moment and turned back to the water, "You look weary, dear. Did you sleep well?"

She stared at the passing ships, rolling off to Adalon, "I slept fine. Thank you, Captain."

"Are you on your way home?"

"Yes, I am," she lied.

"Are you a student at the university? You look like the sort."

"I am. I study science at the Arcana," she said. Stasia never knew how to answer that question.

"Science, huh? You know I've always wondered, what does your science say about the sun? How do you explain why it turns blue at midday?"

"It doesn't, it only appears that way," Stasia said.

"How's that?"

"The sun appears blue at the apex in the sky because our atmosphere is thin. It's the same reason we have so much mist and seasonal rains, and why our machines produce so much steam or water vapor."

The captain looked at her in a long silence, "Kid, I would be careful who you tell that to."

"Well, you asked."

"I know I asked. I'm a curious old man, but there are some who would say that's blasphemy. There was a time, not so long ago, that you would have been hung for such a statement. I don't care one way or the other, you hear. I'm just warning you. Personally, I like to keep to the things I know and trust. I believe in what I can see with my own eyes."

"That's silly. Why would you ever believe your eyes? Do you see as far as an eagle or in the same spectrums as a bee?"

"Huh?"

"Spectrum, it's a dimension of light. Besides, I find blasphemy is the term people use when they can't reconcile new information with old ideas," Stasia said, slightly annoyed. She hated having to change her way of talking to appease anyone. She caught the captain's look and added, "But you 're right, those times are not so long ago and if reports are true, they're returning."

"It is returning at that. It's a resurgence, but this version of it I fear will be worse. Amongst you youngsters, there aren't many believers in the Sagelight faith anymore. But that makes it worse in some ways. It's almost like pouring firespark on a torch. The opposition of belief aggravates the zealots."

The captain pointed with his good arm to the white arching bridge coming into view. It crossed the river in a giant, soft bow shape. The middle was intersected by towering posts angled to each shoreline. Thick metal braided cords connected down from the apex and spread to the stone road.

"The Trader's Port of Mayfair. As you requested."

They had arrived at the Imperial Road and the small port village. Stasia handed over the second half of her fare, thanked the captain, and stepped off his small vessel to the wooden jetty. The river water sliding beneath jostled the dock slightly below her feet. Floating weeds and rolling murk passed along and clung to the water, as sunken posts and a scent full of thick mud and moss hit her nose. The river smelled worse here than downstream.

In the small village, she walked among the market to find suitable transport to Midway. A signpost near the center of activity held a freshly nailed advertisement for the Show of Wonders. The date suggested it had passed through and they were on to play Nearwin tonight, then on to Grape and Midway for three nights. Stasia was sorry to have missed it but realized eventually she would catch up to it. She smiled and walked into the Mayfair travel office to acquire a coachman.

The coach-finder explained that his prices were double the cost of last month. The beasts along the road had grown in number and aggression, but also many greencoats had abandoned their positions to take up with the Bonemen. Stasia had the amber for it and didn't mind the cost.

She didn't like to talk about her family or their wealth with anyone. Most university kids her own age had never heard the Mimnark name, and she liked that. Stasia had always been an oddity among her kin, where they were all singularly minded sycophants, she was the lone person interested in knowledge, science, and art over obedience. They saw her like she was non-human, and her obstinacy had led them to cut her off. But she had always saved every bit of amber they gave her and had more than enough saved up to pay for her education at the Arcana and still live comfortably afterward.

Stasia boarded the coach and found the interior cabin small but comfortable. The flanking doors in the center were split panels and hinged to swing back. Stasia liked these types of doors best because they could be propped open while they were in motion. With the summer heat, the stone road always reached extreme temperatures. The itinerary had them arriving in Midway in a day and a half. With any luck, maybe her and Learon could see the show when it came. As the coach set off south down the Imperial Road, Stasia pulled out the mechanical contraption she had stuffed in with her things. She had retrieved the device of Wade's making the morning before leaving Adalon. It was a long ride to Midway and Stasia would need all of it to fix these silly wings.

SEVENTEEN
TOO MANY BATTLEFIELDS (LEARON)

T he temperament of faithful men should be gentler, Learon thought while
he watched a file of Lionized arriving at the camp he was scouting. He sat perched in a tree, examining the camp of the Lionized, when a caravan arrived with a wagon full of townsfolk. Pulled by
four houses, the wagon had been modified with bars and benches. The
caged people inside looked like normal families: men, women, and children, all being rounded up as heathens against the Sagean. The hearts of
fearful men are so easily terrified by anything that threatens to shatter the
delusion of their world. Learon could understand and forgive that, but
the horrific tactics for self-preservation of the righteous exposed them to
be nothing more than mindless monsters and their faith a badge of lies to
excuse their lust for violence.

Learon crawled out of the cover and returned to the others positioned behind a hedge of bushes and fallen trees. A strategic spot, three
hundred paces away, that maintained maneuverability in case they chose
to attack.

Learon and Meroha had arrived in Pardona with the Band of
Redeemers the night before. The city looked to be mostly peaceful, but it
was packed with Bonemen and Lionized alike. To Learon's relief, there
were no Rendered machines walking around and they had heard no
reports of Scree in the vicinity.

The first day, the Renegades sent scouts into the city to report on the
situation. Darringer was willing to integrate into the city and protect it
from inside, relying on a series of maneuvers over time to defeat the
contingent of Bonemen. Ronick wanted to lay siege and eradicate the

Bonemen outright. Learon found himself in the middle of their argument. The more reports that came back, the more he began to side with Ronick. However, the Lionized presented a larger problem. Where the Bonemen were the Sagean's men through and through, they were also from all over. The Lionized represented local radicals and zealots. An outright fight with them might turn the city against them. They therefore focused on tracking the movements of the Lionized first.

Learon wound through the back woods and came upon Darringer and Ronick surrounded by a team of fighters. They were huddled on the ground, a crude drawing of the Lionized camp in the dirt before them. Darringer looked up with a small branch in his hand.

"What did you find out, Learon?" Darringer asked.

"You weren't seen, were you?" Ronick questioned.

Ronick didn't trust Learon completely, but Learon respected that feeling. It was an instinct that would probably keep Darringer alive.

"There are thirty of them now." Learon reported.

"Ratspit, Darringer, that's a lot of men to route," a young fighter complained. Learon didn't know his name.

"There's more. The new arrivals came into camp with prisoners," Learon said.

"Who?" Darringer asked.

"Local folk, by the looks of them," Learon said.

"That goes with what we heard. They're relocating any anti-Sagean people they find to Riverride," Darringer said.

"We need to go, now," Ronick urged.

"We're not ready and we now have people to protect," Darringer said.

"Ronick's right, we go tonight," Learon said, and he kneeled among them. He picked up a twig and adjusted the camp diagram to reflect what he had scouted. "The townsfolk will be harder to rescue if they're on the move, and I believe they will move at first light. The camp was makeshift at best. The Lionized are not soldiers, which is good for us because they will not be able to defend their position with any skill or coordinating counterattack. I expect most will be deep into their barrels of ale by twilight and drunk by the dark turn of middle night. If we attack from two directions, we can take them unaware and unprepared."

"What about protecting the prisoners?" Darringer asked.

"We should place some archers, here and here," Learon said, stabbing the twig into the dirt. "Another two men to protect the wagon should sweep in once the attack has begun."

"I hate to agree with him, Darrin, but this trash cannot match up to us. We have just arrived, and word of our group is still unknown, but it won't be that way for very long. We need to take them out tonight," Ronick said.

"We need to disarm them first," Darringer said.

"We won't have that kind of flexibility," Ronick said.

"Fine, we eliminate the men who fight back and allow the others to leave. What do you think, Learon?" Darringer looked over to him.

Darringer's willingness to include Learon's opinion was not unexpected, but it was an unwanted position, and it made Ronick grit his teeth. Learon was unsure how he felt on the matter.

"I'll be honest, I'm torn Darringer. I was in Fort Verdict when these Lionized destroyed the city and set Anchor's Point on fire. I have little sympathy for what's coming to them, but I'm no killer either. There's a thin line between being saviors and being killers. I think the time to strike is now, but I would prefer to protect the wagon," Learon said.

"You'll be in the trees with your bow. I've seen you shoot; it's our best advantage when chaos erupts. We will take the camp tonight. I trust every man here to be men of honor. If someone gives themselves up, we will take them prisoner," Darringer said.

The final preparation for the siege was swiftly resolved, and then the waiting began. At nightfall, the camp was loud and raucous, and the blue fires cloaked a boundary of darkness for them to move in. Learon climbed a tree overlooking the camp. He found a perfect spot for strong footing with room to draw his bow. A couple of fighters in his group waited until he was in the nest before moving on. Whispers among them started when he got onto the tree.

"He climbs like a damned cat," a man said.

"How can he even see the camp from there, let alone hit anyone with his bow?" another man replied.

Darringer heard the last comment and tilted his head up. "Learon, are you good? Can you cover us from there?"

Positioning his feet, the bark of the tree scratched at his back. Learon tried a couple of dry pulls on his bow and looked down,

"I'm fine here," Learon said.

Darringer led the group in closer and surrounded the camp. When the waxing moon rose to the highest point in the night sky, they attacked. Six of thirty lionized men were still awake and on the night's watch. The two monitoring the south woods near the horses and carts must have heard something. They tried to raise an alarm, but it was too late. Darringer's and Ronick's teams swarmed in from two sides.

The Lionized, who were able to mount a defense, met Darringer's squad at the tree line, but were thwarted quickly. As more of the camp came awoke, Ronick's squad burst from behind.

Learon released two arrows during the raid. One man had grabbed a torch and ran to the wagon of prisoners. Learon's arrow took the man's leg in stride. The torch fell short and Gerald, the man Learon had met at the gate outside of Fort Mare, grabbed the wounded man and drug him back to the group of prisoners.

The second arrow took a man trying to ride out of the camp. The arrow struck through the shoulder and the man fell from the horse. The momentum of the shot launched him off the saddle and into a tree. He died in the fall. Learon waited in the tree for a while longer before approaching the camp.

Ronick met his eyes when he appeared on the trapped grounds, "Nice shot."

It was a swift and decisive rout of the zealots' camp. Of the thirty Lionized, they held twenty prisoners and ten of those were wounded. Darringer walked among them, shouting questions. He wanted to know who their leader was and why they were moving people out of the city to Riverride.

A man spat on Darringer's leg, but Darringer didn't pay it much mind. However, Learon recognized him. He was one of the men that attacked outside the gate of Fort Verdict: the one who had threatened Tali and whom Kovan had nearly shot. Learon tapped Darringer on the shoulder and told him as much.

Learon approached the man. A small gash dripped blood at his temple, and he eyed Learon with disdain, a hardened defiance set in his eyes.

"Where is your leader, the one named Aramus?" Learon said.

Either from the fact that Learon knew the man's name or the sound of the name itself, shock rose in the man's eyes, and he immediately re-evaluated Learon. He hadn't placed him.

"Aramus. You dare speak his name, you heathen?" He spat again. Learon jerked back, "For one so unclean, to speak his name, your tongue should be removed. I'm not going to tell you anything, heathen. We are dead either way."

"I think something can be arranged."

"You don't get it. To be a Lionized, you must forfeit your life in this world. For in the Divine Light of the Blue, we will be reborn!" he yelled. It was a signal of some sort, and four of the twenty grabbed something hanging round their necks.

Another Lionized man screamed, "No!" and tried to run.

Learon turned back to see a grin on the faces of the zealots still on their knees. He spun and grabbed Darringer and dove away as four explosions rocked the area. Large fireballs decimated the entire band of Lionized and took three of Darringer's men in the blast. Most had reacted to Learon's panic and backed away far enough to receive only minor burns or scrapes from colliding with surrounding objects when the detonation threw them.

Darringer was grateful for Learon's quick actions, but mostly he peppered Learon about Aramus and Anchor's Point on their return. Back at their own camp outside Pardona City, they regrouped with the rest of Darringer's band of followers. Learon found Meroha to tell her he was fine. She was sitting in their small tent reading a book. He dropped his things with her and told her to get ready to leave. He had helped Darringer take the camp of Lionized, but they needed to move on to Midway. They still had a full day's ride to reach it, and that was if they didn't stop. He helped Meroha start packing when one of Darringer's men retrieved him.

When Learon reached Darringer's tent, Ronick was furious.

"What the torqued death was that. We have fought the Lionized before. Never that many, but they never had those things on them?" Ronick was barking.

"Maybe they're escalating their own tactics. I'm more concerned about Riverride. Shouldn't our scouts be back by now?" Darringer said.

Ronick stuck his head out of the tent and came back. "They are returning now, Darrin."

Darringer sat behind his table and made notes on his map. Learon stood in the corner, curious to hear what the riders had discovered.

"Thanks for sticking around Learon. I wanted you to hear the same reports I did before you take off," Darringer said.

The first man that came in was a young and skinny kid, maybe one of the youngest in Darringer's band. He had short-cut hair, and he spoke before he was fully inside.

"Darringer, sir, I returned this morning before your own squad came back."

"What is happening in Riverride?" Darringer asked.

"Nothing sir. I saw no Scree, and the city is operating almost like normal. The Lionized are not as organized as they are here, and the Bonemen stick mostly to the docks. They are more interested in regulating the river traffic than the city," the scout said.

"What of the people being relocated there?" Darringer asked.

"I didn't see any. I know that was the report we got from Pardona, but I didn't see anything to back that up," the scout replied.

"What do you mean you didn't see them?" Darringer asked.

"I asked around, but there was no trace of them. If they were headed that way they never arrived," the scout said.

"All right, thank you, Jaylon. You can go back to camp."

After the kid left, Darringer sat back in his chair, his hands pressed to his eyes. Ronick paced behind him

"Maybe he's mistaken, Darringer?" Ronick offered.

"No, I picked Jaylon because he's an excellent rider and he's likeable. He would have found if anything was amiss."

"Then what are they doing with the people? We know they have gone missing. We just rescued a whole wagon full?" Ronick said.

"I don't know," Darringer sighed.

The tent flap pulled to the side and a second scout came shuffling in. It was a young woman. She had honey-colored skin like Tali and her long brown hair was tied in a braid under a wide brimmed leather hat. A pair of tattered goggles hung on her neck. She removed her hat and glanced at Learon, before speaking with Darringer.

"Darrin, I rode as fast as I could. The city of Shale still stands, but most of the people are leaving for Pardona. There are Scree in the city, but the beasts have claimed the tree-lined road to Jenovee and are filtering into the city."

"That's disturbing," Darringer said.

"It gets worse, sir. When I was there, a man arrived from Delwell."

"Delwell?" Ronick said.

"Yes, he said that those automatons have come down from Anchor's Point. They arrived in Delwell with Bonemen, and he ran to the river. The current landed him on the west bank, and he headed for Shale. According to him, they had already claimed Maiden's Crossing and continue to march south. He said that the machines are as terrible a sight as has been said. They walk ten feet tall in skin of bronze and breathing steam. The worst part was, they came with wolveracks on leashes," the woman said.

"Thank you, Vera. Please go and get some rest," Darringer dismissed her.

She smiled at all three men, turned, and left. In the turning, Learon spotted a pulsator gun holstered inside her coat.

Darringer ran his hand through his hair, a similar tick of nervous energy he shared with Learon. "Ronick, gather our best twenty men and tell the camp leaders to pack up. We are leaving."

"And where should I tell them we are going?" Ronick asked.

"I don't know yet, but we can't stay here camped out near the city like this," Darringer said. When Ronick left, he turned his attention to Learon.

"What would you suggest I do, kid?" Darringer asked.

"I'm no leader, Darrin," Learon said.

"I didn't ask you to lead, I asked for your opinion."

"Honestly, I think you must take Pardona away from the Bonemen, but even if you win it, you can expect the Sagean's Rendered automatons will come down that river any day now," Learon said.

"So how do I keep my men safe and fight a battle against the Sagean?"

"You need a bigger army and to get a bigger army, you need to offer something the Lionized and the Sagean don't."

"What's that?"

"Safety and freedom. Take your army back to Fort Mare. The Resistance built that place to withstand the Empire's full force from the river. Offer the people a place of refuge; you control the only passable road to the west. If you choose to take the city or go after the Rendered, I cannot fight with you. I'm on my own mission."

"I understand. Do you know anything about the machines?"

"I fought them. They're nine feet tall and they are hard to bring down, but not impossible; aim for the eyes. Also, they carry an odd rifle that also has a long lancing blade. The Creator be with you, whatever you decide. When I can send help your way, I will."

They shook hands for parting. "Learon, tell me one last thing?"

"What's that?"

"Who are you? I've hunted my whole life; I've never seen a man as good with a bow. The men said you move like a cat, and you see farther then most men. Twice over. So, who are you?"

"I'm a friend. Beyond that, I'm trying to figure the rest out myself."

Returning to Meroha, he found her sitting outside the small tent they had been given by Darringer's people. Her short cropped brown hair was pulled back by a headband, and she was drinking tea observing the large camp. She smiled at him.

With a quick look around Learon discovered she had already packed their things.

"Everything's ready to go?" Learon asked, evaluating the straps on their bags.

"Almost. Just waiting for Elias's mystcat to return. It likes to patrol the camp," Meroha said.

"Learon?" Gerald called, riding toward them on horseback.

Learon finished strapping down the supplies on Meroha's stallion, "What's happening, Gerald?"

"Darringer has decided to take a team to Rask and cut off the Rendered coming down from Delwell. He wants you to come," Gerald said.

"He has my answer, Gerald," Learon said.

"He knows, but he wanted me to ask again," Gerald said.

Learon locked down his own things a second time and lifted his weight into the saddle, the leather stretching with a subtle creaking. He looked at Meroha a long time and the mystcat came out of the field. It jumped to Learon's lap and squirmed in the saddlebag.

"I'm sorry, Gerald. I am needed elsewhere. Tell Darringer I'm sorry. Tell him I'm searching for some old warriors that can help us," Learon said.

"I will. Go and may you find peace wherever you are, my friend," Gerald said.

"You too," Learon clasped arms with his friend and began to trot away, "Gerald. If you face the Rendered, they have only two weaknesses: their eyes and a long, glowing vein. Also, stay clear of their lance-bombardier. The shots are powerful, and the blade has a massive reach."

"I will let the others know. May you live and die under the Blue," Gerald said.

Learon nodded and watched Gerald ride away before pulling the reins back to Meroha and the Imperial Road.

Her eyes bounced from him to the gathering riders and back to Learon, "Was that hard for you?" Meroha asked.

"Yes," Learon admitted.

"You want to follow them into another fight, why?"

"I believe in Darringer. Not his opinions or his methods necessarily, but the man. Mostly, I am tired of running. It felt good to fight back."

"I always thought of you as a protector more than a warrior, Learon."

"I didn't go with them, did I?"

"But you feel you should have."

"I do. I know I would be useful there," Learon said.

"You are useful here, Learon. I know no one else is here to say it but thank you for staying the path. You can't fight battles on every front and hope to survive." She said, and it sounded like a quote.

"Where did you read that?" Learon asked.

Meroha opened her bag and pulled a book free. Elias's artificer bat Jules clutched to it until almost tumbling out. She showed him the book. *The Accounts of the Great War, by Arlene Kent; with Analysis of the War Tribunals.*

"It's a quote from Ellaria," she said.

He thought about asking her where she had gotten the book but decided against it. They crossed the river and headed to the city of Prine. Darringer and his team crossed the river shortly after them and rode north through the hills and river valley. They were avoiding the main roads in a direct line to Rask. Learon looked on as the squad galloped into the valley, Darringer at the head and the woman Vera leading sixteen soldiers. He stared at them until he couldn't see them anymore, wondering if he had made the wrong decision, worried he had just watched them ride to their deaths and he couldn't save them.

EIGHTEEN
A GAME OF PERIL (TALI)

The morning was still dark as they readied to leave. Even the early brightening was an hour away from tinting the sky. Wade's father was up before them and had hot coffee steaming from a glazed ceramic pitcher. It was ready on the counter near cups for each of them. Tali helped herself. She took comfort in the steam and warmth of the cup. Holding it gently with both hands, she looked out over the farm, the large water wheel turning at the hillside where a stream came through. When Aaron came in, she thought it would be Wade and began to speak but swallowed the words before they were expelled.

"Good morning, Tali," Aaron said.

"Good morning, Aaron, thank you for the coffee."

He filled his own cup and gazed out the window. Wade came in shortly thereafter and poured himself a drink of the hot liquid.

"Any chance I could convince you not to go, Son?" His father asked.

"I'm sorry, Dad. No. We have to get the artifact back."

"I didn't think so, but I wanted to ask. Here," he handed Wade a shining silver gun, much smaller than the electric crystal-charged pulsator gun.

"I didn't know Grandpa left you a gun until last night. You sure I can take this?"

"You would be doing me a favor. I want to help. When my father, your grandfather, was killed in the Battle of Last Ride, his body and things were sent back home. While he never served directly under Ellaria that I know of, her forces were stationed outside Atava, preparing for the last battle. That's why they call it Fort March. They were preparing to march into the Valley of Thorns. That whole area is now called the Dragon's Spine.

"General Ellaria Moonstone had a long-standing practice of making sure all the soldiers under her charge would be returned home in case of their deaths. Since Grandpa's regiment crossed the Warhawk, she saw to every one of them, when really, she didn't have to. And she did it while preparing to go into the last battle against the Emperor. I believe any fight she has chosen a side in is the side your grandfather would be on, and I'm proud you're on that side as well."

They hugged and Tali excused herself to sit on the porch. She didn't want to intrude on their time. She had heard nothing else, either real or unreal the rest of the night, but was wary of hearing something she wasn't supposed to. The morning air was fragrant with the scents of the crops and dew-covered grass carried on the wind. Wade came out to the porch, followed by Aaron and Lorea. Both Wade's parents gave her a hug as well. Lorea hung on a bit longer to whisper in her ear.

"Protect each other."

Tali thanked them both and Aaron helped her get atop one of the horses he brought around the front. Wade mounted and adjusted the straps to his liking, almost over-evaluating his saddle and supplies to avoid saying goodbye.

Aaron stood back to let them go. "There was one thing your grandfather used to say to me. Only one that I remember the words of. You see, when you grow older, you forget the words. What you remember of the best of times is the feeling of the moment, the energy of people. The words, even if elegant, are typically immaterial. Usually if you hear someone say they remember what someone said, don't believe them; it's their own words. But in this I do remember the words. In greater part, because my father wasn't a man of words. He said, *the only thing that has power over you is that which you give power to, including your fear.* Wade, everyone's path is unknown, and every path is filled with trials to test your soul. Both of you, travel with courage, and keep each other safe."

They left the farm without looking back. The sidetrack had brought Tali closer to Wade, and for that, she was grateful, but she hoped they hadn't mis-stepped in their pursuit of Nyra.

WHEN THEY MADE IT TO CORMA, THE SUN WAS GOING INTO THE BLUE. The hilltop town was confusing with the meandering roads that wound around hills in steep, sloping trails. The buildings were more varied in color than the cluster of white and burnt orange that made up the Eye of Adavan.

Here, the buildings were much smaller, but each had a band of thin metal balconies. The black metal bars gave the otherwise simple buildings a gilded look. The balconies were all shallow, providing nothing more than a standing space, but they allowed the cool breeze to carry inside. The inn they sought was right inside the east bridge, as Aaron said, but the proprietor was not the man with whom he had told them to speak. They were given lodging all the same.

In their room, Tali stood on the balcony staring at the main road into the city. There was a tavern not far off that held her attention with a slew of armed men coming and going, but her view of it was slightly obscured by trees. Wade knocked twice and came in. He was returning from the stables.

"What did the Inn Keeper say about the city or that tavern?" Tali asked as he came through the door.

"Nothing. He gave me the room and told me where we could stable the horses. I didn't like the look of them, though. Right across from the tavern. So, I stabled them a few buildings over. That tavern looked like a gambling den to me."

"You don't think we missed her, do you?"

"Impossible. We left before dawn and our ride was shorter by a few hours easily."

"How long do we wait up here, before we—" she stopped as something moving outside caught her attention, "Wade?"

"What is it?"

"I think I see a coach arriving."

Wade came to stand next to her on the balcony.

"Who are they?" Wade pointed to a group of mounted riders charging out to meet the carriage at the bridge.

"I bet it's the Reckers. That's her, let's go," Tali said, turning from the opening.

"Wait, you want to fight all of them?"

"Hello. Luminary," she said patting her chest, and pointing outside, "Regular criminals."

Wade shrugged, unable to mount a counterpoint, but just then, three men burst through their door with pulsators drawn and humming. A fourth man entered wearing a fancy black jacket with white stitching and a timepiece chain swinging free while he moved.

"And who might you two be?" the fourth man asked, his words drawn in a slight accent.

Wade put his hand to his side and waved off any movement by Tali.

"Sir, we don't want any trouble. There's a young woman riding into town today that stole something from us. We just want it back."

Tali's head dropped. *Why was he trying honesty?*

The man's eyebrows pinched. "Nyra's score is yours you say? Well then, why don't we all wait for her together at my estate. You see, no one comes into my city or leaves my city without my knowledge. I control both the east and west bridge. I opened it this morning for Nyra, but you two came through."

"Sir, we--"

"No. No, let us take leave of this place, for better surroundings," the man said with obvious disgust for the inn.

The group of thugs took them to a large house cresting the hilltop, an old castle by the looks of the ruins. It was now a large estate with three-story columns and smaller stone buildings along expansive, front gardens.

They stepped out of the coach cabin with pulsators still pointed at their chests. The leader stood on a square, stone-inlaid road.

"My home," the leader said, gesturing to the entire hillside. "It was once the location of the Castle of Golia. Two thousand years ago, this great castle stood proud on this hilltop. It was destroyed, of course. Who or what is responsible for its demise, no one knows; and as with most things lost to history, no one cares."

They walked into a main greeting entry. The interior upper levels spanned above them in long balconies. The man turned to them underneath the balconies.

"Where are my manners? I am Calhan Venali. Welcome to my city. Now, who are you? You come into my city unannounced, armed with a pulsator and a fancy silver six shooter. I assume this relic still works, but the silver in it is worth more than the tool it was made for. Most importantly, why would you risk your lives for this thing Nyra has?"

"Nyra took something that wasn't ours to begin with," Wade answered, "We were transporting it for the Sagean."

"Wow," Venali said, laughing to himself, "When you lie young man, you shoot for the moon. And with a straight face, too. Makes me think you're a gambler, son. Do you play Reckoner?"

"I do," Wade admitted.

"And what's your name, where are you from?"

"Wade, I'm from Adalon."

"Do you play the Stones Cascade, too, Wade?"

"Never have."

"You should, it's older than Reckoner. There are similarities in the strategy. They say if you master the Stones, you will master Reckoner. I have a problem; I have restless men. Most are angry at being pushed out of the Eye by the Bonemen. I have to keep them entertained. So, either you can play Reckoner, or you can fight in the arena? You look like you could put on a good show in the arena, strapping kid like you, and very pretty to boot. The men would love to see that face bloodied. Of course, you can keep that gauntlet blade of yours for the fight." Venali said. He picked up Wade's arm and examined the metal and mechanism.

"I've seen a few of these before, but none this fancy. It matches your fancy Adalon look. I'll give you the option, which would you like?"

"I'd like the thing Nyra stole from us and to be on our way."

"I can't give that to you. Even..." Venali paused as men came in dragging Nyra by the arm. "Ah, here she is. The little thief of the hour."

Nyra was brought in with a shove, her eyes full of terror. Tali had remembered her as their same age, but she looked much younger, as frightened as she was. Her hands were quivering, and she tried to hold them together in her lap, but they continued to shake. Nyra looked over to Wade and Tali, and Tali heard the words Nyra spoke in her mind: *why did you follow me here? I'm sorry Tali, I just wanted out. I'm...*

"Do you have the bridge tax, my dear Nyra?" Venali asked.

"I... I do," she struggled to say.

Behind her, the henchmen held up the Stone.

"Oh, good."

"We found this on her, too," a man said. He held out a dagger with a gold pommel. There was an emblem on the seal of the pommel Tali couldn't decipher.

"A relic from another age," Venali said as he admired it. His eyes grew wide with delight but ultimately, he handed it back to his hench-man. "You can return it to her. We are in no danger of her using it, correct Nyra?"

"Absolutely. I would never. I just keep it for protection. I mean, to feel safe," Nyra said.

"You see, give it back to her so she can feel safe. Now, if you don't mind telling me why you thought you could transport stolen goods through my city?"

"I asked for passage with Mr. Redmar. He said I could."

With a nod of his head, Venali signaled his man. The henchmen tugged Nyra's shirt down from her collar, past her shoulder bone. A swollen scar protruded from her skin in a darkly cut *R*.

"She's Redmar's property boss," the henchman announced and released her shirt.

Venali paced, but turned back, his mouth tight with anger. "Did you bother to consider who you might be stealing this from? How do you think these kids got such a valuable and unique item?"

"I didn't think," Nyra muttered.

With an ear-piercing whip, he slapped Nyra across her cheek. It was so hard, it split her lip open, and her face came away red. She stayed on the ground where she'd fallen, crying. Tali felt her fists close and the muscles in her arm tighten.

"Are you stupid, girl?" Venali fumed. He looked prepared to hit her again.

"Why don't you try hitting someone who will hit you back?" Tali barked and the lights in the room dimmed. Everyone looked around to find the source.

"Tali, no. I got this," Wade said.

Venali smiled wickedly, "I'm sorry we're not giving you any attention. But I'm going to deal with Wade here and Nyra, and then you," Venali turned and waved his hand at three men, "Put her in the cool-down room."

Tali could feel the heat in her eyes and was ready to unleash a torrent of energy on them, but she could see Wade gesturing with his hand at his side for her to calm down. Frustrated, she let them escort her to a room off a long corridor. It dropped down to a small, lightless pit; a remnant of the old castle that once stood there. They shut the door, and she waited in the darkness, the mildew smell of old moisture wet in the air.

A few minutes passed, and the door was opening again, with Wade standing in the frame. He held out his hand to help her up. Tali stood with her hands on her hips, peering up at him. Wade's *oh shucks* smirk chiseled away at her indignation, she rolled her eyes and took his hand.

"I made a deal to play a game of Reckoner for our passage," he said, lifting her out.

"Why? What about the Stone?"

"We need to get out of here first, then worry about the Stone after."

"But the Stone is all that matters?"

"Not if we're dead."

Two Recker thugs ushered them back down the corridor. Wade waited until they were walking to continue.

"Also, you can't kill all of them, Tali."

"I can certainly try."

"Once I win, we'll leave and track down Nyra on the road before Amera."

"Just when I think I know how big of an idiot you are, you raise the bar. Wade, you can't trust these people."

"I know, but I'll play their game and you keep your eyes on the exit. If we need to improvise, that's what we do."

"And Nyra?"

"They are making her watch the game. I don't know. I get the sense they don't get along with the bounty hunter that she works for, but they're too scared to take the Stone from her."

"Let's go, you two." the henchman said, and loaded them into a carriage.

THEY WERE BROUGHT DOWN FROM THE GREAT HOUSE TO THE GAMBLING den. It was a large wood building fronted by two-story stone columns and tall windows across the entire upper facade. They entered through an arched double door of vertical wood. The interior was open all the way to the back, and inside was crowded and loud. The sounds of cheering and yelling emanated all over, in waves of emotion, accompanied by the endless clang and chimes of glasses and tin-tanks of ale. Though the bar area proved quiet in comparison to the gamblers and their onlookers.

At the center was an expanse of gaming tables with various groups playing card games, games of Stones, or dice. An open loft was positioned above the gaming tables where people crowded around the balcony looking down on the games being played.

Venali sat at the main table, awaiting them. Two half-dressed beautiful women stood next to him in bright red. Both had visible bruises that Tali could see, and she bit the inside of her lip to keep from lashing out.

Two chairs, obviously meant for them, stood empty before the card table. She took her seat and critically assessed the room for an exit strategy. There were other tables playing cards, but they had the largest crowd by far. Most of Venali's men had pulsators or swords. Tali suspected it had more to do with their ranking amongst the syndicate than their skill with either weapon, since none of the gun carriers were younger than thirty.

"This is Thurman," Venali introduced the man to his left. "He is one of the best players in the house. I look forward to the game. The Light and luck be on your side," Venali said, and he stood, heading for the stairs, Wade's silver gun stuck in his waistband.

Tali watched him walk through the room until he took his seat above, among the balcony rabble. Nyra squirmed in a chair by his side. A new deck of cards was brought out along with an extremely fancy action turner. Thurman whistled a song. He lit his rolled candor leaf cigarette and smiled. The smoke puffed out and clouded under his hat, around his eyes.

"It's a forty-two-standard empire. Thurman goes first," the dealer announced and dealt the opening hands.

There were many iterations of the game and the dealer had announced they were playing with four card fields and two card reserves, using a standard deck. Tali trusted that meant it wouldn't contain any surprises. Many city taverns played *fifty-four special*. Thurman drew applause from the crowd for his field when he laid it down and Wade's field drew quiet conversation. Thurman's field was power-balanced and leaning towards attacking, while Wade's squad was a mix of defense and attack, low on energy power. Tali had seen the game played in Ravenvyre, but in the airship, Wade had taught her much more about the intricacies of the game. One thing he stressed was that the head card mattered the most. The best strategy employed a squad that enhanced your leader to win. What everyone knew was that you typically needed a Sagean Lord head card to prevail. It was the common complaint with the game. As they tended to need squads for power and attack. The look of Wade's field said he needed to draw better cards.

They drew again and replaced their field with each turn, discarding their unwanted cards to the graveyard. Wade kept building a mix, which seemed odd to Tali. Slowly, as their turns dwindled, and the Reckoning became imminent, she began to see Wade had really built a high-defense team. However, it was increasingly obvious that Thurman had a Sagean lord head card. His team of attackers said as much, and at one point he was forced to discard a Tregorean Guardian card with a special attack— one of the strongest cards in the game—because they can never be paired with a Sagean Lord. Some card ranks didn't work with others, a tell if you knew how to watch for it. A few more draws and exchanges went by, and Wade's dry spell of not exchanging any cards continued. At last, he drew a card he liked and placed it in his reserves while discarding a high-power Hazon Woodsman to the graveyard.

Then, the eye with two swords came up on the action turner and the game entered the final round: the time for one last exchange and the reveal. They each picked up their hands and threw one reserve card to the Beyond facedown, their teams finalized. Since Thurman was dealt first, he revealed first. He grinned and, using his head card like a shovel, flipped his final field over and threw the head card down atop the pile with a victorious sort of finality.

Two Zenoch Warriors, with a Tregorean Archer, and Menodarin Lance Guard. His Sagean head card was the fifth Emperor Mikol Jagon, and it contained a red gem and orange power grid. His score multiplied the entire squad to a max of attack and a secondary of a high-power number. It was a good hand that brought whistles and clapping, and Tali was unsure what hands could beat it.

"That's a great hand. Not many can knock it out," Wade said.

Thurman stood and smiled broadly, but Wade simply stared back, never budging, his eyes locked on Thurman. He fanned out his cards but held his head card back.

"It's a really tough hand to beat," Wade said.

Wade's entire field was now heavy defense. He had replaced his weakest card with a reserve, a Zenoch Seal Bearer. A great card for defense.

Thurman eyed him suspiciously, obviously confused by the play. Without an offensive card, Thurman's field and attack defeated him. The Sagean Lord leader card had won.

What was Wade's head card?

"Had I only this defense, it wouldn't have been close, but..." Wade paused and tossed his head card to the top, "... with the Tregorean Priest as my head card, I have one more move."

The Tregorean had a blue gem and power grid for three multipliers, the third corner emblem showcasing the life crystal. Wade was allowed to resurrect any card from the graveyard. He pulled a card from the pile of the beyond, the cards cast off during the exchanges.

"Every defense needs a warrior, but you only need one to win if your defense is strong enough and you have the right attacker," Wade said, and pulled the Tregorean Guardian from the cast-offs, sliding it amongst his army. The warrior wore a blue cloak that matched the blue gem. The corner numbers reduced Thurman's power while adding an attack that Thurman's hand couldn't account for.

Thurman pounded the table. Wade had won.

Tali looked around, but Nyra was gone. In the commotion of the final reveal, she had slipped away. A large man came through the crowd and stepped to them. Tali prepared to fight. She pulled what energy she could feel around her into her well, but let it go when the man placed a bag of coins on the table. The soft cloth pouch clattered in front of Wade.

Tali came to her feet and pulled at Wade's sleeve. "Let's go Wade. Nyra's gone."

Wade stood and grabbed the purse. "Good game. I thank you for the sporting time, but we must be on our way. I trust the bridge is open to us now?"

Together, they backed out of the main entrance and to the empty streets. A horse could be heard galloping off; the hoofbeats in rhythm pounded off the stone road, racing away. At the top of the street, Tali could see Nyra riding to the west too fast for them to keep up. They circled around to find their horses where Wade had originally stabled them. Their things remained untouched, and Remi jumped out of the darkness. A huge relief came over Tali. Her mystcat jumped into the saddle bag and they walked the horses out toward the west bridge, the glow of orange globe gas lamps projecting over the shadowed road.

The side streets were quiet. From the darkness, armed men approached from all around. With Calhan Venali at the lead, they came directly down from the winding road and encroached from the sides.

"I've decided I must know. What is this Stone?" Venali demanded.

He checked his watch and four men jumped out of the shadows and grabbed Wade and Tali, holding them up by the arms. Tali's heart pounded. She looked at Wade and her mind raced where to find energy and where to channel it.

Tali closed her eyes and blocked out whatever Venali was saying. She pulled all the energy from every lantern flame she could feel. It wasn't enough, and she searched desperately.

Venali approached and placed the tip of his knife in front of Wade's face.

"What can I say? It's a special rock," Wade said.

"Why does Razor Redmar want it!" Venali shouted and with a flick, he nicked Wade in the eyebrow. Blood sprouted from the small cut and dripped into Wade's eye. Remi emerged from the bag, jumped to the ground, and stretched.

"Venali, look at that cat. Have you ever seen a cat like that?" A man holding Wade exclaimed upon seeing the animal.

Tali's heart stopped at seeing Remi. But there was something else, something stirring inside her furry companion. For a moment, she could sense the link Remi had with her, the pull and charge to their bond that she had never felt before but always knew was there. Through it, Remi held a surge of heat and energy. Suddenly, she was flooded with power.

Tali released a torrent of heat into the men holding her. The men screamed at her side and their eyes burst into flames. Venali spun and backed away, as the men dropped dead to the ground, after which Tali withdrew the heat. She put the energy to work as kinetic power and blasted the men all around them off their feet. She sent the wall of air at everyone except Venali. She left him standing there, his arms over his head for protection.

Tali walked forward and picked up Remi. Wade scrambled to grab a pulsator dropped by a now-dead henchman. He pointed it at Venali and took back his grandfather's gun. Wade appraised Tali and his eyes went wide.

His gaze fixated on Tali's eyes and her surge scars. She could feel the flame marks glowing with her rage and even saw a slight reflection in her hair at the edge of her vision. Venali shook with terror.

"She a Luminary!" an unseen man squawked. Boot heels scampered on the run, "Close the bridge."

"Tali, we have to go," Wade pleaded with her.

Tali ignored him and lifted Venali's knife off the ground without touching it. It drifted into the air on its own and began to spin.

"If you kill me, you won't make it out of the city, girl. You've started a war with the Reckers and someone will take my place and see that you're hunted down," Venali said.

"Let them come," Tali breathed, "I'm tired of hiding. If this is a war, like you say, then let it be a war."

The blade stopped spinning in the air and slammed home into Venali's neck. All around her in the surrounding buildings, she could feel pulsator guns charging and probably taking aim at her. She almost wanted them to fire, confident she could stop whatever they tried.

"Why did you do that?" Wade cried.

"Any enemy you leave alive in war is a threat in the future," Tali said, and mounted her horse. It was a cold rationalization, but she didn't care.

Wade gazed at her with a look of concern, but his eyes spoke of pity. With the energy swirling inside her, she let the sting of his expression slide away. Wade mounted and they rode for the bridge. Coming down the hill, they could see the ridgeway was full of men, at least thirty deep and waiting. Wade steered them off the road to the north.

"Where are we going?" she said.

"Please Tali. Let's cross upstream somewhere. I don't want to kill all of those men." He said and charged ahead. Tali reluctantly followed, but her thoughts persisted, *why was Wade afraid of a fight and for whose sake were they running away?*

NINETEEN

THE KNIFE'S EDGE (ELLARIA)

A fog drifted amongst the looming masses of tents and travel-crafts.
A man stepped from shadow to shadow with a blood-soaked
knife. Ellaria could feel him stalking her, but she couldn't see
him. A slight disturbance in the grass, a crunch in the dirt, whispered of
his position. But the sound was lost in the wind before she could locate its
source.

Where had everyone gone, she wondered. The entirety of the fairgrounds
was empty. With a lantern in her hands, she weaved around the trampled
paths through the large field, the darkness of the night yet to give way to
the morning light.

No matter where she looked, she couldn't find anyone. She heard a
sharp ringing sound from the caravan circle, and she rushed from around
a carriage house to the center space.

At the center was a tall man with a top hat. The soft glow of the
surrounding carriages provided only enough light to softly illuminate the
fog and patches of the ground, leaving the man mostly disguised. He
leaned slightly on a cane and his right hand at his side held a long-curved
knife.

In succession, the lanterns started to wane and extinguish from
behind him. Gradually, each light winked out of existence in a progression toward her and the darkness consumed the circle yard.

Her own light held, and she lifted it forward to see.

A sinister smile on the pale man was now only a few feet away. She
couldn't breathe. She tried to scream, but nothing came out. The man's

face appeared, and she almost recognized him, but his eyes were missing. Like they had been burned out of his skull.

"Hello, Ms. Moonstone," he spoke in a smoky voice that sent a shiver run down her spine.

"Who are you?" Ellaria said.

"Don't you know? Don't you recognize me?"

"No."

"What a shame, after so many encounters, too," he said, and lifted the blade. A reflection appeared in the steel of a man she did recognize: Elias. And the pale man laughed. A dark mocking laugh that made her skin crawl. Her hand trembled and Ellaria threw the lantern at his feet.

The body was engulfed in flame, his laughter stopped, and his face split apart as though large gashes had cut across it and were pulling away. The noise of the blaze was replaced by a screaming. But not from the man, from a voice not her own, and Ellaria startled awake.

She was in a cold sweat on her bed in the upper loft of her carriage house. The room was quiet, and it was still early morning. She adjusted the horizontal band of windows above her head and looked out. They weren't moving anymore, so they must be in the city of Grape, but there was a thick fog outside. The air smelled fresh, and she breathed in deep. It was another nightmare and one more vivid and real than any nightmare had the right to be. She struggled to remember the last night she had without one, but the screams this time had seemed so real.

Scanning the haze, a figure in black passed through the mist and her breath caught. It had only been a moment, but she was sure she had seen something. Ellaria got up, threw on a coat, grabbed the silver-handled knife, and rushed outside.

Out amongst the carriage houses and flatbed wagons, the mist was thicker than she realized. She took the hanging lantern from the hook beside her door and ventured out. She held out the lantern in front of her, but it really didn't help with visibility. She tried to stay near the other cabins to guide herself and wound her way around each one. On her fifth pass, she saw the shape again.

"Stop right there. Who is that--Who are you?" Ellaria called out, but the figure backed away and around the carriage. She began to hear voices and moved toward them. The crew was setting up a tent. The fog had slowed their efforts, and they mostly stood around smoking rolled weed and complaining. When she came upon them, they faltered from her sudden presence.

"Don't be sneaking up on people in this fog, lady. Did you need something?"

Will was with the men, directing the crew manager where to set up. He was already dressed for traveling. She saw him infrequently but favored his company when he was available. He had the soft words that each subgroup spoke between themselves but never breached to outside ears. But he was not a gossip. The entire troupe should have loved him for that alone, she thought. She knew well how rumor killed the squad from within easier than an enemy at the door. When Will heard the commotion, he came over.

"Aria, how are you? Are you all right?" Will asked.

"I'm—did a man come through here. In a black cloak?" Ellaria said.

Will looked at her curiously, then spoke to the crew, "Anyone see a guy running around with a black cloak?"

Most of the men shook their heads *no* and a few voiced the same. A loud crash rang out from something hitting the ground and Ellaria shook.

"It's just the crew dropping the poles for the eight-tip tent," Will observed. "You sure you're all right?" he asked again.

"I thought I heard a scream and when I came outside to check, I saw a man. But maybe…" Ellaria stopped short of saying maybe she imagined it.

"We've been at this most the morning and things are slow, but we haven't heard anything. Of course, sound doesn't travel the same in this mist. It's possible what you heard was on the other side of camp. Max, Garret, come with me; I want to check something," Will said, and he invited two of the bigger gentlemen to walk with them.

A weight lifted as Will took her seriously. She supposed it was out of respect for his elder, but she liked to believe she still had a command to her voice. They were only a few paces away from the staging area when a loud scream bellowed out.

They ran toward the noise. The screaming continued but had changed to a loud whimper by the time they arrived. Jolee stood comforting Desee against the house. Ronee crouched down over a body in the grass. Ellaria could see by the man's pants that it was a security guard. Ellaria helped Ronee out of the way so Will could check on the man. With a slight lift, a pool of blood beneath extended, and he let go.

"Garret, Max, run and get Archibald and tell the crew someone else has been killed," Will said.

Once again, Archibald arrived and told everyone to go back to their duties. This time Ellaria stuck around.

"What the underneath is happening around here, Will?" Archibald exclaimed.

"I told you, Archibald, I can vouch for every man or woman in your troupe. None of them would do this," Will said.

"Both murders look like someone was caught snooping around. Do we have a stowaway?" Archibald asked.

"Unlikely, but I'll have everyone turn out their crafts," Will said.

"And double check all the utility vehicles. The flat beds, everything. Do an inventory, too. I want to know if anything is missing, no matter how insignificant," Archibald said.

"I know you were reluctant in Nearwin but it's time to bring in the greencoats, Archibald. They can assign more security and an investigator. If nothing else, it will boost morale," Will said.

"Fine. See to it. I don't want to take these bad omens with us to Midway. Make sure those greencoats know they can't get in our way. I don't want some investigator interrogating my performers. And no Bonemen. You tell the damned peacekeepers of Grape that if I see Bonemen, we'll pack up. How many nights did you negotiate for our stay in Midway?"

"Three nights," Will said.

"Go back to them this afternoon and get a fourth night if you can. And I expect to play in that damned fancy Barrel Mosaic Theatre, not the Old Stone Ear. Got it?"

"I'm on it, Archibald."

When they finished and Archibald turned to leave, he saw Ellaria waiting nearby. "I thought I told everyone to go back home?" Archibald said.

"You did. I don't always jump when people call to see my heels," Ellaria told him, scowling with her arms folded.

"No. I don't suppose you do. No matter. I wanted to talk to you about your show. Walk with me," Archibald said waddling away and waving her on. They headed back to the carriage field together, the fog lifting with the sun.

"You have some explaining to do, Aria. You undersold yourself. I hate to admit it. I should have known. If you knew Manus, you would know some great tricks, but your show is actual magic," Archibald said.

Ellaria simply smiled and said, "Is there a question in there?"

"I want you to perform two shows a night. Word of your show has traveled fast and your first show tonight is sold out already. I expect the second to sell out before we open."

"Two shows. I can manage that," she agreed.

"Good. In Midway, I'd like to go to three."

"Three, but I'm only doing one night. Don't push your luck, Archi."

"One night?" he growled.

"I told you, I need to catch a winddrifter out of there. I don't expect to be able to find one the first day, but by day two, I'm gone," Ellaria said.

"I understand. But don't call me Archi again or I'll push for seven shows."

"No, you won't. You know as well as me that the best way to maintain the mystery is to keep the shows to a minimum and sell them out."

"You are correct. I do want to talk about our deal, though. You were supposed to deliver a ravinor. I don't believe you can, but if you can teach the Elustri sisters your act, I'll call it even. Can they do your act?"

"I will have to work with them. They know some of the furies of alchemy, but I will have to test them to see which has the skill to do it."

"Test, test away. Have them readied to take over in Midway, but don't—"

"I know—don't let it get in the way of the shows tonight."

"You catch on quick, Aria."

Back at her carriage house, she hung the lantern back in place and entered. Elias was drinking tea and letting the steam wash over his eyes. Seated at the small table, he startled her, but she couldn't say why.

"What made you go running out into that fog?" he asked flatly.

It was a curious thing to ask, and she looked at him sideways before speaking, "Another member of the troupe was murdered."

"Who was it this time?"

"A security guard was killed," she said.

"Is the camp in chaos over it?"

"No. You know how performers are. The theatre is more cold-blooded than a squad of executioners. It's the great show, the *Show of Wonders*. And no matter what, the show must go on."

As the day wore on, her assessment proved true. The crew and performers went about their day as though it was only a pebble in their shoe. Every little detail was seen to, and the circus was set up once the fog was gone. The greencoats showed up soon after. A murder investigator named Hark interviewed everyone in the troupe. By the time he came by the Elustri sisters' carriage, Ellaria was there with the three ladies reviewing their knowledge of Alchemy. Hark was disheveled and yawning while he spoke to them. Ellaria had the impression he had endured many a dramatic telling of the murders from each troupe member already and each, no doubt, focused on how the slayings affected them. Inspector Hark interviewed them individually out in the field.

When it was Ellaria's turn, he asked her about that morning, but it was his questions about Elias that had her concerned. He seemed to accept her explanation that Elias was sick and spent most of the time asleep. It wasn't Hark's suspicion, but Ellaria's own answers that worried her. She couldn't recall if Elias had been in his bed that morning. She had never looked for him. His increasingly erratic behavior felt like residual effects of his sickness, but she had to be honest with herself: she didn't know what was wrong with him. He was almost acting like how he used to a long time ago. *Could it be the Wrythen, The Ancient Evil that he feared? Had it somehow taken hold of him?*

She had taken for granted that he was bedridden, but that had changed. Back inside her carriage house, she found Elias sleeping. It was a restless sleep. He turned and moaned under his breath. His temperature was cold again, and she heated more crystals for him. Ellaria had tried every treatment she knew with little results. The crystal so far had the best effect. She could hear him talking again while she placed the crystals with him.

"You can't know for sure. There must be another way. There are many paths. This can't be her destiny. I won't let you do this. I can't, I…" Elias murmured.

He calmed once the crystals were next to him and by the time Ellaria's call came for showtime, she decided to give him some burgin tea, a sleeping aid that would allow him to rest.

She performed her first show without a hiccup and when she reappeared at her carriage, she checked on Elias to find him sound asleep. After her second show, she found Elias awake and partially sitting up in his bunk space as she climbed up the steps.

"Elias, I thought you would still be sleeping? How are you feeling?" she asked.

"I've been sleeping all day, it feels like. I feel… Where were you?" he asked.

"I was on stage. I had two shows tonight."

"Oh."

"I was planning on seeing Archibald's version of *The Echo of Silence* tonight, but since you're up, I'll stay here with you."

"Can I get some food?"

"Yes, definitely. I'll get changed and go get some."

"Thank you," he said.

She changed and when she was stepping out, she noticed he had slunk back flat into his bed. She hustled over to the fair grounds for the best local fare. The Joybirds tent was exceedingly lively this night. Housed in one of the larger eight-post tents, it was the only bar serving sprits anywhere on the grounds. But that was only part of its allure. The real attraction was the open stage for local acts. This should have led to a cacophony of shodders and rags. But all the performers were vetted upon arrival, and some were quite good. Some of the best each town had to offer showed up, hoping to catch on with the show or simply excited to have the biggest crowds they would ever see.

The tent was packed and, in a city known for its wine, she imagined the night had only begun. Upon her return, Archibald stopped her.

"Aria, Great show tonight," Archibald said, his face beaming behind his chubby cheeks.

Ellaria thought he seemed very cheerful for a man presiding over a carnival with a murderer. "Thank you, Archibald, but aren't you worried?"

"About what?" he asked.

"About the murders," Ellaria said.

"No. The inspector believes it was a thief. A dangerous one to be sure, but he believes the threat is gone."

"Why?"

"The prop car was rummaged through and a few of the carriage houses showed signs of forced entry."

Someone was looking for something, "That doesn't have you concerned?"

"No. We'll be in Midway tomorrow, and I can employ extra security. Besides. It's not all bad. Our elixirs have never been more popular. The Zenoch's protection elixir is just juniper and honey and we sold out before the sunset tonight," Archibald grinned.

Ellaria scanned around and realized the circus was more packed than ever. She gave Archibald a hard look.

"I must be going," she said, and stomped away.

WHEN SHE RETURNED WITH THE FOOD, ELIAS WAS SITTING IN THE doorway, his feet on the front steps, his body half slumped into the frame. His eyes stared off at the night sky and he was mumbling under his breath,

"You can't escape me. We are not done yet. You can't escape me. Can't you see the truth? Can't you see what must be done. You are slipping, you're not as strong as you think, you…"

"Elias?" she whispered.

He shook his head and his eyes slowly focused on her. "Where did you go?"

"To get you some food, remember?" she said.

He took a deep breath, but it seemed he couldn't fill his lungs, and he coughed. She touched his forehead, and he shied away from her. Ellaria gave him a stern look and put her hand to his forehead. It was hot enough to warm her hand.

"Trying to cool off in the doorway?" she asked.

"I think so."

"Let's get you back inside. I'll split the door for more air."

Elias stumbled, trying to climb to his feet, and clutched to anything he could to make it back to bed. She nearly carried him the last few feet and heaved him into the blankets. It was a wonder he had been able to get out of it. She wiped the sweat from her head and realized her friend was getting worse. She had been blind to it, but he was worse. She was so concerned about doing whatever the next thing was, whatever it took to get through the day, she had lost sight of the bigger picture. Less than a week among the circus, and she was lost in its routine. Caught up in the scene.

It wasn't until then that she realized how badly she missed Kovan. *Had she given up?* She slid to the floor and wept. The illusion she was hiding in had swept her away from the reality that the love of her life was gone, and her best friend lay dying in the bed next to her. She let her guard down to feel normal and still death followed her. So, she cried, the tears she never let anyone see. The ones of sadness for the world falling beneath the shadow and for her own inability to change anything. But also, she shed the tears of failure and feeling small. Her helplessness was staggering and confronting the disappointment she had in herself had wrecked her. The mistake was in trying to navigate every step and stone along the path. One step at a time had allowed Fate's hand the chance to take hold, and now she was mislaid. *It was time to take back control, time to rejoin the fight.*

She allowed this sorrow to consume her only for a moment, for the span of a breath of wind through the hills, and that was all. *Let it live on in the wind,* she thought. And if it comes again, she could accept it once more when she had more time for tears. For now, she had wasted enough time hiding, but that ended now.

She rushed to find the communicator watch she had put away. She dug out the enchanted pen that went with the communicator and scratched out a message. Maybe the young rogues would receive it, wherever they were. Maybe they had fixed their watches by now, and if not, she would send a message again and again until she knew for sure. Lifting the enchanted pen from the parchment, her own watch lit up in a soft glow of blue and the words formed.

We're not dead yet. Find us in Midway.

TWENTY
THE SILO (TALI)

The cool crisp morning seemed a peaceful beginning with the soft drone of the country coming alive. The birds' chirp and cackles in the spread of trees chattered their opinion of the dawn. A warbler's laugh chimed out from the tree above her, adding another layer to the ambient orchestra playing the new day. They had slept beneath the limbs of a large tree she didn't know the name of; the boughs extended off the trunk ten feet all around, and the lowest ones sagged to touch the ground. It created a canopied void with room enough for Tali to stand without her head touching a branch. The ground inside was soddened, and too soft in areas, but it was better than sleeping out in the open, and the light rain during the night barely touched them.

They gathered their things and left the confines of the shelter, the horses waiting a few paces away. The ground around the small batch of trees showed no signs of anyone having ridden through. They mounted in tired silence and Wade kicked his charger into a trot. They followed the river upstream most of the morning until they found a safe place to cross. With the sun going into the Blue, they traversed the Turen river and rested on the western shore.

Tali worked on the communicator watch and Wade went for a walk along the bank and when he came back, he carried something in his hand. He sat down next to her on the hill and showed her the fishing pole he had found.

"Think I'll try to catch us some lunch. I've never been very good at fishing, but I've caught a few," he said boldly and unwound the line. Everything about it—the line, the wood rod, and reel—appeared dried out and old. She thought she might get a splinter just looking at it, and didn't think it was salvageable, but she was no expert. When Wade thought he was ready, he stepped to the bank and attempted to cast the white slug he found in the grass.

He flung the pole overhead a few times and snapped it forward to throw the line out. Instead of casting into the water, Wade had hooked himself on the back of his pants and he nearly fell over into the river.

Tali couldn't help it. She chuckled softly under her breath. Wade turned to look at her and for the first time she could remember, she saw him embarrassed.

"That didn't work," he declared. Awkwardly he unhooked himself and tried again. This time the line didn't go out anywhere because it had knotted at the top. But it took Wade a moment to see his line wasn't in the water.

Tali chuckled again, a little louder.

Wade fixed the knot and looked at her. "Stop laughing. You want to eat, don't you? I told you, I'm no great fisherman. I think the trick is getting out into the water a little," he said confidently.

Wade strode into a shallow part of the river, where the surface was still. He stepped with deliberate care to maintain his balance in the current. Tali really was hungry and as he prepared to try a third time, she found herself hoping he would catch something for them to cook.

Wade flung the rod backward and whipped it with a bit of extra power to cast the line. The line flew a good twenty feet out, but he had broken the rod and the top half sailed past his cast line twice as far, hitting the river with a triumphant splash.

Tali doubled over laughing. When she stopped to look at Wade, he was standing in the river staring at the broken tip in disbelief. *Maybe I shouldn't let him lead anymore*, she thought.

"I don't know my own strength I guess," he shrugged, and he climbed out and back to her, laughing to himself as a sat down. "I guess Learon is the better fisherman. What did he do, catch five that day?"

"He caught six, actually, but he lost it when you got there," Tali said.

"Six? Well, we should have known right there we were going to lose the Stone. The number six is cursed," Wade said.

The talk of Learon made her miss him and her smile faded.

Wade threw the remaining pieces of the fishing rod into the river, "Are you all right?"

"I'm fine," Tali said.

"You did great last night. I'm sorry I didn't say so before. You were right, too, you know."

"Was I?" she tore a long piece of grass in her hand into tiny bits.

"You saved us. You saved me," Wade said.

There was a tranquility by the river, and a loneliness too, if not for the companionship of friends. The peace of the moment was welcome and her growing frustration with Wade vanished, but she still couldn't shake the violence from the night before.

"Did I make things worse?" she asked, still fidgeting with her hands.

"Who knows? All we can do is one thing at a time. If we can get the Stone back, then we will worry about the next thing. Speaking of that, did you fix the communicator?"

"I did. But I haven't sent a message yet, since we have nothing to report. *Still looking* or *got away again* don't exactly inspire confidence," she said.

"I guess they don't."

"I'll send a message when we get to Amera tonight," Tali said standing, "We should get going."

"Let's rest a minute?" Wade said.

"No, we can't just sit here together, watching the river flow. Kovan died saving that torquing Stone, and I have to get it back."

Either Wade registered her tone or her glare, but he stopped arguing and followed her to the horses who drank by the river's edge.

"You're right. You sure nothing else is wrong?" Wade asked.

Tali didn't know how to explain feeling like a killer. When she attacked and killed the Bonemen in Aquom, her powers had unleased beyond her control. Then again inside the Sagean Tomb, she had lashed out, after watching Kovan get killed. This time she had been in complete control, and the worst part was not in taking the lives of those men, but in the empty feeling that accompanied it. If Wade had let her, she would have slaughtered every man on that bridge, too. Still, she felt no remorse, and the absence of remorse had her chest tied up in knots. Throughout the morning, she was consciously taking deep breaths to clear her lungs.

Crossing up from the river, the terrain turned stark with the lush grass and abundance of trees becoming a land of dryer weeds and dirt. They made their way west into the setting sun, hoping to find a proper road on which to travel. When the dark clouds overhead started to gather, they picked up their pace to reach Amera before nightfall.

Amera was known as the most lawless and untamed city in all of Tovillore, a climate created by the many crystal mines in the region.

Crystals had always played an important role in the world, but the Great War brought crystal-powered devices to the world and a boom to crystal mining. The crafters in Ravenvyre, that Tali knew, always said it was an old technology only rediscovered. Alchemists and healers had been using crystals for centuries. With the crystal mines came the Mining Guild, and people trying to find they're fortune. The resulting prosperity bred corruption and opportunists.

When they arrived, they had just enough time to locate the headquarters for the Bounty Hunter's Guild before the storm hit. It started slow, and they didn't immediately look for shelter. The clouds rolling overhead came with wind gusts as they scouted the largest buildings and found swarms of armed men and women. At the center of the city, past the foundries, were two dominate structures: The Mining Collective and a sprawling gambling den.

It was obvious from the moment they arrived that they stuck out, a fact exaggerated by their snooping around as the downpour of rain began.

"We need to get off the street," Tali finally admitted.

"Agreed," Wade said.

The many inns surrounding the heart of the city were all crowded with suspicious looking people. Tali got the feeling everyone in the city was secretly watching everyone else; as though information was the main currency, not crystals.

The first three inns they attempted were out of rooms. Wade tried a fourth but quickly came sprinting back to the horse shelter under which Tali waited, shaking his head in defeat.

"Maybe we should look further out of town?" he suggested.

The many muddy streets were starting to be washed out and Tali's skin tingled with the sensation of more energy building in the sky.

"We need to hurry. It's only going to get worse," she said.

Wade got to his horse, and they started toward the south. The rain was pounding all around now and the streets that should have been deserted suddenly had a small band of men standing in the middle. Wade pulled up. The rain soaking in and weighing her clothes down, Tali couldn't see the men well, but the metal of their pulsators glinted in the lamplight.

"Where are you going?" one of the men said. He walked toward them unconcerned by the rain, his eyes focused on Wade.

"Wade?" Tali growled. She was growing tired of being pushed around.

"What?" he said.

"I'm done with this."

"What do you want me to do?"

"I don't need *you* to do anything."

Overhead, the storm had grown strong, and Tali tapped into it. To her, the atmosphere was sizzling. The lighting in microbursts was firing in the highest parts and she could feel it. The war of energy, alive and swirling.

The men kept closing in. They were shouting something at them, but Tali had blocked them out to concentrate. Wade was yelling her name and she put her hand out in front of her.

The men stopped.

She saw a grin crest the face of the leader, whose beard was tied into two obnoxious points. She closed her hand into a fist and pulled the lighting down between the gang of men.

The blinding thick bolt of energy hit with a blaring crash. She winced at the sound and her horse cried and lurched backward. She clung to the straps and pommel and held on. The immediate rush of air was followed by a shower of mud. When she opened her eyes, the men where gone and giant crater swelled the dirt road, water pooling in.

Wade rode near and pulled at her sleeve. She rounded on him, but his mud-drenched face soothed her wrath. They galloped away.

To the south, the rain was still raging, and the buildings of the city were now behind them. The houses and farms were sparse. Rain made visibility in the open country difficult, but Wade pointed to a silo and small house on a hilltop a league away as a destination.

It wasn't until they were right at the foot of the old silo that they could see it was both abandoned and in shambles. Wade jumped down and led the horses into the house. The roof looked to be barely holding together. Between the various holes in the roof and missing windows, the rain was hardly kept out at all. The first floor was flooded and muddy, but the walls were brick and sturdy.

Tali looked at Wade with a pinched nose and skepticism.

"Maybe the second floor is dry?" he said, climbing the rickety old set of stairs. She heard him slip and fall at the top.

She couldn't help but laugh. "Are you all, right?"

"Fine."

"We should find somewhere else to stay," Tali said.

"No, it's not so bad up here. It's dry at least."

Tali sighed and went up the old stairs. Her skin prickled and lightning flashed. The sky burst with light and sunk back into the night. Her body surged with energy again and she tried to control her breathing. She closed her eyes and exhaled. She steadied herself with her hand on the old newel post where a faded red paint had almost entirely peeled away. The walls on the second floor were in better shape. An old and beautiful wallpaper remained, and the smell of mud and mold from the first floor was gone. The second level smelled like the large trees nearby.

Wade took her hand to lead her away from the top of the stairs, "It's slippery at the top. Are you all, right?"

She smiled, "I'm fine, thank you."

In the back room, there were two windows busted out long ago where the rain blew in; otherwise, the room was dry.

"So, what do you think?" Wade said.

"I think we'll be lucky if the place holds together through the night," Tali replied.

"We can keep riding, but I didn't see anything else out there."

She looked at him. They were both soaked head to foot and she smiled. She knew if she said *no*, he would run out into the storm to look for another spot. She smiled and pretended her words were true.

"It's good, Wade," she said. *Maybe he needed a win as bad as she did.*

"Oh good," he said and began to unpack their things to sleep. When he finished, Wade began ringing out his shirt.

Tali retrieved her watch and messaged the others then put it away to sink against the old wall.

"What did you tell them?" Wade asked.

"That we tracked Nyra to Amera and need their help,"

"What do we do until they get here?"

"Tomorrow we can find a place to stay outside of the city, maybe closer to Arrow Bay if we have to," Tali said.

"Then what?"

"Then we'll start scouting the city until we find Nyra. I know she came here to try and pay for her freedom, but I doubt this Redmar is going to just let her go. Not after they hear about what happened in Corma."

"How do you know she's paying for her freedom?" Wade said.

"Something she said," Tali said, and Wade's eyebrow raised in confusion. She ignored him, "You saw the branding. She wants to be free of this Redmar."

"Yes, I saw the scar, but is it wise to start snooping around this city after what happened? We couldn't even get a room without raising suspicion. I'm pretty sure they noticed a crater in the street," he said.

"We're so close to getting the Stone back, I'm not sure I care," she said.

"But we're severely outnumbered," Wade argued.

"Now we are," she snapped back, "If you had just let me lay waste to the estate in Corma, we would already have the Stone."

Tali walked to the far window to look out at the city, feeling that perhaps she had spoken too harshly to her friend, though she wasn't wrong. She pulled at her soaked and heavy hair, trying to squeeze the rain away. Tali always liked her thick black hair, except when it was wet.

"I'm sorry," Wade said

Tali turned back to him, awaiting more, but he just looked at her.

"What's going on with you Wade? When we were stranded on the mountains with Learon, you were intent on going to Adalon. Then you let Learon go get Stasia in your place. And ever since your parents' house, you seem like you lost your nerve. I know you, Wade. You're no coward. You can play like one and you like to complain, but you're no coward. What is it?"

"It's the Scree," he said picking at the wallpaper with his fingers, avoiding eye contact.

"What about them?" she said. It was not what she expected him to say. If anything, she thought that after seeing Tara, he would have been more energized to keep going.

"We can't do anything for them, can we? For my sister."

"I don't know, Wade. I was hoping there would be an answer somewhere in that Stone. We saw how it contained a library of information. All of it from the Eckwyn Age. And we found Tara. We can save her."

"You don't understand, Tali. Tara is worse than dead. Her essence is gone and what remains is a horrific imitation," he said, his eyes filling with tears.

Tali came and sat in front of him. She leaned in when he still wouldn't look at her,

"All the reason more to fight, Wade."

"But it's my fault," he said.

"How is Tara your fault?"

"Not Tara. Nyra."

Tali rolled her eyes and nodded, "Well, you did invite her to come with us, but—"

"I know, and I'm sorry."

"I appreciate it, but losing the Stone is on all of us. I could have said *no*. Same with Learon. I think we all wanted someone else with us. To help us. We were all missing the band of crazies, and none of us knew what to do. We were so desperate; we didn't see the desperation in her. That's a failing all three of us share," Tali said.

"Band of crazies?"

Tali smiled, "That's what Learon and I would call Elias, Kovan, and Ellaria," she said, but thinking about Learon brought Tali to a silent pause.

Wade reached for her hand, "Hey, I'm sure he's fine."

She looked up at him, smiled, and shifted to sit beside him. The rain had died down some but now the wind was whipping it against the outside walls.

Tali rested her head on Wade's shoulder and listened to the repeating patter, "I hope so," she said.

The world was in the jaws of madness, on the brink of death. But the night, nature, was still alive. Something about that calmed her and she closed her eyes. Then she heard Wade's thoughts, *it feels good to have her here. She's so beautiful and...*

Tali twitched away a moment, rolled her eyes and rested her head back on his shoulder.

"Go to sleep, Wade."

TWENTY-ONE
MANIPULATIONS (VERRO)

On the island of Denmee, Verro Mancovi stood in the dimly lit library on the sub-level floor of the Well. The library was the private collection of the Court of Dragons, the room small and hexagonal in shape, with wood timber underbracing the stone floor overhead. Amongst the bookshelves were collections of artifacts on display, either encased in glass or on simple stone plinths to view.

Verro was searching for a specific book about the lineage of the Sagean Emperors. It was a very old book with a worn, smooth leather-bound hardcover, tattered by the twelve hundred years since its making. The details of the original cover drawing had faded, but it contained a decorative raised gold stamping of the Eye of the Sageans that remained. The two-thousand-year-old original sat on a podium encased in glass. The original seal-skinned cover and papyrus pages had not lasted the test of time. During the reign of Emperor Marghast, in the twelfth epoch, the use of human skin bindings was introduced. They held up about as well as the seal skin had but the practice was abandoned by the next ruler. Some texts remained from that era, but many were burned. The Linage Book included alchemist sigils and illustrations, but what Verro was really interested in was the Accounts of Talents. Each Luminary had talent beyond their abilities to harness energy, and the book detailed many of them.

He heard Aylanna's heels shuffle along the clean-cut stone from beyond the doorway before she spoke.

"Are you still searching for the Rune Book of the Sintering Fountain?"

Verro knew she would come along at some point. Aylanna was one for whom libraries were built. She could pore over every book three times over and still find value in subsequent passes. She would scold anyone for pulling a book off the shelf by the top spine and she demanded the servants keep fresh dry towels on hand to be replaced daily. *Clean hands keep books alive*, she would say. Among the Court, Aylanna Alvir had no rival in alchemy skill and probably sheer intelligence and knowledge as well. Unlike her supposed equal, Shirova Edana, who was hungry and deceptive, Aylanna was measured and thoughtful. While none of the acolytes were friends, there were some more trustworthy than others; Verro always placed Aylanna into that camp.

"No," Verro said with a sigh, "I've given up that search. I am looking for the book on the Sagean lineage. Have you seen it?"

"Yes. Well, *brilliant minds make bitter competition*," she quoted, "As it happens, I have it in my study below. Shall I have it brought to you?"

"No, let us adjourn to your study. There is no one better versed in its contents, and I would be happy if you would allow me to pick your brain, so to speak."

They exited the library together and into the open rotunda. Along the filtered rays of light, their feet stepped over the fallen green oblong leaves from the castana trees high above. At the final step off the winding stone stairs, they went through the lower ring of arches and into Aylanna's study. The Well had many rooms, but to Verro, at times it still felt like one big cellar, and they were the ones being preserved. Not every Court member had a chamber in the Well: only himself, Aylanna, and Batak kept rooms within. The others preferred their chambers in the Grand Estate on the ocean side.

The orange glow of the Caliber Stone Orb illuminated at their entrance. There were finely threaded tapestries on the walls amongst paintings and private bookcases. Some of the art had ghastly images and depictions of alchemist spells older than the Empire. Aylanna had done her best to furnish the cold space, and as a result, it was the warmest room in the underground complex despite the oddities inside.

She motioned for him to sit on a side chair, and she brought the book over to him, carefully placing it out in front of him before taking a seat at her writing desk. She spun the chair to face him.

"You will not find what you're looking for," Aylanna said dryly.

"And what is that?" Verro replied. He always tried to form his words into questions when he spoke to any of the Court members. Subtle questions in place of answers were the best way to reveal what his fellow acolyte was truly thinking. They were all constantly scheming and getting to the heart of those schemes took practice. Aylanna was notoriously the best at hiding her thoughts.

"A connection to the last Sagean Emperor, Mayock Kovall," she answered simply.

So, she did know what he was looking for, but what else did she know?

"I don't understand why. We know a connection must exist. There are too many signs that point to a shared lineage. Are they father and son, brothers, second cousins? How can the trail go cold?"

"My opinion is that it was expunged from the record," Aylanna said.

"Expunged?"

"Yes, redacted by someone purposely covering the trail."

"Who would have done such a thing or could have?"

"I have a few suspects."

Verro pondered a moment. *Who would have wanted such a thing erased from the record? Someone close to Mayock or Mayock himself, or someone interested in the destruction of the Empire.*

"The Traitor?" Verro said.

Aylanna smiled at his deduction, "That was my leaning as well. It's the obvious suspect and I believe the right one," she said.

"You seem to have thought this through, but that's not why you have the book in your study. What were you looking for?" Verro asked.

"I was curious about Edward's possible talents. Sometimes—not every time—but sometimes, the talents can be inherited. They can even skip generations, especially when it's not a direct line, as it's not with Edward."

"Do you worry about his effectiveness to rule? If his only talent is glamour shaping?" Verro asked.

"Of course, but I'm more worried about what he may be keeping from us," Aylanna said.

"Edward does as he is bidden. He went to Adalon as we asked and is now escorting the Soul Gem along the shallows of the Mainsolis Sea, is he not?"

"I am uncertain. But my misgivings cannot be substantiated. I am sure it is as you say."

"Why the misgivings in the first place?"

"Something my daughter, Shaylani, said. It's nothing to be concerned with. Please take the book with you and return it to the library," Aylanna said, and there was a sense of dismissal to it. He stood and slightly bowed, making to leave. At her door, he paused.

"Do you think the other book was taken by the Traitor?"

"I do not know what happened to the Dragon's Awakening Book, but I don't think the Traitor took it."

"You mean the Rune Book on the Sintering Fountain?" Verro said.

"Of course."

Aylanna apparently knew the book by a different name.

"I would feel better if we could find that book," Verro said.

"I agree."

"The Fountain was built by the ancients. You are the only one of us who has read the book before it went missing. What do you recall?"

"I read it once many years ago. It was written almost entirely in the dead language. So, I cannot say I know the contents, nor do I recall it clearly after so many years."

"That is a sloppy lie, Aylanna. I will be damned if you don't remember every word of every book you read. I don't care if you were a babe in your father's arms; when you read it, your memory's as certain as the sunrise."

"Please stop, you will make me blush, Verro. I recall parts vividly, but what I recall most is that the author of the text didn't truly know or understand the Fountain. In the two thousand years of Sagean rule, no ruler ever sought it out. It was known to exist, and its use described, but the Fountain was never activated. That worries me. Perhaps it shall be as we expect and perhaps not," Aylanna said.

"What are you afraid of?"

"I fear the Old One is playing us for fools as we played Qudin to access that Tomb. A ploy also devised by the Old One, I might add, when the thing was still communicating with us. The Old One is not to be trusted."

"What does the Orb of Delawyn say?"

"It has not worked in many months. Without a true prophet to attune with it, I fear the charge within has expired."

"That is unfortunate. I will think on what you have said. You are possibly the smartest one among us and we would be fools not to heed your warning. But you still intend to go through with it, correct?" Verro asked.

"I do."

"What do you think of Batak giving his position to his son?"

"Honestly, I have to wonder if it was his idea," Aylanna said.

Verro stepped out of the room, but placed his hand on the closing door, "By the way, what talents do you think Edward has that he has yet to reveal to us? You don't believe he has Mayock's dream walking, do you?"

"No. I believe he may have the ability of his great uncle, Emperor Sage Junhar: mind influencing."

"Interesting, and what would he use such an ability for?"

"Loyalty," she said simply.

Verro eyed her quizzically but understood the one-word explanation as the last word on the matter she was willing to divulge. "Good afternoon, Aylanna. Will I see you on the airship for Merinde?"

"I will be aboard."

He smiled at her answer and took his leave to wander the depths of the Well. His conversation with Aylanna left him curious. Inside the main meeting chamber, he went to the back of the room were the alchemists' pool of ghost sands resided. The sands were fine white granules of crystal and bone. A powerful medium for any alchemist sigil, exceeding blood by some measure. Verro inspected the sands, and a symbol was drawn within. He was no expert, but unless he was mistaken, the sigil in the sand was an innovation of sight. Aylanna was apparently keeping an eye on their new Sagean, tracking Edward through their connection to the ring.

Up on the surface, the afternoon light was casting long shadows in the gardens. Verro left the Well and its complex of chambers for the sunlight and fresh air. On a bench beneath the purple larch trees, Batak was talking with Herod Mimnark.

Herod sat resting his arms atop his silver cane, his manicured grey beard hiding his expressions. Herod was wise and amicable and the oldest of the acolytes. He was also the most trusted, but Verro was always suspicious every time he found any of the Court speaking in secret. He had to calculate what each was gaining from such a conversation, always determining motivations and positioning. In this case, he was sure their conversation centered around who was taking Herod's spot in the Genesis Chamber. Verro noted to himself to ask Batak later. Batak was as strong and determined as any of them. His power and wealth were unmatched, and his very nature made him probably the most feared and thus, the unelected leader of the Court.

The most suspicious was Herriman Nagal. Not that the man himself was suspicious or even very dangerous; it was because he was the one most used as a puppet. Everyone abused his spineless nature to sow seeds of rumors and false trails. When any of the Court were seen talking with Herriman, Verro knew they were up to something.

Verro strolled to the far edge of the gardens where a stone bench, chiseled in flowers and vines, was positioned to look out over the sea. It stood near the cliff's edge with a cropping of lush green cloud maples that gently swayed with the ocean breeze. When the sun had set and the lanterns in the garden lit, Batak came over and sat down.

"Good evening, Verro," Batak said.

"Hello, Batak. I saw you speaking with Herod, has he rethought his stance on the Sintering?" Verro asked.

"No. He doesn't believe he will survive the process," Batak said.

"He may be right. If I was seventy-six instead of fifty-six, I would have trepidations, too," Verro said.

"It was a factor for me in choosing to give my seat up for my son," Batak admitted.

"Has Herod decided who he is giving his seat to? Does he not have anyone in his family he wants for the selection?"

"He has a granddaughter named Stasia. Herod says she is the only one worthy of the position, but apparently she despises the family."

"What do you know about her?" Verro asked. He of course knew about the girl, but he wanted to hear what Batak knew.

"She goes to the Arcana and is top of her class. My spies tell me the professors believe she is the brightest student to come through there in years. Herod has made it clear that while he is giving up his seat on the Sintering Fountain, he doesn't want to give up his position with the Court."

"And do you feel the same?" Verro asked.

"I have no such delusion that once the Court is full of Luminaries, I will have the same standing. My intention is to serve as an aide to my son; help him navigate the Court while I maintain our investments," Batak said, rubbing his chin. He stopped and pointed back to the Well, "We saw a Warbird drift into the Well. I assume it's an update on Ellaria's movements?"

Verro opened his hand to reveal a small scroll in his palm which he handed to Batak. The Warbird's arrival had spurred him to the library that night.

"Ellaria was found traveling with the Showman's troupe on the Imperial Road," Verro said.

"What is she up to? Is Qudin with her?" Batak asked.

"Hiding, I suppose. I can't get a clear answer on Qudin."

"And Aramus, is he controlling himself?"

"Aramus is holding back on my orders. I've already sent word for a team to apprehend Ellaria in Midway. He is supposed to wait for them to move in. We could use her as a Cast for the Fountain," Verro said.

"Why the hesitation?" Batak asked.

"His last communication was odd."

"Odd how?"

"He cryptically said if bidden to act otherwise, he couldn't defy the Light."

"What does that mean?" Batak said.

"I don't know, but it is nothing to worry over. I have spies besides him. Aramus will behave himself."

"How can you trust him, Verro? Aramus is a weasel who thinks he is a wolf. I do not believe he will simply sit on his hands awaiting the intercepting force. Does Edward know about this?"

"He does. It was his idea."

"Interesting, I wonder if he believes Herod might choose his mother Helona, and therefore wants Ellaria for a Cast?"

"It wouldn't be a bad choice, but it is Herod's to make," Verro said.

"That may be so, or maybe we should track down this Stasia. Theomar wants Rotha, which is enough for me not to want that," Batak said.

"I agree. That is why I sent a squad of men to pick Herod's granddaughter up and bring her here," Verro said.

"Where is she?"

"It appears she is as smart as they say and has left Adalon recently, but my agents will catch up."

Batak gave a slight chuckle and smiled at the news. A servant came toward them, and they turned from their shared amusement.

"A ship called the Hollow-Dawn has arrived in the harbor, great Sirs. Three men are being escorted to the palace. Also, Lord Batak, you asked about the second ship in the harbor? The Wave-Feather set sail two hours ago."

Verro thanked him and they both rose from the bench. Verro knew the Wave-Feather was one of Aylanna's ships. He could only assume her daughter was on board. The second ship had arrived a day early.

"The Hollow-Dawn… is that the bounty hunter Theomar called for? The Rodairean, Razorkurvo Redmar?" Verro asked.

"It is," Batak said.

OUTSIDE THE MAIN HALL OF THE ESTATE, THEY FOUND A SMALL GROUP IN discussions near the courtyard pavilion. Theomar Kyana was speaking with the bounty hunters already and Aylanna stood next to him. She cast Verro an exasperated look when he approached. Though Aylanna was a Rodairean herself, she often distanced herself from brutes like Razor. Theomar's greeting of the guests without waiting for Batak and Verro was a minor insult, one over which Batak could not fully hide his displeasure as Verro was doing. However, Batak's crossed arms and scowl dwindled under Redmar's deadly glare.

Razorkurvo Redmar was large and imposing man. He was a good head taller than the lot of them. His face was stoic, and his golden skin chiseled and scarred, including a long gash down the length of his left arm and three evenly spaced cuts to the left side of his face. Verro was sure he had never met a man with a more murderous glaze to his eyes. The skin that was clear of scared tissue was covered in tattoos characteristic of men from the Zulu Sea.

Razor had two other men with him, both looking like equally serious men, but less frightening than their leader. Theomar turned at their arrival and introduced them.

"Verro Mancovi and Batak Asheen, our guests have arrived. May I present Razorkurvo Redmar, and his associates, Joran Dodge and Targo Shine?"

Verro knew the names of all three by reputation. Razor Redmar was one of the leaders of the Moonstalkers and infamously the best bounty hunter in Amera. Targo Shine was the head of the Deviants' Syndicate out of Eloveen, and Joran Dodge, and his brothers headed the Reckers' Syndicate in Adavan. Word had it Kovan Rainer had killed the younger brother in a duel a few years back. Joran had a medium build and was plainly dressed without much flash or style. He had an empty pulsator holster at his hip and a mustache to go along with his scruff. Targo was a dark-skinned man with a black hat that shadowed his eyes. He was slim, fit, and wore a white pinstriped shirt under a brown patterned vest. Unlike his associates, his clothes were more befitting of the city. His empty holsters were strapped at his back, and he held his brown suit coat in his arms.

They each nodded in turn at the introductions.

"I was thanking them about our cargo coming through Amera unscathed. I didn't hear of any adversarial issues of its transport, and they are here to receive payment for a secure passage," Theomar said.

"All three of you helped secure the cargo from the Red Spear?" Verro said.

"No. Only me," Razor said and his eyes didn't blink, boring holes into Verro before he turned away.

"Mr. Dodge and Mr. Shine will be helping us with the Band of the Black Sails. They have been raising a fit in Aquom recently. Mr. Redmar was invited to receive payment and our gratitude in person before returning to the west," Theomar explained.

"Correction, only Mr. Shine will be aiding you. Joran will be returning with me to Amera," Redmar said.

"I stand corrected," Theomar said.

"Mr. Redmar, you're aware of the Sagean's need for crystals in the coming war?" Verro asked.

"I am. Is our standing deal obsolete?" Redmar asked.

"I believe the parameters of the deal need to be renegotiated. However, I'm sure a man such as yourself can see the benefits of working with the Sagean," Verro said.

"I am a simple man, Mr. Mancovi. I think in terms of assets and value. If the compensation is appropriate, I don't see any reason the Moonstalkers can't work with the Sagean. Since the Sagean is not here, I will wait to discuss the details with him."

"We are the Sagean's Counsel, we can speak for him," Theomar said.

"The Moonstalkers would still prefer an audience with the Sagean himself," Redmar said.

"We will see what we can do then," Theomar said.

"I'll walk you both out," Verro said. Redmar nodded and the three of them moved towards the sprawling landscaped stairs. Redmar was not a businessman or entrepreneur, but he was advantageous. Verro wouldn't be surprised if he had been secretly trying to unite all the Syndicates. They all used the bounty hunters anyway as contract killers. It was possible Razor could see the value in a partnership, but it would have to be negotiated by someone Razor felt had equal power to himself.

"What has you rushing away? You only just arrived?" Verro asked.

"We received word that a lost messenger of mine is returning to me with a gift. A significant item that may be of interest to the Sagean and will increase the Moonstalkers negotiating power," Redmar said.

Verro was certain Razor saw the Moonstalkers as outside the reach of the authority, and he was right. They had made a very smart move in relocating their base of operations years ago from Anchor's Point on the

Uhanni, where they controlled the river shipping to Amera. It was a move purely for greed but now as the Court of Dragons attempted to retake the world, Amera loomed as a large thorn in their side; one that would have to be dealt with eventually. Verro had slowly been maneuvering forces into the surrounding area to retake the city, but his plan wasn't yet ready to proceed.

"Is that so? And what sort of item would be of interest and value to the Sagean?" Verro said.

"I'm told it is an ancient relic," Redmar said.

"The Sagean is indeed interested in all relics," Verro said.

"I suspected as much. I am sure we can find an agreement that benefits all. The Syndicates are very interested in a partnership," Redmar said.

Verro held no doubt that the others had heard about their dismantling of the Supremacist Syndicate in Adalon and were trying to curry favor now as opposed to standing against them.

"After what was done to the other Syndicates that refused to negotiate in Adalon, I am sure they are. However, the Sagean and his Court hold the Moonstalkers in high regard. You have regulated the lawless and it's the Sagean's intention to support your endeavors in the new empire," Verro said.

They halted on the platform above the docks. Redmar told Joran to go on to their ship. When Joran was out of sight, Redmar spoke, "What exactly is the Sagean offering?"

"Continued prosperity, Mr. Redmar," Verro said.

"And extermination if we decline?"

Verro didn't want to let on how much the new empire needed Amera's crystal mines; almost equally important, the Moonstalkers familiarity with the New World and the prospering underground crime industry across the ocean.

"The Sagean doesn't want that, Mr. Redmar. We are tightening our grip on this world and every hand allows us to hold it tighter, and more importantly, to reach further," Verro said.

"Razor scrutinized him and stepped away, "The Moonstalkers are amenable to a partnership. Let us know when the Sagean is available to solidify a new understanding."

"Mr. Redmar, one more thing. Be on the look out for one of our little messaging birds. We may have a special assignment for you."

"A target you want eliminated?"

"Yes. A very dangerous one," Verro said.

"I see. Send the details to my business partner in Amera," Redmar said.

"We will."

Verro watched Razor board his ship before returning to the others now inside the Estate. Verro said very little throughout the remainder of the meeting, choosing to watch and listen. By the end, the only thing he had discovered was that Aylanna moved her timetable up for control over Rodaire. Everyone on the Court was aware of her plan, but she was now positioning to take control immediately after the Sintering Ceremony. Verro had known for a long time that her heart was set on taking over the ancient palace in Ravenvyre. As far as Verro was concerned, Aylanna could have her home country, Theomar could control the north, and Batak could have his son as a Luminary. Verro had his own goals. He had long believed Edward wasn't strong enough to live through the Machine. After Verro was reborn as a Luminary and infused with the essence of the warrior king, Danehin, Verro would be able to take control of the Court and the New World.

TWENTY-TWO
THE CRESCENT PIER (KOVAN)

Kovan, Semo and the Hazon man Mayzanna Buroga, sailed into the trench between Adalon and the Crescent Pier. A crossway usually restricted to fishing vessels was now a crowded harbor without proper docking for either side, a rerouting of ships by order of the Sagean to leave the main ports open for private shipments. As a result, the fishing ways between Adalon City and the Crescent Pier were overflowing with shipping vessels and passenger ships.

Kovan and Semo spent the early morning aboard their vessel practicing swords until each dripped with sweat: Semo rebuilding his strength and Kovan restoring memory to his muscles. Kovan felt it was almost like reconnecting his mind to his body.

Both men were Darkhawk-trained fighters, the elite squad of warriors headquartered in the New World. There were specific techniques to fighting with different swords, forms derived from centuries old styles. Many of the most unique customs had been lost to history or remained closely guarded teachings of individual nations. The Rodairean's had the most formal style, and they were the most gruelingly trained. It was a style that had evolved from years of use with the same long-sweeping meiyoma blades. The best he could remember, the style was many variations on the same forms, all involving arching strikes that brought powerful impacts, with an emphasis on speed strikes. Unlike the other styles, the Rodaireans' was more a dance with a rhythm and flow. The speed of the fight could be slow with deliberate back-and-forth engagement, or it could flash with blinding speed, but it was all part of a continuous movement, a style called the *Way of the Wind*.

They were sparring using all the styles they knew and the more Kovan practiced with Semo, the more he felt his spirit mend.

In Tovillore, Bonemen soldiers were trained in the style of broadsword and shield. When small uprisings happened during the Empire's reign, the sword and shield combination was vital. The shield offered the essential protection against staffs, lances, and spears— weapons common to the lower orders and outlanders. The Bonemen's style was predicated on leg strength to pair the shield defense with quick sword attacks.

The Zenoch trained with heavy longswords. Kovan couldn't remember the intricacies of it except that it was based on bursts, passes, and drives and warding. But he did recall they were equally good sword and shield fighters because a greater amount of their warriors were axe wielders. The wasteland tribes of the New World had their own style, but it was unknown to outsiders; so too, the Tregoreans. The Darkhawks trained in every method. Kovan could feel the styles returning to him from muscles that slowly recalled how to move.

Kovan knew most of the techniques and it was obvious from his skill that Semo knew them well. Semo was swift and lethal. But he struggled against the Rodairean style, so Kovan continued to employ it until Semo learned to combat that as well.

Sparing like this made Kovan wonder why he grew to hate the sword so much. Whatever the reason was, it was lost in his mind for the moment. *Maybe it is a truth locked away in the second cube, or the third.*

Semo was easily twenty-five years younger than him, but Kovan still found himself growing frustrated that he couldn't land a finishing move. Semo was fast enough to overcome his deficiencies in the style to protect himself. Kovan switched to a style he knew would trip Semo up. Give or take, every technique borrowed from one another and the Darkhawks were trained to handle each one, all except the style employed by the Shadowyn.

The Shadowyn style, like their people and culture, was unknown. The very location of their lands wasn't precisely understood and charted. Their secrecy had held for many centuries, maintaining protection from intruders. Elias was the only outsider to have ever been allowed in. That funny short sword of his, the elum blade, was immaculately made and could cut unlike anything Kovan had ever seen. He had a lot of experience watching Elias and sparing with him. A component of the style incorporated using the blade in various positions to defend and attack as a basis for countermoves. Some strikes were, in a way, a purposeful riposte, a forced defensive clash to generate the intended counterstrike.

Suddenly, the memories of sparing and fighting with swords were with him and Kovan spun and struck. A perfectly placed flick disarmed Semo in stride and with a flash, he swung the practice sword to Semo's neck and froze, stopping only when Buroga's keen eye, watching the fight, called out to halt.

"Kovan!"

The sound broke through his trance and Kovan lowered the sparing sword. His chest heaved from the exertion. Kovan backed away astounded. Not that he had finally beaten Semo, but at how memories had come back to him. Not from some crazy cube, but from somewhere deep within.

"What was that?" Semo gasped for air, "Shadowyn?"

"Yes,"

"I wonder how that holds up to the longsword?" Semo asked.

A well-trained longswords man was difficult to defeat. Their reach and power were deadly and their sword equal at defense as to offense.

"Elias told me once that the Shadowyn way was based on countering all others, through distraction, speed, and most importantly, flexibility."

"Must be why their blade is so unique. But it's all backwards. You're literarily holding it backwards sometimes. Elias was successful with this technique in the War?"

"You have no idea," Kovan said, wiping sweat from his neck with a towel. Talking of Elias and the Elum Blade had him remembering when Elias first returned to the Darkhawks.

After disappearing for a year, he had returned at the brink of war when they were training before leaving the New World. No one remembered him much and few wanted him let back in. Elias had offered them a test: if anyone could beat him, he would transfer to a different regimen. The arrogance and confidence of soldiers, especially hard-trained Darkhawk warriors, was boundless, so they had accepted without a second thought. Elias decimated everyone on the training yard that day. Kovan was the only one who ever came close to beating him. He used to tease Elias that he cheated somehow. They had been friends before he had left and best friends after he had returned. Later, when Kovan discovered Elias was a Luminary, he had teased him about cheating again, that he had used his powers to increase his speed. After their first battle, during the Great War, Kovan saw first hand that Elias had actually held back when sparring. He saw the effects when Elias did meld his powers with his sword. The speed was blinding and the destruction horrific.

The memory gave him a shudder. *Maybe that was why I hate the blade,* but he didn't think that was it.

When their ship finally found a spot to dock, Kovan insisted Semo and Buroga stay aboard while he looked around. He climbed the rocky coastline to the proper island in time to see a large fleet of ships leaving the Crescent Pier to the south. There was one large steam-powered cargo ship being escorted by four navy ships called Mimnark Runners. The Runners were nimble sailing ships with reinforced sideboards and mounted circulator guns. They were easily recognizable as Citadel Navy vessels even if one didn't know the name of them.

Kovan assumed the cargo ship carried the glowing crate Semo had described, and that Danehin was probably aboard as well. It could be the only reason for such extreme measures. The south end of the pier had been shut down all day and it took Kovan awhile to find a way inside. But he was never able to get close enough to see the contents of the ship before it set off. The entire island was crawling with Bonemen and a few of those evil Rendered machines stomping around. The automatons were excellent at crowd control. Most people ran in fear from them and thus, they had cleared the docks quickly.

Kovan was set to go back to their ship when he spotted the Sagean walking the Pier, his contingent of guards in red cloaks surrounding him. They all loaded into a large carriage and left the Pier, crossing back over the bridge.

Kovan found it curious that the Sagean wasn't aboard the ship. He followed them to the Adalon airfield where he was denied access. The field had been temporarily closed for the Sagean. An hour later, a large airship glider sailed overhead, followed by a giant metal cloudparter. The glider was essentially a wind drifter, only unlike any Kovan had seen before. It had a series of flat sails overhead that stretched from bow to stern, with large propeller fans underneath wide-sweeping wings. The outside shell was a mix of wood and metal, and the hull had an almost threatening shape with three silver spikes from the tip down. Kovan was unsure how it worked but was positive the Sagean was aboard.

He scrambled back through the city and to the boat they had taken from Searest, managing the steep stone path from the barter's bridge to the trench. They set sail and tracked the airship as best they could until it disappeared over the land. They had traveled nearly to the shores of Ash Field when it was lost from view.

Based on the trajectory, Kovan reasoned the ship could be headed for Pardona or Amera. The captain took them to the cape town of Arvenee. From there, they would have to continue on horseback. His eyes flashed over the land that stretched before them, and his vision was filled with a sight that wasn't there: the green fields in sway with the breeze evaporated into a mass of banners and soldiers riding over the hills, trampling the fields that would soon need harvesting to feed the people, captives inside war-torn cities under siege. It was an image from the past, the start of the Great War, before the entire nation had blood in their eyes and black in their hearts.

"Kovan Rainer?" Buroga asked.

The noise jarred his attention and his mind cleared to see Buroga's large hand on his shoulder. Kovan was unsure how long Buroga had been calling his name.

"Yes?" he answered.

"Are we perusing through the valley or returning back to the coast?" Buroga asked.

If they sailed to the south after Danehin, the navy escort would most likely blow them out of the water, and they would be moving further away from his friends. He was sure they were still on the mainland and taking the path that wound around the same crossroads as his group, increasing their chance of finding each other. For him, that was more important than following a curious object, the Sagean, or Danehin.

"Through the valley," he said, and charged ahead.

MIDWAY

To Adalon

To Avence

To Anchor's Point

The Farming Fields

4
3
1
2

To Valley Point

The Airfield

The Imperial Road

To Hazel Point

1. Factory Row
2. Market Clearing
3. The Barrel Theatre
4. Fiar Grounds

Map Commissioned By
The United Scholars Guild

TWENTY-THREE

MIDWAY (LEARON)

Midway was a large city along the Imperial Road that marked the midpoint from Adalon to Hazel Point, a hilltop crossroads city in the south. The people of Midway were often referred to as the *forge-born*. There were more forges, factories, refineries, and manufacturing companies in Midway than in any other city in the world. The name Midway sounded like a simple pass-through town for travelers on their way to other places, and the city had developed a sort of underdog spirit, based on a perceived sense of inferiority. There had been many attempts to rename the city: Copperville, Tinker's City, or Steeltown, for the many smelting factories. However, no other name could ever stick.

Learon had longed to see the city of the forge-born. He explained as much to Meroha as they entered the city limits. It was a city of copper, bronze, and steel. Artless stone foundations with four-story buildings of wood-framed simplicity, all clad and ordained with metal; siding, panels, hammed and bolted. Learon marveled at the details.

Their first stop was the travel office on the northern end of the city. Learon asked around for a young woman with blonde hair that would have been traveling alone the last few days. It took most of the day, but they found someone that had seen her at the fourth station they tried. She had asked for a hotel recommendation and the man remembered her because she was adamant that she could afford one of the nicer inns near the heart of the city. He suggested two places: The Imperial Inn and The Bronzedale. They left to track her down at either place.

Outside the Imperial, Learon thought they would have to start over when a woman's voice called out his name. Stasia was rushing down the street with a drink in one hand and food in the other, but she threw her arms around Learon as though they were long lost friends.

"Learon, I can't believe you are here," Stasia said sincerely and pulled away, "Thank you for coming."

Meroha stood by waiting to be introduced, as Stasia ignored her completely.

"Stasia, this is our friend Meroha. She is from—"

"Kotalla?" Stasia finished, "Your friend is from, I mean? I'm sorry. Hello, Meroha I'm Stasia Mimnark. I'm excited to meet you. I'm excited you both are here. Let's get off the street and up to our rooms."

"Rooms?" Meroha said.

"Yes, I got two rooms on the fifth floor."

A doorman opened the great gilded doors and they passed inside. The lobby of the Imperial was dark and faintly lit by golden wall sconces and recessed ceiling lights. The interior was a mix a smooth-stained wood, dark blue wall fabric, tinted glass, and metal accents. A lattice of thin bronze was fixed to the ceiling, and it rolled down to frame the various openings to adjacent rooms and hallways. A large common room was set to the back beyond the front desk.

Stasia led them to a set of doors where a man awaited them. He pressed a button on the wall to call the lift.

Up at the rooms, the mystcat jumped out from Learon's bag to inspect. Stasia unlatched bolts at the wall and pulled the large panels free to the connected room. She turned back and her eyes lit up at seeing the cat.

"Oh, my Blue Sacred Light, that's a mystcat," Stasia said.

"It is," Learon said.

"Is it yours? Those are supposed to be attracted to Luminaries. They're very rare."

"Stasia, you should probably sit down while I catch you up. First, I wanted to ask if you've seen Ellaria Moonstone?"

"No, why?"

"We received a message from her last night. She said she was heading here. I think it's why the cat is so frantic. She's trying to find her Luminary."

"And who is that?" Stasia asked, wide-eyed and intent.

"Qudin Lightweaver."

"You have Qudin's mystcat? Alright, tell me everything. Start from the beginning, and don't leave anything out. Otherwise, I'm going to ask a million questions. Well, I'm still going to ask a lot of questions," Stasia said.

She looked at him suspiciously, but she sat with obvious excitement from her curiosity. Learon told her everything. From the moment he met Elias Qudin, the Quantum Man, to Tali discovering she was a Luminary. He told her about the wave gates and the fight inside the Sagean Tomb and Edward being the Sagean. The largest gasp was when he told her how they had broken into the Arcana Archives and stole a bag full of books. Somewhere through the telling, she stood and paced around the room. After he had finished with their trip through The Jaws, she was quiet.

"I'm going to kill Wade. It's as simple as that," she said fuming.

"Don't be mad at him, he—"

Stasia cut him off, "No, no. Don't defend him. Friends share their burdens, only enemies keep secrets. He should have told me and let me decide, but he didn't trust me."

"I think he was trying to protect you," Learon told her, but she shrugged it off with a constant shaking of her head, "Wade is good man. If you want to be mad at him, fine. But we are all in this storm together and we need every one of us to get through it."

She looked like she wanted to argue, but she sat down and pulled at her blonde hair. "I was in a carriage with him you know. A few days ago."

"Who?" Learon said.

"The headmaster. I mean the Sagean Lord—Edward Knox."

"What?"

"He gave me a lift to the Crescent Pier. He was creepy. He offered me a job, actually."

"Really?"

"Yes. He said if I wanted, I could work with scientists on a new branch of science that he knew they were developing."

"What was it?"

"My guess, something to do with crystals and energy. He didn't go into the details, and I didn't ask because he made me uncomfortable. These Scree, their souls have been taken?" Stasia said.

"That's what we believe. Tali said they felt empty to her," Learon said.

"I can't get over Tali being a Luminary. That poor woman, I bet she's freaking out," she remarked, "So the question is, what are they doing with the souls?"

"We don't know, but it can't be good. That's why we need to find Ellaria and Elias."

"Maybe they haven't arrived yet. I don't know how the Imperial Road was in the south but coming in from north, it was packed. We should go out tonight and look for her. Here, I thought we might go to the see the *Show of Wonders*."

"We saw posters for that around the city," Meroha said.

"Apparently they have a magic woman they call the Great Avari Nova. She is supposed to be amazing. Her first shows are sold out, but I thought we might be able to get in. Sometimes you can find street-winks that sell the tickets," Stasia said.

"I'm ready, let's go out and look for them. We need to see if Bazlyn's ship is in the airfield. I expect we beat him by a day, but I don't know. If we wind up with nothing, we can check out the Showman's *Show of Wonders*. I need a break, as it is," Learon said.

"I'll stay with the cat if that's all right, Learon," Meroha said.

"Of course, Are you sure?" Learon said.

"I'm exhausted from traveling and traversing the city all day. Honestly, I don't know how you have the energy," Meroha said yawning. She pulled out her book on the Great War and crawled into bed.

Learon and Stasia left the Inn with clouds gathering in the evening sky and a light rain falling on the stone walks and paved streets.

On the outskirts of Midway, the buildings were relatively small. There was an edge of cottage style houses amongst factories. Everything was built in tight, but not to great heights. At the heart of the city, the height of the structures grew, and Learon could see the influences of Adalon on the industrial city. Open rooftops linked to adjacent buildings in a massive web of raised communities. Unlike Adalon that had large, elevated walkways to traverse from one end to the other, these were all constructed organically as buildings were so close together. Short bridges crossed over and back and the upper levels were like a whole other city.

Everywhere he looked, Learon found the dominant detail was the many open, steel-webbed structures. Most were green in color or faded blue and at the merchant's park, the giant steel struts held entire buildings high above the ground, the space below left open for a community of merchants, a diverse emporium scattered between the steel skeleton.

They walked the city for hours, stopping at various inns, hoping to find some trail of their friends but came up empty. The refineries and forges pumped steam and heat into the city and the many globe gas lamps struggled to sufficiently light the streets. Eventually, they made their way to the airfield in the south of the city, but the station was closed.

"No one's allowed in there this evening," the station teller told them.

"When does it open?" Learon asked.

"Tomorrow, ships can land again," he said dismissively. They pried for more information, but the teller wasn't talking.

They left and decided to give up their search. Stasia took them back to the heart of the city and toward the circus grounds. She had a good feel for the city already, even though she had only been there one day. Midway was relatively flat, but the west end pitched slightly to the river and some open fields were found in between the richest buildings in the city.

When the lights of the circus tents came into view, they stopped on the sidewalk to look at it all. There were a range of giant striped tents and a huge crowd of people. All of it was positioned next to the renowned Barrel Theatre, a round monolithic building with arches all around the outside and colored panels of stained glass in every other opening. Stone columns ran from the base to the domed roof. Even from three blocks away, Learon could see an intricate carving in the stonework.

They admired the sight that lit up the city night and embarked toward it.

Stasia was starting to speak while they walked, "That's the theatre. There is a—" but she never finished her sentence. A man lurched out of the alleyway shadows and grabbed her. His hand clamped over her mouth, stifling her scream.

Learon reached for her, but another man charged into him. Learon could see the shape coming and tried to sidestep the man, but he had grabbed Learon's shirt and tugged him to the ground.

When he got to his feet, the man had drawn his sword. The hilt was gold and the handle wrapped in red. Learon recognized the sword, a replica to those carried by Bonemen soldiers; but this man was not dressed like a soldier. He wore plain clothes and long coat for the rain.

"Stasia!" Learon called out and the man pointed his sword at him. Learon pushed the flap of his jacket aside and drew the Elum Blade. It was not an intimidating sword with its small stature but when the patterned steel caught the light, it commanded reverence. The man facing him looked at it quizzically and attacked.

Learon blocked a range of swings and attempted jabs. He tried to counter, but he was not a skilled swordsman. His attacks were easily blocked, but he was fast with the short and light blade. Learon could see no quick end to the fight if neither man could land a blow, and he needed to catch up to Stasia who was being dragged off into the night.

He noticed the man kept their fight under the light of the overhead lamp. When the opportunity came, Learon baked into the darkness of the alleyway from which the men had sprung. He hoped his eyesight would give him an edge and he was right. His attacker followed but was soon blinded by the darkness. Learon's eyes adjusted and he could see the man walking forward with his sword held in front, looking blindly for Learon. When he passed, Learon ran the Elum Blade through the man from the back. He stabbed and withdrew it in a quick motion. The sharpness of the curious sword cut without resistance. Learon was running to the far end of the ally before the man had fallen.

At the opposite side, the man was still dragging Stasia against her will and trying to pull her into a black carriage that waited at the walk. She was putting up a fight. She kicked another man in the face as he tried to force her into the cabin. He reeled back and the man holding Stasia whacked her over the head with the handle of his pulsator.

Learon's pulse quickened and he burst out of the alley, sliding low into the man with the gun. He came up with the point of his blade into him. The man convulsed. The stunned look of the second attacker kept him from pulling his own gun for a moment. It was a moment of hesitation that killed him. In a seamless motion, Learon slid the blade from the one abductor and threw it into the chest of the other.

The man had a hold of Stasia with one arm and dropped her once he was wounded. Stasia fell onto the side of the carriage. A trickle of blood rolled down her check from the top of her head.

"Stasia!" Learon said, and he caught her from completely falling limp into the gutter. He got her to her feet, but her eyes struggled to focus on him. Learon retrieved the Elum Blade, cleaned the blood with the dead man's coat, and housed it back at his hip. He put an arm behind Stasia and supported her as she stumbled forward. A sudden sense of dread washed over him as he appraised their swords. The Sagean symbol of an illuminated eye was etched at base of the steel. He had killed three men in public and from what he could tell, they were most likely Bonemen soldiers or Sagean guards.

"We need to get back to the inn," he said, "but I don't know the way. I can carry you, but you have to point out where to go."

"I can walk," Stasia said weakly.

They rushed along the softly lit streets. Stasia had them take a few alleyways while they weaved back through the city. When they finally reached the open merchant's field, Learon found his bearings and helped lead them back to the inn.

Stasia made it to the lift before she passed out in his arms. Learon carried her into the room, kicking at the door for Meroha to come. She opened it and was quickly startled upon seeing Stasia's limp form.

"What happened?" Meroha said moved aside to allow them through.

Learon laid Stasia down on the bed and looked back at Meroha, "Can you get me water and a small towel?"

While he propped Stasia's head atop pillows and covered her with a blanket, Meroha reappeared with a cup of water and a towel.

"Get the cloth damp for me," Learon took off his crystal necklace from around his neck. Meroha handed him the cloth. He laid the crystal on her forehead and the cloth overtop.

"What happened?" Meroha said.

Learon than went into detail about the night, the airfield, and the attempted abduction.

"Then Stasia said she was dizzy, and she passed out in the lift," he finished.

Meroha listened to his story and rushed to his side when blood dripped from his wrist. "Learon, you're hurt!"

Meroha rolled his sleeve back with a fearful look demanding an explanation.

"I'm not. It's not my blood."

" Did you kill the men?" Meroha asked, as she handed him another towel to clean himself.

"Yes," he said looking around, "Did the mystcat take off?"

"No, Merphi is on the balcony. She was frantic at one point but then calmed as if she lost her connection. Since then, she has been out there, staring into the city."

Learon pulled a chair close and sat with his feet propped up on the windowsill. Elias's sword leaned up on the wall. Sometime in the early morning, before the sun had come up, he heard Stasia stir, and his eyes popped open.

"Learon?" she called out in the darkness of the room until she spotted him and smiled.

"I'm here, what do you need?" he said at her side. She lifted her hand up and he took it gently.

Stasia smiled softly and locked eyes with him, "I was looking for you is all. I never said thank you. You saved me. Thank you."

"I'm here. Get some rest. You still owe me a night at the show, and I expect you to take me tomorrow."

Stasia softly chuckled and closed her eyes to go back to sleep. Learon turned to his chair again and found Meroha sitting in it.

"I'll sit by her side for the rest of the night. You look exhausted, Learon. Go sleep in the other bed."

"Thanks, Meroha."

Learon returned to the adjacent room and stretched out atop the bed. It was thick wood with multiple layers of silk sheets, though he did not cover himself with them. He did not want to be encumbered by sheets if something happened; he was also growing used to the idea of leaving as small a footprint behind as possible. He was already leaving a trail of blood and that was enough. The rain had begun again and was even stronger now. He opened the window slightly to listen and smell the rain. That cat had come back and rested beneath the sill. Learon returned to the bed. The sound outside was magnified by the abundance of metal and tin throughout the city and the smell was bright with a fragrance of metal and rust. Periodically, the rain hit against the window and the breeze blew cool though the opening. Learon listened to the sound of it until he fell asleep.

THE MORNING LIGHT WAS MET WITH A KNOCK ON THEIR DOOR. LEARON sprung up and snatched the blade from its leaning. Meroha looked up at him with her eyebrows drawn. She had the same curious thought he did. *Who could be at their door?*

The knock came again, and Learon reached the main door. He put his ear to the wood to try and listen for how many people were in the hall.

"Learon, are you there?" a woman's voice called but he didn't recognize the sound.

Learon opened the door to find Darringer's scout, Vera. As soon as she recognized him, she pushed through the opening and took off her hat.

"Close the door," she said. Learon's confusion only escalated.

"What's going on. How did you find me?"

"I tracked you in the city yesterday. But lost you. It doesn't matter; Darringer's hurt."

"What? What happened?" Learon asked.

"We went to Seflor to intercept the Sagean's troops coming down south. Those Rendered were as you said. They were like walking night-mares. We were easily defeated and had to retreat."

"How many made it out, where is the rest of the squad?" Learon said.

"Most of us. Darringer was wounded in the leg, but it will heal. We are camped in the south of the city."

"Why haven't you pushed on, back to Pardona?" Learon asked.

"We needed supplies and Darringer wanted me to warn you. The army is coming."

"Army? How many?"

"At least ten legions worth, and two Rendered with each."

"Ten thousand soldiers are headed for Midway. Why?"

"Darringer believes they want to control the Imperial Road"

Learon nodded at the assessment. At some point, Stasia had sat up and listened to their conversation.

"Learon, what if they're coming for Qudin?" Meroha said.

He turned back to Vera, "When will they be here?"

"Is that who you're working with? Vera said her eyes wide, "Dar-ringer said it was someone important, but—"

"How long?" he asked again, impatiently.

"Two days."

TWENTY-FOUR
THE FINAL CURTAIN (ELLARIA)

Ellaria was furious with Archibald. They had arrived in Midway the day before and she immediately asked the sisters if they could check in on Elias while she went to the airfield to schedule a winddrifter out of the city. She trekked across the steel city, only to find out that the airfield had been closed for the arrival of a ship coming in that night. Ellaria had never heard of such a thing. She didn't waste time worrying about what it meant, but she had a feeling Archibald had somehow arranged for the airfield to be closed. She couldn't prove it, but she wouldn't put it past him either. Even though two people had been murdered, Archibald was still singularly focused on the three-night stay in Midway. All he could talk about was performing at the Mosaic Barrel Theater. The building was giant and almost too fancy for the city of metal and steam.

Ellaria had been to Midway many times, often on trips between Adalon and the southern cities. The industry and manufacturing in the last ten years had turned a small town into one of the larger cities in Tovillore. The opulent city surroundings made the troupe temporarily forget about the murder amongst them. Archibald had hired additional greencoats to patrol the tents and fairgrounds, but Ellaria was worried that the perpetrator was cloaking their movements with magic.

Because she had no other choice, Ellaria performed her show that night to a sold-out crowd and because she couldn't take Archibald's pleading, she performed two additional shows that night.

Her frustration with being trapped boiled over and she couldn't conceal it anymore. She was done with hiding; it was time to escape from

Tovillore for good. Time was running out to heal Elias and she had a growing sense that the world was on the precipice of war. What she couldn't understand was what the Sagean was waiting for. Civil unrest on the Mainland was unorganized and while every city, would soon experience massive upheaval, it wasn't going to amount to anything strong enough to stop the Sagean, not with the Citadel's full backing. The new Sagean's forces were established and powerful enough to thwart any rebellion. The war for the New World had to be the next move, but something had kept it from happening.

When the dawn came up on day two in Midway, Ellaria dressed and left the fairgrounds early. Again, she asked one of the sisters to watch Elias while she went to the airfield to purchase a winddrifter's service. Her path was diverted to avoid a murder investigation that had greencoats and Bonemen blocking off a few streets up the road from the circus.

At first, she feared that the murderer had struck again, but a quick examination of the incident and rumors from the watching crowd suggested three men had been killed in a sword fight, though no one had seen or heard anything.

She moved on to the airfield. The pickings were slim, but she found a shabby winddrifter with simple yellow sails and dual balloon lifts that could get them at least as far as Adavan. From there, they would probably have to find a better winddrifter and a skilled aeronaut willing to take them across the Zulu, and one brave enough to risk their life for money and take them over the guarded Nahadon coast into the Tregorean Province.

She paid for the flight and returned through the city. The winddrifter wouldn't be airworthy until late that night, but she intended to get Elias and head back to wait. There were only two other ships there and both were under contract. She didn't want the pilot to take another fare. There was a large cloudparter and an expensive looking winddrifter taking up half the field.

Elias had been peaceful the last two days. His tendency to sleep, eat, and move around had not increased, and neither had his condition progressed or deteriorated. He still mumbled at night in his sleep. Ellaria couldn't interpret much from the mumblings, but she heard it all. Her own sleep was still nightmare-filled. Elias's temperature still incomprehensibly fluctuated from freezing cold to sweating hot. She supplemented the usual crystal treatment with a warding spell, but nothing she tried helped. His sleep was more restful with the spell and when he woke, he was more lucid and more like the man she knew. Sometimes when he woke in the night, he was frightening. His eyes glazed over like she had seen the illness do to him and he would babble nonsense. Things she didn't understand. She used to think he was talking to her, but she'd come to realize he was talking to himself or to someone else he perceived was there. At times she found he was reliving memories. Old memories, that she had no recollection of herself nor were they memories from the War.

They all had those. Moments from the War that stained their dreams, warping the nature of ordinary dreams into troubling fragmentations of old worries and old transgressions. These recreations from Elias were personal memories.

In one instance, she was sure he was talking to his wife, Mia, like she was in the other room standing next to him. He was shouting as if they were arguing.

He pleaded with her. *Don't you trust me? I know you think what you found, what you see is inevitable, but you know better than anyone else these things are not set in stone.* He continued to cry for her to listen to him, continued to counsel the ghost in his mind, *People change. The world changes. Time moves and the world changes with it. How can you be so certain? Please don't do this.*

Ellaria didn't know what was scarier, the reliving of the conversation, the tone of his voice, or the way his body froze up motionless each time, like some unseen force kept him paralyzed.

When she got back to the circle field of carriage houses, she was surprised to find him sitting outside, talking with Desee and Jolee.

"Eric, how are you today?" Ellaria said to Elias.

"I'm good. I feel good today. The sisters were telling me all about your show. Very interesting. I was wrong about how much skill you had. I mean to say, I knew you were an expert in alchemy and all the many paths to magical things, but I didn't know to what extent your skills had grown." Elias commented. He eyed her and the sunlight sunk into his glazed eyes. The man looking at her gave Ellaria a chill.

"You should see it, Eric. When she disappears from the stage, everybody in the room is left with their mouths hanging open for a solid two minutes before they burst into roar of clapping; hollering and cheering as you've never heard before," Desee said.

"It's unlike anything we've heard before and I know it's unlike anything Archibald's seen before, because I've heard him complaining about how much applause she gets. He was saying the other day that he needs Poe to write him another play, otherwise he's going to have a hard time keeping people coming to the show after Aria leaves," Jolee said.

The sisters knew she was leaving but most in the troupe expected her to stay all three nights in Midway. She had worked with them over the last two days figuring out how to do her act. They only had some of the skills required and none of the three had figured out how to disappear and reappear themselves. They could do it with large objects, but not flesh and blood. Together, they modified the act to be an object instead. It involved a mannequin, lights, and some interesting distracting techniques that were a bit lewd for her own show.

"If you go inside, I'll make you something to eat. You should be resting; we have a long night ahead of us," Ellaria said.

"As you wish," Elias said.

"Bye, Eric," Desee said to Elias.

Ellaria walked the ladies to their carriage house, "Thank you both for keeping an eye on him."

"Sure, he seemed well today. I know he hasn't been out of that bed much in the past two weeks, but he looks like he's on the mend," Jolee remarked.

"I hope so, but I'm afraid he has his relapses."

"I didn't know he was such a religious person, or that you were, for that matter. I fear I haven't been very cognizant of that possibility. We don't have many Faithful in the show," Jolee said.

Desee leaned in and lowered her tone, "Too much deviant behavior."

"What are you taking about?" Ellaria said confused.

"Eric. He must have quoted the Sagelight Codex at least six times while we talked." Jolee said.

"Eric did?" Ellaria said.

"Yes. You know, some of the more famous lines that are common enough, but some obscure lines, too," Jolee said.

"Oh, well he came to it only recently," Ellaria said.

"Because he's sick?" Jolee said, "I've seen that before. It's common for the sick and the lost to seek guidance from higher powers."

"Exactly," Ellaria said, and she tried to hide how quickly she rushed back to the house. She found herself nearly running. She bounded over the threshold, but Elias was fast asleep again. He was cold to the touch and every bit of suspicion drained from her. *What was happening to her friend?* She heated the crystals and pricked her finger for blood. She drew out a sigil on the towel placed warmed gems inside and placed them atop

Elias's chest. He stirred but didn't wake. When she was done, a light from her bed brightened the low enclosed space.

The watch, she realized, had a new message. The others had finally responded to her. She scrambled up the skinny stairway and snatched the watch from where she left it near the bed.

"Wade and I are in Amera."

Amera? Why are they—

"Long story, Learon is in Midway with Meroha"

Meroha? what was she doing away from Polestis?

"Find each other and come to us"

Go to Amera. The nerve of that girl.

Ellaria didn't know if she was proud or annoyed. Mostly she was happy someone else was so close. She tore through her bag to find the enchanted pen and scribbled out a response.

"Learon, come to the Barrel Theater."

She waited for a response but received none. She hoped he got it. A knock on her door startled her and Archibald poked his head in.

"Aria, are you dressed?"

"What do you need, Archi?"

Archibald stepped in and his shoulders slumped, "You're really leaving then?"

"Were leaving tonight," she said.

"And I can't persuade you to stay? I will find the best doctor in Tovillore for your friend and pay for them, too, I suppose."

"No. We must be moving on. I've stayed too long with you as it is. I don't know how you did it, but you held me here another night, but we have to move on."

"I heard the airfield was closed. I had nothing to do with it," Archibald said rolling his mustache in his fingers.

"Sure."

"Honest," he said, hand over his heart, "However, since you're here…"

"I'm not doing another show. I'm waiting to meet up with a few friends and we are leaving, tonight."

"I know you are. However, I wanted to invite you to my show tonight. I will be doing *The Twilight of Nevermore*."

"In the mosaic?"

"Yes," he beamed. "The first showing will be over after nightfall. You can still catch your flight out afterwards."

"If I can, I will be in the audience, but I can't promise you anything."

"I knew you would say as much," he said and produced two tickets from his sleeve, "Which is why I went ahead and got you two seats on a mid-balcony."

"Thank you, Archibald. For everything. You didn't have to let us ride with you."

"Of course, I did. It is not every day that Ellaria Moonstone asks for your help."

Her face flushed, and her heart began to pound. *If he knew who she was, did that mean he knew who Elias was?*

"Don't look so worried. No one else knows who you are," Archibald said.

"When did you know?" Ellaria asked.

"I suspected from our first meeting. Very few people knew Manas Zabel so well, if at all. He told me you rode with them. It was one of his proudest achievements, your apprenticeship under him. Anyway, I was positive when I saw your act. You have Manus's flair for theatrics and unmatched alchemy skill."

"Then I can't thank you enough. I fear I put everyone in danger."

"I'm not the great man my uncle was, but I am happy to help the heroine of the Great War. However, if there is to be another war, promise me something."

"What?"

"Get the aftermath right this time."

"Agreed," Ellaria said.

"Now, if you will excuse me. I must get ready. As the Master of Ceremonies, and a stage player, I have much to do before showtime," Archibald said, and left her cabin, shuffling off in the slight wobbling way of his, a walk owing to his bulky form.

BY THE TIME NIGHT HAD FALLEN, ELLARIA WAS COMPLETELY PACKED AND
had their horses ready to leave, but she had yet to hear from or see
Learon. Elias awoke and felt rejuvenated. He didn't recall the morning at
all. His temperature leveled out and his energy level was as good as she
had seen.

With everything ready, they made their way to wait outside of the
Mosaic. The evening light was fading, and she was beginning to worry
that Learon wasn't coming.

"We can't have people loitering around out here. Do you have tickets,
miss?" a security guard asked.

"We do." Ellaria said, producing the two Archibald had given her.

"Great, if you would please head in, the show is about to begin."

Ellaria wanted to argue but pulled Elias forward with her and
stepped into the theatre's concourse. A wide ramp wrapped the
perimeter to both sides. The outside wall of arches and stained glass
threw the sunlight in a jumble of color along the walkway and bathed
the interior wall of sculptures in bright hues. They headed up the ramp
and Ellaria removed a small notebook, and the enchanted pen, and
wrote a message for Learon.

*"Waiting inside. When you arrive, ask the ticket agent to send a message to Aria in
balcony box 1129."*

The watch was safely inside their supplies with the horses, and she
couldn't verify if the message had been sent.

They reached their balcony level and an usher escorted them to their
seats. The box had ten padded seats and thick curtains draped at the
ends. The draping cloth was pulled back and clasped to a column on the
wall. Adjacent balconies were all nestled side by side nearly around the
entire interior circumference. Ellaria thanked the usher discreetly.

"We have friends who are meeting us. Can you please have the ticket
master send us a message when they arrive?" She slipped the usher a
piece of Adalon amber. He took the coin, smiled, and nodded his head
enthusiastically. Once intermission came, they could stand outside the
theatre again.

The stage was sparsely lit. The many lanterns and gas lamps were
covered with black fireproof cloth and controlled by a series of levers and
pulls. The stage loomed large and intimidating even in such an immaculate room, or maybe because of the room. There were a few hushed
whispers and the sound of something dragging through dirt came from

the stage. A few lanterns were unveiled, and the thief came limping across the stage.

"When we were born of shadow, we were renewed in dreams and the sway of light blinded us," The actor began.

The play was underway and still no sign of Learon. Ellaria continually checked behind her for the usher, but none ever came.

The show was magnificent, and Archibald perfectly played the Merchant of Dying. As it wore on, she noticed Elias had grown more invested in it. His energy had surprised her and she trusted it to last until they made their flight. His attention was especially drawn to the show; he bent forward, chin in his hands and elbow on his knees, intensely watching.

She observed him from the corner of her eye and tried to watch the show simultaneously. If Elias was having an episode from his illness, she wanted to rush him out of there. Finally, she decided they couldn't wait for Learon any longer. He would have to find them at the airfield. It was a logical solution she had come to already. She began to tug at Elias's sleeve when suddenly the lanterns dimmed throughout the theatre and winked away. It was still too soon for intermission; *what was going on?* She touched Elias's arm and felt the chill consuming him. He didn't stir.

A lone gas lamp high above remained, still lighting the set's backdrop wall. It gave off only a minimal amount of red ambient light. On one of the set's cliff platforms stepped a cloaked man from a stage-draped cave. He wore the demon mask from Ellaria's show. She had left it in the carriage house, along with a *thank you* note to Archibald. The small light there was reflected in the knife the figure held at his side. The glinting dagger was hard to miss.

Ellaria wasn't the only one to see him. A gasp from below was audible and small whispering trickled throughout the audience. The stage lamps flickered, and he was gone. They flicked again and Ellaria could see Archibald searching around in confusion. The theater plunged into complete darkness, then the lamps were brought up and the demon was on stage, standing behind the Goddess of Light dressed in layered ethereal clothes. Ellaria stood abruptly and screamed out a warning, but the masked man thrust the knife into the actress' heart. The audience screamed and Ellaria's shriek was drowned away.

Half of the crowd thought it was part of the show and the other half began to panic. The demon figure pointed at Ellaria and fled into the back. Ellaria watched it disappear and grabbed Elias, roughly pulling him to his feet to exit. He stood and sagged into her.

"What's going on?" he mumbled, "Is the show over?"

Sweat fell from his forehead and the cold had overtaken him again. In the hallway, a man waited for her. Dressed in a dark blue suit and a high-topped hat, Edward Knox bowed slightly and tipped his hat in greeting.

"Miss Ellaria Moonstone, I've been looking for you. My colleague Aramus," the Sagean pointed back to the stage, "Told me, I could find you here."

Ellaria froze in her steps, stunned by the man before her that she never expected to see. Elias, behind her, was slow to find his footing, and his weight almost toppled her over. At the sight of him, Edward snarled. His face contorted into a beast like growl.

"Aramus lied, you are with her," Edward muttered.

Edward threw his hand out toward Elias. A bolt of light, not quite lightning, shot out of the Sagean's hands and struck Elias. The focused beam of light and heat carried Elias backwards over the balcony to the benches below. Ellaria screamed and withdrew her small knife, but Edward grabbed her arm. She tried to fight back but a prickle to her skin made her shudder, and it was like all the energy was sucked from her body. The spot where Edward gripped her burned hot and her neck drooped. She stumbled forward and he pulled her away and down the corridor. A blaring sound and a shockwave rippled the air behind her. From behind her shoulder, she saw Elias flying back atop the balcony. Edward waved his guards forward to attack as he pulled her on and away with him into the night.

TWENTY-FIVE
THE FIELD OF LIGHTNING (KOVAN)

He was ten feet inside the theatre when the roar of the crowd enveloped the concourse and people began spilling out to the exits. Panic-stricken and crazed, the crowd was shouting something about lightning and Luminaries and the Quantum Man. Kovan couldn't see where he was but was certain the Sagean had gone inside. He followed, slipping past the ushers waving people to the gate. On the winding ramp, a mass of people charged toward him. Kovan tried to fight through the stream but crashed into the fleeing theatre goes, one after another.

A small group of security guards and Midway greencoats came running up behind. The crowd cleared for them and Kovan followed at their heels. A few levels up, he rounded into an empty door to see the stage. The great theatre contained a radial arrangement of benches and aisles on the lower levels encroaching up to a massive stage, where a huge set was still lit with lantern projectors in shades of red. Above him were twenty flights of balconies. On the far ledge, almost ten floors up, Elias was climbing into a balcony opening and yelling. Kovan couldn't hear what, but it sounded like he was calling out for Ellaria.

"Elias!" Kovan cried out, but it was no use. His voice traveled in the room, but Elias was too focused to register anything.

Kovan ran back for the perimeter concourse. People were still streaming down from the upper floors. *What the underneath is going on? Have they decided to take in a damned show?* Kovan cursed under his breath.

He scrambled up the corridor ramp but slowed when the amount of people coming down had trickled to a few only. He rounded up further to see a scattering of the greencoats and security guards strown on the ground, all of them knocked unconscious. He continued up slowly and spotted Elias standing on the sill of a tall opening, the archway at his head.

"Elias, don't," Kovan said.

Elias's gaze was focused on the ground outside and he jumped without looking back. Kovan rushed to the ledge. Elias had landed softly somehow and was gathering himself to run. Kovan followed Elias's line of sight and in the distance, toward the large colorful tents of the Fair, he spotted the Sagean dragging a woman away: Ellaria.

Kovan ran back down to the entrance, cursing the chase. At the front gates, a squad of Bonemen had gathered and were flowing into the arena. Kovan changed course. He dashed to an open archway and jumped through. The height was a minuscule drop compared to the one Elias had vaulted though, but Kovan landed with a hard plop. The twelve-foot drop rattled his legs and Kovan winced. He knew he was lucky he hadn't broken anything. He was too old to be jumping out of balconies and expect to come away unscathed. Simple bruises at his age lasted months. Running around the ramparts had him gasping for air, his old lungs crying out with strain while he tried to catch his breath.

He picked himself off the ground and continued toward the tents of the main circus. Arriving at the fairgrounds, the carnival roared with life, still beating to its own weird drum. The chaos of the theatre had not reached the fair at all. The crowd still lingered amongst the tents, Men, women, and children watching the jugglers and eating candy. The growl of a lion was heard, as were calls of animals behind a fire-eater and knife-twirler. The circus was packed, and many seemed to be looking to the sky, awaiting something.

Kovan scrambled through, his head spinning as he looked in every corner and crevice for any sign of Ellaria or Elias. Beyond the large colorful tents, he noticed a dimly lit field and a caravan of huge carriages positioned in a back lot. He charged forward towards it. He tried passing between tents, but before he could emerge into the back staging area, he saw the heads of two Rendered Beings stalking around.

Kovan drew his pulsator and hummed on the priming power. He crept behind them, and they split in two directions as the crowd he left behind him chanted something. The Rendered machine stopped and spun to look back. The cloak draped at its back shifted and Kovan could see some of the inner workings of gears among a pump and reservoir for the curious glowing liquid, housed behind a plate where the steam exhaust puffed out and tubes angled over the thing's shoulder to its face. Kovan took aim and fired. The first and second shots destroyed some of the machinery, but the third shot found something inside and a spark ignited throughout the automaton. It tried unsuccessfully to move and fell hard to the ground, fire and sparks shooting out of it.

The sounds went unnoticed by the circusgoers and a fireworks show began above. The first few orange blasts were small and low. Then a large blue explosion with shimmering white sparks lit the night sky and Kovan could see the clouds above were swirling around unnaturally. The bulky clouds that had shielded the moonlight completely were now a funnel above the entire park.

More fireworks and the crowd cheered. Some noticed the clouds but thought little of it amongst the excitement. It was only an odd curiosity proceeding a spectacle of curiosities.

Kovan ran to the open field. The traveling village took up more room than the show tents. The closer carriages were jumbled in their arrangement, but he could tell there was a center expanse of grass and it aligned perfectly below the spiraling clouds. Here, the wind was thrashing, and his coat flapped. He found his way through the congestion of structures and set eyes on the open center. Three figures stood opposed to each other. Ellaria seemed to be in a daze, but Kovan was focused on the man's hand tightly gripping her wrist. There was a glowing barrier between them, like a wall of soft light. The ground rumbled and Kovan hesitated in his steps. The fireworks show was culminating to a finish. The noise and chaos pounded in his head.

The man pulled Ellaria reluctantly away and the field swarmed with bonemen soldiers. Fifty men in full armor shuffled closer, their gold face-guards reflecting the light and their red capes waving in the wind. They all carried pulsators or the larger surge-rifles.

Kovan started to sprint to Elias who now stood alone. Slowly engulfed by soldiers with their guns pointed at Elias, they unleashed a barrage of charged and glowing rounds.

A loud crack concussed the air and echoed out, and the sky folded over, and darkness became light. The bullets gathered at their mark but became a great beam of light hurled from the center of the field into the air, like a column of blinding white energy reaching to the stars.

Above him, Kovan could see the clouds were now moving with a violent speed around the column and the wind had tripled in its intensity. It began to lift the tents, and a series of screams from showgrounds called feebly into the night. The heat from the column made Kovan sweat, but once the firing from the soldiers stopped, the column of light evaporated. It was replaced in the sky by long tentacles of lightning. They started small but soon stretched out overhead and the field before him erupted.

Kovan was lifted off his feet. One moment the sound was blaring in his ears and the next, a blast of heat had decimated the field. The ringing in his ears kept revolving in an endless drone and someone was helping him up. Kovan's eyes slowly adjusted back to the darkness.

Learon's eyebrows were raised and his mouth open. Learon was saying something, but Kovan couldn't hear him. He motioned to his ear and shook his head. He tried to say *I can't hear you* but wasn't sure the sounds came out.

Learon, hugged him, looked at him in disbelief and Kovan smiled, then pointed to Elias. They rushed to the center of the field, where Elias was crumpled on the grass. A young blonde woman came running toward them and a cat flashed to Elias side and started licking his cheek. Elias's eyes opened.

"Elias! Are you hurt?" Learon said, his voice still muffled in Kovan's ears.

Kovan could see a dazed look of confusion in Elias's eyes. But the longer the cat sat with him, the more the paleness evaporated from his face and arms.

Learon patted Kovan on the shoulder, "I can't believe you're here. How?"

"Yeah, I'm a wonder to behold. I'll tell you later, right now we need to go," Kovan said.

"I'm glad to see both of you. I must get to Nahadon. I don't have much time left," Elias said.

Why didn't he have time left? Kovan scowled, angry that he may have survived his whole ordeal just to watch his friends die.

"What's going on Elias. Why would the Sagean take Ellaria, where are they going?" Kovan said.

"We should head to the airfield, I have an airship that's ready to take us to Amera," Learon said, lifting Elias to his feet. Kovan was surprised to find him here, but maybe more surprised to hear the confidence in his voice. His eyes lingered on Learon a moment before his worry about his friend took over. Normally, Elias and Learon would stand at about the same height, but Elias couldn't lift his head or straighten his back enough to stand tall. Instead, he hunched over onto Learon, holding his cat like he was ready to pass out.

"The stables," Elias mumbled, "We have horses in the stables."

They followed his suggestion and found the white mare of Elias's next to a brown charger in the back. Supplies were stacked and ready for traveling in their stalls. Kovan only needed to tie them on. Elias got atop the white Nyrogen, and Learon and his blonde friend mounted the charger.

"I have some friends camped outside of town. I need to go back there and get Meroha." Learon said, and he pushed his hand through his long hair. Elias's blade was strapped at his hip and Kovan could see some of the glowing blood from a Rendered on Learon's pant leg.

"Where's Tali?" Kovan asked.

"Amera," Learon said.

Kovan didn't ask why. He could get the full explanation later when they weren't in a hurry, but he understood a little better why Amera was their destination. He stole a third horse for himself and followed them outside the city.

Camped beyond the city and off the Imperial Road was a small band of fighters. The group looked exhausted and weary like they'd recently been in a battle. When they stopped, Learon didn't dismount, instead leaning down to one of the guards. Two men at the front held what looked like jagged shovels, but he guessed they were spears.

A short time later, three people emerged from a tent. One man had serious eyes and two blades strapped at his back. His dark beard was better manicured than any man around him. Kovan assumed he was the leader. He was accompanied by a Rodairean woman and Meroha.

"Meroha, we're leaving. You can ride with Kovan," Learon said.

"Kovan!" Meroha cried. She ran to him and Kovan pull her up, where she leaned in and hugged him tightly.

"Learon," Elias said weakly from his saddle. "Can I leave my horse with them?"

Learon looked at him sideways, but said, "Yes, I trust them."

Elias dismounted and held the white horse's head close to his own. He whispered to it, before addressing their curious looks.

"We're leaving on a winddrifter. I would prefer Ghost stay with someone I might one day be able to track down again. I can't simply sell her to the stable trader," Elias said.

The leader agreed and he whistled for another horse to be brought over. A man brought over a saddled brown and white horse and helped Elias's move over his supplies. When Elias couldn't quite get back in the saddle, the man helped him with that, too.

"Thank you, Gerald." Learon said.

"Learon, we will be riding at dawn back to Fort Mare, like you suggested," the leader said.

"Good," Learon replied.

"By tomorrow, this city will be lost and under the Sagean's control. If you can, send help our way. We'll need it," the man said.

"I will. May you live and die beneath the Blue, Ronick. Tell Darringer we'll be in contact," Learon said.

There was a story there and Kovan's head ached, he was playing catch up on his past and current events.

They left the band of rag-tag soldiers and headed for the air station. Kovan retrieved Semo and Buroga who waited nearby to watch the airfield for the Sagean in case he came back. When Kovan arrived, they told him the Sagean's ship was long gone and the giant cloudparter with it.

They regrouped at the stables outside the air station and sold their horses to an angry trader, made so for being awoken in the night and therefore refusing to budge on his price for thieves, as he called them. From there, they proceeded into the airfield and Kovan followed Learon's lead toward the last winddrifter.

"I recognize that ship," Kovan said.

"Bazlyn's helping us," Learon replied.

"Why is Tali in Amera?" Kovan asked.

"It's a long story and I'll explain onboard," Learon said.

Kovan watched everyone climb aboard the Ragallia Savona. Standing alone in the dark and empty airfield, he pulled out the small tin box and removed a colored cube from inside. He climbed aboard, hugged the tall aeronaut who beamed at seeing him, and found a spot on the bench. Learon began his explanation and Kovan nudged Buroga. He flashed the cube in his hand for Buroga to see, but kept it hidden from the others. Buroga nodded his understanding.

The ship lifted into the sky and Kovan put the cube in his mouth. The hard edges lasted only a couple of seconds and then the bulk of it dissolved. He put his head back against the hull and watched the stars swirl.

TWENTY-SIX

HOSTAGE (ELLARIA)

Unconscious time was a sea of uncertainty for Ellaria. She was cognizant of moving, but not how, or where, or in which direction. She wasn't even sure how much time had passed since the theatre; Edward had syphoned away all her energy and it produced a lethargic sickness which overwhelmed her. She slept and she forgot, but she didn't rest. The panic and fear had an awareness all its own, pulsing in her muscles and skin.

At some point, she found her head was swaying. It dipped from side to side, and she came to. Ellaria opened her eyes and stared at the slatted wood a few fingers from her nose. She caught her breath and her muscles jerked on instinct; terrified Edward had locked her in a box.

Her limbs flailed and she tumbled out of the top bunk of a small, bunkered space, slamming into the floor and wall unceremoniously. The door came ajar in the crash. She picked herself up and crawled into a tight hallway. Her elbow screamed from the fall. A bruise had formed quickly, and the ache weakened her whole arm. The hall connected to larger one. As soon as she crossed into the corridor, she heard his voice.

"Did you hurt yourself?" Edward asked.

Ellaria peered down the hall to a brightly lit cabin, and Edward sitting within. Ellaria exhaled and climbed to her feet, but the floor lurched below her and her stomach leaped into her throat. Everything was falling and she braced herself with her hands on the paneled wall.

"You see, there's nowhere to go. The pilot says there are storms he must navigate around but not to worry," Edward said and closed his eyes,

"I can feel the energy of the storm is concentrated many leagues from us. We will be fine."

Ellaria looked around. *Of course, she was on an airship.*

Edward waved her forward, "Please come sit with me. We have much to discuss."

What could they have to discuss, other than her release? She came into his main cabin and found the empty chair that awaited, including a cup of tea on the adjacent table, still steaming. Her first thought was she should throw it in his face, but she wasn't sure how to land an airship. Now was not the moment to act. She reached for the cup and looked at him. The heat of the ceramic warmed her cold hands.

"What do you want from me, Edward?"

"I need you, Ellaria."

"You *need* me?"

"Yes. as you no doubt need me to keep you alive, I need your help with my Court."

"What Court?"

"They are my advisors. A group of wealthy merchants that I believe plot against me."

"I'm plotting against you. Maybe I should be working with them?" she said.

Edward smiled, "That wouldn't work. They want to use you as a Cast for their little spell."

Ellaria knew spells of all kinds and had never heard the term before.

"A what?"

"My Court of Dragons are preparing to becoming Luminaries, and they need Casts as capacitors for the spell."

"Impossible," she said instinctively. *How could such a thing be possible?*

"I would normally tend to agree; however, there is an ancient temple hidden in the jungles of Nahadon near the Black Shore. It is there that such a thing can be done. An ancient structure called the Temple of Ama awaits, forgotten in a forbidden area the Tregoreans call the Shadow Field. There's a chamber inside one of the structures that was built for this one use. A machine of sorts, ancient in its construction and difficult to operate. It is called the Sintering Fountain. But for a human to survive the transformation, there must be a surrogate person who serves as a conductor, a Cast, through which the acolyte is shielded. The magic of the machine is filtered through their Cast and protects their rebirth. As you can imagine, those who are chosen as Casts are important. You are gaining their essence in the Sintering process. It is believed the Cast imparts something of themselves."

"Danehin, the King?" Ellaria said with understanding.

"Yes. The Peace King was highly sought after, as you can imagine."

"And how does the soul-stealing come into all of this?"

"The machine requires various components to operate. Along with a few other elements, the souls power the machine."

"That's sick."

"Hush. You more than most know how much blood stains the path to rule."

"And so, the cycle continues. We invent the means of our own demise and then we learn how to deploy it, then we argue how to protect ourselves," Ellaria said.

"What are you saying?"

"Isn't it obvious? The machine is dangerous. If the ancients sealed it away, they knew the dangers. If we're lucky, a machine like that gathers dust until it decays with the expiration of time, never seen again and never used."

"Your warning is noted," Edward said.

"What do you want from me?" Ellaria said.

"Well, Shirova Edana or Aylanna Alvir will probably want you as a Cast. Most certainly Rotha Durrone, though I'll never let that happen."

"Wait Alvir and Edana—as in Alvir Pulsators, Alvir Steam Engines, Edana Metals Company? That Aylanna Alvir and Shirova Adana?"

"But of course. Did you believe the Court of Dragons a simple, scared Syndicate hiding in the shadows? A rabble like that could never execute such an ambitious plan. No, the Court, my dear Ellaria, is made up of the most wealthy and powerful men and women of the world."

"They are corporations?"

"Yes, and they want to control the world as they did when serving the Emperor. What I need is someone on my side. My mother is obviously on my side and thus, they don't provide her the same leeway. She is a great woman, but she handed me over to them when I was young before realizing what she had done. She did not think what would happen because she wasn't one of the acolytes like my father had been. She was, for all intents and purposes, an outsider."

Why would she be on his side? Either power or suspicion had made him delusional. Ellaria was tentative how to respond. She wanted him to divulge as much as she could coax out of him, but she could almost feel the noose tightening around her neck the longer their conversation progressed. *What she needed was facts.*

"Where are you taking me?" she asked.

"We are going to a meeting in Merinde. We need their help to safely reach the Temple. I have heard that things have changed drastically there in the last month. I believe my Court will be as vulnerable as ever, and I want you to observe them all closely. I must know who I can trust and who I cannot."

"I don't understand their games of power."

"But you do. You outsmarted the Emperor. You're the leading expert on Alchemy in the world, and you're an excellent judge of people."

"I'm not. I thought I knew you and you turned out to be the person we were looking for."

"That's not your fault. I never lied to you. My involvement with the Guild and the Arcana was, and is, genuine. I also have a certain talent to see things in others and project an image they find to their liking."

"How many are on the Court?"

"There are seven, not counting Queen Rotha. They plot like thieves and bicker like old hags, but beneath it all, there are relationships of trust based on mutual beneficial advancement. I have never been able to read them."

"Why don't you read them as you do me?" she said.

"This," Edward said, lifting his hand to show her his dragon ring.

"The ring?"

"This ring is their hold over me."

"You can't take it off?"

"I'm working on that, but no."

"How is it this is the first time I'm seeing the ring? Another trick?"

"Yes."

"How does it work?"

"You see, the acolytes were never meant to be in control. Over the histories, they would guide the Sagean as his council, but ultimately their role was to train the new Sagean once an heir came along. These rings are very old—from before the Eckwyn age. They help contain the Luminary's power so that the Illumination Surge doesn't burn them out. Typically, there was one for the apprentice and one for the master. After the Luminary Wars, most were lost or destroyed. But the Sagean order found seven of these rings for their acolytes to use and control any of the apprentices under their training. When the line of Sagean Luminaries began to die out, the monasteries became unnecessary."

"The acolytes probably shouldn't have hunted down and killed all Luminaries, as some records say they did," Ellaria admonished.

"The Sagean Order could not allow Luminaries to be born outside of their order. Any one of them could be a threat to the empire."

"So how did Qudin slip through the cracks?"

"He didn't. Not really. But the acolyte's method of locating luminaries was stolen."

"Stolen by whom?" Ellaria asked. Hoping short questions would keep Edward talking.

"An acolyte betrayed the order. He stole some magical artifacts and helped hide Qudin away."

"Why?"

"I think he simply wanted to see the Empire fall. Others believe he had a personal stake in the game."

Ellaria sipped her tea and looked around the room. Edward had already revealed more then she thought he would, *but what else was he hiding?* If she could get him to truly trust her, perhaps she could manipulate him into his own demise or take him down while standing by his side.

"I suppose I don't have much choice?" she said.

"Don't do that. You don't have to lie to me, Ellaria. I know you. You want to do this because you like the challenge, and you have a hatred of people like this. Now that you know about them, you will do whatever it takes to bring them down. Why else would I tell you everything? I need you at your ruthless best," Edward said.

She bit her tongue. "You're right, I will never stop trying to bring you down and now them, too. But you all dance to the tune of darker power, don't you?" she said. Edwards's eyebrow lifted.

"Yes, I know of the Wrythen," she said.

"Don't say its name," he scolded her.

"The Old One scares you too?"

"Too? Who else does it scare? Qudin? Has Qudin seen the Old One? When?"

"I don't know."

"Don't lie to me," he said darkly.

"I don't exactly know."

"Yes. We serve the Old One, and so do you. You were all unwittingly serving its will when you entered the Sagean Tomb."

"What?" she said. That was a terrifying proclamation she needed explained.

"We needed inside and Qudin was needed to accomplish that."

Something about that didn't feel right, she thought. "What did you need from inside?"

"A scepter rested inside in the arms of the long dead Empress Corinsura. It is another component to the Sintering Fountain."

"A black scepter. Like a pitch-black void?" she said, recalling the scepter inside the tomb.

"Yes. That reminds me, I have questions for you. Where is the glove Qudin wore? And where is his apprentice?"

"Apprentice?"

"The young Rodairean woman who killed the Prime, where is she?"

"I don't know. We escaped Marathal on different paths."

"And the glove?"

"Lost in the lake. My guess is it's probably leagues away by now, down the Uhanni river. Maybe to the Zulu Sea. It is very shiny, so maybe the river folk found it," she said, trying to hide the image of it from her mind in case Edward had other powers she didn't know of.

"Do not mock me, Ellaria. You may have been powerful once, but your time is over, and your friends are not here to help you. Though I must say, I respect your restraint."

"For not throwing this cup of tea in your face?" Ellaria said. "It's only because I can't land an airship on my own."

"No. Because I thought the first thing you would ask me would be to explain what happened in the field. To explain why Qudin let me go."

She could only vaguely recall the scene in the field. Her exhaustion had overcome her by then and standing on her feet had strained every bit of strength she possessed.

"I know what you did. You manipulated his mind like you did mine," she said.

"No. It's a lovely thought, but no. He already has the master of manipulation inside him."

"What does that mean?"

"You'll see. At the end, you'll see."

She didn't know what that meant but if this was to be an uneasy partnership, she needed to ask some uneasy questions. "I do have a few questions for you."

"Ask. I'll answer how I choose."

"Does your Court communicate with the Old One or just you?"

"Both."

"If you're afraid they're plotting against you, why agree to the Sintering Fountain?"

"It was the Old One's bidding, and not the Court's."

"We learned that the Luminaries of old fought this Old One once; why would the Old One want more Luminaries? And why has the Old One chosen now to come back?"

"I have no answers for you concerning the Old One. I have seen its immense power and witnessed its abilities."

"Why partner with such a dangerous being—" she paused in recognition of the irony at work and changed subjects, "I assume once the court is full of Luminaries, the war with the New World is next on your agenda?"

"That is the goal, yes, but you should be happy; a band of Luminaries will bring a swift end to the war. I have no doubt the New World will have prepared an array of war machines to deploy against us. We are preparing our own and other additional methods of attack, but a group of Luminaries will not be defeated."

"I understand being suspicious of your Court. Have you gathered other allies or am I your only hope?"

"Don't flatter yourself, Ellaria."

"So, you do have other's helping you. Which means you have a plan to thwart them besides me?"

"I believe I have told you enough," he said, and stood to lead her back to the small quarters.

"You've given me a lot to think about, but why send a murderer to terrorize me if you wanted my help?" she stepped inside the cramped space.

"Aramus was under some else's control," he shut the door, locking her in.

There was barely enough standing room, no light, and one bed atop a chest of drawers. For all intents and purposes, she *was* trapped in a wood box. In the darkness, she searched her wrist wrap and cloak. Not for the vials or the knife, she knew they had taken those, but for the enchanted pen. She found it still tucked inside one of her inside pockets. Without paper to write on, she scribbled on the wood wall. If Edward was confident enough to tell her everything then she was going to relay it all back to her friends. She could play as his confidant while angling others toward their path and still defeat him in the end.

AMERA

To Turgo

Passage to Echo Canyon

Map Commissioned By The United Scholar's Guild

To Corma

Millers Rise

The Crystal Mines

The Pinch

Bounty's Fold

Pliers Point

Miner's Run

East Town

Refinery Row

Old Town

Air Field

The Tailfeather Mountains

To Axern

To Duma

W E
N
S

TWENTY-SEVEN
REGROUP (TALI)

When Bazlyn's ship finally arrived in Amera, Tali ran toward it before the skis had safely settled on the dirt. From the fence line of the airfield where she would wait every day, she saw them approach, the Savona's faded maroon sails falling from the clouds and a full hull like she couldn't believe. Without a pen, Learon had no way of contacting her. But she had read every line of Ellaria's messages the night before and anticipation had built up for their arrival.

Beneath the ship, the wind blew through her loose short cloak and pants. The ladder popped out of the hull and the cabin door in the side-wall sprung open, and the first one down was Meroha, followed by Stasia.

Learon stood at the top and looked at her waiting on the ground. He smiled brightly when their eyes met, and he turned back to discuss something with someone on board.

At the sight of him, something stirred inside her. She didn't realize how much she had missed him until now. She wanted to confide in her friend everything that had happened, to laugh at bad choices and share each other's burdens; but seeing him, she suddenly didn't know what to say.

She greeted the women when they reached the ground and was turning to see who was coming next, when the sight of something around Stasia's neck caught her attention: the leather-bound crystal hung at Stasia's chest and Tali was certain it was Learon's necklace.

Semo suddenly appeared next to her, and she was startled out of her trance to hug him. He was shocked by the greeting. Semo was not the hugging type and Tali wasn't sure what she was more surprised by: that Semo was there or that Stasia was wearing Learon's necklace. Tali kept looking at it even as Learon came down. She ran up to him and hugged him before he was firmly planted on the territh.

"Hi, Tali. Did you miss me?" He asked, his hair pulled away from his face she saw he had a new scar above his right eyebrow.

"No," she lied, and hugged him again. She pulled away and touched his scar, "What's this from?"

"That's nothing. Just a scratch from battling with a Rendered in Midway. But Tali, you might want to brace yourself—" Learon was trying to explain something when the sight of a huge man appeared behind him. They were traveling with a Hazon man? *Why were they traveling with a Hazon man?*

"Tali, this is Mayzanna Buroga," Learon said, introducing them.

"Hello, Miss Tali. I have heard much about you on the flight here. It is my pleasure to meet you," Buroga said. His voice boomed a deep timber, but he had a soft manner to him. A hand tapped on her shoulder, but she kept staring at the Hazon man, so far from his homeland. It was the first of his kind she had ever met. *How had they met him?* She put her hand over the hand on her shoulder, but the hand was colder than Learon's and rougher.

"Hello, young Raven."

Tali spun and nearly collapsed into Kovan. Tears filled her eyes before she could blink, and her throat suddenly bound up.

"Kovan," she whimpered into his shoulder. Kovan buckled slightly from her weight and Learon came to steady them. She came away reluctantly and wiped her eyes. He was alive, and he looked... *tired.* His eyes were drowsy and far away, "What's wrong?"

"I'm fine. Just tired," Kovan said, but she could see something had upset him and she didn't think it was their reuniting. She smiled anyway, a joy deep inside was breaking free and she surrendered to it.

"He's—" Learon started to say and Kovan punched his gut lightly.

"I'll explain when we're somewhere safe," Kovan assured her.

Tali nodded and embraced him again. This time climbing to her tiptoes, "Thank you. Thank you for coming back."

He winked at her, "I'm a tough old dog to kill, Raven. Where's Wade?"

"He's back at the inn. Where's Elias?" She asked, realizing he had never come down. She could see Bazlyn moving around above securing his lines.

"He's sick. He's real sick and we need to get him south as soon as we can," Kovan said.

"I want to see him," Tali said, and she climbed the ladder up to the main hull. Elias lay covered up with blankets and his mystcat Merphi, sprawled over him. The cat perked up at her arrival and its ears winked as though talking to her. He didn't stir.

"Don't worry, I'm watching him," Bazlyn said. "You get back with you friends. I'll be here preparing the ship to leave again at dawn tomorrow."

She thanked Bazlyn again and descended from the ship with a hardening shell of determination enveloping her. Tali told the others to follow her. Outside the airfield, they procured a carriage to take them south. The inn in which they held a room was in a tiny town called Garrison. It was a good distance outside of the Amera and closer to Axern and the Arrow Bay.

All of those shocking revelations in one instant had Tali in knots as they traveled. Her two mentors had returned and there were two challenges ahead of them. She knew that meant splitting up again, and she didn't like it. One team would have to accompany Elias while the other stayed to capture the Stone. Since arriving in Amera, Wade and Tali had made no headway in retrieving it themselves. The streets were guarded with twice as many men as in Corma, and everyone here carried a gun. Outside of locating Nyra at the Miner's Collective, they had managed to do little else. For the past two days, Wade had pleaded with Tali to wait for the others. She waited, not to appease him but because she wasn't sure of herself and didn't trust Wade to have her back. Now with the others here, she knew they would get the Stone back, but she didn't care as much any longer. She had back what she wanted: her friend.

At the inn, they sat in silence in the small room; Learon on the floor beneath the window, Stasia and Meroha on the beds, Buroga filling a chair, and Kovan looking out the window. Semo had left to scout around the small town to ease his restlessness. Wade sat against the bed.

They seemed tired and dragged under the long pathways they had all taken to get there. It was clear Elias was leaving at first light for the Tregorean Lands, and that whoever traveled with him had two goals: to heal Elias and to convince the Tregoreans to venture into the neighboring mountains of the Black Shore. If they could, they could thwart the Sagean and his followers, and save Ellaria.

The second team was equally against the knife: they had to retrieve the Tempest Stone from the Bounty Hunter's Guild and its maniac leader, Razor Redmar. Tali knew how the division of efforts must be done, but she didn't want it to be so.

Kovan was the key. He would want to pursue Ellaria, but he was the expert on Amera and the best warrior among them. Tali had power, but it was unpredictable. Her control was shaky in the best of times and stress brought it forth, but also limited her capacity to control herself. She didn't want to admit it, but until she learned control, she was a liability.

"Well, I know I'm going south with Elias. The question is, who's going with us?" Learon said.

"You're going? Who decided that?" Tali said.

"Elias," Kovan said, turning from the window, "It was one of the few things he did say when he was lucid. He told us he had to go the Tregoreans and Learon had to come with him."

"Why Learon?" Tali asked.

"Come on, it's Elias; he doesn't explain things, even when he isn't sick," Learon said.

"I'm staying to go after the Stone. I've chased it this far," Wade said. Tali understood the importance of the Stone, but it didn't outweigh that of saving Ellaria and Elias, nor that of stopping the Sagean and his acolytes.

"The only one I'm uncertain of is Semo," Kovan said, "But I will ask him when he returns."

"How do you know what I've decided to do?" Tali said.

"You're going to the Nahadon, Raven. If they can heal Elias, we need the Tregoreans to help us capture this, Temple. You have a knack for gathering allies, but more importantly, I want two Luminaries going up against the Sagean and his men. We don't know for sure Elias will survive and even if he is healed, I don't know if he will have the strength to fight. Mostly you're going because I must stay here. I know this sewer of a town and all the rats that live in it."

"And Semo?" Learon said.

"I believe he will want to go with you, but I could use him. I need four to retake the Stone from the Moonstalkers. I want him to stay, but he will insist on going so he can save Danehin, his King."

"If you need four, maybe I should stay?" Tali said.

"No. I have an acquaintance that might help. A bounty hunter that knows the city, knows Razor Redmar, and is also great marksman. I need a rifleman; I was probably going to ask him anyway," Kovan said.

"Can you trust him?" Wade asked.

"No. He's not a man of trust or honor. Just a hired gun. His oath is to himself, but if he takes a contract, he's reliable."

"How comforting," Wade sighed.

"I will stand with you, Kovan Rainer," Buroga said, looking up from the book he was reading, given him by Meroha. Kovan smiled and slapped the big man on the back.

"If that's settled, I'm going to the other room to rest before I ride with you guys back to the airfield," Kovan said.

Kovan left, the contemplation was over, and Tali couldn't say she disagreed with the division. *Reunited only to be split up, again.* A bitterness came over her and she wanted to go for a walk, excusing herself to leave. Wade followed her out the door but she ignored him and scampered down the steps through the common room and out the front.

"What do you want, Wade?" she said behind her when he continued to give chase.

"Would you hold up a moment? I need your advice about something," Wade said.

"What?" she said, finally stopping to address him.

"Are you alright?"

"Yes. I'm not happy that we're splitting up again, but it couldn't be any other way," Tali said.

"Why do you think Learon has to go?"

"Your guess is as good as mine. So, what did you need my help with?" she asked.

"Stasia."

"Oh, did you see she was wearing Learon's necklace?" Tali said.

"What?" Wade said.

"What do you mean, what? Isn't that what you're talking about?" Tali said.

"No. Wait do you think they. . ."

"I don't know. She seemed to like him when they met that night in the tavern, and they were in the Midway a few nights together. I don't know," she said tersely.

"Wait. Are you mad her or Learon or me?"

"I'm not mad at anyone," she snapped, "The situation. I'm mad at the situation."

"The situation or *their* situation?"

"Oh, by the Great Blue Sun of Forgiveness, you're impossible sometimes, Wade Duval," Tali said.

"What did I do?"

"The situation *you* created Wade is that you let Learon go in your place to retrieve your girlfriend. And you're wondering why she's mad at you? You're an idiot. Stasia was obviously in love with you, and—"

"Wait, was?" Wade interrupted her.

"Was, is, I don't know. I don't really know her. Maybe she's in love with Learon. Honestly, I don't care. I don't want to care. We don't have the luxury for these distractions. That's what I'm mad at. You created a distraction; you need to solve it. But if it turns out Learon and Stasia are a thing, don't you dare blame Learon for your own choices," she said.

"What if they are *a thing*?" Wade said.

Tali threw her hands up and grumbled under her breath as she stormed off down the street. Her anger had surprised her, but she was mad at Wade for letting Learon go, and she realized she was mad at Wade and herself for their failure to retrieve the Stone. If they had it in their hands, they would all be going to the lands of the Tregoreans, together.

Around midnight, when she had wandered long enough and the rain which threatened all day finally began, she returned to the inn. Stasia was sitting outside on the long-covered walkway. There were no chairs on the thin boardwalk that fronted the building, but Stasia sat against the wood siding, her legs crossed beneath her, and her hood pulled over. Tali was almost unsure who it was except for the strands of stray blonde hair sticking free of her hood.

"What are you doing out here?" Tali asked.

"I couldn't sleep. I told the others I would wait for you. Though I'm sure Kovan is waiting up in the common room still," Stasia said.

Tali noticed Stasia was rolling the crystal necklace in her fingers, and she was on the brink of asking her about it when she heard Stasia's voice beneath, *why am I so jealous of her?*

"Jealous of me?" Tali blurted out and froze—realizing her mistake.

Stasia starred at her dumbfounded, "Can you hear my thoughts?" she asked with a slight recoil, though her question also had an edge of excitement.

"Lately, I have started to hear people's thoughts," Tali admitted, exhaling with a cringe, but she rushed to add, "—I don't mean to. It just happens. I don't know why or when. Things that seem to be at the front of their mind, almost like the phrases people want to say, but don't."

"Is this a thing for Luminaries that I didn't know of?" Stasia said.

"I don't know. I think Elias can do something similar. Did Learon tell you about the One People of Wanvilaska?" Tali asked.

"A little."

"All of them could talk to each other that way. With their minds. I think it's something like that," Tali said.

Stasia appraised her explanation, but changed the subject instead, "So, you and Wade?"

Tali's eyes almost popped out, but instead of rushing to denounce the accusation, she threw Stasia's question back at her,

"So, you and Learon?"

It was a petty response, but with the question asked, Tali found she wanted to hear the answer.

Stasia looked at the necklace and dropped it, "No." Stasia said.

"No?"

"He saved me in Midway and gave me his necklace to heal. That's all," Stasia explained.

"But you like him, or do you like Wade?" Tali said.

"How could you not like Learon? He is one of the kindest, most protective people I've ever met. You know when we walked around Midway together, he would always switch which side he walked on next to me based on where he thought danger might come from? It took me awhile to understand what he was doing. I mean who does that?" Stasia said.

Tali remembered Learon doing the same thing when they walked around Adalon.

"I thought you two were a—" Stasia started to say.

"No," Tali cut her off, "He's never shown any interest in me," Tali said.

"I don't think that's his way, he's too conscientious to be. . . forward," Stasia said.

"I suppose you're right. In Ravenvyre, men are not so reserved. But Stasia, there's nothing between Wade and me. Truth be told, he infuriates me, and not in the good way," Tali said.

Stasia laughed.

"What's so funny?" Tali asked.

"I know that Wade very well," Stasia said.

"I know you're mad at him, but I don't think you have to be. He thought he was making the right choice sending Learon. He probably did, considering what Learon ran into," Tali said.

Stasia shrugged, "He's my best friend. Maybe my only real friend. I kept telling Learon how I was going to punch him because of how mad I am that he left me in Adalon. But my anger evaporated at seeing him.

And yet, I don't know, there was something different between us. I figured it must be you. You're so beautiful and special; if it was you then I would understand it."

Tali had never been called beautiful or special by anyone and to hear it first from a woman whom she found fit both those descriptors was empowering.

"Your words flatter me, but I promise you, it's not like that. He's all yours. I don't have time for romance. I can't add that to saving the world," Tali said.

"I've always kept him at arm's length. He's the best friend I ever had, and I didn't want to ruin that, I guess," Stasia said.

"I've not had many friends, either," Tali admitted, "Not the real kind anyway. The only solution is, we need to be friends, Stasia. If you haven't noticed, this world is starting to crumble, and those fighting to save it share a bond," Tali said.

"When you put it that way," Stasia said with a smile, "We should be great friends. Whatever relationships we can strengthen will only serve us well in the future."

"I agree," Tali said and she hugged Stasia. Stasia jerked slightly but hugged her back. "Sorry, I'm a hugger. That's the first thing you should know about me," Tali said.

"The first thing you should know is that I don't trust people. It's a learned behavior that I'm working on," Stasia told her.

"That's all right. I'm an expert with people who don't trust others. Especially the grumpy older ones, like Kovan and Elias."

They walked toward the entrance and Tali wasn't sure if everything was smoothed between them, but she felt better. At the door, Stasia put her hand on Tali's to keep her from opening it.

"As your friend, I should tell you that I've come to realize: if you do like someone and it's a man, then you need to tell him straight out. They're too thickheaded otherwise," Stasia said.

Inside the common room, Stasia slipped away up the stairs, and Tali found Kovan waiting by the hearth. He was spinning something on the table and looking into the fire. It was a tiny case with a grooved lid. He held one point with his finger and spun it on end. Though he never looked up to see them enter, Tali was sure he noticed, and she sat down across from him.

There was a glass half-full of some sort of spirit and many rings of precipitation on the wood table. Kovan was at least four drinks deep.

"Raven, I'm sorry," he said.

She didn't expect that to be the first thing he said to her, "For what?"

"I'm sorry I wasn't there for you these last few weeks. Wade told me of the Reckers, and Learon told me how panicked you were to catch this thief. And I'm sorry to send you to Nahadon. But I think that's where you're needed most. I know Ellaria will need you and I need you to be where I cannot be," he said.

"Learon, he's going through something isn't he?" Tali had noticed something different about him since they departed in Atava, like a shadow had been cast over him.

"He is, I think we all are, *Such is life but the struggle of time and strife,*" Kovan quoted.

"How long will it take you to get the Stone? Once you're done, you can meet us, right?" Tali asked.

"I hope it works out that way, tomorrow night. We can't wait any longer. It's a miracle you and Wade weren't captured yet. I'm sure the Bounty Hunters' Guild know we've arrived by now, or they will soon. Honestly, it's good you all fly out at dawn. They might think we all left. At least it should offer enough confusion to hold them at bay for a day while we get ready," Kovan said, and downed the rest of his drink. He held it up for the server to see, and continued, "But what can you do? There's no hiding a Hazon man in Amera. We were bound to be noticed. Once we have the Tempest Stone, we'll set sail for the Tregorean lands. Make sure you leave a watch with Wade so we can have some communication."

"I will. He can have mine and my pen. I'll take Ellaria's with me. It was in her pack," Tali sighed, "I wish things were different, I hate splitting up all the time," Tali said.

"Me too, Raven, me too. There's nothing for it but to do what needs to be done. War is not fought on a single battlefield," Kovan said.

"Doesn't mean I have to like it."

"True, Ellaria always struggled with it, too."

Kovan had stopped twirling the case, but it still rested beneath his palm.

"Kovan what's in the case?" Tali asked, she wasn't sure he was going to answer, but he slid it to the center of the table and opened it. The lid folded over smoothly and Kovan lifted a small piece of silk away to reveal a single colorful cube. There were swirls of all kinds of colors in fractal arrays and curiously branded symbols on the faces.

"That, Raven, is me. Well, a small part of me that I've forgotten. The last part," he said.

"What is it?" she asked.

"When I told you on the ride here that I was hurt and lost my memories and that they were coming back slowly, I wasn't lying. What I didn't say was that they were never coming back. I found a man with a device that extracted my memories so I could relive them and remember everything I was, and am. I didn't really want anyone to know about the cubes. Buroga knows, and Learon, but only because he saw me take one and was worried when he saw me pass out," Kovan explained.

"That's crazy, and that cube is your memories?"

"Yes, this one is the last dose."

"Why haven't you taken it?"

"Well, they incapacitate me when I take them. The first one knocked me out for a day. The second one I took when we got aboard the Savona to come here. That's why I didn't want anyone to know. I knew it would knock me out. I'm still not great, but I'm almost there."

"Kovan, I can't leave you like this."

"I'll be fine by the morning. It's true this second dose was harder. I feel a lot more has returned to me. More than I ever cared to think about again. Each dose has gone deeper and... Well, I must wait to take the third when I have time to recover from it. I'm not quite sure what will come of this last dose," he said, and he closed the lid and tucked the case away in his coat pocket. "We should sleep. You're better I trust? The walk cleared your head?" he asked.

"I'm fine. Confused is all, and I'm seldom confused," Tali said.

"You know, sometimes we can go great distances with people and still feel lonely. That's part of life. It's humanity's great curse. To be connected to each other but ultimately feel totally alone. Remember whatever happens, we are all entwined. Elias used to tell me that the energy of life was the strongest energy in existence and that it's all connected like a web of four dimensions. Whatever that means."

"The energy of souls. From Ellaria's messages," Tali said, "The Sagean knows this, too, and is harnessing that power."

"No, not our souls exactly. That's not how Elias explained it. He was talking about something else. He said it was the realm that our souls were made from and connected to. The *essence of eternity*, he called it. Ask him about it when he's healed. Maybe you can get a better explanation than I ever did. I have only recently thought on it again," he said tapping the case in his pocket. "The point is, even when you may feel alone, do not despair. We are connected, we just can't see the connection. Maybe one day with your abilities, you'll be able to see it."

"I'll remember that," she said, and she lingered by the fire a moment longer before heading to her room.

In the early morning, six of them left the inn for the airfield, Wade and Kovan coming along to see them off. Kovan said he had to find his acquaintance to get the fourth gun he needed, as Semo had decided to fly to Nahadon as predicted. Meroha, too, choose to follow Tali and Learon.

At the airfield, Semo hefted the bags to the hull above. The sunlight was dawning on the low dry desert hills. Zephyr stood barking at Tali to come up. She held Remi in her hands and hugged Kovan tightly, not wanting to let go. Learon and Wade were talking about something amongst themselves, then said their goodbyes. When Learon came over, he shook arms with Kovan, who pointed to the Elum Blade strapped at Learon's side.

"You best go unarmed into the Tregorean's land," Kovan said. Learon removed the straps and handed the bundle to him.

"Understood," Learon said, "Any other advice?"

"State your purpose and tell them who Elias is. They know him. They will help," Kovan said.

"Got it."

"I wish I could tell you both more. Something that would help you. But with all the memories I've had returned, much of my time with the Tregoreans was not one of them," Kovan said.

"Thank you, Kovan," Learon said.

Learon turned to go but Kovan caught his arm for one last word, "Protect Tali. You want to rise above the violence you've wrapped yourself in. You can't and you never will. You wouldn't have survived the fights you have if it wasn't who you are. Coming to terms with that isn't easy, but you may find relief in your honor, in the protection of the people you love. Trust yourself because you can't run from who you are," Kovan said.

"A code of honor, does that work?" Learon asked.

"Not really, but it will hold you together. It's a solace you can wear like a shield," Kovan said.

Learon thanked him again and climbed the ladder to the airship. Tali hugged her friend again and went to Wade.

"I'm sorry I let you down, Tali," Wade said.

"Get it back, Wade. Watch Kovan's back; and Wade, don't be a hero. If things go sideways, run."

"You know me. I'm not a hero," Wade said.

"I do know you, Wade, and I know you won't abandon a fight. I'm trying to tell you, sometimes it's all right to run," Tali said.

"I'm fine with running. Like I always say, you can't win the game if you're dead," Wade said.

"When have you ever said that?"

"I'm saying it now."

"Bye Wade, we'll see you in a few days," Tali said, and she handed him her watch and pen. She turned to leave but something she remembered came to her, "Also, for what it's worth, Nyra is not evil. She's scared. I never told you, but when we were with her in Corma, I could feel she was sorry. She told me so actually. She was terrified of this man who held her. This Redmar. I wanted you to know, I think she might help."

"I'll remember that," Wade said.

Tali climbed up and found herself a spot near Elias on the back bench. Semo and Learon emptied the sandbags and the winddrifter lifted up into the sky, another trial awaiting them in a foreign land.

TWENTY-EIGHT

JOKERS AND THIEVES (KOVAN)

Kovan and Wade watched the scene from their scouting position. Far down the dusty street atop the roof of a mining supply store, Kovan could see Redmar mulling around outside the large brick building. He was impossible to miss. He stalked the grounds like he owned everything. In some ways he did.

Three men approached Razor Redmar outside the Miner's Collective, two with their guns drawn and the third man holding double blades. The swords swiped at the air hastily, in shaky hands. The slashes fell out of sync, but Kovan figured they were in line with the man's rising pulse. Razor only tilted his head to eye their approach. Kovan remembered how deadly Redmar was and if this group thought to attack him, the three of them would not be enough.

"Maybe this is it? These fellows will kill him, and we can get the Stone back." Wade suggested. He watched with eager anticipation, but Kovan shook his head. Wade was about to find why Redmar was considered *the demon of the south*.

In a flash, Redmar had drawn his pulsator gun and fired. He didn't waste time talking to them. The first shot blasted a man's hand where it gripped the handle of his pulsator. The next round shot a hole through the other man's head. Then his barrel came to a rest, pointing at the man with swords.

Redmar holstered his gun and drew his meiyoma blade, the traditional sword of a Rodairean, except meiyoma blades were long and single edged on the subtle arch and Redmar's had several backward notches cut into the top length, like barbed hooks.

Holding his sword in one hand, Redmar's empty hand waved the fighter forward. The dual blades man charged forward, and Razor pivoted. Blades clashed. Over and over the two swords slashed and Razor continued to block both easily. Kovan had a sense Razor was testing the man, studying him.

Suddenly Redmar struck like a snake. Three successive deflections, a slash to the man's wrist, and an arching upward sweep drew a long deadly gash through the man's neck. The swords fell from limp hands and the man went to his knees, bleeding out. The rage in Razor's eyes burned like a wildfire. Even from the distance, they could see his temper was spiking and he circled the kneeling man, his chest heaving in anger. He was a big man and Kovan remembered the demon that lived in him.

Razor stopped in front of the dying man and threw a needless left cross punch to the man's face. It sent him sprawling backwards, blood splattering to the dirt.

Wade turned away from the gruesome sight. Kovan watched as Razor's wrath continued. When he was through, he let the first wounded man run away. *This fiend deserved whatever evil fate the great energy beyond had in store for him; perhaps they all deserved their fates.*

Kovan sat back behind the ridge with Wade. He could see from Wade's expression doubt had settled in that they would be the ones to bring Redmar's fate to bear.

"He's an animal. He's the head of the Bounty Hunter's Guild?"

"Kind of. There's a man that runs the business side, but basically yes."

"No wonder Nyra was scared of him."

"I've been all over, and I've met all kinds. Some people have their own demons inside. Sometimes it's evil, sometimes a pain; you can be born with it or someone can put it inside. To keep the beast contented, they drink spirits or work from dawn to dusk; maybe they sink into religion. Razor Redmar doesn't bother to feed the beast inside, he allows it to live on the surface, where it can feed itself. He is a demon in the flesh," Kovan told him, and he could see his words didn't comfort Wade, though they didn't scare him either.

Earlier in the day, Wade had taken him to the buildings to which they tracked Nyra and now that Kovan had seen the layout, a plan was forming. He had spent many years in Amera, but it was smaller then and the Miner's Collective wasn't the dominant force it was today. There were maybe one or two gambling dens then and now they lined the streets, huge buildings, and new ones in the process of coming alive. The one thing he didn't see much of were Bonemen or greencoats. They had spotted a few of both, but their presence was scarce. With his eyes on the situation, they needed to get back to the inn and plan how they were going to capture the Stone and keep from being killed. First, they had to find his old friend, Mason Blackwell, and hope he still took contracts.

BACK AT THE ROOM WHERE THE OTHERS WAITED, WADE PACED WHILE Kovan sat down at a table with a pile of small rocks he had put there. He explained the fight to Buroga and the bounty hunter, Blackwell. The young woman, Stasia, sat to the side, looking disgusted at hearing the details.

"The dead swordsman was Gaunmeer. His crew came from Zawarin about a month ago, escaping the Viper Lords there," Blackwell said. He fiddled with his mechanical leg contraption while he talked. He had not been surprised by the tale or worried from hearing it, still the cold-blooded killer Kovan knew.

"Was this Gaunmeer skilled, Kovan Rainer?" Buroga asked, his deep voice had a way of silencing the others.

Kovan thought a moment. Replaying the fight in his mind, he reluctantly admitted he had been a decent swordsman.

"So, what's the play here?" Wade said, still moving around.

"First, would you sit down, Wade? Now I know how Ellaria always feels when I would pace about," Kovan grumbled, and he pushed the empty chair with his foot. Wade sat and Kovan began to move the stones around to crudely model his plan.

"Blackwell, you take a highpoint behind here. While I would love to have you on the street with me, it's your rifle skills I need. You'll only manage to get off three, maybe four shots before they will scramble behind cover. So, make them count."

"That's why you hired me, Kovan. Each shot will count, you have my word."

"Make sure you wait until Redmar's reinforcements come."

"You think he'll signal his entire band? That's not his style." Blackwell said.

"I think he may try capturing me. Redmar is no dummy. I'm sure he's in contact with the authority and possibly the Sagean himself. He knows they'll be interested in me. Though I can't be sure he will care if I'm alive or dead."

Wade looked at all the small rocks along the table and the lone rock next them. He picked up the small black pebble that stood alone, "Is this one you?"

"Yes. I thought you would be happy you're way over here at the den." Kovan said pointing to the small white stones.

"And Buroga?"

Kovan lifted two larger rocks, "He'll be by the fountain with the wagon to provide fallback fire."

"Kovan," Wade said annoyed, and put the rock back, "This is stupid."

"I told you I had a plan. I never said it was a good plan." Kovan said and he turned to Blackwell, "You said Redmar will be there, right?"

"Yes. He always meets the last wagon coming from the hills. They take their cut and let them continue on to the Crystal Exchange in the east of the city," Blackwell said.

"How many men with him?" Kovan asked.

"Tough to say. Sometimes two, sometimes ten," Blackwell said.

"When we saw Redmar before, he had the same two guys with him," Wade said.

"The kid's right, Kovan. Dodge is usually one of those men. He was out of the city for a time, but he came back a few days ago," Blackwell explained.

"Good," Kovan said.

"This is crazy. I wish we had Tali or Elias here, we could—" Wade started to say, but Kovan kicked his chair to shut him up. Blackwell didn't know they traveled with Luminaries, and he meant to keep it that way. There were rumors that before the Great War, Blackwell was once hired in his youth by the Emperor.

"Or Learon," Stasia said.

"That's right. Learon's possessed by some warrior's spirit. What am I doing in this fight?" Wade complained. While it was a simple deflecting comment, Kovan sensed both a tinge of jealousy and despair coming from the young man.

"You're our Light of Luck, Wade," Kovan said.

"Those aren't real. You need fighters for this. Not luck."

"You always need luck on your side, and we are going to need all the luck we can get on this one. Besides, I don't want you in the fight. I want you focused on getting inside and retrieving the Stone. You tracked the girl there, right?"

"She's usually there, or in one of the gambling dens that's connected to the main building. But I'm sure the Stone is there."

"Charm and luck are going to get us that Stone, not guns."

Wade shrugged off his words and began rummaging through his supplies. He removed his pulsator and holster and put it on. In the many things spilling out of the bag, Kovan saw the glint of steel.

"What's that?" he said, pointing to Wade's things. Wade reached inside and withdrew an old hammer firing gun and handed it to Kovan.

"It was my grandfather's. Aaron Duval."

It was a Resistance-issued silver six gun, with a wooden handle, and someone had taken great care of it. Kovan looked at it and repeated the name in his head. An image of a man with a mustache and blonde hair came to him. A memory he had long forgotten, but one the second cube had brought back.

"I remember him. He fought in Flynn's Legion in Rodaire."

"Yes. That's right. You never told me that before?"

"I . . ." Kovan didn't know how to explain. "I seem to be recalling more and more from those days," he said simply.

Kovan popped the chamber open and emptied the bullets into his hand. With the chamber in place, he spun the gun forward and backward a few times testing the action, cocked the hammer, and released. It was a little stiff, but in fine condition for a forty-year-old gun. The holster leather was worn and in need a little care, but it, too, was in good condition. This was the sort of thing that might be handy if things depending on how things played out.

"You know, they didn't make too many of these, hammer-firing guns. Even then, most of the ones produced were rifles. There was only about a hundred pistols ever made."

"Why?"

"Weapons of war were a new idea then. Subjugated beneath the foot of the Empire, uprisings were rare. The Empire had a powerful army, and most revolts over the centuries were dispatched with ease. All those battles were fought with simple weapons of steel. When our Resistance began, we had the freedom of the New World to plan, train and develop weapons. Projectile weapons were the innovation we thought would win the War. But we were experimenting with everything at the time, including the uses of charged crystals. We had plenty of smart minds but not much money to manufacture. These guns had their time, but they were flawed. The pistols were only good for close combat, but even then, they were notorious for misfiring, and they weren't very accurate. The bullets caught too much drag, and most would go askew. By the time you had reloaded, your enemy would have charged you and ran you through. The rifle was a better weapon, but the battles became so large that they amounted to an opening volley like archers. More defensive than for attack. Except arrows were cheap and more people were skilled with bows... This was your grandfather's? Would you mind if I used it?"

"Sure. But why, if your pulsator's the better gun?"

"This gun inferior in every way but one."

"What's that."

"You can draw them three times faster than a pulsator."

"Is that something we're going to need?" Wade asked.

"I don't know, but if we do, I'll be glad to have it."

"Then it's yours. Until we're through with our task, that is."

Kovan nodded.

"You've seen what Redmar can do; you know how dangerous he is. How do you stay so calm?" Wade asked.

"My mind is set, is all. I can see a clear path ahead and I mean to follow it."

"Even if it's the last path you ever take?" Wade asked.

It was a hard question to answer for Kovan. The old him would have simply said *you're damn right* and left it at that, but things had changed. Reliving his life and revisiting who he was had him questioning things he wasn't used to questioning. He used to think he was in control of his destiny but now he wondered if that was true. *How can you control your own destiny if you can't even control the influences that weave your path and shape your person?* Every path he had taken had left its mark. Marks he never gave much thought to, but now he wondered if the scars of life penetrate the soul or the mind or both?

"Kovan?" Wade said, noticing him lost in thought.

"We take the path that's before us, come what may," Kovan said.

"You alright? You seem different or distracted?" Wade asked.

"I think I am different; we are all different, every day that passes makes us a different person than the day before."

Wade didn't add anything else; he strapped on his pulsator on and went to talk with Stasia. Blackwell tinkered with his machined leg and looked up. His slicked-back hair was mostly grey, with his mustache nearly silver.

"We're going tonight?" Blackwell confirmed.

"We have to," Kovan said. "They will have figured out that we weren't on the winddrifter, and they'll be knocking on our door by tomorrow."

"You thought about your escape?" Blackwell asked.

"I figured we would catch a ship out of Axern in the morning."

"That reminds me—Tali scouted the docks," Wade chimed in, "And she said she thought she saw a familiar sail heading into port. I forget the name of the boat, but she said the captain was named, Moralas."

"See, you are the Light of Luck, Wade When we're done here, I'll ride out there and see if we can't bargain passage with him. If nothing else, he can recommend someone."

"Kovan Rainer, are you worried at all about reinforcements by the Sagean, or even the Scree?" Buroga asked.

"The Scree?" Blackwell said.

"He means the people who were abducted and have now come back," Kovan said.

"Oh, those soulless things. Most people around these parts call them *the plagued*," Blackwell said.

Kovan could see something Blackwell had said upset Wade, who left the room.

"What's wrong with him?" Blackwell asked.

"Don't worry about him. Any of these Scree in Amera?" Kovan asked.

"No, most of them are in Duma. I heard Turgo was overrun with them. If it is a plague, it's rolling across the frontier like the wrath of God," Blackwell asserted.

"God's wrath has never scared me," Kovan said.

"Then what does?" Blackwell said.

"God's indifference."

Kovan was sure his plan was flawed. But he wasn't sure it mattered. Chaos had a way of straightening the path for him. The one thing he was surer of than ever was that he was made for chaos and when everything inevitably went wild, he was confident in his own ability to navigate the swirling fire. The men they were preparing to face were cold-blooded from head to toe. They were not men of purpose, but aimless beings at the mercy of their greed. Redmar was something worse than all of them. The longer Kovan was in this game, the more he realized how little people valued life, *but who am I to pass judgement?* He wasn't focused on judging these men, only eliminating them. If Kovan had learned anything from war, all the endless fighting and ruthless combat, it was that sometimes the only way to win a battle was to be the last man standing; and sometimes that meant being the one willing to face death with a smile.

TWENTY-NINE
PASSAGE (TALI)

They passed over the Zulu Sea together, Learon still stoic in his demeanor. Not cold exactly, but certainly distracted. Tali couldn't understand what had changed with him, but he was different. More serious and somehow, she could tell, more dangerous. His posture was tight like a ship mainline nearing to snap. He had told her about the fighting near Pardona and his killing of soldiers in Midway who had attempted to take Stasia. It wasn't the stories that worried her, but the matter-of-fact way he told the events. It was a detachment that matched her own feelings about her actions in Corma, and lately when she did have an emotional response, they quickly skewed to anger or to despair. Maybe it was like the stories she had read about the Great War, where the phrase *battle hardened* was thrown around. Whatever it was, it was emptiness, like a void imprisoning compassion.

Learon stood holding the loft ladder that led to the blast plank, the warm waters of the Zulu sea spread out below. Tali watched him hoping to hear something from him, something of his thoughts, but she couldn't hear anything.

Sometimes when Tali listened to Elias sleeping, she heard things. Like voices calling out from deep caves, but the words were jumbled by the time she could make them out. Elias did look better than when she first saw him on the ship. Periodically, he would wake and eat and investigate the sky, but he didn't say much. Beyond a short conversation when they had launched from Amera, she had started to speculate if he was even aware of what was happening. Kovan's description of the power he rained down at the fairgrounds made her wonder if that was all he had left. His mystcat Merphi never left his side, but oddly Tali's cat, Remi, stayed away from him.

Over the next day, they sailed on until the ocean waters began to turn a greenish hue. In the morning, with the sun dawning on the water, they saw land again. Meroha exhaled with excitement, she was uncomfortable in the sky, but Bazlyn kept her busy working the sail lines, pullies, and the engine controls. He frequently commended her for being a natural.

With land in sight, Bazlyn said they were flying over the City of Tycan. The lush continent of jungles and rivers stretched out before them. High hills of tangled and packed green wilderness were marked with wisps of mist that hung to the trees and meandered through the jungle top layer like a snake.

When the clouds cleared, Tali could see the mountains and flat plateaus in the greater distance towards which they headed: The Tregorean Province. The morning sun had yet to illuminate the full magnificence. The clearing of clouds also brought Bazlyn to a harried state. The aeronaut wasn't happy they were now visible to the city below. His nervousness was palpable, and he retrieved his old hammer blast rifle, handing it to Learon.

"Look out over edge, and if you even think that they have spotted us, let me know. You too, Semo."

From there, Bazlyn bounded over to the valves controlling the steam and lifting gas and he spun both rapidly.

"What's the matter?" Tali asked.

"All of the coastal cities controlled by the Viper Lords are notorious for shooting down airships."

"I thought the Tregoreans were our biggest concern?" Tali said.

"Oh, they are. No one flies into their lands. They have weapons that the Viper Lords could only dream about."

"So how are we getting there?"

"I'm going to land on a plateau south of Xavole. From there, you will have to raft into their land down the Tyn River. It's the only spot I know of between both borders."

"Bazlyn!" Learon called out.

Bazlyn abandoned what he was doing and rushed over the edge to see what Learon was pointing at. Tali looked from the opposite edge to a sprawling city of territh-mounded roofs and villages of thin-wooded structures. In the hills, she spotted a series of tall wooden towers spaced hundreds of feet apart and tiny dots of men atop them. The ship was still a league above them, but that didn't stop the tower guards from sounding an alarm. Tali followed the guard's flag and found the contraption at which Learon pointed. On a far tower, a giant ballista machine was rotating atop flat gears. The catapult had a huge arrow pulling around to aim at them. The machine had what looked like two bows drawn vertically and a third larger bow drawing back horizontally, each bow in concert with each other to launch the iron headed arrow into the sky.

Bazlyn sprinted to the lift valve and the air release lever and looked back at Learon.

"Tell me when they fire, and I'll launch us up as fast as she can climb."

They released the wench pen, "Now, climb!" Learon said.

Tali heard both his thought and words. She couldn't hear or see the release, and she didn't know how Learon could, but she could see the arrow flying their way. The Savona climbed and the huge arrow narrowly missed them. Bazlyn swung the wheel and shifted the sails to send them further away. Tali looked to the new direction where another arrow launcher wheeled toward them.

"Bazlyn!" Tali called, "Look."

Bazlyn slammed the steam engine level down for full depression and the ship lurched under their feet. Another large arrow flew at the bow of the ship. It clipped the rear boom and cracked it in half. The sail folded, the winddrifter jerked then teetered

Meroha ran to steady the pullies and Bazlyn rushed to the wheel. "Don't you go over!" he shouted to Meroha, "We have to put her down. If they hit the balloon, we're dead," Bazlyn said.

"Wait. Do you have—" Learon began but Elias interrupted him.

"Tali," he muttered, and she hurried to his side. His voice was soft and breathy as he spoke, "The arrows have kinetic energy. I can feel them. So can you. Before they are released, they have a buildup of potential energy. Tap into that. You can't absorb it or manipulate it, but you'll feel it like a beacon. When it releases, when it changes, you'll have a split second to capture it. Got it?"

No, I don't have it. He waved her away and she went to the edge to find the next arrow. The first tower was reloading, and the lines were pulling back. She didn't feel anything, except stress that she was going to fail.

"They've locked it. They're spinning to target." Semo said. He had climbed up almost to the ballast plank to lookout.

She focused on it, searching—then there it was. Like the tension on a spring in her hands. She held it tight.

"Something's wrong," Semo said. Tali opened her eyes she didn't remember closing and let go.

"It's away." Semo called.

"No!" Tali shouted.

The arrow flew directly through the sky to where they had been, missing them. In the confusion, they had failed to adjust to the moving target.

"The second one is about to fire," Semo called.

Tali ran to the other sideboard and snatched the releasing energy in her grip. She felt the energy fill inside her veins. The arrow and lines slowly slid back to place. The arrow feebly went to the edge and tipped over the top. The winddrifter was still going at full speed and the wind passed through her hair. She held it a moment to feel the energy beating in synchronicity with her heart and she flung the energy into the tower behind them. It was enough force to splinter the top battlement and the launcher there crashed.

Tali breathed heavily. She turned back to see stunned faces on everyone but Elias. He was sitting up now, watching her.

She looked out at the second tower, but they were past firing distance now. Bazlyn looked very concerned when he looked at her, but he went to work adjusting his gears to bring the ship back under control.

"That was amazing! From so far away? How are you feeling?" Learon come over to her, his hands on the rail.

"I'm—I'm fine," she squeezed his hand. She was always grateful for his kindness, "Thank you."

"Everyone, find a seat and secure the cats. Semo, come down. The Savona is all over the place without the rear boom and sail. I'm doing my best to keep us in the air," Bazlyn held tight to the wheel, "I'm going to try to get us outside the boundary, but it's going to be bumpy."

They all sat down at the back bench next to Elias. Learon was staring at her.

"What?" she said.

"Your eyes are so. . ." he paused.

"Weird?" she finished.

"No, they're wonderful, but it's more than that… they're comforting," Learon said.

"How's that?" she asked, her eyebrows lifting.

"I've seen Elias use his powers before and the only sign that accompanied the magical feats were the color in his eyes, but that came afterward. Your eyes and the flares off the sides, they glow when you are doing it. It's awe-inspiring and comforting to witness the cause and effect, even if I don't understand it," Learon explained.

"He makes a good point, Tali," Elias said, his face a little more colorful than before, "You must learn to control that somehow or your enemies will always know when you hold energy and when you're using it."

"But how am I supposed to do that? I don't even know it's happening?" Tali asked.

"You don't feel anything?" Elias said.

"No," she said. But that wasn't exactly true, she could feel the heat of them when they glowed, "Maybe" she corrected herself.

"Focus on the *maybe* and try to temper it. It will take time, but like all the unseen forces we are connected to, you will be able to control it," Elias said.

Tali touched her eyes and the flare that reached to her temples. The subtle skin change was barely visible during the day. Sometimes, it looked like a blemish; sometimes it was imperceptible. She had grown used to letting her hair cover it when possible. She always worried about it, even though Learon and Wade always mentioned how amazing it was. She felt like it was an ever-present scar that signaled how different she was. As much as she hated the idea of another problem to solve, she agreed with Elias. It could be a liability in the future amongst people she didn't trust.

The winddrifter dipped and swayed and she gripped the seat tightly. It would seem they had other worries.

After an hour of some of the most nauseating flying she had ever experienced aboard the Savona, Bazlyn called out that he had to land. They had gone as far as he dared both toward the Tregorean border and before the ship failed them. He set the winddrifter down on a low plateau of wild grass and weeds. Bazlyn cursed that he couldn't get them further south, but Tali was happy to be safely on the ground. There were many higher plateaus to southwest and the river was close enough to access.

"You'll have to go down the hill and approach on foot by the river. I don't know this land, but I've seen good maps and the Tyn River will take you to the heart of their province."

"He's right," Elias said, "If we follow the river south, we'll get there."

Semo hauled out the makeshift raft he began crafting during their flight. He lowered it to the ground below. They had convinced Semo to stay with Meroha and Bazlyn while she and Learon took Elias into the Tregorean lands. Mostly they feared the ship might be attacked, but Tali also thought that without him, they didn't appear as imposing a threat to whomever found them.

With the raft on the ground, Learon and Semo finished its construction. What started out as a litter on which to pull Elias was modified into a raft with which they could navigate the river. Tali scouted ahead for the best route to the river. It took some effort to get Elias down; Learon brought him to the sloped path Tali found. With Semo's help, they launched the raft with Elias on it.

Each got on and felt the precarious nature of their craft. Semo returned with a long, somewhat sprightly branch that he had cleaved clean. He pushed them into the river and tossed the pole to Learon. Tali waved goodbye and Learon continued to push them along the lazy current upstream. Tali watched at the front, with their two handmade paddles resting on her lap.

"You sure we'll find them following this river?" Learon asked

Elias opened his eyes to respond, "They will find us, kid."

The jungle was wild and thick and foreign in every way to her. There were various trees Tali didn't recognize. They sprouted from the land and spread out with multiple trunks extending back to the ground, supporting the huge limbs that extended in all directions. One tree could spread for a hundred feet. Other trees looked like they grew from a nest instead of a solid trunk. The trunk branched out at the base like a huge cage, large enough to build a tent underneath. Green vines draped all over and wild animals moved in the thicket unseen, but the sway of leaves betrayed their movements. Birds of bright colors perched calmly and other wild cackles and sounds filled the landscape. Tali was both in awe and terrified to be lost in such a strange land.

IT WAS MIDDAY WHEN THEY WERE SPOTTED. THE SUN SHINING HIGH above, Blue and sweltering, made the river surface sparkle in color, enhanced by the reflective rocks beneath and the iridescent algae. Tali was mesmerized by it. Learon tapped her on the shoulder and motioned her to look.

"We're not alone anymore," he said softly.

On a huge tree ahead, where a branch crossed over the river and smaller trunks punctuated the water to hold it up, a slender figure sat in tight clothes. Tali assumed by the slender shape that it was a woman, but she was almost impossible to see amongst the foliage. Her skintight clothes were colored to blend into the trees, but it was more than that. They somehow shifted in color to match her surroundings.

In the high branches, they could see she had a bow, but it wasn't yet aimed at them. Instead, she simply watched them float by, her bright eyes staring at them from behind a fabric veil that covered her nose and mouth. She wore a hood; as they passed directly below, Tali could see a lock of bright red hair tucked underneath.

It wasn't until they passed below that she spoke, "You are very brave, very stupid, or very desperate?"

"We're desperate," Learon called back.

The woman sprinted off the branch and disappeared in the trees. Tali had trouble following her, but Learon eyed her progress and Tali matched her line of sight to his. Sure enough, the woman appeared a short time later a hundred feet ahead of them. This time, she was on the shore perched on a half-submerged tree trunk.

"You won't get far. Our archers will kill you before the next bend."

"Help us," Learon pleaded.

"Why would I do that, bohoja?" she said. Tali found it an odd name, but Learon didn't even register it.

"This is Qudin Lightweaver, and he is dying. Help us," Learon asked again.

The woman removed her hood to reveal her vibrant red hair. Her ears angled to a point at the top. Her green eyes had a piercing quality. She pulled an arrow from her quiver and nocked it to her bow. Tali began to fill herself with light, but Learon waved her off.

The woman fired her arrow up the river. It slammed into a tree there and another man appeared. The woman waved to him. Then she put her cupped hands to her mouth and made a whistling, melodic call. The man upriver called back in a similar sound.

"Bring your raft to the shore by the man there," she told them.

"Thank you," Learon said.

In the distance, they could hear more calls continuing up the river. They came to the spot where the woman told them to stop and were met by two men similarly dressed to the first woman. Their bows drawn, arrows nocked and pointed at them, they each had a darker skin tone than the young woman.

"Tentarans, lower your guard," the woman said, stepping through the brush. Her veil was still up. It was a satin silk but even with it up, Tali could tell she was beautiful, as were the archers. All three of them had a pristineness to their skin that Tali couldn't describe. The men looked at the woman with red hair and lowered the bows to the ground, arrows still nocked. A large ship came rushing toward them on the river and everyone turned to watch it. The vessel was long and slender, sitting only two people to a width though at least thirty could fit to the length. It approached at a speed Tali thought beyond the pull of the current, powered instead by something below the surface.

The red-haired woman whispered something to one of the archers and he took off running into the jungle. She turned and addressed them.

"I am Echoryn. You have entered our lands unbidden."

"Our friend is dying," Learon said with an edge to his voice.

"So, you said. And you believe he is the Quantum Man?"

"This is Qudin Lightweaver."

"For your sake, I hope that he is. It is what. . ." Echoryn paused midsentence, staring at Learon. She squinted her green eyes and whispered under her breath, "Dooko kara kitano, Kyode?"

"What?" Learon said.

The archer next to her spoke up. "She wonders, where you have come from?"

Whether that was what the woman said or not, Tali saw her flash the soldier a glare that could cut stone.

"We brought Qudin from Tovillore. Our airship is down steam," Learon said.

"Not Qudin—" the archer started to say but the young woman cut him off.

"Are there more with you?" Echoryn said.

"Yes. Our airship landed on a plateau. There are two men and a young woman, waiting there for us. We come in peace. They are good people, and they are unarmed."

"We will find them, and we will see," Echoryn said.

The boat arrived and men helped pull Elias aboard. Tali and Learon followed, and the red-haired woman stepped aboard behind them. A mechanical noise below Tali's feet clicked in place and a low rumble started up. The boat proceeded back up the river, having never turned around.

She looked up at the woman, "Is there a steam engine that propels us?" Tali asked.

The woman eyed her a moment before answering, "A propeller tube. It is not steam-powered."

"Crystal?" Tali guessed.

"Yes."

They progressed along the river a long way, allowing Tali the opportunity to figure out what about their skin was so odd: none of the Tregoreans seemed to sweat. After a series of winding turns, she began to see figures moving in the rocks above them. Tali noticed the shimmer of the afternoon sun off their nocked arrows.

"Learon," Tali uttered his name to look.

"I see them," he said.

Their aim tracked the boat through the river, eyes locked on target and ready to kill. She observed at least nine archers but felt there were three times as many unseen. Some stood among the rocks and some in the trees. The river bent sharply, and they turned to the west, toward the towering formation of mountains. The water was slowing, and the formation of cliffs towered around them, promising an expansive meadow beyond. The sheer sides of the mountains turned from green to exposed rock. The trees and bushes and grass that filled the mountainside were replaced by chiseled stone, and the river took them under set of crossed giant stone-carved swords which spanned the chasm from one cliff to another. The river soon unfolded into a massive lake and the mountainside to their right became a city; one made of elaborately built façades, carved directly into the mountains, with endless arching stone openings and columns.

Giant sculpted figures stood proudly in the façades, as cleanly cut and polished as any modern building she had ever seen. Green vines hung through the openings and strung across the elevations. More figures moved in the rooms through the openings and over the terraces beyond, their shapes appearing and disappearing through the archways.

"No sudden movements. If the archers even think you're acting with aggression, there will be ten arrows in your chest before you can plead for them to stop," Echoryn warned.

The bank of the lake became shaped rock and soon, clean-cut stone, everything meticulously hand-placed. The rock beyond the edge solidified with a mud substance that was impervious to water and formed a flowing dock that lined the river's edge. There were a few other ships docked, all similar in shape to the one they were in. A man jumped out and took the ship lines to tie off at skinny stone plinths with lanterns at the top.

A large group of armed warriors had come to greet the ship and they carried a litter for Elias. Before they could step off, a sharp-pointed boot slammed on the deck.

The boot belonged to a tall woman dressed in tight green clothes overlapped with scaled armor and solid veil across her face. Unlike the other soldiers, her veil was not fabric but a jade plate. Her eyes were painted vibrantly, and she glared at them.

"Where have you been, young Solhara?" She demanded, releasing her vail. She was a stern-looking woman, with a scar at her lip. By her lead, most of the Tregoreans removed their veils. Echoryn was the last to do so. She let it free and wrapped it back behind her hair to re-pin at the front. Tali was surprised by how varied the skin tones were among one race of people, but she knew almost nothing about the Tregoreans, and they all had a look of agelessness to them. The armored leader was one of the older-looking Tregoreans in the bunch.

Echoryn stepped off the boat and the contingent of soldiers behind the stern-faced warrior all kneeled in unison, clattering their spears to the stone.

Learon and Tali looked at each other. This Echoryn was someone of importance, they realized.

"Echoryn Solhara, you are an infuriating young woman. I curse my charge as your guardian," the lead warrior said.

"Nokha, this man they bring to our province is the Quantum Man," Echoryn said.

"Your runner said this. Monk Hira Zadar has been informed of the situation and prepares for him now," Nokha said.

Echoryn nodded and walked toward the tall arches.

"Come with us. We have many questions for you," the woman called Nokha demanded.

They followed the full squad through the building frontage and into the heart of the mountain where an expansive city thrived within. Tali and Learon stood equally stunned at the world before them.

"This is the city of Sualden. Keep moving," Echoryn said.

Tali had thought at first how the front-terraced design reminded her of the temple beneath the falls of Marathal, but where she expected to enter a large building, they entered another world, as though the whole of the mountain was hollowed out; the city of the Tregoreans lay before them, an endless weaving of streets. Villages and large buildings were lit with lanterns and orbs, but the sunlight, too, streamed down from openings high above. Among the rock and stone, there were trees and grass, like the jungle wrapped in and around the mountains, cradling them in green vines and life. The squad walked down a series of stairways to a small canal where a boat waited for them at the water's edge. It was a much smaller boat but equally interesting as the first. The ferryman held a long pole with a small hanging lantern at the top and a series of levers were at the stern of the vessel where he stood.

When they were aboard, the driver manipulated the levers and the ship lurched into motion. The canal weaved through the city among a series of additional riverways snaking all over. Then, they were disappearing into a cave and the view changed. The lantern at the head of the ship was the only substantial light. They merged with other canals at some point and continued deeper within the territh.

Finally, the cave ended, and a light was seen at the mouth of the tunnel. The air had become stifling, and they emerged into a new giant, cavernous space. A still lake spread out at the foot of a large gleaming palace. Multiple tunnels funneled into the lake from various darkened caves. The mountaintop above was gone, like a hole had been scooped out of the rock, with the sides cut and sloped in ridges. The palace was at least seven-stories in height and the top spires failed to reach halfway to the surface above. Large statues at the sides stood like proud sentries with stone-shaped cloaks and lances angled at a tilt.

The light in the sky looked to be fading when they reached the edge. They filed in through tall wooden doors ornately decorated with silver and jade.

"Where are you taking us?" Learon asked, annoyed.

"To our master healer," Nokha said curtly. It was a tone to suggest she would not answer again.

The entire palace was sculpted and polished to the point Tali could see their reflections in the columns as they passed. The Tregoreans had always been known as people of the trees and wilderness, skilled fighters, and archers, but from what she had seen, they were masters of stone.

Echoryn left the escort and disappeared down a hallway while they were led into a small room where the ceiling rounded from one side to the other and an old man in robes stood over an old, frayed book. Small orbs lit the space and the man turned to accept their entrance. He paid little attention to Tali or Learon. His eyes found Elias first and he attended to him without hesitation. Tali found a small comfort in his actions.

They moved Elias from the litter to the table inside and he groaned. The healer held his arm and checked his eyes. He rushed over to his table of instruments, vials, and powders. When he returned, he blew some fine purple powder over Elias's head. It evaporated in a mist and Elias fell unconscious.

Learon made a move to get closer, but the guard stopped him force-fully with the end of his lance.

"How long has he been sick?" The healer shuffled through the room, precariously filling his hands with supplies.

"We don't know exactly. Eighteen days, give or take," Learon said.

"He doesn't have much time."

"Can you heal him?" Tali asked.

"I can, but I don't have the ingredients on hand that I need."

"How can we help?" Tali said.

Four armored men entered the room, each as serious and dangerous-looking as Semo. They had swords at their sides and long-bladed lances each with a crystal housed in the steel. They were followed by three people in immaculate clothes and jewels: an older man and woman followed by a young woman with red hair. It was Echoryn, but Tali hadn't recognized her. She now had on a purple dress that was mostly sheer. It wrapped around her body and her arms, and up over her neck where it was clasped with a jade leaf.

Learon's mouth was open, and she honestly couldn't blame him. Everyone in the room went to a knee except Tali and Learon, though she felt very strange not doing so. Their clothes almost demanded respect.

The woman who had some gray in her hair, spoke first. "I am Aruna Solhara, the Queen of the Kihan, what you call the Tregoreans. This is King Talus. We do not allow strangers in our borders. Our daughter tells us you bring Qudin Lightweaver?"

Daughter? Echoryn was the princess?

"We do. Elias—I'm sorry, Qudin—told us that your healer was the only one capable of saving him," Learon said.

"Hira Zadar, can you heal him?" Queen Aruna asked.

The healer lifted his head, "I can. What's been bound by the Shadow can be undone by the Light, but we must move him to the dusting cham-ber. And I require a shroom of the Red Moon for the elixir. It grows on the Wunri perch in the Turquoise Flats of the Kaze Valley."

"We will send a squad immediately," Queen Aruna said.

"I'll go." Learon said. The Queen paused but didn't address him.

"Master Hira, if it grows on the flats, then it must be harvested in the night." Queen Aruna asked.

"You are correct."

The queen looked to the king for his input.

"They will make it there," King Talus said firmly.

"I can help," Learon spoke again.

The Queen nodded and King Talus said, "You may."

"I can show him there," Echoryn said, speaking up for the first time.

"No," The Queen said definitively.

"There's no time to argue, Mother. We must go now, and I know—" Echoryn said

"No," Queen Aruna cut her off, "Escort him to the Western Walk and wait for the Renja Guards. They will take him from there."

"Come on, bohoja," Echoryn said to Learon, and she stomped out of the room.

"I'll go, too," Tali said.

"No, I need one of you to stay if Qudin awakes," the healer said, "A familiar face will be needed to calm him, and another Luminary may be of use."

He knew she was a Luminary, but from the look on the Queen's face, she had not known.

"We will leave you to it, Master Hira," the Queen said and left.

Men followed inside after the queen and king and lifted Elias back on the litter.

"Follow us," the healer said.

They led Tali into a circular room that opened in the center to accommodate a towering contraption with a pit full of crystals. Elias was lying on a table in the back of the room, a thousand tiny particles surrounding him. Tali stepped though the opening and toward him. The instant she stepped inside, she felt a tingling along her arms and the back of her neck. It glowed with hues of purple and magenta. It didn't hurt but it did itch at first.

"What is this, what's happening?" Tali said, her eyes darting all around, her breathing short and racing.

"This is the dusting chamber. The circulating crystals are attracted to your powers. Don't worry, they drift away after a bit. Please take a seat. The others will not be back for a while and there is nothing for you to do but wait."

Tali found a chair against the dark gray stone wall. A low glowing lamp nearby provided a little warmth in the otherwise cold cave. She watched the master healer prepare items on a table near Elias, wishing she had Remi with her to keep her company while she waited. A tightening in her chest was making it hard to breath. Worry for the people she loved was mounting and now her concern for Learon was making the nerves in her hands tense. She closed her eyes, rubbed her hands, and wished her anxiety would drift away, too.

THIRTY

TURQUOISE FLATS (LEARON)

earon waited on the endless rampart the Tregoreans called *the Western Wall*. Echoryn brought him through the interior mountain canals to an arched cave, the walls of which were lit by orbs on angled sconces. At the top of the cave were doors that led out to the guard walk. The sun was low on the horizon, but vibrant and brightly illuminating the rampart. Echoryn left him there and told him not to move. Learon stepped to the stone hedge of the battlement; it came chest high. His chin to his hand and elbow on the stone, he gazed down from the massive stone wall at the endless coast, and out to the Brovic Ocean beyond that. The Tregorean's Western Wall was an endless lookout along the mountainside, facing the Drycoast and the Brovic Ocean. *What were they watching for?* Learon thought.

He heard someone approach and turned to find Echoryn coming toward him, clutching a pack in her arms with a second thrown over her own shoulder. A short walking staff was tied to hers. She wore her tight green outfit again and pushed the extra pack into his hands.

"I told you not to move. You moved," Echoryn said.

Did she mean from the wall to the edge? He thought, but didn't respond.

"Well, let's go. It's a long walk to the Turquoise Flats and we need to get there and back by morning," Echoryn said.

Learon looked around but it was obvious no one else was coming with them, "We're not waiting for the others?"

"Do you want to wait? More importantly, do you think your friend can wait?"

"No," he admitted.

"Neither do I. I know our lands better than any *ranger* and I know the Turquoise Flats and the perch of which Master Zadar spoke. I told my guards to meet us on the north trail. They will be right behind us."

He swung the pack over his shoulder and followed her. They walked a long time along the Western Wall. The air was thinner here than in the jungle, which was to be expected, but it was as thin as the air in the White Hawk Mountain where he was used to hiking.

"You breathe loudly, bohoja. Are you going to make it?" Echoryn asked.

"Sorry," he said, embarrassed to be winded. "My name is Learon, by the way, and I prefer that to bohoja."

She smiled but said nothing.

"You change clothes more than anyone I know?" Learon observed.

"I prefer my scouting outfit; I had to change for my parents," Echoryn said.

He noticed symbols carved into the mountain above every door they passed, some simple and others intricate.

"What do the symbols mean?" he asked.

"They tell where every passage leads."

"I understand that, but why do some of them repeat?"

"There are many canals within our land, within the mountains, and not all of them flow together or with the same speed. Sometimes the passages behind the doors have many tunnels connected; some tunnels will take you to the Loren, some the Lagrin or some to the Veerin. The many canals of the Corridon are intricate but efficient."

"Corridon? Is this the name of your province?"

"No, our province is called Ammadon. Corridon is the name of the system of canals that connect all of Ammadon, from Tarhallen to Sualden to the Averient, to Saber's End and Moorlon, which is where we are headed. To reach Moorlon, the farming plateaus, we must walk the Wall."

"We can't take a river there?" Learon asked.

"The Wall is quicker than navigating the Assemblage, where the river would take us. It's extremely crowded in the evening, and we need to get through the farmlands quickly."

"Your healer, Master Zadar, said we have to find the mushroom at night. Why?"

"It glows in the dark. That's how we will find it," Echoryn stopped at a set of doors and pushed. The great battlement wall continued leagues further. "Come we have far to go, and it will take most of the night to get there. We cannot be on the flats when the sun is out."

THEY WALKED FOR HOURS, LATE INTO THE NIGHT, BEFORE RESTING. IT had taken them a long time to climb through the farming plateaus. It covered most of the northern half of the province. The system of stairways and bridges allowed them to pass by and, for Learon, the chance to admire the agricultural ingenuity of the Kihan people. When they reached the jungle, Echoryn put her hood up, tucked in her hair, and clasped the veil over her face. She handed Learon a mask and told him to put it on and cover his mouth. They stood at a precipice above a darkened valley where, even in the night, the space below looked darker by degrees of shadow repelling the moonlight.

"This is the Kaze Valley. Among other things, the green leopard stalks the night. It is very dangerous; even the Ravinors don't hunt here."

He had forgotten that the Nahadon jungles were the home of the Ravinors, too.

"Echoryn, why do we have to cover our faces?" he asked.

"There are many animals in the jungle that hunt by the smell of our breath and others are attracted to the moist heat of it. There are also some pollens in the far east that, should you inhale them, will make you very sick. It is better this way. Trust me."

Whether it was her eyes or the way she spoke to him, he did trust her. It was an odd realization to come to, having only just met a person.

"Thank you," he said, unprompted.

She looked at him and started to hike down the slope, "Don't thank me yet, squirrel."

Learon cringed, he had graduated from bohoja, *whatever that was*, to squirrel. They trekked through the jungle and Learon had the sense the whole of it was alive, like eyes watching them pass. He made a point to step where she stepped. He knew how important it was to follow the lead of any guide in their homeland. No wilderness was alike, and no trail existed without reason. So, he stayed to the path she set and the pace she set.

Echoryn was nimble on her feet and didn't seem to tire. As the night wore on, he thought they would never come to this Turquoise Flats when suddenly from the thick trees, the land opened and the ground before them shone in hues of green and blue. Something unfamiliar stretched over the field like a blanket of glistening melted sugar, only turquoise-colored instead of amber. He didn't know why that was what came to mind other than that it looked brittle and thick at the same time. It didn't escape his attention that Echoryn had not ventured into the flats and instead, skirted the edge, looking for something.

"What is it?" Learon pointed to the colored ground.

"It's a peculiar lichen that grows here."

"Is it dangerous?"

"Yes, kind of. It's very sticky. A little exposure to it will not harm us, but a lot would kill you; and if you stand in it too long, it gathers."

Echoryn picked a path along the side until she stopped, "There. There is the Wunri Perch."

Learon had been so focused on following Echoryn's steps exactly that he hadn't noticed the glowing plant life around them. Now that he looked, the phosphorescent vegetation was everywhere, and it glowed in all kinds of amazing colors. He looked where she pointed. It was a mounding rock formation about three hundred feet from where they stood. The mound crested above the blanket of lichen and atop was a small patch of glowing flowers, plants, and mushrooms.

"There is where you'll find the mushroom of the Red Moon," Echoryn said.

"What do they look like?"

"They are red-capped with orange stems. You must go slowly across the flats and return slowly, but don't linger. Find the mushroom and come straight back. The sun will be up soon."

"What happens when the sun comes up?" Learon said.

"The lichen changes. Now go," she urged him scanning the wilderness beyond.

He stepped slowly on the fragile surface expecting to sink in, but he didn't. The turquoise blanket beneath his feat bellowed and creaked, but his foot didn't penetrate the surface, yet the weight of each depression and shift exhibited a groan. On the surface, he didn't see any cracking but underneath, he feared what fractures had formed. As Learon made his way to the perch, he began to understand the darker patches were less brittle, but more suspicious. He was reminded of the pool inside the Sagean Tomb that had solidified to walk atop. He had the same nausea in his stomach now as he did then, the impending doom of a false step knotting his insides.

Midway across the plane, one of his steps was followed by a blast of steam ten feet away. Step after step shot puffs of hot gases from beneath the surface. At the brightest point near the center, he finally saw what lay underneath.

The turquoise lichen there was so brilliant and clean, it became glasslike, and he could see below. It was an expansive cavern of nothingness. A thousand foot drop at least. The lichen had formed over a huge opening in the land and the depths of the void shone with hues of green and blue until it became darkness, the light failing to reach the bottom. Learon's pulse quickened.

He was close to the mounded rock formation of glowing plants. The vines sprawled over the surface like lace. He reached the solid ground and breathed heavily. There were hundreds of mushrooms all over and at least seven varieties growing in the thicket. The mycelium undergrowth pulsed with color. He found a patch of the Red Moon mushrooms as Echoryn had described. Their stalks glowed orange to the gills where it turned red. Gently, he removed some and put them in his bag. But he couldn't take his eyes off a patch of mushrooms at the center. The brilliant blue mushroom was hard to look away from. It glowed like it had a sound to it. More alive than the rest of the jungle, it shimmered with faint pulses running through it. He had never seen anything so ethereal.

"Learon!" Echoryn called from the edge.

He looked up to see the morning brightening had begun in the sky. He needed to return to the edge more swiftly than he had come. He grabbed what was needed and threw everything securely in his bag, turning to make his way back and almost forgetting to breathe as he went.

The once taut blanket of lichen suddenly began to droop. It hung like a failing net below his feet, the chasm looming below.

Echoryn saw the failing, too, "Run!" she screamed.

Learon looked up to her and sprinted. The green slime began to part and peel away at every step. It quickly disintegrated. Learon's heart pounded, and his blood pumped furiously. He ran as fast as he ever had in his life.

He sprinted from stretched piece to piece and when each tore away, he stepped to the next. The pieces falling away and disappearing into the dark abyss. His focus became connected to picking the safest path back to the edge. The gap to solid ground was widening and Echoryn was now above him. With a final leap he bounded from the last patch of lichen and lunged.

Learon reached the brink with the first sun rays at his back. He clung for the edge and Echoryn dove for him. His feet, kicking beneath, caught in the sludge of lichen, thick at the perimeter. Echoryn pulled and Learon clawed at the territh until he found purchase, and he was freed from the turquoise web.

His knees on solid ground, he turned over and breathed heavily. Echoryn hit him in the stomach. She looked distraught.

"How?" she said out of breath, like she had been the one running, "I can't believe what I just saw, stupid Squirrel."

"Next time, I'll let you go," he exhaled through gasps of breath.

Echoryn bounced up and brushed herself off. She stood running her hands over her face and sighed. She took a deep breath and handed him a large leaf she tore off a nearby plant but avoided eye contact, "Here, use this to clear the lichen off you and let's go. We must get back before the Blue."

"Will Qudin die by then?"

"No, by then my mother will have discovered I took you and the entire order of Renja will be out looking for us."

THIRTY-ONE
MASKS OF MERINDE (ELLARIA)

E llaria figured it had been three days since her abduction, but she wasn't positive. Edward had kept her confined in the cabin aboard his winddrifter the entire time. She knew they had landed once. She felt the fall in her stomach and heard soldiers piling in, along with cargo. The sound of the wheels rolling over the wood deck above was unmistakable.

After their brief stop, they had been flying a very long time; longer than most winddrifters were typically capable of. She had to assume the ship was an example of the innovation coming out of the Citadel. It was common knowledge amongst the Guild and the now-dissolved Coalition that the Citadel was investing heavily in advancing aircrafts, with the goal of military use.

A knock on her door opened to a soldier who escorted her for another audience with the Sagean Lord. This had happened a few times, but today inside the main cabin, Edward had the shutters on his windows open and she could see it was light outside.

Edward lifted a finger for them to wait. She stood in the doorway as he read an old book. She could tell he was deeply studying it, whatever it was. She had seen it out the last time she was inside his room. Her only glimpse of one of the pages had shown a scepter with multiple markings. He closed the book and looked at her and the guard by her side.

"Good morning, Ellaria, we will be arriving at our destination short-ly," Edward said and stood up. He retrieved a bundle of clothes and handed them to her, "Please get changed and meet me on deck."

The guard escorted her back to her cramped bunker. She changed and was promptly escorted above. The dress was Merindean in style, a colorful ankle-length dress with an evolving pattern that shifted at her thighs and varied again at her waist and bodice. It was amber in color and the neckline embroidery resembled a magnificent necklace, with one shoulder left exposed. Ellaria wrinkled her nose at the shoulder reveal. Most woman her age were satisfied to conceal everything they could. In this instance, she didn't care that her thick arm and shoulder wouldn't appease an appraising eye, she cared that she was offering more skin for the Kalihjan sun to burn. The continent of Merinde was a desert and the sun here was relentless.

On the main deck, the heat was stifling and made breathing difficult. Ellaria kept her eyes on the smooth wood planking to avoid looking out past the ship. At the sidewall, the guard shoved her slightly when she stopped. Edward looked at her curiously until it dawned on him why she hesitated to come to further.

"You're afraid of heights?" he said.

Ellaria nodded confirmation. He stepped toward her and walked her back to the middle column. The canopy of layered sails above were all full and tightly stretched while the ship descended from the sky.

"When we land, we are heading to the palace for a meeting. The others are aware I have you, but they will expect me to leave you aboard or escort you to the prisoner's ship. Personally, I'm not fond of shackles, leashes, or cages," Edward absentmindedly rubbed the ring at his finger, "We are above such things, correct?" he said.

"Yes, I think we are," she answered as confidently as she could.

"And you will behave?" Edward said.

"Do I have a choice?"

"No, I can make your blood boil whenever I like."

Ellaria rolled her eyes. She knew he meant it, but it was her natural reaction to all superfluous masculine boasts.

When they were a few hundred feet from the ground, Ellaria finally peeked out to see the great old city of Kalihjan and all its congested glory rising toward them. Every foot of the city seemed inhabited; people jammed in amongst the chaotically arranged, sandblasted, white-plastered buildings. A mix of flat roofs draped with colorful sails, and green oxidized copper domes dominated the landscape, with the richer estates brightly decorated in tile arrays showcasing intricate patterns on the exterior walls and colonnades. Near the harbor, she noticed a larger number of swarming birds, a sight she didn't remember from the previous time she had been here.

The instant Ellaria stepped off the ship, it was like she had entered a world of breathing steam. The air and heat consumed her and sweat emerged unannounced in uncomfortable places. The full punch of the humidity had been concealed while in the sky. This was the land where the zenithal season lasted all year round, a city of eclectic traditions, where the High Order wore ornate masks in public; a result, most likely, of the country being conquered by the Menodarians over three-thousand years ago. With most histories lost, the origin of the tradition was unknown and the Menodarians had abandoned the continent centuries ago.

The airfield was adjacent to the harbor and the path from the landing field led into the old docks. A thousand masts of various sizes rose and fell in the full marina. Navigating down the aged wood pier, they marched past crews of men offloading crates held aloft with wooden poles. The masked men and women were an unsettling sight which Ellaria would never get used to, giving the old city an aura that everyone had something to hide.

Beyond the harbor's main palisade, a large contingent of soldiers awaited them. They stood in full gleaming armor on the sunbathed walkway of crushed white stone, the hoard of birds behind them. To the people of Kalihjan and all of Merinde, the Sagean was the manifestation of the Creator among men; they had always been one of the most faithful countries on Territhmina.

At the sight of Edward in his striking white cloak and blue suit beneath, the contingent knelt. Their crouching to the ground came in a unified clatter and revealed the gruesome sight beyond. Two rows of tall poles lined the walkway, with bodies or heads atop every post. The vultures swirled around in disgusting delight. Ellaria felt her stomach turn and averted her eyes.

It was a short walk from the pier past the spread of the impaled, but with the heads of dead men and women stabbed atop each, it felt a lot longer. At the far end, they were met by two men dressed in suits, each holding their jackets with sweat visible at their shirts and forehead.

One man was older than Ellaria; he had grey hair and a muscular jawline and carried himself like a trained fighter. She noticed he held a cloak and not a suit jacket as she first thought. The other was a skinny man with a shrewd look to his eyes and sharp facial features. The first had a bigger reaction to seeing Ellaria, but neither said anything.

"We are blessed—" they began, but Edward interrupted them.

"Dispense with the customs. What has happened here, Verro? One of those heads was Delusa," Edward demanded in a tone more akin to the voice she remembered in the tomb, the tone of a Sagean ruler.

Delusa was the ambassador of Merinde in the now-dissolved Coalition. He had argued with Ellaria at court those many months ago in Adalon. If his head was on a pole, she had missed it, not wanting to see.

"The entire council here has been dispensed with," Verro said.

"Then who leads here?" the Sagean said.

"A woman named Moria Ghulshan. The people call her the Mistress of Merinde, though she says that she is but a servant for the Old One," Verro explained.

"What?"

"That's not all. She has a. . . A thing by her side. A beast we know nothing of," Verro said.

"A beast?" the Sagean said.

"She called it a *Mirthless* and said that the Old One has blessed her with the power to take over this continent. She says she has many of these things, an army." The second man said.

Edward flagged down a soldier nearby.

"By the Light, my Lord," the young soldier said.

"Lieutenant, please return to my ship and prepare my automatons. I want them on the march and ready to take this city if called upon," the Sagean said.

The lieutenant left quickly, jogging back the way they had come.

"That is prudent, My Lord, but ultimately unnecessary, I believe. Moria said she will support us. They are eager to help, in fact. But they do want the pleasure of your company before they release the ships to us," Verro said.

"Fine, let's proceed. I must get out of this sun before I melt," The Sagean said.

The two men turned and led the way to the palace. Edward pulled Ellaria back to speak outside of earshot.

"The skinny man is Verro Mancovi. He is smart and the unofficial leader of my Court. The brutish one is Batak Asheen. He is probably the most feared."

She nodded and kept walking. They had discussed his entire Court in depth during their meetings aboard the winddrifter, but it was good to put faces to the names. She was still astounded that the Court was made up of the most powerful businessmen and inventors in the world.

The palace was one ornamentally carved surface after another. There was an old grit to the city that carried into the palace itself. The coarse stone floor was a magnificent collection of huge stones with patterned inlays and colors. The walls were all covered in mosaic tiles and the coolness of the corridor was an amazing relief from the stifling air outside.

They reached a large room on the second floor, full of people. The left wall was lined with arches and windows. Above every arch was a circle of stained glass. The view beyond showed the thick sandy city and where the heatwaves were visible in the blistering air.

Two expertly-crafted heartwood chairs stood at the center of the opposite wall, both illuminated with colored light. One was empty and in the other sat a masked woman. She wore tightly wrapped red and gold clothing with exposed stitching around the patterned cloth. The effect of the dress made the woman almost look like a patched machine. She sat with one leg up on the seat and her arm resting atop of it. She was partially sunken in the large chair and behind her mask, she could have been asleep. The mask was unlike any Ellaria had yet seen. It was angled to a ridge at her nose and mouth, but from that, gold lines stretched like a web to edges where the mask fanned out like a crown of gold in the shape of a large spade. Her eyes were in there somewhere, but the dark patches between the webbing made it look like she had many eyes. She also wore gloves of gold with fingers elongated to sharp points. Her fingers impatiently tapping on her knee were the only sign she wasn't asleep.

Beside her chair stood a tall, ghastly-looking beast. Ellaria mistook its beige head and smooth face for a mask, but it was more like bone. It almost resembled a ravinors lizard form, but the bone features of its face were pronounced and swollen. The sunken eyes were small and red beneath the bone's brow. It looked blankly at the room, but Ellaria had the sense it was aware of every movement in the chamber. It carried a long-bladed lance.

The many surrounding chairs were occupied, but she followed Batak and Verro to seats around the outside of the center space and the large red rug that dominated the floor. This Mistress of Merinde looked uninterested by their entrance. They waited a moment more before the Sagean came in, announced by palace guards in robes.

Edward showed himself to one of the chairs. Everyone in the room knelt and to Ellaria's surprise, the Mistress joined them. Edward settled into the oversized chair and spoke to the woman in red and gold.

"I am told you are the new ruler of Merinde, Mistress Moria?" the Sagean said.

"I have been given this land by the Old One, my Lord." Moria answered.

She still called him Lord, which Ellaria found interesting, and she could see that Edward found it reassuring.

"The Old One's hand is behind the changes here?" The Sagean asked.

"But of course, My Lord. I was but a simple woman living in the small village of Embree when the Old One came to me. It spoke of a ship arriving at night and bringing me its army of Mirthless. I was to meet this ship in Vemabest. It promised me powers to lead my people and promised that through my journey, I would acquire a following.

"The Old One spoke no lie. From the next day, I did possess powers I had never known, and, on my journey, I met many people who for unknown reasons began to follow me. We met the army of thirty-one Mirthless in Vemabest. Thirty-one may not sound like an army, but each Mirthless is as strong as any three soldiers and worth ten in battle. From there, we set out and reclaimed Merinde, from the city of Desmar to Kalhijan. I had the power to expose the ambassador and his council for the imposters they were, and we took the palace," Moria concluded.

"I see. And the people of Merinde follow you?" The Sagean said.

"They do. They have not resisted my coming or the words of the Old One. But we are loyal to the Sagean Order, My Lord. Merinde was once the most trusted lands of the Sagean's and so we are again. We are at your service," Moria said.

"So, you will give us ships to go to the Black Shore?" The Sagean asked.

"I have an armada of four ships awaiting to set sail as we speak, My Lord. Your success at the Temple of Ama is of the utmost importance to the Old One and I am to aid you as you wish."

"What of these Mirthless, do you control them?"

"They follow my command and yours, My Lord. Would you like them to accompany you to the Black Shore?"

"I don't believe that is necessary," The Sagean said.

"Please My Lord, take A'garik with you," Moria said pointing toward the beast standing next to her, "They are elite fighters and equally blessed by the Old One."

Edward reluctantly agreed and stood to leave. The Mistress of Merinde stood next to him, her face still hidden behind the mask; she leaned close and whispered something no one else in the room could hear. Edward's face looked back at her quizzically. Whatever she had told him, Edward had found it intriguing.

They filed out of the Palace and back to the Sagean's glider craft. Back at the airfield, there was now a second ship next to the Sagean's. They climbed aboard the Sagean's ship, followed by the entire Court of Dragons. The guard made to take Ellaria below deck when Edward stopped him.

"Leave her with me," The Sagean said, and then he addressed the Court gathering on deck. Their small conversations broke away with the sound of the Sagean's voice. A woman standing with her hands on her hips stared at Ellaria. She had blonde hair and wore an obscene amount of jewelry.

"I see you have brought me a Cast for the fountain, Sagean. I am grateful. But shouldn't she be in with the other cargo?" the woman said.

"Enough, Shirova. I will determine Miss Moonstone's fate when we reach the Temple. Now, who here knew anything of this power shift on Merinde?" They all looked at one another, but no one answered. Ellaria thought she saw Shirova grin.

"It's unsettling to say the least, but we have not had contact with the Old One for some time now. It is possible that It fears our efforts need assistance," Verro suggested.

"We have known for a long time that the Old One has more power than we realize," Batak suggested.

"Yes, but this is extreme," a man said. He wore a black cloak and top hat and he looked oddly familiar. Ellaria was sure he must be roasting in his attire in the sun, but he showed no sign of being uncomfortable. He did, however, keep his fingers pressed to the dragon ring on his right hand. She assumed this must be Theomar. None of the men present were old enough to be Herod. There was another man squirming and shying away from the discussion, probably Herriman. He stood so close to Theomar they could share an umbrella if it started raining.

"We will deal with the Old One together after the Temple. What is the status of the barge out of Adalon?" The Sagean asked.

"The last communication we had, the Gem had made it through the Neck of Aquom," Batak answered.

"The Band of the Black Sails offered no resistance?" the Sagean said.

"No, My Lord, they requested a transport tax, but that was all. It seems the other Syndicate leaders were able to convince Mr. Barragan," Batak said.

"And your play to capture the Tail Feather Cities, Verro?" The Sagean asked.

"It is underway. I have sent Duraska to personally control the Scree and the Rendered. They are starting in Duma," Verro answered.

"Why Duraska? I thought he was leading the army from Anchor's Point?" the Sagean said.

"I sent Alden Vick to take over, and Duraska to the south. He knows the Zulu better than Vick. Also, I received a report from the south about a young woman with Luminary powers. Some say her name is Rue. But we haven't had that verified yet. She was seen traveling through Corma. Apparently, she defeated a large contingent of the Reckers Syndicate there. I sent additional men and some Rendered automatons," Verro explained.

Ellaria's heart fluttered at hearing Tali's alias, Rue, spoken amongst the Court.

"What about Razor Redmar? Is he aware of your schemes to take over his stronghold on the crystal mines?" Theomar asked.

"Razor has been warned, and we have an understanding," Verro said.

"You mean when he was at the Court Estates? I remember he wanted an audience with the Sagean," Theomar said.

"Theomar is correct, but when Redmar sees firsthand the force of the Sagean's power, he will wisely fall in line," a dark-haired woman said.

Ellaria recognized her as Aylanna. Not from Edward's description but from her own past, before her family relocated from Ravenvyre. A time long before the war, just two young girls playing in the gardens at the palace of Redvine. Ellaria remembered Aylanna and her family and their love of Rodaire. Aylanna had, for the most part, stood back and watched the rest talk; never registering Ellaria's presence. It was curious she chose this moment to speak, and the question had been addressed to Verro, but the others accepted her statement and moved on.

"Aylanna's airship and my ship will fly to the lowlands east of the Black Shore and lead our teams in on foot from there to the Temple. One or two of you should sail out with the Merinde ships," the Sagean said.

"I will go," Theomar said.

"That's good of you, Theomar. I noticed your son is not here. Did he miss his flight?" Verro asked.

"If he made his ship to Aquom, he will be arriving with the transport team, but I haven't heard from him since Midway," Theomar said, and he looked at Ellaria as he said it.

"*I* would prefer to fly," Shirova said.

"You're welcome aboard my ship." Edward said. Shirova bowed her head slightly but said nothing, nor did she smile. Aylanna, however, smiled.

"I think Herriman should sail with the fleet and I will, as well," Batak said, "I want to meet the transport team and my son on our way into the Temple. Transporting the Soul Gem through the jungle must be carefully seen to, in case the Tregoreans contest our passage."

Ellaria looked around and from what she knew of the Court, she found it curious that they had all entrusted their children with the transportation of the Soul Gem. She wondered if that was where Aylanna's daughter was as well. She was surprised Edward hadn't asked about her, but maybe he already knew the answer.

"Then it is settled, Verro will fly with Aylanna. As soon as my pilot tells me we're ready, I'm calling the Rendered back aboard and we are taking off," the Sagean said.

"By the Grace of the Blue, safe journey to you all," Batak said.

Edward motioned the guard to take Ellaria away as he went to speak with Verro. She was escorted down the center steps into the belly of the large ship and to her disbelief, the guard left her in Edward's quarters. He shut the door and stood outside. Ellaria froze a second, contemplating what she could accomplish here. She rushed to the desk where the book Edward had been reading was situated.

The old leather cover was faded, and the front image almost worn away. It showed four dragons flying around a circle that seemed to swirl. The center image was either a temple or a volcano, it was too worn to see. The spine read *The Sintering Fountain*. The first few pages were unlabeled drawings of the fountain and a gruesome-looking mask with tethered wires attached, but the first page with writing was boldly titled *The Dragon's Awakening*. Ellaria turned through page after page. It was an ancient book on the Temple of Ama and the Sintering Fountain. There were drawings and depictions of the machine and the Soul Gem. There were many drawings of maps from the Black Shore to the Temple and instructions on how to operate the machine, with incantations and symbols Ellaria decided referenced specific Luminary powers.

Oddly, there was also a mix of languages. Some of the passages had been deciphered, but poorly. She found the section on the Black Scepter that she knew Edward had been studying intently. It spoke of binding souls, and it looked like the Scepter was crafted with the Soul Crystal. She remembered seeing a picture of the Soul Crystal in Elias's library. It had been part of one of the crystal amulets meant to trap the Wrythen. She flipped further and found some undeciphered descriptions about a warning, the advanced make-up of the Genesis Chamber that housed the Machine, and its unknown origin.

Outside, she heard footsteps and an argument. Edward had slapped the guard to the ground, and she heard him scream out. She closed the book and dashed over to the chair in which she always sat. The Sagean burst through the door with obvious anger coloring his face. He squinted at her and sat down. She wondered if he really cared that she was in there alone or that he didn't have control. He sat down and smoothed out his clothes to regain his composure.

"What do you think? Who can I trust and who is out to supplant me?" Edward asked her.

"I'm not sure you can trust any of them. Maybe Batak," she said.

"Batak? But he's the most dangerous."

"In a fight, certainly he is. If I wanted to go to battle, I would select Batak to lead an army; but in terms of positioning against you? No. Don't get me wrong, Batak is still a danger to you, but he is also the most content with his position as your council. The two you should worry about are Verro and Aylanna. They're smart and calculating and I believe they're closer than you realize," Ellaria said.

"What makes you say that?"

"They purposely sat away from each other in the palace, but I caught them looking at each other at various points while you spoke with Mistress Moria."

"And Shirova?" Edward said.

"Shirova would slit your throat if she dared, but she is also desperate for the powers the Fountain will bring her. Theomar, he is your biggest threat, but I think he despises the other Court members more. Is his son disliked by the Court?" Ellaria asked.

"His son is Aramus."

"The murderer?" Ellaria said.

"Right. Aramus is not liked by anyone. Tell me more about Verro?" Edward said.

"Verro and Aylanna are both probably better allies then enemies. They both scheme, that's clear. Verro is intelligent and meticulous. He is too smart to be careless. I could say the same for Aylanna. I know I would not want any of them gaining Luminary powers. Most I believe will work with you, for a time," she said.

"Even if they lost their control over me?" Edward tapped his ring.

It was an interesting question, and she wondered if Edward had found a way to remove the ring. "If that happens, Theomar will move against you first and he will have Herriman by his side. You asked if Herriman's personality was an act, and I don't believe it is. He is genuinely uncomfortable and scared, and he will follow Theomar before anyone else. He chose to stand closer to him on deck just now and sat behind him in the palace," Ellaria said.

"Thank you, Ellaria. Most of what you observed align with my own conclusions."

"What did the Mistress whisper to you?" she asked.

Edward locked eyes with her, as though weighing whether to tell her the truth, "She offered some insight on the Scepter which she thought I might find useful."

"I see," Ellaria said. It was worth asking; half of a secret was better than nothing, she supposed. And insight from Moria meant it was probably insight from the Old One.

"One more thing I was curious about: is Aylanna's daughter also accompanying the transport?" Ellaria asked.

"No, she's off doing her mother's bidding," he said, and she was certain she sensed a tinge of annoyance in his voice. Edward had previously explained that all the sons and daughters of the Court were close, having grown up together. Ellaria was uncertain if it was Edward or the Sagean who was mad about the refusal from Aylanna's daughter to journey to the Temple.

Edward stood to show Ellaria out. Still, one thing was bugging her; one thing that stood out from the day. The Court had been taken unaware by the change of power in Merinde, but she wasn't sure if Edward had been. He had acted like he expected it but was unaware of the extent.

"Do you trust the Old One?" Ellaria said.

"I trust no one."

THIRTY-TWO
LARK OF THE DEAD (WADE)

The foundry smoke streamed free into fading light. The muddy streets of the Bounty's Fold, the west region of Amera, were emptying out. Merchants locked up and commoners hid inside the many courtyard inns or returned to the outlying homesteads of Old Town. The gambling dens doors were closed, but they would still be operating late until morning. The night winds blew the dust from the Drylands in from the southern plains. It piled on the windowsills when the small dust-driven tornados developed and tossed enough of the dirt.

They got into position in the early evening's emerging darkness. Kovan positioned each group strategically along Miner's Road. The main street snaked through the Fold to the center of the city known as the Pinch. Placed to triangulate their attack, Blackwell took the highest position atop the roof of the High Horse Inn, his foot atop the parapet where he stood looking out toward the road, puffs of steam from his mechanical leg evaporating before it passed his silhouette.

Kovan came back to their position behind a stack of slate stone, part of the mixture of materials set in heaps for the construction of yet another gambler's den to be built. The foundation and first floor, damp from the past day of rain, was caked in a mud wash.

"Almost time," Kovan said as he sat down with his back against the stack. Wade looked at him checking his weapon and followed his lead.

"How are you feeling today?" Wade asked him.

"I feel stronger than I ever felt. How about you, something on your mind?"

"Besides life and death?"

"Yeah, this may be your last chance to ask me something and take advantage of my years of wisdom."

"In that case, I was just thinking. Why are women and men so different?" Wade asked.

Kovan removed his hat and wiped his forehead with his arm, "I have no idea. But it's one the first questions I'm going to ask the Creator if I ever meet the torquing fool."

Wade laughed.

"Seriously. When you get inside, lie low until the shooting starts, then tear that place apart until you find the Stone. If you see the thief inside, hide your face," Kovan said.

"What if Nyra offers to help?"

"Great. But it's up to you to find that Stone."

"Got it."

"And Wade, whatever happens, get that Stone to Ellaria."

Wade nodded as he stood and sauntered over the Best Bet gambling den. The place was lively with all sorts of rabblerousers, most of them already half-rats from ale or stronger spirits. The front of the den had breaker games and the tavern, whereas the back rooms housed the serious players. Wade could see tables playing Stones Cascade and some playing Reckoner. There were dice games and even pitch games in the back, too.

Wade found a seat at an open table and was promptly greeted by a woman in high-laced boots that came past her knee. He ordered a tin of their house ale and leaned back in his chair. In his right hand, he practiced the card shuffling trick Tali had taught him.

At the bar, Nyra found his eye and looked like she'd seen a ghost. She took the drink intended for him and hastened to his table.

"You need to go," Nyra said, handing him the drink.

"I can't. I'm not leaving without the Stone," Wade said.

"I don't have it anymore."

"I know it's here. Where is it?"

"There's an upstairs office, top floor, but you have to go. They know who you are," she said urgently.

Wade scanned around the room and noticed three men standing on the far side, looking his way. An urge to run pulsed through him, *but where?* He needed Kovan to cause his great distraction already.

Suddenly a loud voice he recognized rang out in the den. Stasia's laugh broke the subtle sounds. She reached the bar in the arms of a young man. *This wasn't part of the plan, what is she up to?*

"Go, now," Nyra insisted and pointed to a back hall.

"What room?" he demanded

"Room 401. And Wade, I'm sorry."

He stood, downed his drink, and headed to the hall. A single stairway was there, off the kitchen entrance. He didn't know where they went, but they went up and that's what mattered. *By the Blue, Stasia better know what she's doing.*

Wade scrambled up the steps two at a time. It wound back and up in a tight shaft where it stopped at the third floor. He walked the hall to the main staircase and past a small sitting room with an open window. From outside, he heard a wagoner calling a halt. Wade dashed over and opened the window further to look out, gun drawn.

A wagon, pulled by four horses, was pulling to a stop. A trail of dust blew from where it had charged into town down the Miner's Road. The cart rattled with the heft upon the back bed, the sound creaking loudly in the quiet of the evening.

Razor Redmar sat at the front of three other men on horseback, ready to meet the wagon as Blackwell had said they would be. Each of Razor's men were heavily armed and Kovan said they were all sharp shooters, some former veterans of the War, but most washouts of the Citadel's Cloaked Knife, hired to protect the interests of Amera entrepreneurs and merchants beyond.

Wade checked his gun again and again; the thought that this plan was a bad idea entered his mind. Kovan was either as good as he said he was, or they were all dead. From the porch below him, he heard Kovan's voice call out loudly.

"Redmar!"

The group in the street turned to see who dared to call out to them. Even the noise from the gambling den quieted below him. On the dirt-covered road, Razor Redmar recognized Kovan immediately and he smiled; a wicked smile meant for his own twisted mind. Before the bounty hunter could issue orders to his men, one of them had jumped from horseback and charged Kovan.

"Dodge, wait," Razor hollered out.

"I've been looking for you, Kovan!" the man called Dodge shouted, a red rage visible in his face even in the darkened street.

"Why Joran Dodge, you sound like you want to duel?" Kovan said.

"Dodge," Razor shouted again, "We should take him alive."

SHADOW BOUND SOULS 303

"He needs to die, Razor. I will avenge my brothers—" Joran Dodge spat.

"I'll send you to them," Kovan said, walking off the porch and to the street in Wade's view. Even in the limited light, Wade could see his grandfather's gun in Kovan's hand.

"A silver six? You are not too long for this world Kovan. Those don't shoot straight and you're too past your prime to hit anything with one," Dodge warned.

"I have six bullets to try," Kovan said.

"Let it whirl then, old-timer," Dodge said with his arms spread wide like he was bullet proof.

"Who's the amber-man for this lark of the dead?" Kovan asked.

Another unannounced man dismounted and held an amber coin high, "I'll throw the amber," he said. Kovan and Dodge each flipped the man a coin of their own.

They circled around the street, facing each other. Yesterday's dirt roads were swathed in streaks of drying mud, where the flow lines of draining water visibly crossed. Kovan had Wade's gun strapped to his right hip, the wooden handle reversed, and his pulsator holstered up tight near his left arm. The gunfighters shuffled in the soft clay street, but Kovan's eyes never left Dodge. They glared with a hawk's intensity.

Finally, Dodge nodded to the third man, who flipped the amber coin high in the air between them and ran out of the firing line. The coin hit the ground and both men drew their guns. A loud bang—and Dodge fell to the ground before he could fire his pulsator. Kovan's draw had been so fast, the small puff of dust from the coin's landing had yet to settle.

Razor's men watched their friend fall stiffly off his heels and in the momentary pause as the sound of the shot still echoed, Kovan unloaded the remaining five bullets of the chamber. He aimed the second shot at Razor, but Razor had moved back behind a post before the duel and his shot missed. Kovan quickly changed targets. He slew the man that had thrown the coin and shot the fourth man still on horseback, unloading three shots into him. The man went falling from the saddle and Kovan scrambled down the street.

Hell consumed the streets. Wade could hear Razor shouting and more men piled out of the Miner's Collective, opening fire at Kovan. Blackwell, from his high perched point began to pick men off who ventured into the open, his bronze scope glinting in the moonlight.

Wade pulled himself from the window and ran up the main stairs. Sounds of the tavern's own chaos below clashed but no one seemed to be heading up the stairway. Wade bounded to the top floor with his gun ready to meet any resistance. The hall was empty, and he found room 401, with a pair of double doors, cream-painted and golden-handled. He tried the handle, but the door was locked. He fired his gun at the lock and blasted the wood to splinters. He kicked the doors open and fired on the man inside. He was standing at the window observing the fight. Wade's blasts took the man into the glass with a crash. Kovan had told him not to hesitate, and he hadn't.

Wade searched for the Stone and pulled the vials of fire spark he had brought to blow through a vault door. But there was no need to break into anything. The Stone sat inside a small chest with the lid up. The triangular shape wrapped in the cloth was unmistakable. His rising panic subsided, and he breathed easier for a moment.

The sounds of a war outside were hard to ignore. Wade looked to the window and found the streets were full of Bonemen now fighting in league with the Bounty Hunters. Kovan was pinned down and Blackwell must have been spotted and either killed or retreated. The aid of his rifle assault had ceased.

Wade grabbed the Stone and headed for the door. In the hall, Stasia was running at full speed toward him.

"Run!" she yelled as she headed to the opposite end of the hall.

Wade followed, "Where are we going? There's only one way out?"

"Here," Stasia said, pointing at a closed door. Wade was confused but he broke through the room anyway. They burst through as guns fired on them. Wade turned back and fired his gun blindly.

"Ratspit, we're trapped."

"No, we're going to jump," she said, and she threw a chair through the window. Wade's eyes bulged, but the shock of seeing her throw a chair came from him questioning her logic, rather than her radical behavior.

"We're four stories up?" he said.

Stasia removed her coat and had something strapped to her back. The contraption connected to the leather cuff on her left arm.

"Come on!" she shouted at him.

Wade stopped firing and ran to the window, realizing what it was.

"Hey, that's mine! Those are my wings."

"Be quiet and hold on," Stasia said. She hugged him and pulled them both out the window. The instant she was clear, a sound depressed, and the crafted wings expanded in a sharp snap. They fell fast and then slowed as the fabric caught the air. Still, they were about to crash hard and Stasia hit another trigger that fired jets of white gas from bottom-angled nozzles. A second longer and they would have wrecked into a heap of broken bones, but the jets slowed their fall to a rough slam.

Wade hit the dirt on his hips and rolled a few feet. When he picked himself up, he found they were in an empty alley between two buildings. Stasia stood hunched over sucking wind. She looked up and laughed at Wade. Another flick of her wrist and the wings retracted back into a tight bundle at her back. She had fixed his wings and improved them in every way. They were now housed in a thin leather shell that also held canisters of whatever gas she had used.

"How?"

"I'll explain later," Stasia said and looked above to the top window. Wade pulled her down the alley, against the wall and out of sight.

"I thought machine-crafting was your worst subject?" Wade said, with his head against the wall.

"Oh Wade, you simple man," she sighed.

Gunfire continued to flash and blaze in the street and Wade tentatively crept to the main road. He assumed since the gunfight was still raging that Kovan was still alive. A quick peek around the edge of the building revealed Kovan was pinned down behind an overturned wagon. Crates of rock and crystals were strewn about the dirt. The horses were long gone. Among the bounty hunters firing at Kovan were a small group of Bonemen soldiers.

Buroga fired his gun from the fountain, but Kovan couldn't get there. Kovan spotted them and threw up his hands in a questioning way. Wade nodded back that they had the Stone. Kovan smiled and laughed to himself.

Wade turned back against the wall, "How are we getting out of here?'

"Nyra," Stasia said.

"No way?"

"Yes, she helped me get upstairs to you and said she would pick us up here."

Wade hoped it wasn't another way for her to steal back the Stone, but they had no alternative. From the streets, the gunfire died down and the noise was replaced by a mechanical sound followed by growls.

Wade looked again and at the end of the street, four Rendered walked with their long weapons and each held a wolverack on a leash. The glowing eyes of the pair together stood as phantoms of terror. Wade looked to Kovan whose head was against the upturned crates, his eyes to the darkening sky.

From the opposite end of the alley came a carriage. Nyra, sitting at the driver's bench, yelled, and waved.

"Come on!"

Stasia pulled Wade's sleeve, but he couldn't abandon Kovan. The look of desperation on Wade's face told Kovan all he needed to know, however. He waved to Wade to go. Then he unlatched the old silver gun and threw it over to Wade, holster, and all. It hit on the ground not far from Wade, the gun sliding out of the holster. Wade sprinted for it. He picked it off the ground and dove back to the alley. A volley of charged rounds destroying the space from which he had jumped. Kovan put his hands up, his gun hanging loose on his finger. He was giving himself up.

Stasia pulled again, and Wade ran for the carriage. They jumped inside and Nyra snapped the horses to go, screaming the command.

"Don't forget the big guy," Wade told Nyra.

"He won't fit," Nyra said as she turned the carriage to get Buroga.

"He can sit at the back cargo for two blocks to where his large bay is waiting."

They pulled behind the fountain and Wade yelled at Buroga. The huge Hazon man rambled to the back. He rapped on the side when he was ready. The carriage sunk slightly, but the axle held, and they charged down the road. Wade caught a last glimpse of Kovan, his hands held high and his gun hanging upside down. He had emerged from his bunker and was slowly being surrounded by soldiers, Rendered, and wolveracks. Razor Redmar looked pleased, but to Wade's relief, Redmar held a set of handcuffs.

THIRTY-THREE
OLD MEDICINE FOR OLD WOUNDS (TALI)

T
ali waited for Learon to return to the healer's hollow as the next day approached midday. She had sensed a growing anxiety among the Tregoreans, but no one was telling her anything. Sometime during the night, the head guard had come in to tell her that Meroha, Semo, and Bazlyn were taken prisoner and were resting in the cells. However, her cat Remi bounced through the opening into Tali's arms. The guard explained that they weren't hurt and took her to another room to rest.

The curious combination of distrust and hospitality continued in the morning. Someone brought her food but kept her locked in the room. No one came to talk with her, and no one knew where Learon was. There were bells somewhere deep in the city that chimed the hour. By her count, it must have been close to the Blue Hours when the door opened, and Learon came in.

"Did you get it?" Tali rushed over to meet him.

"Yes."

"It took all night. Did everything go well?" Tali asked.

"It's a long way from here. Echoryn and I went as fast as we could."

"Echoryn?" Tali said confused, "She was told not to go at all!"

"She didn't want to wait for the rangers. I'm glad we didn't; the trip there is long and, well, I'll explain later, but it's not a place you can access in the daylight. What's going on in here, where's the healer? Where's Elias?"

"He's in another room on the other side of this complex."

"Why did they bring me here then?"

"I don't know. Learon, they also found the airship and captured others."

"Are they alright? Where are they?"

"As far as I know, they're fine, but I haven't been allowed to see them."

"They're not a very trusting people, are they?"

From the open doorway came the head guard, Nokha. She had a fierce glare to match a sharp jaw that could intimidate anyone.

"Come," Nokha commanded.

"Where?" Learon asked.

"I will take you to Qudin."

In the hall, there was a small squad of armed guards and beyond them stood the young woman, Echoryn. She was dressed in traveling clothes, and she stood next to the King and Queen. There was dirt on her face and her eyes darted around as though she were nervous.

Nokha did not wait for them to keep up, but it was obvious they were expected to do exactly that. Down the short hallways that switch back and forth, Tali continued to look behind them at the group. The royalty accompanying them was plausibly explained; it was the full squad of armed soldiers behind the King's guard that Tali couldn't account for.

"Learon, what's going on? Why are their leaders coming?" Tali nudged him as they shuffled along the polished corridor.

"I don't know. Maybe they want to see if Elias is healed?"

"I don't think so. It's possible, but I was under the impression it will take a while before Elias is back to full health and before they can speak to him," she said. The healer had explained as much to her the night before. There was something else going on, she could feel a tension amongst everyone in the hall except Learon and herself. *What are they worried about?*

Tali tried to calm her thoughts and allow someone else's in. She wasn't sure how her talent worked exactly, but she believed if she could push her own thoughts aside, then she was receptive to someone else's. But she couldn't sift through the incidental noise that filled the hallway, the stomping of boots on the stone, and the ruffle of armor. It all eliminated any chance for something so quiet as thoughts to drift to her.

They stopped outside the paneled door and Nokha knocked. Master Zadar opened it and he looked more exhausted then when she had left him the night before. Nokha held them back with her spear and allowed the group behind to go inside first. Tali scrutinized them with distrust, but Learon was simply annoyed by their customs and the delay. His stance was restless, and a sigh escaped his lips. When everyone else was inside, Nokha lowered her spearpoint to the floor. During the procession, Tali had not missed the fact that Echoryn had looked at Learon and smiled, but her eyes looked regretful. With the path clear, Tali stepped into the domed room of the dusting chamber and the particles of blue and white light swarmed over her. She could feel the eyes of everyone watching her.

Learon followed her in, "What's happening, why does it tingle?"

"I know—" She turned abruptly to look at Learon. Someone in the room gasped, possibly the Queen. She looked at Learon and the cloud of glowing dust that enveloped him. It was green and blue, red, and even purple, all swarming him and the pack on his shoulder.

So, it's true, a Trinity arises. Tali heard someone's thoughts in her head.

"He has been marked." Hira Zadar said.

The contingent of soldiers all shifted on their feet and pointed their spears at Learon in a line that began to surround them.

"Don't," Echoryn said, "I'm telling you; he is Kihan."

What did she mean he was Kihan? Tali thought.

"Who are you, young man?" the King asked.

Learon stammered to answer, obviously confused about what was happening. From the table on the other side of the room, Elias began to cough loudly and mumble. The Tregorean healer pushed through the soldiers to Learon.

"Question him later. We need to see to Qudin before he succumbs. Where is the mushroom of the Red Moon?" the healer asked

Learon pulled the pack off his shoulder. He looked inside and took out a handful of glowing orange and red mushrooms. The particles returned and swirled around it but in less density than before. The healer took them and hurried over to his station of tubes, percolating steam, and drips. Whatever elixir he was making was being mixed through the contraption.

Learon looked at his hand where the glowing dust still floated, his eyes fixated.

"Will he live?" The King asked Zadar.

"We will know in an hour or two. It is old medicine for an old wound. The spirit needs to mend and regain control."

"And what caused the imbalance this time?" the King asked.

"Best I can tell, he must have exhausted his powers and when that happened, the seal was broken," Zadar said.

"Wait, what seal?" Tali said.

"It is a long story, young Luminary, but your friend has had a great darkness living inside him for many years. This is not the first time I have healed him. Though his memory of the last time was simplified to ease his burden by—"

"Enough!" The Queen shouted, "Continue your work and let us know when he is healed," she commanded and rounded on Nokha, "Please take our guests to the Grand Hall. His Grace Raza Derasi is awaiting us there."

Learon's arms were crossed, and he looked reluctant to move. Tali was equally frustrated with being commanded about. *Who was this Derasi, and why were they being brought to him?*

Echoryn pushed away from Nokha's grip and came to Learon's side, "I know you want answers, Learon. You can trust us; you can trust me. Come, we will explain."

Learon relaxed at her words, and suddenly, Tali felt like the only outsider.

From the room of Dust, they were taken to the Palace's Grand Hall. The large greeting room was a wide-open space, with only a few stone columns marking the different sections of seating areas; each column fluted up and sprouted at the ceiling like a tree. At the sides of the room, the ceilings were low, but they raised much higher above the center walkway and then again at the back, where a platform awaited with more soft-covered chairs in plush fabrics. The back stone wall was draped in banners, and in the high-lofted space, there were windows to the jungle beyond. It looked to Tali more like a chamber for discussions and large parties than a Grand Hall. She had been inside the Palace of Redvine once and this was nothing like that.

At the upper platform, a man in large green robes awaited them, draped with a decorated gold shawl over his neck and around each arm. He turned to scrutinize them as they entered. Most of the Tregoreans had an aura of youth to them—even the older ones with graying hair seemed youthful somehow—but not this man. This Raza Derasi was by far the oldest Tregorean Tali had seen since their arrival.

Tali and Learon stepped to the platform before the old man. He immediately began to appraise each like they were horses for purchase, doing all but checking their teeth. He walked around them and at one point, held up a circular piece of colored glass with which he inspected them. It looked like glass to Tali, but it could have been finely polished and shaped crystal. The old man was protective of it, as he carefully placed it back into a soft pouch around his neck.

He glared a long time at Tali's own necklace. The obsidian stone coin with the amethyst sigil that Elias had given her hung over her green cloak. The old man was drawn to it for some reason and instinctively he reached for it. Tali flinched slightly.

"I wouldn't do that if I were you," Learon warned.

The old man looked at Learon and back to Tail, then he backed away immediately. It was then that Tali realized she held enough energy inside that her eyes were glowing. Feeling like a trapped animal had her gathering energy. She had found it very easy to find energy all around and inside this place. As she thought on it, she could feel more energy in the Tregorean Province then anywhere she could remember, outside of the Sagean Temple in Marathal.

"I am sorry, dear one. I did not mean to offend you. We have seen so few of your kind in my lifetime. And we have longer lifetimes than you. I was curious," he spoke in a gravelly voice that was also oddly off-key, his speech lingering on sounds longer than normal. "I am Raza Derasi, the Grace of the Kihan people. What you would call a priest in Tovillore."

"You are a priest of the Sagelight Faith?" Tali said.

"Not exactly. The Sagelight has never been our religion of choice. Otherwise, we would not have been exiled from the Mainland. While many of our number practice the Faith of the Fates, most Kihan people follow the Faith of the Severin."

Tali had heard of the Faith of the Fates, but not the Severin.

"Your Grace," The Queen interrupted, "Please, the young man… tell us what you see?"

He acknowledged her and stepped closer to Learon, "Who are you, where are you from, young man?" he asked.

"I am Learon Everwyn, I was born and raised in West Meadow. It is a small mountain village near Atava in Tovillore."

"I know this place from our maps. What can you tell us about your parents, Learon Everwyn?"

"My mother is Cara Farlon, a weaver from West Meadow. My father was Rylan Everwyn. He worked for the Scholar's Guild before he was murdered by the new Sagean lord, Edward Knox."

"Did your father travel? Perhaps here or to the New World, or—"

"Yes," Learon interrupted, "What is this about? What did the healer mean when he said I was marked?"

"You are of the Kihan blood, Learon Everwyn. A Tregorean man to be sure. Though your features don't show themselves in your ears or your face, your blood is our blood, Kyode."

Tali looked at Learon with wide eyes, but he didn't respond.

"Kyode? What does that mean? Echoryn said that at the river." Tali asked.

"It means *brother* or *kin*."

"And Bohoja?" Learon asked.

"This means *protector* or *guardian*."

Had Echoryn known from the moment she saw him? Tali wondered.

"Impossible, neither of my parents have ever been to Nahadon, and I can tell you neither of them are Tregorean."

"That is not all, Learon. We know you have Kihan blood in you, but we believe you are more. You are special among our people. You have the Mark."

"What mark? I have no mark on me," Learon resisted.

"It is not something on your skin, but of your spirit. The Dust Room revealed this."

"Special how? Like a Luminary?" Tali asked.

"Not exactly, but the two beings are linked. In ancient times, it was said there were three and together, they formed the Trinity Guard. A Luminary, a Fusion Mage, and a Nimbus Warrior. Each of these beings could come from any of the races of Territhmina, but historically, certain races produced more of one then the other."

"This is crazy," Learon said dismissively.

"Which do you believe Learon is?" Tali asked.

"Come on Tali, you believe this?" Learon said, agitated.

"I know Elias thought you were a Luminary, and he said you must come here. I want to hear them out."

The old man studied them both and answered, "From what Echoryn described of his speed and agility to escape the collapsing lichen, we believe Learon is a Nimbus Warrior. While humans tend to produce more Luminaries, the Kihan people were known to produce both the Nimbus Warrior and Fusion Mage."

"What about the Zenoch and Menodarins?" Tali said.

"We are not certain. While our histories stretch much further than humans, our knowledge ends at the birth of the Sagean Empire when war ravaged the world, and much was lost to magic and deception. We believe the Menodarins were known to produce Fusion Mages and the Zenoch more likely to produce Nimbus Warriors."

"What was the purpose of the Trinity Guard?" Tali asked. While Learon was struggling to hear what the man was telling them, she found herself excited. Like when they had devoured the books in Elias's library, every bit of information on her kind came as a comfort to her.

"There was once a place where all three beings of the Trinity were trained together. What we know is that every Trinity was bonded. There are many things we don't understand about this bond. In our library, there is a book that tells the story of a Nimbus whose Trinity was killed. As the lone survivor, the woman warrior fell sick for no reason. She had no symptoms to suggest an illness, but nevertheless she died, a result of the bond either being broken or carrying to the afterlife. To their true purpose, we have only myths of wars. Wars involving beasts and animals long forgotten: Dragons, Meeraws, Mirthless, Hellfiends, Syrowings, and Torakumas."

"You're saying my parents weren't my parents?" Learon said.

"I'm positive at least one of them was not. I know that is not an easy thing to hear, but understand *we* are also scared of what this means. A Luminary and Nimbus together? I fear something grave is upon our world once again."

"How is this such a rare thing? What could be graver than an Empire that enslaved the world? Where was this Trinity Guard then?" Learon said.

"There are many things your people don't remember, many truths erased. When the Sagean's acolytes became intent on hunting all Luminaries and in that, all potential challengers to the Empire, a rift was created, and the resulting imbalance led to a decline in all three Beings of Power. The Sagean Empire also outlawed all mystical arts, alchemy, and any exploration of the furies. It's possible that without the Luminaries and without the knowledge to train a Mage, the Nimbus who were born never found their Trinity."

"Every other word from you is what you don't know. How can I believe the little you say you do know? I am not this Nimbus thing, and I am not a Tregorean. My parents were Cara Farlon and Rylan Everwyn." Learon said defiantly. He was shouting by the end and when he turned to leave, Tali felt nervous he would attack the guards. The room behind them, however, had swollen with three times as many soldiers as they had arrived with. Learon appraised the wall of forty warriors, spears, lances, and bows aimed at him. He turned back to Tali and the Tregorean priest. His eyes stormed with a rage she had never seen. He was not scared of the warriors, he only feared what the old man had said. Tali knew what Derasi had said was true. She knew it the moment she had seen the dust glowing around Learon and if she thought about it, she had known for much longer than that.

The Wanvilaska wise woman's words haunting her, Tali stepped toward her friend to calm him, "Learon, it's all right. Whatever the truth is, we'll find it."

"I'm sorry Tali. I just. . . I need some air," he said, shaking his head, "I need to get out of here."

"You may go. We are not holding you here," Derasi said.

Learon turned and motioned toward the armed guards as a counter argument. But they parted when he pointed, allowing a gap to form to the exit. Learon eyes darted around, but he didn't hesitate. He strode for the door.

"Where are you going?" Tali asked.

"Outside. I can't breathe in here," he barked and left.

Tali turned back to the Grace. The King, Queen, and Princess had all joined Derasi on the platform.

"I have to follow him," Tali said.

"It is better if you stay, Tali. Our lands are not safe for strangers to wander through. We will send for a ranger to follow him," the King said.

Tali lightly touched Echoryn's arm, hoping to have an ally in this. Echoryn convulsed slightly and her eyes closed. Tali withdrew her hand quickly and Echoryn looked back at her with her eyes wide and piercing. It all happened in an instant and the others almost didn't notice.

"Echoryn?" King Talus said.

"Father, I'll go after him," Echoryn said, and she pulled her hood up over her red hair and the veil over her face, "I'll make sure he doesn't walk into something that could kill him, and I will lead him back."

"Wait—" Tali started to object but was cut off.

"Will he listen to you?" The Queen said.

"Yes," Echoryn said, and she started to walk away. Tali grabbed her by the arm. This time, every weapon in the room raised to aim at her and six soldiers closed on her. Tali let her go, but she could feel the heat of her scarred eyes.

"He needs time. I will go after him," Tali offered again.

"Tali, it's all right. I'll keep him safe and bring him back. I can't explain but trust me, it's better this way. As you say, he needs time, but when he is ready to accept the truth, I can answer questions for him and lead him back. You don't have to worry."

Tali stared at her, dissatisfied by her response.

"It is better if I go," Echoryn repeated, "I promise, nothing will happen to him."

Reluctantly, Tali nodded and Echoryn rushed out and after Learon. Tali turned back to the Tregorean leaders.

"I need you to release my other friends, now. They pose no threat to you. It is as you say Grace Derasi, the world has come under the cloak of darkness, and we stand against it. Once Qudin Lightweaver is healed, we must search for the Temple of Ama in the south of your province."

"The lands there are forbidden," Grace Derasi said.

"Do you know of the Temple we seek?" Tali asked.

"There are many ancient places there, but by old law, no Kihan travels beyond the Wall of Nagari and into the Shadow Field," the Grace said.

"What about the Black Shore?" Tali said.

"We do not go to the Mountains of Fire, either. What sends you there?" The King asked.

"The new Sagean Lord gathers his forces there. A Temple somewhere in the jungles holds a device that can transform men into Luminaries."

The King looked to the Grace Derasi who seemed to be contemplating her words.

"If this is true, then we are all in grave danger. Our ancestors forbid us from venturing in the Shadow Field for a reason," Grace Derasi said to his King.

"Then we must send scouts at once to find this Temple," the King said.

"And my friends?" Tali asked.

"They will be brought up here to wait with you," King Talus said.

"Thank you, King Talus," Tali said in a slight bow, "Your Grace. I didn't know there were many Tregoreans living outside of the province?"

"There are not."

"Then how could Learon be Kihan?"

"There is one we know of," he said, and he looked at the King and Queen as though for permission to continue, but simply said, "She left here many years ago; we believe she is Learon's mother."

THIRTY-FOUR
IN THE SPLINTERED LIGHT (LEARON)

L earon didn't know where he was going, he only knew he couldn't stay there. Lies upon fragments of truth piled together and suddenly he had inherited a life not his own. *How can I trust who I am? If Rylan wasn't my father, then who was?* He had a million questions, but now he only wanted to be somewhere he could breathe. The simple smell of the jungle and moist heat allowed his body a semblance of ease. The sounds of nature had always been a comfort to him and even here, where the strange bird calls and cascade of noises sounded vaguely threatening, Learon found a sense of peace returning to him.

It had taken him a while to find a way out of the interior complex and once he did, he began to pick his way through the jungle following an old but walkable path. He eventually crossed the river in the high ravine, stepping gingerly onto a rope-and-wood bridge that barely swayed from his weight. After he had been walking about an hour, a loud crash sounded in the wilderness a few hundred feet from his position. Learon took it as a sign to change directions. He turned to the east and the jungle began to subtly change: the trees grew taller and the under-brush of the jungle, thicker.

It wasn't long after he had turned east that he knew Echoryn was stalking him. *If I am this Nimbus being, I'm not very good at it. How long had she been tracking me?* Learon let her follow, curious if she would abandon her pursuit, but she never did. It wasn't until he crossed a small stream into a valley of curious trees with thick foliage that she sprang out.

"Stop, squirrel. Can't you hear me telling you to stop?" she said scrambling out from the jungle.

Learon glanced at her and slowed but he didn't stop. "I heard. Why should I? I've come this far without anyone dragging me back."

"That was supposed to be my job, but I was letting you *breathe*. But we must turn back. You've taken us across the boundary," Echoryn shifted her bow off her shoulder to hold.

"The boundary to where?"

"We are in the Ravinors' land. While they don't have regular patrols this close to the border, we don't want to be caught on this side of the jungle. They are clever, quiet hunters and they attack with impunity. They have not developed the ability to reason with enough logic to outweigh their instincts. They are emotional creatures, and dangerous ones."

"Fine," he admitted and looked around. The darkness of the jungle thickened. The canopy of trees only allowed pinpoints of light to filter down and each beam was losing intensity.

"It's oddly dark here," Learon observed as he stepped from lighted spot to spot. The ground was much thicker with layers of vines; roots and weeds pilled thick beneath their feet.

"You know there are bugs under there, in the shadows, that would kill you? Snakes, too." Echoryn warned.

"Good thing you're here."

"It is a good thing. You might try to nap beneath the wrong tree where the goreadoom ants burrow. You would die a horrible death, squirrel."

"Quit calling me squirrel."

"You don't like that. I think it suits you fine. I like it. Squirrels have amazing balance and they're curious little animals. That curiosity is part of their survival."

Learon shook his head, "You know I came out here to be alone, Echoryn?"

"I know. I also know from taking you to the Turquoise Flats that you're oblivious to danger, squirrel. You expect if you fall, you'll find your feet at the last second. I had to ignite some of the hollow boom stems near the nil wasp swamps, or you would have walked right into it."

"That was you?" he stopped and she gave him an exacerbated look.

"Time to turn back," she pulled at his sleeve, and they reversed direction. In their short conversation and the shaded light, Learon realized his sense of direction was skewed. A mounting sense of danger came to him, either from instinct or unfamiliarity with the surroundings, but he began to examine the area more closely while they walked.

"Do your people have dealings with the Ravinors?"

"Very rarely do we trade with them. Mostly we leave them alone and they leave us alone. I am curious. You and the Luminary, Tali. How did you find each other?" Echoryn asked.

"Actually, it was just coincidence. It's a long story."

"Are you two lovers?"

"Excuse me?"

"I mean no offense; she is a beautiful woman. Strong and willful. Our Grace said she is very powerful, too. She's very lovely, but what does she see in you, squirrel?"

"She doesn't see anything in me. I mean, we are not lovers. Tali's my friend."

"Good."

"Good? Why is that good?"

"You are a Kihan and a Nimbus."

"So, what does that have to do with who I'm allowed to love or be attracted to?"

"I suppose it doesn't. Are you starting to acknowledge who you are?"

"I… I don't know. I have also done some things recently that I couldn't believe. I don't know how to reconcile one truth with another."

"That's fair."

"How did you know?" Learon asked.

"You were a Nimbus? I didn't until I saw you escape the flats. But I knew you were a Kihan blood when I first saw you. You were driving that small raft and you were not sweating as much as you should have been. You also spotted us in the trees much faster than any human would have."

"But you were out in the open."

"We weren't, and as soon as I knew you had discovered us, I signaled everyone to reveal themselves. It was obvious from the moment I saw you that you were dangerous. I didn't know your friend was a Luminary until later."

"You think I am this Nimbus thing?"

"I do. From what I know, only a Nimbus could have done what you did. You know, it is our belief that the Nimbus were born to protect the Luminaries. This is why I asked about you and Tali. You two are intrinsically bonded. If you were lovers, it would make sense. But as you say, you are not."

"No, we're not."

They were almost out of the thick jungle when he heard something creeping from behind them. Learon stopped dead in his tracks. The approaching person was heavy on their feet and their movements were odd. The steps sounded like they were accompanied by a light scrape on the ground.

"What is it—" Echoryn voice cut off when she heard it, too, a sweeping rustle to the ground. "Run! It's the Ravinors!"

She tugged at his sleeve as she launched into a run. They ran through the splintered light in the dark entangled jungle and turned at a cluster of thick trees. A splatter of darts plunged into the bark, whistling at their heels.

They entered a grove as the evening sky was coming on, Echoryn pausing to catch her breath. The bugs and snakes moved in the thick ground cover. It made stepping from patch of light to patch of light even more important. Learon stood and listened for their pursuers, but the jungle betrayed nothing. In the cloak of the trees above, it was difficult to see far into the tangle of wilderness behind them. Something about this moment felt familiar to Learon, but he couldn't make it clear in his mind. A sound emanated from the brush and an arrow shot toward them. Echoryn's attention was attuned to the shot, and she reached to snatch it in the air. Learon felt the moment slow, and he moved within that time freely. Before the arrow had arrived, Learon pulled Echoryn down to the ground atop him.

Reality sped up and the first arrow flew past. It was followed by a second arrow exactly where Echoryn had stood. She lay atop him, breathless. She smelled of sweat, sweet flower, and fresh mountain air. Her eyes bulged and she spun off him pulling her bow free in the spin. She released an arrow at one of the two Ravinors walking toward them. Learon suspected that they thought they may have hit the targets from how slowly they approached. Her arrow pierced the first Ravior's neck. Echoryn turned to aim at the second. Learon pulled her boot knife free and flung it at the tall lizard-like beast. The blade caught the thing in its clawed hand that was preparing to fire another dart at them.

The huge creature roared. It had scaled greenish skin and a face like a flattened lizard. Its cry was full of sharp teeth. It turned back to charge them, huffing out its nose. Learon scrambled to the first Ravinor to retrieve the beast's spear. The one still standing leapt through the air from ten feet away. It crashed into Learon and took him to the ground. The free spear plunged into the monster. The heavy animal lay dead atop him. Learon crawled out and had to brush bugs off his arms. He looked at the second motionless Ravinor and found two more arrows from Echoryn on its side.

"Are you hurt?" Echoryn asked.

"I'm fine," he answered, and, in the distance, he heard more coming, "We need to run."

Echoryn nodded and they scrambled out of the area. In a short sprint, the land began to turn uphill, and they were clearing the canopy of thicker jungle, rising on a mountain more dispersed with trees and bushes. They had cleared the boundary.

Learon now understood how dangerous the Ravinors were. The huge muscular creatures blended in with the habitat and could hunt prey with equal parts stealth and ferocity—*they had been lucky*. Even though they were clear inside Tregorean borders, Echoryn kept a fast pace until they had crossed the rope bridge and the ravine over the Tyn River.

They neared the high side entrance from which Learon had left. It was a tall, sheared edge of the mountain where sentries flanked the outer edge. When they reached the opening Echoryn spoke to one of the guards.

"Seal the passage after we're through."

A few feet inside and a large slab of stone started to lower behind them, closing the exit behind rock three-feet thick. A depression of air sounded, and steam filled the hall from nozzles at the ceiling. Echoryn continued without noticing and Learon followed. She turned at a side hall and he wondered if she was taking a short cut. The interior complex of their protected city was a maze, but Learon was sure this was not the way he had come. When she led them down a hall lined with statues, he finally slowed to ask where they were going.

"Come on, I want to show you something," she said, noticing him slow to look at the statues.

"What is this?" he asked. There were many statues all around the province. More statues than Learon had ever seen in his entire life, in fact, but this hall was different.

"It is the Hall of Prophets. Come on. We don't have much time in here. I need to tell the guard about the Ravinors, but I wanted you to see this."

He followed her impatient waving to a tall circular metal door. Echoryn removed a thick rod of gold that fit in her palm. With a flick of her wrist, a half arch of flat perforated metal released. She placed the metal into a slot in the wall, nudged it to align and pulled down. It was a key, Learon realized, as the door mechanism came free with an escalating clacking. Echoryn pushed the door open and entered.

The sound of a water fountain and birds flourished from inside, but there was an echoed silence of abandonment punctuated by the plod of their boots on the marble floor. Echoryn found a plate on the wall that brought orbs to life within. A bronze statue at the center caught Learon's eye first. It was a celestial sculpture that stood on a large set of gears serving as a pedestal, the sphere of Territhmina in full shape and splendor. Instead of land and sea, the ball was covered in various lines and patterns, all of it adjustable.

Directly above the moving statue was an open dome to the night sky. The oculus opening at the top was framed by a lattice of steel that spread around the perimeter as though a structural cage. Where it met the floor, there were alcoves. Two on opposite ends of the room had small water fountains, and the others were full of books and scrolls. Each of those were locked behind caged doors.

"Why did you bring me here?" Learon asked, admiring the space.

"I wanted you to see something unique of the Kihan people. Your people. And I wanted to explain a little about myself. I know you are overwhelmed by the news that you are a Kihan, but we are a people with a prodigious acuity for the nature of things, both seen and unseen."

As she spoke, Learon noticed the many layers of dust around the room and even on the glowing orbs themselves, "This room doesn't look like it has been used in decades?" he said.

"Our last prophet left almost thirty years ago."

"Why did they leave?"

"Some say she disappeared on a quest to fix the future, others believe she was driven mad and sailed the Brovic."

"What do you think?"

"I don't know. But I did find a note the last time I was in here. I think she went to the New World to find something she called *The Hyperion Compass.*"

"What's that?"

"I think the word *Hyperion* has something to do with the Fates, or watchers of fate—I don't know. Certainly someone must know what happened to the last prophet, and where she went, but no-one will tell me."

"Derasi?" Learon asked, but Echoryn didn't respond. Given the state of the room, the opened books, and papers on the desks, it looked like everything had gone untouched since the prophet had disappeared, "But you have the key?"

"Grace Derasi has held it many years, but he believes I have the calling to prophecy. Me, I would rather be a ranger like my brother, Zorick."

"I didn't know there was a prince, too?"

"A prince?" she laughed, "No. No. Do you believe I'm a princess?"

"Well, yes."

"It doesn't work that way here. My Mother and Father were chosen to lead. The Grace nominates a select few worthy of the position and then our people chose."

"The people chose your father to rule?"

"And my mother."

"Are you saying they are a publicly arranged marriage?"

"That's correct. While it's possible I could become Queen one day, it is not a birthright. We Kihan have long lives and a rule of lineage would be unwise."

"That's interesting," he said, though the word he wanted to use was crazy.

"It's our way," she shrugged.

"Where is your brother? Why haven't I seen him?"

"As a ranger, Zorick seldom visits the palace. He is stationed in Tarhallen."

It was hard for Learon to wrap his head around how large the Kihan province was. It was like one vast city of many cities. He watched Echoryn run her finger through some dust and meander around the room and he understood.

"You can't be a ranger, can you? They won't let you, they want you to be a prophet?"

She looked up from something that held her attention on the desk and nodded, "They believe I will be one. I have struggled to believe it. As you can see, I haven't even been inside here to clean things up yet. This is only the second time I have been inside, and the first since Derasi gave me the key."

"Why do they believe you are a prophet? What did you foresee?"

Just then a call came from the hall outside.

"Echoryn Solhara?" A voice called.

She looked up, puzzled, and went to the door. Some muffled conversation continued and Echoryn came back.

"Learon, we must go. Something is wrong with Qudin Lightweaver."

THIRTY-FIVE
THE SCREE (WADE)

T hey returned to the small town of Garrison in the night, a red and orange glow ominously punctuating the southern horizon. The little town was swarming with people and the inn keeper was not happy to see them.

"I was preparing to give your room away. Now I suppose you all want to stay?"

"What's happening?" Wade asked.

"The people started showing up after you and your friends had gone, most of them willing to pay triple for a bed. That was the start of it. They say the plague has taken over and it's coming this way." The innkeeper hollered to a man sitting at the bar. He had to shout loud enough to carry over the crowded room, "Mark!"

A scruffy-looking man came over with dust covered clothes. The black ink covered his forearms and hands.

"Tell this man what you told me about Axern and Duma," the inn keeper asked.

The man looked Wade over, who himself probably looked the most intimidating he had ever looked in his life. He had both guns strapped around himself, his gauntlet blade at his right wrist, and his usual shirt and vest was frayed and dust-covered; additionally, Wade was sure that it was splattered with blood on the bottom.

"You came out of Axern? My friends and I are headed there tonight to board a ship. Is it safe?"

"We came from Axern this evening, by way of Duma. The docks and bayfront properties were still intact, but some of the buildings on the outskirts were in flames. You might make it to a ship."

"What's going on? Who started the fires?"

"The plague, that's what. Those suffering from the spirit killer, those cursed few that were abducted and came back, they started attacking in Duma. At first it was the Syndicate buildings they attacked, but soon it got worse. The fires in Axern, that's regular folks did that. These people that act like they're dead inside, the peacekeeper of Axern called them zombies. Well, fire is the way to kill zombies, everyone knows that. Ain't that what happened to the City of Ashalon? So, the legend goes. I've heard these things called the Scree in some places, too. Whatever they are, when they started to attack, they did so with determination and a complete lack of fear. The fires didn't do anything."

"Did these Scree go from Duma to Axern?"

"No. A lot of people got out of Duma as soon as the fighting started, but once those giant machine beings showed up with Bonemen soldiers, every able-bodied person hit the road. It didn't take long for people to raise the alarm in Axern. But Axern has their own Scree, don't they? Like most the coastal cities."

Wade turned to the inn keeper, "You can have our room. Once we have all our things we'll be on our way."

Wade pushed through the throng of people in the common room and up the stairs. He gathered their things and left, throwing the innkeeper their key, and slipping out the back to the stables where the others were waiting. Nyra sat atop the carriage she had stolen. She looked sullen and sat with her arms crossed while continually kicking the wagon with her foot.

"What's happening?" Stasia asked.

"I'll explain on the way," Wade told her.

"What are we going to do about Kovan?" Stasia asked.

Wade didn't respond, because he didn't have the answer.

"Wade?" Stasia asked.

"We need to find a ship in Arrow Bay like we planned and get the under-death out of here," Wade said.

"If you want to go after your friend, I can help," Nyra said from the carriage.

"We can't go back to Amera," Wade said.

"I don't think they're holding him there. I think they'll be transporting him into the Tail Feather Mountains. They have a high-security prison that's through the mountains. I heard it's deep within the rifts of Echo Canyon. They call it the Red Spear," Nyra said.

"Are you sure?" Stasia asked.

"I think so. I saw them transporting people through Amera the last few months. Razor would usually escort the caravan from Amera through the pass."

"I believe she is right, Wade Duval. We heard of this Red Spear in our travels here. Kovan Rainer said he knew of this place from his past, but he couldn't recall much about it at the time. They discovered it during the War. We will never catch them following behind them, but if Kovan Rainer found a route to the Red Spear through the canyon rivers, maybe we can find the same route?" Buroga said.

"Why are you helping us, Nyra?" Wade said.

Her head slumped and she focused her eyes on the reins clutched in her hand. "I'm sorry Wade. I was trying to get free of Razor, but I underestimated the extent of his reach. One of his men found me in Atava. I was desperate, and I hoped that relic would buy my freedom. I was wrong."

Wade was becoming increasingly exhausted by the disease of desperation permeating this lost frontier. What he really wanted was time to think, but there wasn't any.

"It's settled, we ride for Axern and find a ship like we always meant to. When we can find this Morales that Kovan spoke with, we'll ask him to take us into the canyon."

"If I saw a map, I could figure out roughly where this Red Spear is. I know how long Razor would be gone on these trips," Nyra offered. "It was the only relief from him I had. Believe me, I know exactly how long it took. I escaped on a winddrifter for Atava during one of them."

Once they were all saddled and riding out, Wade handed his grandfather's silver six to Stasia and she gave him puzzled look.,

"You need a weapon. A man inside said that Axern is on fire because the Scree have started attacking," Wade told her. He turned in his saddle to Nyra, "Do you want a weapon besides that golden dagger of yours?"

"This was my father's," Nyra drew the knife free to show off the golden sun pommel. Then she sheathed it again. "It may not be the best weapon in a fight, but it makes me feel safe. Anyway, I don't like guns."

An image flashed in Wade's mind, of bursting through room 401 and shooting the man at the window. The simplicity of it and coldness washed over him again and he shuddered,

"I'm starting to feel the same way."

THE FIRES WERE ALMOST ALL EXTINGUISHED BY THE TIME THEY REACHED Axern. Wade hoped it was a good sign that the city had come under control. They rode in on silent and empty streets, past the towers and foundry to the lowlands and the docks that edged the western shore of Arrow Bay.

The city was mostly a port town, where the streets went from dirt-filled to stone-paved the closer they came to the pier. An hour through the city and they hadn't seen a soul. A dog barked at a smoldered building, blackened, and collapsed. With the sun still a few hours away from rising on the bay, patches of embers remained visible. Smoke floated around them along with drifting ash and soot, but no people.

They found the Scree standing on the docks which stopped them in their tracks. Wade dismounted to get a better look.

"Wade," Stasia whispered.

He waved her off, "Stay here," he said.

Wade wanted to see the harbor, but he didn't want to raise any awareness of their arrival. He approached the warehouse and the docks beyond. The creak of leather stretching alerted him to someone else dismounting after him.

"What happened here?" Nyra said in a hushed tone.

"I don't know, but we need to get on a ship."

They had slunk to the edge of a warehouse to get a better view of the entire harbor. The Scree stood unmoving and staring east like they awaited the sunrise. Wade's heart sank. Except two ships and several sunken vessels clogging the waters, the harbor was empty. Both ships that remained were anchored offshore and far apart from each other. The one closest in view was called the Hollow-Dawn.

"That's Razor's Ship," Nyra said, and she picked a necklace up in her hand and kissed the swirling symbol on it. Like the dagger, it belonged to a very obscure religion called the Fates.

They backed up and skirted behind three structures to the south to get a better look at the second ship. It was well past the end of the wharf with a set of three lanterns hanging on the masts. The script on the boat read *The I'Varrin*.

"Is that the ship we are looking for?" Nyra said.

"I believe it is."

"How do we get aboard? I don't think they're coming back to dock anytime soon."

"I think we need to steal a small boat from the marina and paddle out to it."

"Two boats. That Hazon man may need his own."

"True."

"The marina is crawling with those things."

"They're not beasts or demons. They're people, Nyra."

"I know they're not demons—I've lived amongst demons—but they're *not* people. They're closer to things than people. The Creator help them, they're beyond the hand of Fate. Something else manipulates them now."

"My friends are working on it," Wade said.

Nyra smiled, "I'll go. I have some skill sneaking around. I'll pull the boats back here."

"We'll both go. As you say, we'll need two."

They returned to the others and told them of their plan. Stasia fought him on it, but the necessity to remain quiet left any arguments useless and muted.

Nyra and Wade walked back to the main harbor. The brightening sky brought a new horror that had originally gone unseen: the many Scree standing on the docks were covered with blood.

They tried to spot boats in the water worth stealing before venturing through the throng. Once they had located two, they started out on the pier. The sun was rising and began to shimmer in the waves of the bay. At first, they slowly tiptoed past the frozen Scree, unsure what the reaction would be, ready to sprint away at the slightest movement. The eyes of the first one they passed looked completely cloudy and glossed over.

At the dawning of sunlight, they began to move slightly. Wade's heart seized in his chest, but the Scree remained in their stance. He could see they were breathing normally but like his sister Tara and the people of West Meadow, they ignored everything around them.

Nyra and Wade crept along as quietly as possible, growing more terrified that nothing seemed to disturb these things. *Had they killed everyone in the city or had everyone simply run?*

Nyra lowered into one of the boats below. Wade unwound the tie for both crafts.

"Wade, hurry," Nyra whispered, pointing toward the Scree. They had begun to walk around and were approaching the short dock on which Wade knelt. He started down the ladder in a hurry and slipped on the second rung, falling with a loud crash into the boat below. Nyra was starting to paddle, and he heard her sharp inhale.

There was a moment of silence followed by a clatter of stomping feet running to his position. Wade used the paddle to push off from the pier and looked up to see a hundred pale faces staring at him, eyes cloudy but focused on him and Nyra.

The Scree piled together on the pier until they covered the entire thing. The old dock creaked from the weight, but it held. Wade paddled as fast as he could, moving his arms faster than he ever remembered doing anything. They both rowed out to the open waters before angling back to the south end, the silent crowd watching them as they left. At first, they watched intently but the farther Wade and Nyra got, the things eventually lost interest.

They retrieved the others and rowed out to the I'Varrin. From the small rowboat, Wade could see a few people moving aboard the elegant ship. When they were close enough that the waves knocked the boats into the hull, a rope ladder was thrown down to them.

Wade was the last to climb aboard and found Stasia already conversing with the captain. He held his hat in his hand and slapped it hard against his thigh. Then he beckoned them to follow him.

"Will he take us inside Echo Canyon?" Wade asked, catching up.

"He will. I think. There were a lot of curses in what he said, but yes."

"He wants me to find the spot on one of his maps," Nyra said.

Inside Morales's cabin was a small bed to one side and a desk to the other. The desk was full of loose drawings: maps, small arial drawings with extensive notations, and a mound of scrolls besides. Pinned above the desk and covering the entire wall was the most intricate map of the Zulu Sea coastline Wade had ever seen. It stretched from Aquom to Talon. Wade stepped closer and realized there were many sheets behind it that detailed other parts of the world.

"Wow," Stasia exclaimed, "These are amazing. Did you inscribe these yourself?"

"Thank you. They are my life's work. I don't let anyone inside here usually, but when Kovan Rainer tells you that the fate of the world rests on your shoulders and your ship, well I'm reevaluating the parameters of my service."

"Aren't we all," Wade said, "So, Nyra can you figure out where the prison is?"

Morales picked up a long, smooth stick and used it to point to a place in the canyon, "I would assume it's somewhere in here?"

Nyra approached the map and traced her finger from Amera through the mountains drawn on the map, then she stopped.

"What's the scale? How far is it from Amera?"

Morales produced a ruler and handed it to her, "Each notch is a quarter of a league."

"By horse, they would be able to travel close to eight leagues a day," Wade said.

"No, it would be less, given the terrain. Maybe six," Morales corrected him.

"It's closer to seven," Nyra corrected both of them. She put the ruler on the wall and marked out a passage with her finger. Pulling the ruler along, she settled on a point where the drawing showed canyon lines spreading around an expanse.

"That's it," Nyra said.

Morales stepped close to inspect the point and followed a different path from the Zulu,

"We can arrive there in a day and a half. The last part of the trip will be accessed by those small boats you brought out to us," he tapped on a small number written in the water lines, "I can take the I'Varrin to here. And we can reach the canyon by this river."

With the timeframe set, it would leave them half a day to scout the area and figure out how to free Kovan. Wade mulled the possibility that they were missing the best people to pull off such a thing. Namely Kovan himself, but it would be nice to have a Luminary or Semo.

"Captain what do you have aboard that could help us get Kovan back? Guns, shadow dust, anything?"

"We have some star-powder," Morales said.

"Not what I had in mind but—"

"No, Wade that's perfect. I think I could make an explosive with star-powder," Stasia said.

Wade exhaled a long slow breath and checked his watch again waiting for word from the others, some sign that they were doing better than he was. But no message came.

THIRTY-SIX
AWAKENING (ELIAS)

E lias felt like he was living in dream, walking through fog-filled streets, searching for a path that would lead him out. Sometimes people appeared in the mist, and he would talk with them. Sometimes the haze itself turned black and there was nothing to see. The world became a frozen void of wandering.

He heard voices now, calling him, pulling him to the correct route and free of this maze. He walked an empty trail now, trees and a forest beyond sight; but now a light of warmth and air lurked within his path. He found himself before the light, and behind him, though he didn't look, he knew was the darkness and another voice. It mocked him and threatened him. It was familiar and entwined deep inside his own voice. He couldn't look, but he wanted to. He wanted to know whose voice it was that had accompanied him so long and haunted his every waking breath. He knew who it was, but sometimes accepting what one knows to be true when the truth is wrought with peril can be that hardest thing a person can do.

The friendly voices called again from the light.

"If you go into the light, you will never live, Elias Qudin," the Dark Being behind him warned. "I will win."

Elias hesitated. There was no way in knowing. No way to tell, but he couldn't remain in this fog any longer, of that he was certain. If the light was the end, then let it be the end.

"No!" The dark voice screamed. "I have tasted freedom now, Qudin. I have lived again, and I will find a way to return, or I will destroy both of us!"

Qudin stepped into the wall of light.

His eyes flickered and blinked with need. The universe stretched out before him, the great young star burning bright white and the planets alive and spinning around it. Then time plunged into a whirlpool of dark space and the dimensions of reality branched in infinity, the crossroads of fate bound in the wrappings of time, space, and energy. He glimpsed visions of every route and every choice that splintered the universe. He stood at the precipice of time, among the loom of souls, and understood the future like a warm embrace.

The swirl of energy evaporated, and the edges were consumed by a dark energy; an omnipresent purple light swallowing the world.

A flash of lightning and sear of pain snapped the ethers away and he awoke to see the face of a child he once knew in the face of the young woman who looked upon him with great concern and glowing eyes like flames, the wind blowing back to her temples. The many pathways of fate remained a burned image in his mind. Tali smiled at him, and she slumped back.

The visceral state of reality was uncomfortable. Pain returned in spikes and aches and spoke of a weakness set deep in Elias's bones. His body almost required death and rebirth to function properly again. *He'll never live. Indeed.* Elias squinted at the glowing dust above his face and found that his eyes hurt. He rested them.

"DRINK THIS," A CLOAKED FIGURE SAID.

Elias looked at him and drank from the ceramic cup. The liquid was warm and tart with an herbal quality that was covered up by some fruit. Dreamer's Berry if he wasn't mistaken. The Tregorean healer had saved him again.

"It's been a long time, Hira Zadar," Elias said.

"Not as long as I would have hoped, Qudin."

Elias finished the drink and handed it back. It had replaced whatever horrible taste he had in his mouth before.

"What did you give me?" Elias asked, still rolling the remnants of it on his tongue. He handed back the cup. His mystcat, Merphi, took it as an opening and jumped up to his lap to nestle down.

"The mushroom of the Red Moon has brought you back to us, though I believe you owe the young woman your life. She did something to jolt you back."

He spotted Learon standing against the wall, a small steady cloud of glowing dust drifting around him. Elias smiled, the truth of who Learon was laid bare before his eyes. Elias wished he had put everything together sooner. He could have guided the kid differently. Now that he could see things the way they were, Elias realized Learon really did look like his mother.

"Master Zadar, I need to speak with his Grace Raza Derasi. Does he still live?"

"He does, and I'm sure he is waiting to speak with you. We will move you someplace more comfortable and he will be brought to you."

"Thank you and thank you again for saving me."

"You should thank your friends. How they dragged you across the world to me, I'll never know," the healer said. He waved a group of three attendants to come closer. They helped Elias to a private room. It had been many years since he had been inside their lands, but he remembered some things. The rock had different coloring and striations the closer to the surface or deeper under the mountains one went, and he recognized his room was near the surface.

Tali and Learon accompanied him to the room, explaining the situation as best they knew, recapping for him everything that had taken place since they escaped the Temple beneath Marathal falls. The larger pieces missing from their story concerned how Elias and Ellaria had come to Midway. Elias could recall some of that, but not clearly. The other missing bits all concerned the Sagean and his Court of Dragons. All they knew was what Ellaria had told them in an endless stream of messages.

Elias had heard of this Genius Chamber before in his research, but he also had abided by the Tregoreans warning to stay out of the Shadow Field. No one was sure how long it had been since one of the volcanoes there had erupted, but one thing everyone agreed on was that they were all active.

Elias understood what was to come next but wasn't sure how to explain things to these two. How much he should tell them and how much he should keep to himself? He could see the journey had aged them both. They looked almost like different people than the youngsters he watched escape through the wave gate. Learon looked especially stressed. He had apparently not taken well to the news of his parents and who he was. His eyes refused to settle on any one spot in the room and his leg shook unconsciously.

It had taken Elias longer than it should have to figure out what Learon was. He wanted to attribute his slow realization to distractions, but it was a reluctance to see the truth. He regretted not being there to tell him. Coming to terms with the meaning of truth is never easy. *Why didn't you tell me?*

"Did you say something?" Tali said from her chair.

Elias looked at her quizzically, but a knock came at the door before he could ask her if she had found a talent.

"Come in," Elias said.

The old man he remembered came through the door and closed it behind him. Elias stood and bowed to the wiseman. Then he turned to Learon and Tali each in turn to dismiss them.

"I will call for you soon. Please get your things ready. I am sure we will receive word by this evening that they have located the Temple. It's a long journey to the south," Elias said.

They both left and Elias sat back on the bed. He knew now with a certainty what had happened years ago on the plateaus of the Dragon's Spine, but that's not what he wanted to talk about with Derasi. Grace Derasi sat in a chair near the door, his hands folded together, he looked like Elias remembered him.

"Your Grace, I have had a vision," Elias said.

"That is not uncommon, if you were given the mushroom of the Red Moon. What can I advise you on?" Derasi asked.

"I wanted to talk to you about time and future events. Your people know more about prophecy and fate than any I have encountered."

"This is true. Though it is believed we once worked very closely with the Menodarins to unravel our prophets' words."

"If I ever find their lands, I will relay what they know."

"That would be of much help, Qudin."

"I had a glimpse of what will come," Elias said.

"Have you ever seen this before, the future?" Derasi asked.

"No. Though as you know, I am no stranger to the dangers of prophets and foresight, but what I want to know is: can the future be changed?"

"Time, Qudin Lightweaver, is neither a circle nor a straight line, but it is progressive; it is dimensional. A common misconception is that the legend of the Great Tree of Life symbolizes life and nature; the greater meaning, however, is that of time. Time branches and splinters and gives birth to new realities, all born of deep roots."

"You know the true threat I face, the Old One. Not long ago, I spoke with a wisewoman of a forgotten people. Based on what she told me and my recent experience, I now believe the Wrythen is an energy. But unlike the energies that are born of life and give birth to life, I believe it an energy born of death," Elias said.

"It could be as you say. You know better than anyone alive the nature of energy. But as to your first question, the future is guided by the vast web, but every event has multiple paths and each path a dimension. The unfortunate truth of living things is our propensity to repeat the past. This is the vulnerability of our world, with the history of all the steps that came before having been washed away. Our path can very easily circle back on itself, and we wouldn't know until it is too late. These dimensions—they aren't planes of existence in separation but in a tangle. Think of it all like a crystal of ever-changing shape. Those few legends great enough to fight against the lattice can merge paths or destroy branches, but the crystal's structure simply adapts. Everything impacts the whole and some pulses can travel the full expense, the energy breaching the void."

"That's what I'm afraid of. I fear there are gaps that have started to unravel, cracks in the structure. I believe the Luminaries were born to repair those holes and the Old One is a creation of the void itself. It is the echo of the destruction, and it longs to unravel the web for good," Elias said.

"Thus, the Trinity Guard returns?" Derasi said.

"Yes."

"I shouldn't be telling you this, but we have a new prophet," Derasi said.

"You do?"

"Yes. The King and Queen are adamant that you two not see each other."

Elias wanted to ask why, but he didn't, "Does she have bright red hair?"

"She's young, about the same age as your companions. She. . ." Derasi stopped. He seemed to be picking around what he could and couldn't tell Elias. "She has been slow to trust her abilities and so she is slow to see, but she did foresee you coming here. And…"

"And she has seen my death?" Elias finished for the old man. He didn't have to look his expression to know it was the truth, "It is alright, old friend. I have seen my death as well."

Maybe it was the shock of hearing someone say something like that without worry or maybe it was the slight smirk on Elias's lips, but Derasi reeled back with arched eyebrows, awaiting an explanation.

When they had finished their conversation, Elias knew they would be leaving soon for the temple, and he quickly jotted down some notes he wanted to leave for Derasi. Elias thought he knew how everything might play out, especially if the Sagean had the Black Scepter as Ellaria said. Events inside the chamber would present each of them with choices. He didn't want Learon's mind conflicted in any way. Though their journeys might diverge and take them into different directions, it would be their ability to come back to each other that would save the world. Elias had seen it. His wife Mia had seen it, too, but her vision had been corrupted. The connection Learon had with Tali was evident from the moment they sat together on the bank of the river that morning. She would do whatever it took to defeat the Wrythen and Learon would do whatever it took to protect her. He only wished he had more time with them. If his plan worked, he would, but he was unsure what was going to happen once the spirit he held back was released. Elias hoped Learon would forgive him one day, but he knew what was to come next had to be done.

Learon walked in shortly after the Grace left. He carried Tali's myst-cat, Remi, in his arms but was otherwise by himself. A marksman bow was strewn across his back, and he looked more upbeat than he had before.

"They have found it," Learon announced and laid the cat on the bed, "Just as you said, Elias. We are gathering and heading there within the hour. I told Tali we would meet her and Semo at the canals. The Kihan have chosen to help us."

Elias smiled at his preference to call them the Kihan. It was his right. Kihan should call their people Kihan. "Let me guess, Tali convinced them?" Elias asked.

"I guess so. She told them all about the Sagean and the Old One and the leaders of the Kihan were persuaded," Learon looked at Elias with concern, "Can you make the journey?"

"I have to. Don't worry, I am regaining my strength with each moment that passes. By the time we reach the Temple, I will be ready," Elias said. It was the truth and Learon looked relieved to hear it. Elias didn't think Learon needed to know the rest. He stood clumsily on his feet and walked with Learon out into the palace complex, leaving the cats behind. He was surprised there were no guards with Learon. The Kihan had accepted Learon.

"Do one of you have my Elum Blade?" Elias asked.

"No, I left it with Kovan. I even left my bow on the winddrifter. This is a ranger bow," Learon said.

"Whatever happens at the Temple, you need to get Ellaria out of there. The Sagean's next move will be all out war against the New World. It's essential that Ellaria makes it out and across the Anamic," Elias said.

"Understood."

"You should go with her," Elias said.

"What?" Learon said surprised.

"I know you will want to stay here with the Kihan, but I want you to go to the New World and seek out the Shadowyn."

"The Shadowyn?"

"They are blade masters without equal. They trained me and I believe they will teach you."

"Where are you going?" Learon asked.

"I'm unsure what fate has in store for us, but I believe the first Nimbus Warrior in a two thousand years should seek out the Shadowyn. They are very secretive people, but they can teach you what others cannot."

"If they are as you say, why would they let a stranger into their land? Won't they kill me?" Learon asked.

"No. Show them the Elum Blade and they will let you pass."

They continued through the halls in silence until they reached the main entrance and the lake in the mountain. Boats full of soldiers and one with Tali and Semo awaited them. Meroha sat on the steps. She stood when they emerged through the doors.

"Elias, how are you?" Meroha asked

"I am well, thank you. I am glad you're here. Could you also watch out for Merphi while I'm gone?"

"I thought you might ask. Yes, I can do that," Meroha said.

"I hope you understand how much this means for Tali and me. Our Mystcats are more than just pets," Elias said.

Meroha nodded her head yes, "I have your bat, Jules, also," she said, opening the flap of her pack for him to see. The little artificer bat squirmed and squeaked its disapproval being stuffed in a bag. Elias placed his finger on the bat's head, and it calmed.

"Then I would ask that you keep her safe, too," Elias said.

"Jules has been acting funny. Does the bat need tinkering?" Meroha asked.

"No. Most likely she just needs something to do. Please don't let it out of your sight, she is one of the few keys that will open my vault in Polestis."

"I won't," Meroha said. Her sorrow filled eyes spoke of having traveled one of the hardest paths of all and he was about to leave her with one of the hardest missions.

"Was there anything else?" Meroha asked.

"Yes. I have left instructions for you with the Tregorean's priest Grace Derasi. It's very important that you both follow my directions exactly. Understand."

"No, not really."

"You will. I know you worry about your home, and your people. For that I'm sorry. Remember, family is more then blood. I speak for all of us when I say you are part of our family."

"Thank you, Elias," Meroha said, and she hugged Learon before she escaped back inside the palace. They turned to head for the boats, and Learon tapped him on the shoulder.

"Elias, did you know about me?" Learon asked.

"I knew you were special."

"Did you know I wasn't human?"

"You're still human, Learon. All the races of beings in this world are kin of humanity. We are all fundamentally the same species. Even the Zenoch with their blue skin, they bleed red blood. The Menodarins with their tall slender bodies and flat faces or the Kihan with their skin and ears: it doesn't matter. We are all unified in our humanity. What binds us is not our physical differences but what's inside us. The energy of all beings is both, unique to the individual *and* from the same source."

"Did you know?" Learon said.

"I didn't know until the wisewoman of the One People told me."

Learon nodded and descended the steps to the waiting boats. Elias was relieved he hadn't asked the question he expected. At the boat, Tali hugged Elias, obviously excited to see him up and walking. Semo gave a slight nod and Elias stepped inside the boat.

"Bazlyn is staying behind," Tali said.

"Probably for the best," Elias said.

Something shifting around her neck caught his eye and he tapped his own neck to ask her about it. She removed the necklace and the obsidian coin he gave her on a leather string. In an instant, a plan B formed in his mind.

"I fashioned your coin into a necklace," she explained.

"I see that. It reminds me of the amber coin necklaces from the Great War, where soldiers would punch a hole in the amber and put them around their neck," Elias said.

"I've seen a coin like that before. They're old and I thought it was bad luck, so I got rid of it as soon as I could," Learon said.

"You still find some in circulation, but they're very rare," Elias said.

"Why did they do that?" Tali asked.

"Do you really want to know?" Elias said.

"Yes, of course," Tali said.

"Because..." Semo said and he lifted an amber coin necklace from under his shirt, "If they were found dead, the coin was to be used to pay for a burial. All Darkhawks still follow this tradition."

"It originated with sailors when they began to search for the New World. Many vessels wound up shipwrecked, and the crews' bodies would float to shore. It was a major problem during the Brovic fever when, for a time, there was a contest to see who could cross the Brovic. Of course, no one ever has," Elias explained.

"I know about the Brovic Fever, but I had never heard about the coins before," Tali said and she looked at her own necklace a little differently.

"Do you remember I told you how that coin was more than just a compass? Did you ever discover the meaning behind the symbol?" Elias said.

"No. I even searched once through your library," Tali said.

"Well, the properties of the crystals do many things, but the intent of the sigil was meant for transporting. I made it long ago when I first started studying the wave gates and how they worked with magnetic waves in unison with the magic of the furies. You should have Ellaria study it. I bet she would find it fascinating."

"I will. Elias, did you know about the Trinity Guard?" Tali asked.

"I did, but I..."

"Didn't believe in it?" Tali said.

"No, I didn't concern myself with it. I figured something like that was beyond my control. In a way, I had a Trinity Guard. Kovan is as fierce and deadly a fighter I have ever encountered or seen on a battlefield, and Ellaria was, and probably still is, the foremost expert on alchemy and mystic arts. I would say she is as close to a Fusion Mage as there has been in a thousand years," Elias said.

"I didn't think about it like that," Tali admitted.

"There are many mysteries of life and the universe that can never fully be grasped. That's the vastness of reality. Each step forward in knowing is only a new perspective. Knowledge is not a path, it's a viewpoint of the endless horizon. The better the viewpoint, the more of the horizon you can see, but there is always *more* to see. Even death can only be another viewpoint. We are not cast out of existence, only ushered into a new realm of it," he said.

"That's the Elias I know," Learon said.

"It is also entirely possible we are all trapped in the event horizon of existence from which we can neither escape nor perceive what's beyond, because it is beyond time itself," Elias offered.

They left his words to linger, and the boat powered on through the snaking canals. Over the course of the day, they traveled the many districts that made up the Tregorean lands. The full Ammadon Province spanned a traveling distance close to a hundred leagues from the northern farm plateaus to the southern villages of Tarhallen. It was much larger if the full expanse and spread was considered, but still the hundred leagues on horseback would have taken almost five days. The Kihan's powered boats and canal system had cut their time to a little over a day.

On the night of the first day, they rested from the boats outside of the main transport district of the Averient. The markets stretched from the river, to the Twin Lakes. Elias was given a room in a rustic village, in one of the *akoya huts* that sprouted all over the hills of the district where it bordered Tarhallen. It was possibly the most peaceful area in all the province. Most of the districts where full of people, artists, merchants, crafters, and builders. Here, the *akoya huts* scattered the slope, each an elevated space, lifted on engineered bundles of wood and providing a view of Lake Azeerall in the distance. The huts were like manmade trees, ovoid shaped, with thatch roofs comprised of tightly woven leaves.

Elias surveyed the hillside of glowing orange lanterns. The moon above was waxing to full in the coming days and the land stretched out beyond with vibrant light and shadow. He had spent time here before and always found the tranquility of the jungle and mountains were best found in the border points.

Tali and Learon came over to say goodnight. They sat together, their feet hanging over the edge.

"They are a beautiful people, aren't they?" Tali admired.

"They are," Elias agreed.

"Coming here has changed everything for me," Learon admitted.

"So much of our mind is made up for us even before we begin to think on something. Belief is more penetrating than truth. It's neatly simplified for our own comfort. When something challenges that, we can either change or fade away," Elias said thoughtfully.

"Is belief more powerful? Before we left, the Mainland was on the precipice of war. Once again, hordes of people are willing to die for their belief in the Sagelight Faith," Tali said.

"It is more alive than truth, but it's not more powerful. Discovering the truth of things beyond one's own belief requires an acceptance of reality few are willing to see," Elias said.

"It's almost like the Great War was meaningless," Learon said.

"Never look for meaning in war. If I've never said anything you will remember, remember that. The Great War left things untethered. In the end, we didn't save the world when we overthrew the Empire, but we did awaken it. In that freedom, there is still the freedom to believe as people want, and people will always want to believe what's most comforting," Elias said.

"It's probably natural for the conflict to arise from the ashes and rubble of war, but I can't help feeling ashamed of our generation for squandering the freedom," Tali said.

"We fight a darker threat now, one I believe, is manipulating all of us. It will only be through unity that we will prevail. To do that, we must forgive others their beliefs, their differences, and unite in an oath for truth. The energy of life is in us all and it comes from the same source. It makes no difference what you call that source, just as it makes no difference if that energy is wrapped in a different skin color or gender. We all strive for the pursuit of life and in that, we can and must stand together against the darkness," Elias said.

"How? How do we fight all these battles and unite people to one cause?" Tali said.

"I don't know. But if anyone has the strength and ability to unite people to a common purpose, it's you Tali. I believe you'll find a way," Elias said.

"Where would I start?"

"You have already started here, but I believe that the Tempest Stone could still be our greatest asset."

"I hope Kovan and Wade got it back," Tali said.

"I am sure they did. We should get some rest. We will reach this passage point tomorrow and traveling the jungle will be much harder from there," he said.

"Here," Learon said, and he handed Elias his old satchel. "I almost forgot."

Elias opened it to find his diffusion goggles and journal, "Did you find the glove?"

"No, it wasn't with any of your things, or Ellaria's."

"Thank you."

Tali and Learon's watches lit up.

"Another message from Ellaria…" Tali paused.

"is that it? What happened?" Learon said.

"What's wrong?" Elias asked.

"The message cut off," Tali said.

"What did it say?"

Tali showed him her wrist,

We've landed northeast of the Blac...

"What do you happened?" Tali said.

"Best not to speculate, but it sounds like we may reach at the temple after them," Elias said.

"Is that bad?" Learon asked.

"Can't say for sure, but the second army to arrive at battle field usually arrives exhausted. We should get some rest," Elias said.

They parted for the night and Elias watched them walk back to their akoyas. He gazed at the night sky, thinking about Mia and thinking about his friends. He wondered if they would ever forgive him.

THIRTY-SEVEN
THE RED SPEAR (KOVAN)

T he cage rattled and swayed on the trail, coarse dirt of rubble and granite. Every bump, rock, and dip in the mountain route reverberated through the wagon bed and jostled Kovan around. He was content with being captured. In fact, he had anticipated that it might be a possibility before they even attacked that day. The bigger problem was, he had forgotten to give Wade the little tin can of his last memories for safekeeping. When they surrounded him, Kovan was smiling as he watched his compatriots riding away, but as Razor stepped up, a sunken feeling hit Kovan's stomach. He realized Razor was about to find the only thing precious to him. He reached for the can to try and take the cube and Razor pounced on him, ripping the tin box free. Razor then looked at it with curious suspicion. Razor opened the lid and his forehead creased. A slight relief flooded Kovan: he didn't know what it was. Razor closed the lid and waved his hand in the air—cuffs were put on and a short beating ensued.

Throughout the journey through the pass, Kovan watched every move Razor made, trying to see if he had done anything with the cube, but he hadn't. Redmar had placed the tin in his vest pocket and never looked at it again. He may not have known what it was, but he knew it had value.

It was a long ride to the Red Spear and Kovan had a lot of time to sit in his cage with nothing but his thoughts and the sky above. In the day, the sun scorched the wagon bed and everything in it, including Kovan. The intensity of the sun in the elevated mountain pass was brutal. Kovan would huddle up as best he could to shield his face from the harsh rays of light. At night, the star-filled sky stretched out above and the cool mountain air provided a splendor in his solitude. With the cubes, his memories had returned, but they had come slowly. As a result, so too had his sense of urgency for the frailty of the future. He had struggled to correctly appreciate the future and plan for it. With no memories to guide his thoughts, he wasn't appreciative of how events unfolded in time.

With the first cube, his memories had come in a rush that exhausted him, but they were mostly jumbled in their return; more emotion than images. The sequence and nuance of the events came later when the impact of a lifetime returned.

Poe had been correct; the second cube was harder to take and harder to reconcile. Kovan had no choice in the matter and the flight to Amera had provided the only opportunity. Necessity to know more about the Bounty Hunters and the Red Spear outweighed his trepidation to live in his past. That was what taking the cubes were: a total immersion in his past reality brought on like he was in a dream.

Major events felt sped up in his recalling, but they also still felt to him like he had spent most of the time actually there. The experience, the exhaustion, the joy, or heartbreak, all hit with equal measure. The battle of Zulu had taken ten days, and his revisiting the memory made him feel like he was there the full ten days again. Years of his life relived in a day. It was exhausting and it left much of reality a confusing mess.

He had forgotten how much memory could make him feel old. The weight of life is in the experiences, all stacked inside, and that alone ages the mind. The jumble of time was the worst part. It wasn't as though each cube had simply revealed thirty years at a time. Each revealed memories from throughout his life. He now remembered why he hated swords, why he didn't drink mulberry wine, even what his favorite star constellation was.

The night before the shootout in Amera, he had been blasted with fragments of his daughter and his life with Ellaria. It was enough for a man to want to drink himself to blacking out. The nature of the return always brought the emotion of the memory back to life and only later, the memory of how to live with his failures. He realized now sitting in the cage, he had almost wanted to get caught.

Now his only thought was getting to Ellaria. Nothing would keep him from her. No armed guards, no shackles, or chains, and certainly no great prison in the vast canyon. With a new purpose, Kovan began planning for his escape.

Two men driving the wagon, two front riders, both Bonemen with pulsators guns, three riders behind, and a squad of six soldiers further back with two Rendered machines struggling to keep pace: and Razor riding back and forth between all of them. If he didn't count the automatons, he was outnumbered fourteen to one. And he was in a cage. *Thorns*, he thought, *this could get bloody.*

To make matters worse, once they arrived at the prison, the numbers would grow. But to get inside, they would have to let him out of the cage and walk the steep open-sided stairs where footing and spacing could diminish their advantage.

Kovan eyed his captors through the bars with a grin. They had made a huge mistake in capturing him. They should have killed him.

"What are you smiling at, Kovan?" Razor sneered from his horse trotting behind.

Kovan didn't say anything, but in his mind, he thought, *Dead men, I'm smiling at dead men.* But another voice in his head, the piece of him that would always be Caleb, wondered, *who am I, to deliver such a fate?*

"Since you're awake and in a good mood, I'll ask you now, where's the young woman named Rue?" Redmar said.

Kovan tried not to betray his recognition of Tali's alias and he maintained eye contact without emotion, but his fist tightened on the iron bar.

"Not talking I see, it doesn't matter. Some very important people are looking for her. They've taken out a contract on her and after I have you in the Spear, I'm going to track her down," Redmar said.

In the hills, a flash of light flickered like the sun sparkling on metal. Kovan spotted it and his grin returned. An explosion decimated the valley behind them, and the group of Rendered machines, in its wake. The horses of the caravan all reeled from the caterwaul of sound. Razor Redmar pulled his horse back to inspect what had happened behind them.

"Keep going," Redmar ordered the wagoner, apparently believing they were under attack from behind.

Kovan had to bite his lip to keep from laughing. When the gap between the wagon and the group of riders widened, a second flash of light from the peak shimmered and another explosion blasted rock from all sides. Debris showered down on Kovan, and he laughed out loud. Most of the legion of soldiers in their traveling party were now blocked behind a large mound of the mountain piled high, including Redmar. The cloud of dust from the blast refused to settle and the driver called a halt, as huge boulders tumbled down from the side slopes all around.

From Kovan's position in the cage, he could see they had come upon an overturned wagon on the trail, impeding their passage. As soon as the cart stopped, the wagon bed lifted into the air. The large and wonderful Hazon man, Mayzanna Buroga tossed the cart at the front riders with a destructive crash.

Perched overhead on the higher rocks, Kovan spotted Wade, who launched from the boulders a hundred feet above. Immediately, a set of cream-colored wings sprang out from his back.

Kovan's eyes bulged. Whatever the contraption the kid had strapped to his back, it allowed him to fly. Wade soared in a slow circle, firing his gun into the solders that remained. When he was over the cage, a pulsator dropped drown from the sky and landed in the hay-filled wagon bed.

Kovan grabbed the gun and laid waste to every soldier he could see. Buroga came running over and ripped the cage door off the hinges to free him.

"So much for locks," Kovan said.

Buroga looked at him, "You are free, Kovan Rainer."

Kovan jumped down and looked at the bent cage door bobbing on the dirt road, "You know, I think you could have broken through the bars in Ravenvyre?"

To this, Buroga only smiled wryly. Wade finally landed a few feet away and came running toward them.

"We have to run. They're climbing over the barricade."

They started down toward the far edge of the canyon. The Red Spear was in sight. The canyon there channeled around a large mass of red clay that had long ago been shaped into a prison. Smoke rose from the jagged top. Wade led them away from that canyon to the west bluff, where the edge rose over the river below.

"Let's go, freedom awaits," Wade said, and he jumped from the cliff into the water below. Buroga was next and his splash was large, but not as impressive as the sound of his huge form hitting the surface, or the subsequent gulp of the river accepting him in.

From behind, Kovan heard shouts. He turned to see Redmar cresting the rock mound and pointing towards Kovan. More soldiers followed and the Rendered began lifting the boulders away. Kovan was caught between running for his life and facing off against a small army for the last cube of his past.

"Kovan, Come on!" Wade yelled.

The soldiers fired their guns and Kovan jumped to the river.

He hit the cold waters with moving feet and the impact stung his legs. When his head came clear of the surface, Wade was paddling a boat and yelling something. Kovan's ears were waterlogged, and he could quite make it out, but he got enough from his motioning hands. Soldiers began to fire at them from above. Kovan swam below the surface until he reached the small boat. He lifted himself up and in, where the water from his clothes pooled in the boat bottom. Wade paddled away and Kovan pushed the wet hair from his face, *What did I just give up?* He aimed his gun to the high ledge and fired. The first few shots were almost useless from the water-soaked mechanics, but on the fourth pull, the gun fired true and blasted the rock where the soldiers stood. The boat was being carried off to the sea by the current, but Kovan could tell Wade was angling it back close to the nearest canyon.

"Where are you going?" he asked.

"We have to get Nyra," Wade said.

"She was your spotter?"

"Yes, she volunteered. Stasia watched the boats and kept them from drifting out and Nyra hid in the cliff peak, watching the caravan," Wade explained. Kovan looked over and spotted Stasia at the bow of the other boat, Buroga rowing at a pace they couldn't match.

It was a good plan, a dangerous plan, but so far successful. They could still hear a commotion of yells from the plateau and as they rounded the sunlit rock, Kovan spotted the small young woman moving down from the summit. Even as small as she was, she looked exposed climbing away and to the south slope.

Suddenly, movement on the far side where they had come disturbed the stillness of the rocks. Razor Redmar appeared at a boulder there and fired his gun toward them. The shot went extremely wide of the mark. It ricocheted on hard stone and zipped off into the canyon. He was too far to hit them, and he knew it, but that didn't keep him from trying to find a better perch from which to shoot.

In the cliffs, they watched Razor climb to get a higher position for shooting. To their collective horror, the farther he climbed, the closer he came to Nyra's position. She was busy trying to scramble away without falling to the jagged rocks hundreds of feet below. Even at a running jump, no one could clear the harsh stone shore and make it to the river.

Shots rang out and splattered the water behind them, the sounds echoing into the canyon walls in manner befitting the namesake of the massive and vast land. While the charged tungsten rounds were nowhere close to hitting them on the boats, they all still flinched and ducked on instinct. Their rifles were more effective than Redmar's pulsator. Stasia huddled in the boat's stern, while Buroga continued to row. Kovan tried to take aim at Razor, but he knew his own shots would be equally futile.

Frustrated, Redmar unloaded his pulsator gun. He kicked a large boulder over the side, and it cracked into pieces. Several rock fragments flew far enough, they hit the side of the boat. Razor observed the crashed stone and Kovan's stomach dropped. Not far off, Nyra had found the trail, but in doing so, she had sent some loose gravel tumbling to the shore below and Razor had caught the movement. He walked to the edge and peered around the mountain when he spotted her. Without a clear path to Nyra, Razor disappeared back the way he had come.

"Faster. Row faster Wade. We need to get to Nyra now!" Kovan said.

Wade had missed it, but he rowed with a faster clip, "What's happening?" Wade asked between his heavy breathing.

"Razor is going after Nyra."

The boat moved in the water far slower then Kovan could tolerate. The entire time, his eyes watched the rocks above while also trying to find another possible route to her. The trail wound around with the cliff face and the river. When they were close enough to the shore, Nyra could see them clearly and smiled at their success. A hulking form emerged out of the mountain behind her. Razor must have said something because Nyra froze in place and visibly trembled. In a heartbeat, he was on her and lifting her into the air. His hand around her throat, her feet lifted clear off ground.

Kovan stood and aimed his gun, but there was no clear shot and the momentum of his stance nearly toppled both Wade and him into the river. He watched as Nyra tried to fight back, but Razor laughed at her. In a last-ditch effort to save herself, she pulled the gold-hilted dagger free from the sheath at her back and attempt to stab Redmar with it. He caught her arm with his free hand. She must have cut him because his hand came away for an instant, but it was quickly back, clutching her wrist. With his strength, Nyra could do nothing.

"Kovan, do something," Stasia whimpered. Her and Buroga had drifted further out in the river toward the sea outlet, but they could still see what was happening. There was nothing Kovan could do but end it for both. He aimed his gun to shoot them down. But before he could fire, Razor had driven the blade into Nyra's side and flung her to the rocks below. Kovan heart stopped, and he closed his eyes from the deadly impact.

"No!" Wade cried out.

When Kovan's pulse picked up again, he blasted every bullet in the chamber into the cliff face where Razor had stood. He couldn't say whether he had hit anything, but certainly he hadn't killed Razor Redmar. The demon of the south had fled back into the mountains with Kovan's memories.

THIRTY-EIGHT
SOULS IN THE SHADOW FIELD (TALI)

They stood before the old stone wall in the morning. It stretched through the valley's edge as though it held back an untamable jungle beyond. Expansion cracks in the mortar of the stone spilled dirt and moss. Vines had punctured through in some locations and large stone chunks pushed free to crumble on the ground. There was an opening, but it was blocked off by the jungle. The rangers hacked away at the passageway. Tali hung back while Elias studied the writing in the stone, writing that had illuminated to their presence on the threshold.

The gateway through the Great Wall of Nagari was in the shape of an upside-down triangle and above that, a band stretched wide over the face of the wall like a rainbow. There was writing in the relief that glowed blue through chiseled grooves. Some of the writing didn't glow, but it was so worn away by time that it looked impossible to read.

Behind Tali, a cloaked and veiled woman approached Learon and pulled him away to speak. Echoryn was out of place among the other Tregorean warriors. She was dressed like the scout they had first met, and Tali had not seen her since she had brought Learon to Elias in the Dust room. Tali couldn't hear the conversation, but Echoryn seemed to be introducing Learon to a tall man of some importance. He walked forward and took measure of Learon. He was heavily armed, and his face held a questioning look with arched eyebrows. After the introduction, the man turned to talk with Echoryn and Tali realized they must be brother and sister. They didn't look alike at all; in fact, Echoryn didn't look like either of her parents, but something about the scolding look of annoyance the man gave her while they talked reminded Tali of a mother.

More men dressed like Echoryn's brother came through the throng of archers and Tregorean guards. Five men and two women stood at the head of the squad of soldiers. They each had cast-metal shoulder guards in the form of vines, where a dark green cape was pinned below. It flowed from their side around their back. A vest of armor was yet another shade of green. Unlike the scouts whose clothes were skintight, these uniforms were made for combat. Each looked formidable and all carried a sword sheathed at their side, a bow across their back, and some sort of short-handled scythe that folded closed against their armor.

Learon walked back to Tali, and she watched Echoryn stare at Elias before sneaking away.

"Who are they?" Tali asked when Learon came close.

"Those are the Renja. The tall one is Echoryn's brother, Zorick."

"Renja?" Tali said.

"It means *ranger*," Learon said.

"Why are they here?"

"They know the area beyond the province borders better than anyone. They're going to lead us beyond the wall and into the Shadow Field. The Temple of Ama is far from here, but Zorick said we will reach it by nightfall," Learon said.

Elias waved them forward. Tali and Learon came at his call and three of the Renja came, too.

"Did you find something, Quantum Man?" a female ranger asked.

"Nothing of importance. A cryptic warning about the souls in the Shadow Field bringing life to a demon. Also, the symbols here do suggest more than one Temple is hidden in these jungles," Elias said.

"Our scouts found the Temple by tracking soldiers in red and white," the ranger informed Elias.

"We should go. The day will be long and the jungle beyond this point is very dangerous," Zorick said.

Elias nodded his agreement and they started through the passageway. The jungle proved as treacherous as they had been warned. More than once, the Rangers called a halt to the group to patrol for the Carowdo Python, a giant snake that roamed the southern jungles. There were various signs of an ancient civilization that had disappeared. Everything they found suggested that humans hadn't dwelled there in thousands of years and the jungle had taken no quarter to consume all it could, swallowing the structures beneath the will of nature.

Eroded stone hinted at the thoughtful hands that once shaped the area, but the detail had faded. Crafted corners and shapes made new spaces of creeping life among the crawling jungle plants and foliage all around. Now and then, a statue rose above the tangle, forever stained green and black from the years, and it was obvious through most of their journey that they traveled on a stone walk and stairway. Tali couldn't help but be in awe. The entire jungle was once a sprawling city in equal magnitude to the rest of the Tregorean Province.

They rested in a large clearing with a destroyed fountain at the center. The Blue Sun overhead gave the stone a glow in sections, as though it was crafted with bits of crystal included in the mixture.

They ate what little provisions they had brought, and Tali tried to understand the hierarchy of the Tregorean divisions. She thought the rangers were in charge, but the scouts dictated a lot. The head guard Nokha was with their group, and she commanded the archers and lance carriers but not the rangers. However, the rangers all bowed to her in respect in every interaction Tali witnessed.

Elias ate by himself, and Tali was content to let him sit with his thoughts. When he finished, he came and knelt before her and Learon and waved Semo over to sit with them.

"The rangers say we will be there at sunset. Before we go in, I wanted to talk to you," Elias said, sitting with his legs crossed, "I had a master; he taught me about time and dimensions and realms of being," Elias began, and Learon laughed.

"Sorry," Learon apologized for laughing, "I don't know why I thought we were going to talk strategy. Go on."

"In a way, I am. My master, he told me that there are an infinite number of dimensions for every possible outcome, for every being, for every living moment. Meaning every choice before us, every path diverges to infinity. So, no matter what lies ahead for us, there is an outcome where we fail, and there is an outcome where we succeed," Elias said.

"Do you believe in that, infinite dimensions?" Tali asked.

"I don't know, but I do believe that outcomes can be affected by our perception and our goals," Elias said.

"So, how do we know what path is the right one?" Learon said.

"That's what I'm trying to explain; there is no true choice. We can only do what's right for us; what feels true, inside. Let those other dimensions deal with the outcomes of choices we don't believe in. We are here now, and my goal is to save lives first, not to take them. Agreed?" Elias said.

"Agreed," Tali said, and they both looked at Learon. She understood the point of Elias's conversation now. He feared Learon still held hatred and revenge in his heart for the Sagean and his acolytes.

"Learon?" Elias prompted.

"Agreed," he said.

"Good. You three focus on saving Ellaria and Danehin. I will free the souls trapped in the Gem," Elias said.

Tali had forgotten about the Gem. Kovan and Semo described a giant sphere of souls swimming in a trapped cage, and she realized she knew exactly where the Temple was. She stood and looked to the four archways connected to the courtyard next to which they had stationed themselves. *She feels it.* She heard Elias's thought.

"What is it?" Learon asked.

"I can feel it, the Gem. It's an immense power. There," she pointed through the far opening. "You felt it, too?" she asked Elias, sitting back down.

Elias nodded, "I could feel it at the Wall. Once I figured out what I was sensing, I think I could feel it as long as a month ago."

Tali weighed what he had said and to a degree, understood what he meant. She had sensed something powerful in the east since they had flown over the Zulu Sea.

"The Gem must have been aboard the ship Kovan told you about, at least up until this morning. It's now stopped moving," Elias said.

"Does that mean we are too late? Are they already going forward with the transformation?" Learon asked.

"I doubt it, but we need to hurry. They will wait for the full moon. I don't believe it is a coincidence that they planned the event for a full moon and would not wait for it to be in the sky. I could be wrong," Elias said.

"I hope you are right," Tali said.

"That's a curious talent you have found. Can you hear everything or only single words?" Elias asked her.

"Not everything. I hear full sentences, I guess. Is that my talent?" Tali said.

"Hard to say. I can pick up on words, but it never turned into a talent for me," Elias said.

"What is your talent? You said the last Emperor had a talent for mind manipulation. I think the new Sagean must have a talent for changing his appearance," Tali asked.

"In a way, those talents are one and the same. The Emperor used his for all sorts of things: dream leaping, fear amplification, rage projection, even possession. It's how he subjugated his followers and altered truth for millions. This new Sagean is using the power to alter how people see him, it's called *glamouring*. He doesn't physically change his appearance; it only looks that way. Even so, I got the sense he has yet to master that skill. When he does, he also will be able to create avid devotees. He also has a skill with heat. When he blasted me out of the window at the Tomb in Marathal, it was not a kinetic wave, but my own shield against his attempt to boil me."

"And you?" Tali asked.

"I never developed one particular skill," Elias said.

"Oh," Tali said.

"It's not something you can control. However, whatever skill you develop you can sharpen, and I have sharpened many."

"If you can gain abilities, can you lose them?" she asked.

"I don't believe you can ever lose them, but there are spells that can block them, and sometimes trauma can affect your ability to touch energy," Elias said.

From the far end of the courtyard, the rangers waved at them to start moving again. The sunlight was painting the sky with colors of bright orange and pink when they came upon the towers of jagged stone, piercing above the jungle. The rangers positioned everyone in their traveling party around the mountainside and the head ranger waved for Elias. He was dark-skinned like Nokha, but less intimidating, even though he carried twice as many weapons. Elias spoke with the guard and Tali watched his head nodding as the guard pointed to something. Elias came back.

"Is there some sort of trouble?" Tali asked.

"No. We've come upon something they want me to see. I think we should all go. It's on the hillside below. From there, we'll proceed to the Temple. I've told the Tregoreans to hold their position here for us," Elias said.

Together they slowly traversed down the slope of thick vines. The grade of the hillside was steep and when the jungle cleared, they could see from the hill all the way to the compound of Temples. The path meandered into the darkest corner of the wilderness and Tali could feel another energy emanating in the area. A ranger stood guard on restless feet outside a web of vines, continually scanning all around, and looked relieved at their arrival. Elias ducked inside and Tali followed alongside the others. The inner expanse was occupied by a sea of statues.

A thousand moss-covered sculptures spread out below the trees and through the wild grass, like a beltway toward the Temples. They approached the area with the rangers, but the rangers held back from walking among the stone figures. In the midst was a large statue of an animal raised on a platform like a sentinel over the domain.

"What animal is that?" Tali's eyes were fixed on the moss-stained statue still three- hundred feet away in a tangle of large leaves and grass.

"It's a dragon," Learon said.

Elias looked but didn't question him. They continued to walk between the smaller statues of stone-people scattered around.

"Some sort of guardian?" Tali said.

"I don't know. The people. They are all kneeling," Elias observed.

Tali continued ahead with Elias, and both took in the faces of the statues with the same recoil. The stone-sculpted faces were exaggerated and contorted with wide open mouths, crying to the sky, cheeks puffed and stretched back. A frightening form to purposely chisel, made worse by their grime and weathered state.

"What is this place?" Learon asked.

"The Temple of Ama means *Temple of Souls*," Elias said.

"So, are these the souls in the Shadow Field?" Learon said.

"No. I think we are, The warning was for the living," Elias said.

Elias beckoned them to move on and they proceeded in silence out of the area of statues and reached the base of a tiered structure of spires. The main set of stairs in the west slope was guarded by thirty Bonemen soldiers, but the complex of towers was massive. After scouting the entrance, they slipped away quietly from the way they came. They roamed around the maze of stone that formed various platforms of spaces, including an area of shadow-soaked columns. Each column looked like stacked cubes, and all were covered grime and dirt; they made up a cave-like area that held up the smaller towers. Elias removed the goggles from his neck and put them over Tali's.

"The design and arrangement of this compound reminds me of the Temple I discovered in Echo Canyon long ago. If it is of similar construction: you three will find an entrance on the north side. Use these to find your way," Elias said.

"Where are you going?" Learon asked.

"I'm going to find another way in."

"Why?" Learon said.

"There's something I want to search for. Don't worry, I'll find my way. Stay hidden. The Genesis Chamber and the device will be in the center tower on an upper level. Wait for my signal, then get Danehin and Ellaria out. And remember: the most courageous bend the world to them."

"Understood," Tali said.

Elias started to walk away but he grabbed Learon by the shoulder at the last moment and slung his satchel over Learon's neck, "Take this with you. And Learon, find the Shadowyn."

"I will," Learon said.

"Promise me," Elias said again.

"I promise," Learon said.

"Good. Learon, I... I know you're grappling with who you are. But no matter what changes come, or how others see you, no outside force can change who you are inside. You are in control of who you are. Whoever you want to be, create that person, and be," Elias patted his shoulder and bounded away in a quiet swiftness, disappearing into the dark complex of stone columns.

THEY FOUND THE HIDDEN ENTRANCE AMONGST THE TANGLE OF VINES AND tree roots on the north side, as Elias suggested. The side was the least confined space of the entire complex and opened to the jungle and back up to the hillside where the Tregorean troops waited. The dome-type trees grew nearby; each could easily fit a man standing upright underneath them, and the door sat beyond one nestled against the wall. Tali could feel the energy of the Soul Gem inside slipping through the cracks, and Elias's goggles revealed the energy leaking in an outline.

"There," Tali pointed to a particularly crooked and black snaking set of roots, densely compacted against the Temple stone. Learon pulled an arrow from his quiver and stepped to the section where Tali pointed.

"Here?" Learon verified.

When Tali nodded, Learon stabbed the wall of weeds and thorns to see how thick the overgrowth was. Semo stepped up with one of the ranger's scythes. With a snap of his wrist, the long blade came free, and he hacked away at the vines. The blade was sharp and effective; Semo and Learon removed the overgrowth in short order. Once the wall was cleared, it exposed a depression of brown-stained stone in the shape of a door. Learon ran his hand along the uncovered edge and the panel moved clear on its own. They looked at each other, concerned, but Learon stepped inside.

Through the dark tunnel within, they crept with slow steps in a side-ways stagger. The short passage led to a wider, well-lit hall that split in two directions. They wound around the hall prepared to run into anything, but the path took them to a dead end. Back-tracking around the hall to the other side led to another branching hallway and a set of tight stone stairs. The stair continued up and branched off to another stairs, that again wound around tapered stone walls to yet more stairs. Some stairs ended at doors outside of small dark rooms, but it was the seventh set of stairs that took them into a Viewing Room.

The narrow and dark space was a few paces wide and about thirty feet in length. A horizontal opening in the stone wall provided the perfect view of the main chamber. To Tali, it felt like a sort of control room, but there were no dials or levers to be found. It was their first look at the fountain and each of them stared in dumbfounded awe. The Genesis Chamber was large and round, with a glass-like sheen to the walls. Someone had previously lit torches, the flames flickered from stone sconces. There were several large statues around the perimeter as well. Each held a large sphere upon its shoulders like the figure was hefting them, a grimace on the carved faces. The ground was soot-stained with scorch marks and an etching in the surface of a seven-pointed star. Along the wall at each star point were seats carved into the stone, and ominous masks of metal hung above each station. Cords strung from the ceiling and back to the center where a raised circular platform sat with a smooth bronze finish, connected to the array of components.

Inside the top tier of the platform was a large glowing ball with bands of metal wrapping around it. The crystal ball of blue-white light pulsed and swirled. It omitted a low hum which droned in the chamber. Tali couldn't take her eyes off it. The longer she stared at the glow, the more comprehension of sounds below the hum became clear: whispers.

The resonance of a thousand souls screaming into the void with their voices muzzled. A shiver ran down her spine and she involuntarily trembled. Tears came to her eyes, and she wiped them clear, feeling an arm around her and Learon leaning his head towards her.

"I know," he said in a comforting voice.

"Can you hear them?" She stammered; her voice unsteady.

"No. But I can feel a torrent of torment pulsing from it. You can hear the people inside it?"

"It's not just that," she said and paused, her extra senses prickling at her arms. "I can *feel* them. They're trapped inside that thing, but they're aware. Learon, we have to free them."

"I know. We will," Learon said. He paused and tilted his head to look above.

"What is it?" she asked.

"The carvings all around the upper dome: they're dragons."

Tali looked at the jumble of intersecting lines in the dome. They surrounded the oculus opening in the ceiling and in the moonlight from the opening, she began to see the dragon shapes in the web of lines, circling the opening.

Semo wound up the stairs and joined them after watching the corridor. He began to speak when the sight of the Genesis Chamber and the glowing center stopped him. He stared at it a moment before turning back to them.

"The hall is clear down there. If there is a way into the chamber from that jumble of passageways, I can't find it," Semo said.

"There must be a hidden door," Tali said.

"Without it, I fear we must enter through this viewing channel. It's a long drop to the floor below, but I don't see we have another choice," Learon said.

"Fine, let's go now before the chamber fills up--" Tali paused.

While they argued, the prisoners proceeded to be brought inside by armed soldiers. Each fighter was covered in a thin, silver lattice cloth and a gold face panel that left their eyes clear, as well as the red cape. There were seven prisoners in total and some looked worse than others, but all looked tired and fearful. Danehin was at the front of the line. Ellaria was brought in last, and she looked drugged. The Sagean walked behind her, his stiff posture unsupported by the unnecessary cane he carried in his left hand.

A procession of guards followed him, more with red capes but most with leather-strapped armor, shoulder guards, and shinny metal gauntlets. Tali counted twelve soldiers in all. Four red-caped elite and eight plain Bonemen. With the prisoners in the room and more people approaching from the main hall, the cavernous room began to feel small. They placed the prisoners in small pocketed trenches outside the platform, their connected chain link forcing a clumsy positioning. When one woman fell, a soldier simply kicked her into the depressed floor area. The poor woman was too exhausted to cry out and only a whimper escaped her lips. The soldier slammed her hands atop the individual pillars before a seat and a set of copper rings clamped over her wrists with finality and the soldier walked away.

Once all the prisoners were in place, the Sagean walked around the room. When he seemed satisfied, he raised his hand and opened his palm. Tali could faintly see a mound of dust held there. He muttered words in a language she didn't know and blew the dust into the air. Before the fine particles could reach the ground, they became a green cloud of smoke. The smoke settled into the trenches all around the room and over the prisoners. They toppled over in heaps, hanging limply by their clasped hands.

Semo nearly jumped out from the bunker, but Learon held him back. Ellaria and Danehin slumped in place only a few spots away from each other.

Where is Elias, what is he waiting for?

Each of the seven acolytes had taken their seats at the perimeter stations where a helmet awaited. Seven grim masks of metallic, empty heads hanging on coiled wires were strung upwards and disappeared into the stone, their appearance in stark contrast to the prisoners. Dressed in exceedingly fine clothes, they stepped to their seats and placed the helmet over their heads. The eye sockets looked shielded, and a metal grill extended down to cover their mouths.

"Wait until they're all strapped in, and we rush in. We'll get Ellaria, you get Danehin, and we run out the main hall," Learon told Semo.

"And the Soul Gem?" Tali said.

"We trust Elias will handle it."

The Sagean climbed to the top platform of the machine and looked out over the collection of people.

"Before we begin, there is something I must do first," he said, and Tali feared they had been spotted. "Batak, please come forward; you need to see this, too."

An older man stepped in from the main hall and stood at the Sagean's feet, and the Sagean continued.

"You seven have controlled me for too long now, but each of you mistakenly gave me a key to my freedom. This Scepter has many powers. One of the more curious powers it has is related to the Soul Stone within it. You see, we may be connected though these rings, but I am not your puppet anymore," he said.

The Sagean pressed the Scepter to the dragon ring on his hand, a swirl of energy snaked around the Scepter, and his ring evaporated into black smoke.

"Next order of business; Nathan are you back there?" A young man came into the room and knelt as soon as he entered. "Please take Queen Rotha's place in the Sintering Fountain."

"No——" the voice of an older woman began to protest, but her jaw snapped closed.

"Hush. You think I would allow you to be on my Court? You will be lucky if I allow you to live when this is through. Now with that settled, we can proceed," the Sagean barked.

Ellaria was below them and not far to the right, but she hadn't moved since the green smoke. The woman in front of whom she was stationed squirmed in her seat. Tali watched with suspicion at the darkhaired woman in the mask; whatever Court member it was had pulled something from her cloak and placed it beneath her thighs. Tali nudged Learon to look, but he missed it.

They scrutinized the room, waiting for a sign from Elias, when Learon suddenly pulled them back down. A look of fury from Semo hung dangerous in the silence but Learon pointed to the room. He was afraid to speak. Then Tali noticed it, too. Semo stopped and looked. The chamber was slowly cloaked in darkness—like the shadows had grown thick—which began to consume the room, and a disembodied voice spoke.

"Sagean, the Quantum Man arrives."

Suddenly, a strike of lightning ripped into the room with Elias holding it. He lowered down from it in a blur and the lightning winked out of existence. The blast reverberated in the chamber. When the lightning vanished, the retina burn remained, blinding everyone. A ripple in the shadows and the sound of boots on the stone interrupted the stillness, and Elias stepped out of the shadows. The Sagean, standing ten feet above him, stopped what he was doing to appraise the arrival.

"Thank you for joining us, Qudin. I've been waiting for you. Though you will have to show me how you did that little trick. I assume you've gotten through the small army outside, but it doesn't matter. We will soon be beyond your ability to stop," the Sagean submitted.

"Not likely," Elias said.

"Will I appreciate your bravado; you are the missing piece here. Well, not you. The *other* you. I didn't understand myself until recently. I couldn't understand how you could live for so long without knowing what you are."

'What am I?"

The Sagean smiled, "You are two souls trapped within one man. And I want one of them."

Two souls? Tali thought, and Elias looked up to them. He knew exactly where they were, and more than that, he was not surprised by the Sagean's words.

"I'm not interested in what you want. I didn't come here for you. I came for her and for them," Elias said, pointing to the glowing sphere. A loud thunder ripped the sky apart and shook the entire structure. Lightning struck down into the chamber in all directions. It latched to the walls in blinding light; Learon pulled Tali over the edge, and they jumped down into the chamber.

Together, they landed roughly on the stone floor. Semo jumped down smoothly. No one had seen them yet, most were shielding their eyes or staring at Elias. The Court was blinded in their helmets and Tali didn't think they could remove them now that they were on, as one man seemed to be panicking to no avail.

They ran to Ellaria, unlatched her wrists, and pulled her out. Learon lifted her into his arms, and they looked around for a way out. The lighting stopped striking the walls, but the burn marks remained all over, and parts of the stone structure glowed. The sparks of energy blanked out of existence with a loud pop and the chamber was back to darkness except the glowing sphere.

"Sagean! Intruders!" a guard shouted. The Sagean spun on the platform to see Learon and Tali. Though Learon held Ellaria in his arms, the Sagean eyes fixated on Tali. His cold look caused her to shiver. The Sagean struck out with his raised hand and her body lurched.

One moment she was embraced in fire and the next it had evaporated, leaving her on her knees. Elias stood in front of them, encapsulating the Sagean in a ball of light of his creation.

"Run!" Elias yelled.

Soldiers marched around the machine toward her. They pressed a button on their gauntlets and bronze shields unfurled, a red crystal at the center. Tali tried to throw pure white light at them, but the shields absorbed them. Elias spotted them and flicked them aside with his hand as if they were bugs. An invisible force threw their bodies into the walls. A loud ring echoed out where one body had slammed into something other than rock. Tali ran to it and examined the area. With her hand over the surface, her fingers found an orb embedded in the wall. She channeled energy into it and the wall parted. Dust and dirt fell in sheets as the doors opened.

With the way clear, Learon carried Ellaria out and Danehin hobbled with Semo into the large passageway. She looked back and the Sagean had freed himself from the cage of light. He held the Black Scepter in his hands and looked at them with a murderous gaze. Tali used her powers and projected a wave of kinetic energy into the domed ceiling. Chunks of stalactite rock fell. Elias stumbled toward the opening. She hadn't seen him get injured, but he didn't look strong. But instead of going with Tali, he closed the door between them.

She stood stunned; what was he doing? She looked around for a way to open the door but couldn't find one, so abandoned it and ran to catch up with Learon. The passageway opened out below the main entrance stairs. A small opening there was hidden by the jungle overgrowth at the base of the structure, the gap only wide enough to squeeze through sideways. As quietly as they could, they lurched through along the sidewall and back toward the awaiting army of Tregoreans. When they were clear on the north side, Tali stopped.

"I'm going back, Learon," she said.

He stopped, still holding Ellaria's unconscious body in his arms. He struggled to say anything.

"I have to. We still have to free the Soul Gem,"

"I know, I wish I could go with. No. Actually I feel a pain letting you go," he said.

His words stirred the sense she held in herself, like someone was squeezing and twisting her insides. "Me too," she professed.

"I'm going to take Ellaria up the hill and run back. Stay alive."

"Hurry," she said.

Tali knew Learon would always protect her, Somewhere inside, she knew it for a certainty. Their bond was real and now that she sensed the full impact of it, she found a great energy inside it. She reached for his hand. Once she touched it and knew what to look for, the bond made her shiver from the strength of their connection. She squeezed his hand and ran back toward the north entrance.

TALI SPRINTED THROUGH THE PASSAGEWAY AND BACK INTO THE VIEWING Chamber. She reached the room to hear the Sagean's voice clearly. Elias was frozen in place, unable to move. Held by some unseen force, his head twitched slightly as the only visible signs of the convulsions inside. His eyes closed to the obvious pain. The Sagean walked to him with the Scepter pointing at his face.

"You have accomplished nothing, Qudin. Guards, please detain Queen Rotha and her son and place them in the Casting pits where Danehin and Ellaria were," the Sagean ordered.

The guards moved the older woman and forced her into the pit before the dark-haired woman where Ellaria had been only moments before. A young man with a strong resemblance to his mother put up a fight but the soldier struck him over the head and dragged him to Danehin's spot. Tali put her hand out to channel an attack at the Sagean and Elias made eye contact with her.

With the slightest turn of his head, he spoke to her.

Tali wait. His thoughts cast into her mind, and she stopped.

"Now where was I? That's right: I wanted the soul you hold within, Qudin. I'm sure by now you know the soul of which I speak?" the Sagean said.

Elias didn't show the Sagean the slightest signal he cared and the Sagean carried on.

"I denied it was true for a long time, myself. You see, I assumed the Sagean Emperor was strong enough to consume you if he was inside you, but I was wrong. You were the stronger soul and you have been able to shut him out. Oh, I think he makes an appearance occasionally. Especially now that you have been sick. He, of course, has been the sickness. You see, the years without using your powers kept *him* at bay but he drew the Old One to you. The more interesting thing is not who is inside there with you, but why he was able to share your body."

The Sagean licked his lips and scowled, "You, Qudin Lightweaver, are the true Sagean heir."

Tali placed her hand over her mouth, but she didn't see the slightest change to Elias's expression. In fact, he looked tired, not surprised.

The Sagean continued, "How do you think you were able to enter the tomb? It was not the glove that allowed your passage. Your blood had been the key. My Court," the Sagean motioned to the seven masked people around the room, "They tried to keep that from me. But I discovered the truth."

"If he's inside me, then take him," Elias said. Tali thought it sounded like a dare, or even a plea.

"I think I will," the Sagean said, and he stepped to Elias, placing the Black Scepter on his forehead. Elias screamed. Tali put both her hands to her face and tears fell over her fingers. Elias's head stretched backward in agony and stopped; his eyes flew open. They pulsed with changing colors. Then they bloomed orange and swirled to a sparkling silver, then blue and swirling to silver again. On it went.

The Sagean muttered a chant Tali couldn't hear. The Scepter still pressed firmly to Elias's head, his body lifted from the ground. Elias's feet hovered above the Stone, his toes pointing down in an anguished posture as something bright pulled from his chest. A light emerged, partially whisky smoke and partly solidified droplets in air. It was bright at first, but the luminosity faded as more came free. When it seemed at last that everything had been withdrawn from Qudin, it began to coalesce into a single brilliant red and white ball. It floated between them, and Elias dropped in a heap to the floor. The sphere of light rolled on itself in space and the Sagean clutched it with an outstretched hand.

"Now the last Sagean Emperor will be returned. If you could contain him, then so can I," the Sagean said.

The Sagean brought the glowing ball of smoke to his face and open mouth. It wasn't as simple as swallowing it, as much as the light seemed to attack the Sagean. As though it sensed a safe harbor to live, it poured forcefully into the Sagean's eyes, mouth, and ears. His skin swelled with a red dimness beneath. The Sagean reeled backwards in a shriek and went to his knees.

A new silence came over the room. Tali didn't remember hearing anything during the extraction, but now the new silence made her realize how loud the soul exchange had been. Maybe the sound was her own blood pounding in her ears because she couldn't slow her racing pulse.

"Time to see if this machine works?" the Sagean muttered picking himself up, but the new voice from Edward's lips sounded different in timbre then before.

"Aramus! Where are you!" The Sagean called out.

A man came jogging into the room with a black cloak. He had long blonde hair and he looked around the room as though searching for someone.

"Come here, my servant," the Sagean said

The man kneeled before the Sagean; his eyes were clouded over, but Tali recognized him as the same who had accosted her at Anchor's Point.

"You did well in my service, tracking Ellaria. You were discovered searching for the glove and handled yourself well. Continue impressing me and I will see you are rewarded. Now go and ready my ship," the Sagean ordered, and the man ran out.

It is past time to do something. Tali thought and started to climb through the opening when a bronze panel slammed down, nearly cutting her hand. It shielded the Viewing Room from the chamber completely. *No, no, no, no* she thought in a panic, *Learon where are you?*

THIRTY-NINE
MIRTHLESS (LEARON)

L earon heard Tali calling for him and he froze. It was an odd sensation. Something was wrong, something was terribly wrong. She wasn't in danger, and he now believed the link between them would tell him if she was injured, but she *was* upset. Learon ran as fast as he could up the steep hill, back to the Kihan encampment. The waiting rangers held nocked arrows pointing at him. A ranger with braided hair spotted him and signaled the others to let him pass. Semo and Danehin were behind him on the hillside. Learon laid Ellaria down in the grass. She was starting to come to.

"I have to go back," he said the Semo.

Semo helped Danehin to sit down next to Ellaria. The effects of the Sagean's spell had yet to wear off. Three rangers approached Learon.

"What do you need? What's happening?" Zorick asked. Echoryn's brother had his sword drawn.

"Qudin and Tali are still inside. I'm going back for them," Learon said.

He dropped his cumbersome bow and arrows and he bounded back down the hill. Semo was on his heels and yelling at him from behind. Learon finally turned around to see Semo holding out a sword handle for him to take. Together, they continued sprinting down toward the Temple and passed the statues.

In the depression outside of the Temple grounds, mechanical footsteps on stone echoed through the structures. The sound of the breathing mechanism that made the Rendered move pressed toward them. The Rendered approached from the stairs, their glowing eyes tracked movements in the jungle, and they turned to fire their giant weapons. Learon dove clear of the blast.

The Rendered stomped closer and swung the huge lance to the ground. Learon rolled and it slammed into the weed-covered territh where it remained stuck. He jumped to his feet and raced up the automaton's lance pole. When he reached the bronze head, Learon slammed his sword into the machine's eye. Sparks flared up the steel blade to his palm. Learon tugged his weapon free and dove to the ground. The Rendered fell to the territh.

Bonemen were advancing and firing their rifles at him. Learon sprinted away and from his periphery, he watched as the squad of soldiers were decimated by arrows from the darkness. Semo met him and they rushed toward the north face to get back inside, the chaos of battle rumbling the jungle.

A shape moved fast toward them. The shuffling sounded like a ravinor, only faster. Learon paused trying to locate the sound. On the ledge of the Temple's lower tier, the shape appeared bounding toward them on all fours. In the moonlight, the creature's skin appeared hardened—stretched thin and tight over bone. It leapt from the Temple wall to the ground, and Learon lunged away as the beast swiped with long claws where he had been.

The thing stood tall on two legs and pulled a long sword from its back. The monster before them was neither a ravinor nor anything Learon had ever seen before. The face was all swollen bone and its eyes set deep behind sharp bulging brow bones. It charged at Learon and Semo.

A ranger appeared from behind them to absorb the attack. The huge, long sword swept powerfully at the ranger and the blow knocked the Kihan off her feet.

The thing continued undaunted and Semo stepped next to Learon, ready to stand with him against the beast. In a flash, it attacked Learon and swung back to Semo in quick succession. Learon jabbed in, but his blow was deflected. Semo tried to slash, and the beast caught the blade in its hand. Black blood oozed out, but it twisted the weapon free and flung it away. Semo's eyes widened. The beast's blade swept in a huge downward arch. Semo tried to leap away, but the long blade met Semo's foot as he jumped. Semo screams of pain were drowned out by a rumble from the Temple itself.

The ground trembled and Learon drove his sword into the creature's back. It whipped around and Learon ducked and rolled away. The fallen ranger had recovered and pressed a new attack, but she got too close. The beast grabbed the ranger and threw her thirty feet into the jungle.

Learon scrambled for Semo's discarded sword. The beast was faster than it should have been for its size. Even wounded, it appeared in his path in a flash. Another female ranger came in screaming and Learon grabbed Semo's blade and joined her attack, but the beast spared with both easily. In one contorted motion, it kicked Learon away and slashed a bloody gash across the ranger's arm. Learon felt like he had been hit by solid stone and fell to his knees, dizzy. His heart was pounding, and he could hear the both the ranger and Semo moaning nearby.

The beast turned to finish him and in the chorus of suffering around him, Learon realized he had been surviving these battles on instinct, and suddenly he understood both Kovan and Elias's advice at once. Something pulsed in his blood, something he had been slow to recognize before, but as he knelt with his hand on the ground, winded, he understood. They could call him whatever name they want; his spirit knew who he was and what he could do.

Learon stood on the balls of his feet and waited for the creature's long sword to come. In the moonlight, Learon saw the subtle movement of the thing's muscles, and he reacted. Time slowed and the air stilled. The slash came in a long, slow sweep and Learon dodged and rolled for the ranger's fallen sword. The beast spun on him. Blades in both his hands Learon shielded the blow from the creature at the longsword's strong point with Semo's sword and lurched the steel tip of the ranger's blade up into the monster's head. A loud howl pierced his ears and faded.

Learon got to his feet again and rushed to Semo. He was still alive but had passed out from the pain. Sweat drenched his head. Learon called to some of the Kihan for help. They ran over and looked at the foul beast on the ground.

"Please get him out of here," Learon said and ran for Tali.

The ground below his feet rumbled and the sky cracked and boomed overhead. The trees and shrubs of the jungle all around began to bend toward the Temple, and the wind pooled in from all directions. It carried debris of leaves and dirt and swept up the sides of the structure to the top, kicking up clouds of dust that swirled around them like a tornado forming. Something bad was happening and Learon feared the Machine had been activated. He ran for the Temple.

FORTY
THE SINTERING (ELIAS)

The room shook and the pulses of energy rolled endlessly along the wires strung within the room. Elias was still crumpled on the floor when the shrieks started. He almost didn't dare to open his eyes. The drone of sound blurred the noise of screaming and the buzz of power throughout the chamber.

He was now unburdened by the Emperor's soul tangled with his own, but his body needed to survive the night, and there was still the matter of freeing the Soul Gem. It was a calculated risk to allow Edward to remove the Emperor before activating the Machine, but any other sequence would have led to deaths of Tali and Ellaria.

Elias looked to the platform and could see the Sagean was barely holding on to the Scepter. He had it locked in a slotted position that must be powering the contraption. The bands of metal around the Soul Gem were spinning wildly and the bodies of the masked acolytes labored in their seats, writhing in pain, their voices lost from screaming. The prisoners in the Casting pits were dead.

When Elias was finally able to stand, a wind generated by the fountain pushed him away from the Soul Gem. It took effort to remain on his feet and as hard as he tried, he couldn't step any closer to the platform. A final concussion of air blasted him into the perimeter wall and the noise was gone. The energy still reverberated in the ground and Elias could sense a massive amount of moving heat beneath the Temple; deep in the territh, it stirred like a sea of fire.

On the platform, the Sagean reached for the Scepter, but it had completely melted. Only the crystal of souls remained. Around the room, the acolytes stirred and moaned.

"Those of you who have survived, now is the time to bow to me as your Lord or breathe your last breath," the Sagean announced, and his voice brought chills to Elias. The voice sounded like Emperor Mayock Kovall, now.

Slowly, the people around the room removed their helmets and came to the center. They all looked disoriented, but one Rodairean woman with dark hair stopped and looked around her seat. When she found what she was looking for, she whispered an enchantment and disappeared.

"An astute assessment," the Sagean snarled.

The others looked at the empty space she had vanished from. Two younger men walked around the room and brought everyone before the Sagean, but they left Elias crumpled against the wall.

Elias couldn't be sure which ones now held Luminary powers and which didn't, but none of them were in any state to fight back. Even the young men helping herd the remaining acolytes looked exhausted.

One of the acolytes lay dead in his seat. It appeared like he had attempted to remove the mask and his body was crumpled, one hand soldered to the mask and the other, ash. The Sagean walked to the dead man, brushed some ash from the floor and lifted free his dragon ring.

He turned back to the others and spoke, "Verro Mancovi, Theomar Kyana, Shirova Edana and Nathan Edana, and Delvar Asheen. Your Emperor has returned," the Sagean declared, "And I will be choosing a new council."

The Sagean stepped to the others and pulled a knife from his cloak.

"I can be loyal," a man professed.

"Theomar Kyana, you're conniving and power-hungry. Edward wanted you dead the most and I agree," the Sagean said.

Theomar backed away and put his hand out hoping to channel some energy, but his own skin began to burn. The Sagean laughed and slit Theomar's throat.

"Besides, your son is much more useful," he muttered, and tugged the dragon ring off the dead hand. Turning on the woman, he pointed his blood soaked knife at her and she squirmed against a younger man.

"Please, no! Nathan, please tell him," the woman cried.

"Your son's loyalty is for Edward, Shirova. He was plotting with Edward to kill you," the Sagean said.

The blonde-haired woman backed away from the one she had called Nathan, her face horror stuck.

"I may have use of Shirova, but I have no need of a man who would scheme against his own mother," the Sagean said, and he plunged the knife into Nathan's heart.

Shirova gasped and rushed to her son.

"I don't understand. Why? Edward, why kill your own acolytes?" the older man said.

"Verro, I am no longer Edward Knox. He was foolish, and he cowers in the corner of my Being, unable to mount a threat to me. I am the Sagean Emperor, the Lord of Light, and I will not have a council that plots against me. Edward had derived this plan long ago, but he was always unsure which of his acolytes he would spare," the Sagean said, and he handed Delvar a ring, instructing him to put it on.

"Spare me, My Lord; I can be a great asset to you," Verro begged.

"Maybe you could have been an asset to Knox, I'm unsure of your value to me. However, for the three of you left, I will give you the opportunity to prove yourselves, but not without assurances," the Sagean held his ring up and it began to glow. The remaining acolytes winced.

"Now I will control you," the Sagean said.

Then the wall exploded.

Tali walked through the large hole and flung an onslaught of energy at the standing men. They flipped around the room and crashed into the walls. Elias used the chair near him to climb to his feet and Tali dashed over to him.

"Elias, we need to free the souls in that crystal," Tali said.

Elias looked at her and nodded. They rushed to the glowing sphere, and Learon emerged in the new opening. A thick black ink covered half his body. They turned to him and the relief in his eyes at seeing them both was tangible. But his eyes brightened, and his body soared back and slammed into the dome above, where it stayed pinned.

The Sagean, holding him in place, stepped into the open. Elias immediately recalled the lightning he had stored in the walls throughout the structure, and he blasted the Sagean's back. Learon fell and Tali gasped.

From the far side of the room, the darkness pooled unnaturally. The Wrythen was showing itself. Suddenly, a tendril of black smoke slithered around Tali like a rope. Elias pulled in every bit of energy he could, and light filled the room. His entire body became a bright being of light. The walls began to crack, and the blackness dropped Tali.

She heaved and convulsed on the ground. The effects of being in the clutches of the Wrythen, even for a moment, made her vomit.

Elias went to her even as he could feel the Wrythen gathering again. She stared at Elias, at first shielding her eyes, but then in awe. He knew what he had to do now. They stood at the crossroads of fate together and he was choosing the only path forward.

He placed his hand over her heart and the coin necklace that had settled on her chest. She looked at him in confusion.

"Goodbye, dear one. I promise someone will be waiting to help you," Elias told her.

"What are you doing?" Tali said.

"Remember, you must unite them all," he said.

Elias closed his eyes and muttered an incantation, and Tali vanished.

Learon stirred on the floor. When she disappeared, a panicked look enveloped his face.

Elias looked to him, "Run, kid! Run!"

Learon hesitated but the Temple shook all around them. He started towards Elias, but Elias waved him away, "Run!" he cried.

Chunks of the dome crashed to the floor. Learon stood at the opening, his chest heaving. Elias nodded his assurance, but Learon refused to go, so Elias gently pushed him out with a column of air and sealed the opening. As soon as Learon was clear of the chamber, Elias brought all his energy to bear on the Soul Gem. He would release the trapped souls and bring down the Temple.

On the other side of the platform, the Sagean stumbled into view. He clutched to the Fountain and tried to keep his feet while the Temple rumbled. Elias lashed out with an effluence of light and heat. The Sagean's eyes burst with flame and light and his skull seared in flames. His screams went unheard in the chaos.

The darkness at the edges of the room stirred again. The heat and blinding white fire pulled away from the Sagean like tendrils of pure living energy and gathered into two points in the shadow. The black mist moved around the room like a phantom and the energy reformed into a set of glowing eyes.

The Wrythen grinned, Its mouth alite with fire.

"It's too late, Quantum Man. My children have awoken, and they will free me. For I am alive in them. Your world is now in my grasp. Soon, I will walk among the ashes and you will not be there to save this lost world."

As though beckoned, a loud animal cry and roar pierced the air; a beast Elias couldn't see but could feel. Something being born to the south.

And the Wrythen barked a dark, dead sound Elias realized was laughter. It slithered to the Soul Gem and placed hands of black mist over the sphere. The blue and white pool of light began to turn red, like the Wrythen had cast droplets of dye into the mixture. *It's corrupting them.*

Elias redirected all his energy at the Gem. The metal bands around it bent and broke apart and the crystal reverberated, but it wouldn't crack.

"Take him away," the Wrythen said, and Elias realized it was speaking to the three acolytes who now carried the Sagean's limp form out the far side. The Wrythen turned back to Elias and smiled. The mouth of fire grew rapidly to the size of the chamber and hurtled toward him. Elias put everything he had into the breaking the crystal.

It burst with a roar. Blue, white, and red light showered straight to the sky in a torrent of blinding illumination. Elias fell to his back and watched the stream pour into the night sky and splinter in all directions. His breathing slowed and the image blurred. The structure of the Temple began to crumble, but he couldn't hear any of it. He only stared at the light and the moon and brightest stars that somehow sat in the beyond in endless observation. Bright enough to shine in the darkest times. With his last breaths, Elias whispered into the chaos, *find her, and guide her.* He stared at those stars and stretched out to be among them as the Temple collapsed all around.

TALI'S MEDALLION

FORTY-ONE
MEDALLIONS (TALI)

The hut's grey and white animal-hide door slapped against the thatched walls, producing a distinctly thick, snapping sound. The repeating noise and blast of cold air that followed roused Tali's eyes open. Exhaustion had made her consciousness fleeting and she was drained of energy to the extent she couldn't roll over in the cot if she wanted to. A deep ache radiated in waves, and her body heat fluctuated minute by minute. She could feel the air cold and crisp in the tent but sweat dripped from her forehead. Turning her head to the side, she scanned around the room.

The man who found her was missing from the corner seat where he had been watching over her. Tali had been unable to learn his name, as she had yet to be awake long enough to ask. She had spoken only two words to him, saying *thank you* when he lifted her from the snow, but she passed out staring at his strong jawline and blue skin, before she could ask any questions.

Alone in the strange hut, with a swirling wind outside, Tali stared past the opening into the blowing snow beyond, trying to stay awake for the stranger's return. When a woman appeared walking through the drifts of snow, Tali thought it was a vision. She watched the woman approach; skeptical the person was real.

A fur-lined hood blew free from the woman's head and her reddish-brown hair whipped in the wind. She had lovely soft features and a rosy glow to her cheeks. She looked young, but her age was hard to place, and her eyes looked very familiar. She walked confidently through the drifts with a huge, white furred *torakuma* prowling by her side. The great mythical animal stood taller than the woman's waist and its antlers grew wide, twisted and angling backward like the black stripes of fur on its face.

When the woman entered the tent, Tali realized she may have been wrong about the woman's age, but she couldn't be sure—it was impossible to tell. Her face was young, but her eyes told the story of a much older woman. The longer Tali studied her, the more familiar the woman looked. When she smiled at Tali, realization dawned. Tali knew this woman, having seen her before in a photogram in Elias's hideout.

Tali smiled back. Comforted finally with the knowledge she was safe, Tali closed her eyes. The woman approached her bedside and Tali could feel her pick up and examine her medallion necklace. The woman placed it down gently and then touched Tali's forehead. Her warm hands seemed to wash the chill from Tali's body.

"Rest, child, you've come a long way," the woman said softly.

Tali wanted one last look but her eyelids were too heavy to lift, and she slept. Visions of her friends swam in her mind and memories of energy accompanied her. She reached out for the link with Learon and found only a faint and strained presence. The distance between them was vast and when she tried to hold onto it, the bond stretched and was lost.

FORTY-TWO
THE LAST CUBE (KOVAN)

The lightning continued in the night sky. The charged air had produced only a sprinkle of rain, but the seabed was oscillating between still waters and high chopping waves as if in the middle of a storm, as though tremors encircled the entire world.

The star-filled sky was concealed by clouds of turbulent light that shone with streaks of trickling beams, like slow lightning. The men aboard the Hollow-Dawn moved about the ship in mostly darkness, tending to their duties, all of them fearful of the captain's wrath otherwise. Two solemn lanterns on the masts cast subtle glows.

The night held a full moon if the clouds ever parted to reveal it. The lanterns flickered with the untamed wind that swirled like the water below, in blasts of returning power and violence. The Hollow-Dawn sailed west, most likely to Ravenvyre in an attempt to claim the palace of Red Vine. Almost a hundred leagues out to sea, a man in the high nest called out. He'd spotted another ship on the night cloaked sea.

Razor Redmar burst out of his cabin, annoyed at the disturbance. He looked around the oddly dark deck in surprise and gazed back to the clouds. They began to part almost through his will and the ship once again was bathed in light. A glimmer of the moon's radiance reflected off something on deck, midship, and Razor turned his attention to it curiously.

"Who are you?" Razor said to the cloaked figure.

Kovan sat on the deck upon one knee, holding the sword hilt to his head. The hood of his black cloak concealed his face and the dark fabric sprawled out around him. Kovan looked up from his hood and stood smoothly to his feet.

"Kovan Rainer, have you come aboard my ship to die or join me?" Razor said.

"Neither. I'm here to trade. You have something of mine, and I have something for you."

Razor pulled the small colorful cube from his pocket and rolled it between his fingers. His bare grimy hands on it made Kovan's stomach curdle.

"Do you mean this?" Razor said.

Kovan nodded.

Razor placed it in a high pocket on his sleeve and drew his long sword, the bastardized meiyoma blade with the back-etched barbs.

"Then come get it." Razor said.

Kovan was there in a flash, almost before the words were out of Razor's mouth. Razor stumbled slightly but was saved only by luck. Blocking the first slash, he counter-attacked with a swing at Kovan's torso and aggressively tried to slam the blade down from above.

Everything was as Kovan had anticipated. Kovan ducked away from the first attack and darted away from the second, quickly cutting a slice into Razor's right leg and sidestepping away into the shadows of the ship's corners. Redmar's anger raged, and he charged, swinging wildly. A mislaid blow brought enough force to a stack of barrels that the oak splinted and burst. The violent strikes continued and the barrel full of emberbroth splashed to the deck and began to soak into place. Kovan was well clear, but a swell on the sea nearly toppled both men.

Razor took the moment as an opportunity to strike again, but it was clumsy. The motion of the rocking ship guaranteed it. Razor missed, but his power sliced deep into the sideboard. Wind roared through the masts and scattered loose remnants all about. The ship tipped and a blast of sea spray hurdled aboard with one last jostle before the waters calmed again, the boat settling to a leveling drift.

Some of the ship's crew had come to the main deck now to watch. Razor's chest heaved with anger. He ripped the blade free of the wood and stalked toward Kovan confidently. Kovan spun the Elum Blade tip facing backwards and placed his left hand on the knife he carried.

Through gritted teeth, Razor taunted Kovan, "You want to trade? What do you have for me, Kovan Rainer? Whatever it is, I'll take it from you after I've—"

Kovan rushed toward Razor Redmar, spinning two blades as he

reached him. The edge of his sword clashed against Redmar's blade and as Razor tried to reach for Kovan with his long arms, the knife struck home under Razor's outstretched arm. Kovan drove it hilt deep, the golden sun pommel glinting in the moonlight.

"Justice," Kovan said.

Razor's eyes were a mix of fury and pain and he choked on his words. Kovan spun his sword free, and his violent upward slash found its mark. Redmar's sword hit the deck, his arm with it.

Razor Redmar screamed in agony, but he was too consumed with shock to cry out completely. He stumbled and fell, crashing backwards into the sideboard. Kovan grabbed the second thing he came for from the bloody stump and walked back to Redmar. He stood over the dying man and looked out to sea where the shape of a ship drew near. The I'Varrin had arrived after circling around. He could see Wade standing aboard, awaiting to find out who won.

With a wheeze, Razor slumped over, blood expelling from his mouth and Kovan exited the ship. He tossed a varium crystal of firespark at the barrels and left. The firespark exploded and the barrels leapt into flames. The men aboard, stunned by witnessing Razor's defeat, now panicked, but it was too late. Kovan had seen the provisions they had stacked there, and the cargo directly below. Among the food and drink stores were crates of dynamite sticks and barrels of star powder. The first explosion was small and so was the second, but the third and fourth decimated the ship to pieces. Each one came on top of the next so rapidly, Kovan lost count.

Aboard the I'Varrin, Kovan watched the explosion for a moment, then placed the last cube into his mouth where it started dissolving on his tongue. Wade and Buroga stood near him. Captain Morales cursed from his spinning wheel—something about being too close—and he steered the ship toward Nahadon.

"Wade, you can send the message to the others now; that we have the Stone and are on our way," Kovan said.

"Yes," Wade replied.

"Did you find what you were looking for, Kovan Rainer?" Buroga asked, placing a wide-brimmed hat on Kovan's head.

"Yes," Kovan said.

"You know, you could have just shot him," Wade said.

"I know."

"You are a very good blades-man, Kovan Rainer," Buroga said, appraising the sheathed sword at his hip, "And you say Elias is better?"

"Yeah, but I think he cheats," Kovan said with a smile, but the substance inside hit him. A wave of heat and nausea rushed through his blood like steam ready to burst through his head. Kovan's senses surged beyond his limits, and he staggered on his feet. His hand grasped tight to the edge of the boat, as the strength in his legs gave away.

"Kovan, what is it?" Wade said, reaching for him.

"My daughter," Kovan said, tears in his eyes. He fell unconscious to the deck, the barrier in his mind crumbled and memories flooded in, memories he was never meant to remember.

FORTY-THREE
SHADOWS OF OBLIVION (LEARON)

After Learon escaped the crumbling Temple, he found his way
back to the Kihan soldiers, all eyes watching the sky from the
hillside. Ellaria was awake, sitting on the dirt and admiring the
display of light. She looked at him hopefully, but he shook his head to tell
her no one else was coming.

He expected Ellaria to be more rattled, surrounded by the
Tregoreans in the jungle, but she looked on stoically. He was reminded
that her special ability was adaptability. She had been through a lot and
Learon couldn't let her go any longer without knowing about Kovan.

"Ellaria, Kovan is alive," he said.

"What?" Ellaria clutched his sleeve.

Learon looked her in the eyes and nodded, "He's in Amera trying to
get the Stone back."

Her hand fell from his sleeve and tears streamed down her face.

They sat together on the hillside feeling the trembling ground below
their feet and watched the lines of light zipping overhead in crazy
patterns. There would be time to tell her everything, and she must have
sensed he didn't want to talk, so she didn't press. They sat there until
night became morning. Once the Kihan had cleared the area and
packed up, they began their trek back to the heart of the province.

It took more time in their returning, but Echoryn met them at the
Wall of Nagari and accompanied him back to the Palace in Sualden. She
knew he was heartbroken and didn't pressure him to speak either.
Instead, she did what any great friend would do. She kept him company
and distracted him with talk of drama amongst the provinces. Most of it

concerned the rumor about a Nimbus Warrior; she also kept others away from him.

At the Palace, they received a message from Kovan that they were heading to Nahadon. Ellaria was torn between waiting or leaving immediately to join the New World fleet anchored in the Barruse Islands. However, the weather was a continual torrential downpour and when there were breaks in the rain, the lightning still flashed in the clouds. Bazlyn said any flights with the winddrifter would have to wait. So, Ellaria spent her time pouring over maps and speaking with the Kihan, Elias's cat never more than a foot from her the entire time.

A day later, reports came in from the Kihan scouts that the oceans were turbulent with surging waves that had decimated shorelines on the Dry Coast and to the south. Worse yet, smoke had been seen rising in the sky from the Black Shore. All of it connected somehow the night of splintered light when the Temple fell. The province feared whatever Qudin and the Sagean had unleashed had caused the volcanoes on the Black Shore to erupt. A team was on their way to verify what was going on and Grace Derasi, with Meroha's help was organizing a party to retrieve Elias's body. Derasi explained to Learon and Ellaria that he was making good on a promise but wouldn't say any more. When they were ready to leave, Learon intended to join them.

With the odd weather, Ellaria prepared a group including Semo and Danehin to go east through the jungle to the Barruse Islands, where Kovan could meet the fleet stationed there, and together cross the Anamic Ocean to Ioka. She pleaded with Learon to go with her, but he couldn't. He felt he had to return to the Temple ruins to search the rubble. He refused to believe that Elias was dead.

The return voyage to the forbidden area took two days with the excessive rains, but to Learon, it felt like a blur. A growing sense of aimlessness was settling in, and he couldn't shake it.

In the Blue of the second day, Learon stood beneath the overcast sky atop the mound of rubble, working with the others to lift large chunks of stone and debris and throw them aside. His watch lit up again and he glanced at it. Ellaria was updating Wade on their progress.

Echoryn saw him looking at his wrist, "You're sure you don't want go with them?"

"I'll leave in a few days when Bazlyn says the winddrifter can fly," he said.

Something in the wreckage glinted in the sun and Learon clawed it out. The crystal was large and somehow unblemished. He held it in his palm and rubbed it. The bright blue color within was intoxicating, but holding it made him shiver. He pocketed it.

"You said she just disappeared?" Echoryn asked about Tali for the hundredth time.

"Yes. Elias's hand was on her, and she vanished," Learon said.

"And what's Ellaria think?"

"Ellaria said it could be a spell, but she doesn't know. Given the amount of energy Elias must have been holding at the time, there's no telling where Tali was transported to."

"I'm going to speak with our Grace again. I think he's holding something back," Echoryn said.

Learon appreciated her determination, but he couldn't explain to her how his bond to Tali felt severed and he wasn't sure she had survived the spell.

"Over here!" Someone searching with them called out. They had found something.

Learon jumped from boulder to boulder and helped the team dig. It was the second person they had found, but right away, he knew this was different. All the boulders were perfectly propped up above the body, creating a shelter. It took them an hour to uncover it completely. It was Elias. He was gone, but his cold body was perfectly preserved. They placed the lifeless form in a specially scribed and ordained box that Derasi had the team bring for transporting Elias back.

When they took the body out of the valley, Learon remained at the site, running his hand through his hair, regarding the smoke-filled southern horizon. He was determined to search the portions of the Temple still standing. Something itched at his mind about that night, and where Elias had disappeared to before entering the Chamber.

Lost in thought, Learon was slow to recognize something was wrong, that the jungle had gone quiet. A heartbeat later, a loud roar breached the silence. A shriek cried from the sky, and a huge black shape emerged overhead, flying between the grey clouds. It was as massive, and bigger than any airship. It circled over the Temples and when its wings moved, they beat loudly against the air in an unnatural crash, like restrained thunder.

The Kihan scrambled for cover where they could, under trees or sections of stone. Learon's gaze fixed on the magnificent creature, and he stood motionless atop the rubble, not from paralysis but from wonder. The first dragon in two thousand years soared out across the jungle and Learon's eyes followed it, mesmerized and undaunted. A surge of deter-

388   STEVEN RUDY

mination rose in his blood and tempered his fear, vanquishing the depression of the past few days.

War was coming, and in the face of oblivion, a truth came clear in his mind: he was born for war.

THE END OF BOOK TWO

EPILOGUE

Aylanna reappeared on the deck of her airship a crumpled heap. Her men, as they were ordered, were waiting for her arrival. They spotted her instantly, picked her up, and carried her to the inside cabin. It took all her strength to speak.

"Take off immediately," she grumbled.

"We will be in the air shortly," her pilot said.

Every muscle in her body burned and pulsed. The hundred leagues from the Temple was the greatest distance she had ever traveled using the Spell of Displacement, and combined with the Sintering, Aylanna knew she was blessed to still be breathing.

She had only successfully used the spell once before, but the closer they had come to the ceremony, the more she feared the need for an escape from the Chamber. Her daughter had warned her that Edward's skill for eliciting devotion in others had grown, and that he had recruited all the Court heirs to his plan. Aylanna held out hope for a smooth ceremony but prepared her means of escape in the event Edward betrayed them; she never thought she would be fleeing the wrath of Emperor Kovall.

A kid during the War—she still remembered his voice and his lifeless eyes. Seeing them overtake Edward made her skin crawl. The masks connected to the Sintering Fountain left them blinded during the process but she could hear everything that happened. Once her mask had released itself and the Sintering concluded, she took one look at the Sagean and escaped.

A rustling of noise and shouting outside forced her to try and lift her head, but it was no use. The door to her cabin flung open and her most trusted lieutenant, Owen Dunbar, came rushing in.

"Mistress Alvir," Dunbar said.

"We found an injured man on horseback while lifting off and brought him aboard. It's another member of the Court."

Aylanna's heart stirred, *could Verro have survived?* She liked her lips and muttered.

"Who is it?"

"Batak Asheen. Should we kill him or bring him with us to Ravenvyre?"

"Bring him," she said.

Owen closed the door and Aylanna ripped the dragon ring from her finger and tossed it aside, then she passed out.

DAYS LATER, SAFELY INSIDE THE PALACE OF REDVINE ON THE NORTHERN tip of Ravenvyre, Aylanna was still struggling to walk. She had survived the Sintering Fountain and could feel the charge of energy in the world, but her body was slow to recover, and as yet, she had no sway of the energy she could touch.

She limped around her quarters, dressed in simple clothes, and threw a soft cloak over herself for warmth. Ever since the Sintering, she was always cold, and with the Zenithal season slipping away, Ravenvyre would soon grow windy, cold, and rainy—*well, it was always rainy on the island.* She was sitting beneath her wall of repeating windows, examining her daily reports, when a knock came to her door.

"You may enter," Aylanna called out, hoping it was her daughter—it wasn't. Instead, her maid stood in the opening and a man with black hair and a black cloak stood behind her, hiding his face.

Aylanna gripped her cane and walked over to greet them, finally recognizing the man, when she reached the doorway.

"Morrowmaki Drevoren, I am glad to see you," Aylanna said.

The man withdrew his hood before replying, "Please, old friend, call me, Maki."

Aylanna waved her attendant away, "You may leave us. Go see to our other guest."

Her attendant disappeared down the stone hall and Aylanna offered her arm for her old friend.

"Walk with me to the map room, Maki. We can discuss why I had my agents searching the city for you this last month."

"As you wish," Maki said.

"I am surprised to see you," Aylanna continued, "You are a very hard person to find and seldom come when called on."

"I was intrigued by your letter," Maki said.

"And how is the Whisper Chain in Ravenvyre, these days?" she asked.

"It's close to operational again," he said.

They reached the map room and Maki helped her sit. The map encompassed the entire floor, sunken in the center by a depth of two steps. The polished stone surface painted over with fine details of the world as it was known.

A pair of glass doors stood ajar to the terrace balcony. The light breeze off the Brovic nudged the heavy curtains, producing sporadic flutters.

"I don't know why they always do this," Aylanna complained, "No matter how many times I tell my attendants that the sunlight can ruin the inking on the map floor, they still insist on opening these doors."

"Would you like me to close them?" Maki asked.

"No, leave them for now," Aylanna said. The open air brought the fragrance of the gardens inside, and Aylanna always liked the smell of the redvine trees.

With a heavy bronze positioning pole, she pushed carved stone figures around the map, and moved a few off to the side entirely. Finally, she added a new, polished white stone figure to Andal.

Maki watched her complete the set-up before speaking, "So it's true, the Sagean Emperor has returned?"

"Yes, and I assume he retreated to the Black Spire to meet with . . ."

Her voice was drowned out midsentence by a chorus of screams from outside. Maki squinted toward the open doors but didn't move.

"Help me up," Aylanna said.

He helped her to her feet, and they walked out onto the large terrace overlooking the north gardens. In the air, a loud woosh was followed by a roaring caw that blasted the air and made them duck instinctively. The cries of the city continued, and a huge black-winged beast emerged overhead.

It circled once around the garden and Aylanna gasped. Her mouth stayed open in awe at the sight of a dragon. Something rode on its back: a shifting, formless phantom like a fire of black shadow was stuck to the back. The mythical animal was massive and when it landed, the dragon stomped toward the terrace, the creature's huge feet crushing stone below its claws. When it's menacing face lifted to her, the dragon's eyes alone were taller than any man. A formless black fire of shifting waves and whisps on its back suddenly become solid and turned into a Being, slowly lurking forward.

It joined them on the terrace, and Aylanna realized with a start who it was.

She knelt and Maki followed her lead. His hood was back on now and he eyed the Old One curiously.

"Old One, how may I serve you?" Aylanna said.

The Old One she had seen before when it came to speak with the Court of Dragons was little more than a presence in the room, sometimes with floating eyes of fire. This was a semi-solid Being and looked almost like a giant-cloaked man. It stood eight feet tall, but the shape morphed and streamed in all directions, even against the wind, as though It were made of vapor. At various times, shapes formed in Its cloak that looked like animals pushing through a thin black veil. Even the Old One's face changed position as It walked, the cloak hood morphing and resetting, while a pair of orange glowing eyes within stared at her.

"Luminary Alvir, I have a mission for you. As you can see, my children have been reborn," It pointed a long finger toward the dragon. The finger stretched and formed to ashen skin and then bronze, and back again to liquid smoke.

"Your children, my Lord?" she said.

"There are very few things in this world that can hurt my dragons. One of those things is called the Desolation Blade. Find it," the Old One demanded.

"Me, I . . ." Aylanna stammered.

"It has also been called the Midnight Sword. In another time, the blade was worn by the Radmana King, Roal Oakol, and then by Zelon Marathallor."

Aylanna had never heard either name before but had to assume the city of Marathal was derived from one of them.

The Old One continued, "It was last carried by woman warrior named Avari Nova."

That was a name Aylanna knew: the Queen of Ravenvyre during the Luminary Wars.

"You understand now why I have called on you. I believe it is somewhere on this island," The Old One said, and It began to slide away. The

Being appeared to evaporate when it reached the dragon, and in a blink, it had returned on the dragon's back, more shapeless than before, but Its eyes brighter.

"In return for your service, my children will not trouble your little island. Though you will see them periodically, they must not be bothered or attacked," It said, and the dragon lifted off. The wind from the wings made her stumble, and the energy of the dragon prickled her skin; it was a uniquely radiant power.

The Old One spoke again from the dragon's back and Its words seemed to resonate in the air like It still stood by her side.

"Find me the Desolation Blade, Luminary Alvir, and you may be by my side in Telatheor."

Then the great ancient beast lifted higher and with its formless black rider, it swam the sky and disappeared out over the Brovic.

"Did it say Telatheor?" Aylanna asked, dumbfounded.

"Yes," Maki said.

"Telatheor is a myth. Destroyed by Ovardyn and wiped from this territh," she said.

Maki shook his head, "Myth and truth live in the wind, Aylanna. When a story is told and retold over thousands of years, who can say what's real, what's myth, and what has simply been forgotten?"

The Scepter of Corinshra

GLOSSARY

Note: The current date is the 25th of Savon in the 54th year of the 23rd epoch.

Acarite: A bright blue crystal, also called the soul crystal. Prized for its blue color, which many nations see as sacred.

Afterblue (The afterblue, the blue hours, blue sun): The atmosphere of Territhmina is clear and thin enough that when the sun reaches the highest point in the sky the sun turns a blue color. For the Sagean faith this time is spent in worship. Afterblue refers to the moment the sun leaves the apex of the sky and the color of the sun returns to normal. The thin atmosphere contributes to a high volume of water vapor in the air. More rain and colder temperatures.

Age of Eckwyn (ek-win): The time before the Sagean Empire, spanning the 2nd to the 6th epoch, when the people of Territhmina were unified. See also **Ancients**

Alchemist's Codex, the: Written by Xand Zosimus. It is the oldest and most extensive book on alchemy ever found.

Ammadon: The name for the Tregorean Province

Amadazumi (ah-ma-daz-ew-me): The name of the God of the northern region, near the Gray Sea.

Amatori Market: The great market in Ravenvyre. The market established a wider notoriety because of the large contingent of crafters, tinkers and alchemists found in Ravenvyre, who sell their gadgets and potions there.

Amber Coins: The common currency of the world is stamped amber coins. The amber has an odd bluish tint from pyrite inclusions. Each coin is marked with a symbol denoting the location of its origin.

Anamnesis Vase, the (aka the Eyes of Deja Maru): An ancient vase, with eyes at the top. The vase can extract memories in the form of liquid that pools inside the vase into cubes.

Ancients, the: The common term for the forgotten Age of Eckwyn. A time lost to history. All that is known is that the civilization that existed before the Sagean Empire was advanced and divided. See also **Eckwyn Age.**

Anthracite: A black stone used in fires to ward off the beasts. It burns blue.

Artificer: A machine maker of small lifelike devices, such as mechanical butterflies, bats, spiders and owls.

Ascendency Tower: The main government seat and headquarters for the Coalition of Nations and the Councils Court.

Atlas tablet: A Soft crystal used in the Whisper Chains Melodicure Machine that empowers the machine. An ancient relic believed to possess the ability to find anyone in the world.

Band of the Black Sails: A crime syndicate that mostly operates out of Aquom. They plunder and pirate the Mainsolis Sea and the Zulu Sea.

Band of Redeemers aka the Renegades of Tovillore: A small force of people from the west of Tovillore banded together to protect the country and fight the Scree and the beasts and the Lionized, in order to free the country.

Bards of Renown: Poe Lamdryn, Marcus Shayval, and Antara Ronvia. The three authors are the most well known throughout the world. Creators of the oldests tales, plays and poetry in the world. Including the Lore Tales of Caleb Reaver and the Gaurdianof the Beyond, The Tin City of Telatheior, The Queen Of Ravens; the tales of Avari Nova, and the Radmana Crown. And famous plays, Echo of Silence, *The Twilight of Nevermore*

Barium star-powder: A black powder used for fireworks and explosives.

Barrel Mosaic Theatre: A large round theatre in Midway, with arch filled columns wrapping around the entire structure, and colored glass in alternating openings.

Bogdrin: A swamp creature with a tentacled face. They are a rare creature known to exist in the blood marshes off the western coast of Nahadon. They have been seen as far north as the swamps of Aquom.

Bonelark: A large, featherless flying beast. Fully grown they can reach the size of an adult human. Though rare, these creatures eat human flesh and bone. They first appeared during the Great War and are one of the beasts controlled by the Sagean Emperor. Not much is known about their physiology, but it is believed they don't hunt in numbers and stay close to their nests.

Bonemen, The (The Bloodless, the Bone Army): The Sagean's personal army. The bonemen or also known as the bloodless or the bone army. They derived their name as a representation of last servitude beyond death. For even bones remain after the blood is gone and the flesh has decayed.

Branch Spider: Large poisonous spider with thick brown hair. Typically, found in the forests throughout Tovillore, non-deadly to humans:

Cadowa: A slender boat with a very tall single sail. Used predominantly in Aquam to navigate the shallow and thin canals and waterways.

Calendar Year: The Territhmina year is 396 days long and divided into 12 months. Summer (Jovost, Savon, Shadal), Fall (Deluarch, Harven, Faden), Winter (Emberheart, Hazune, Souludal), Spring (Anander, Thawrich, Reesee). The New Year begins on the first day of summer and is the longest day of the year.

Capacitor gems: Any stone or crystal capable of energy.

Carriage Houses (Circus Caravan): Large moving houses, using a combination of steam power and pull horses. The wood housing structures are built on long wagon flatbeds and coming in a variety of shapes and sizes. Typically, with small sleeping compartments and a main sitting room. Various window sizes are all around the house, with exteriors of wood trim and framing.

Cloaked Knife: An elite group of mercenaries trained at the Citadel. This special military unit grew from the remnants of the Ultrarians.

Cloudparter: Enormous metal airships that transport people and supplies across the mountains and throughout Tovillore.

Confidence chairs: Attendees at the council's court in support of the ambassador who called them there.

Craftcore, The: The center for scientific development in Adalon.

Craftsmith: A crafter of objects not associated with a blacksmith.

Crime Syndicates: There are six known crime syndicates around the world. Most of them originated after the fall of the Sagean Empire. They are: The Deviants Core, The Supremacists, The Guard, The

Shield, The Reckers, The Broken Flame, The Devisors and **The Band of the Black Sails**.

Crystals, Jewels & Gems: Crystals are categorized into five groups based on their use: Energy stones, Power stones, Protection stones, Healing stones and Lore stones. Lore stones are rare or considered myth in some cases.

Energy Stones:
Quantum Stone: a capacitor gem that recharges continually until the stone's integrity eventually degrades, (Extremely Rare).
Caliber stones: orb stones used as lights by luminaries, (Extremely Rare).
Joulestone: crystals that can hold electrical charges. Fragments are used throughout the world to power small gadgets, guns, (Common).

Power Stones:
Turquoise: strength and stamina.
Blue acarite: Spirit, energy and clarity.
Ruby: added skill and movement and agility.
Topaz: inspiration.
Emerald: luck and reflexes.

Protection Stones:
Obsidian: protection and clarity of mind.
Blood stone: protection and cleansing.

Healing Stones:
Jade: healing and wisdom.
Clear Quartz: healing and memory.
Rose Quartz (love stone or heart stone): love bond and blood cleansing.
Amethyst: calms the spirit, dispels anger and fear, grief and stress.
Sun Stone: healing of wounds and internal aliments.
Bismuth crystal: stomach aches and headaches.

Lore Stones: Considered myth and legend.
The Elder Stone: ultimate protection stone and stone of wisdom.
The Dream stone: provides a connection to dreams.

Mistinite Crystal: crystal prisms with a glittering milk like luster, reveals hidden realms.

Gemstar Stone: asteroid fragment used to power the wave gates.

Corridon: A system of canals inside the Tregorean Province, many running inside the mountains. The three main canals are called: the Lagrin, the Loren, and the Veerin.

Court of Dragons: The counsel of acolytes in service to the Sagean Lord. Typically, an order consisting of Seven members as the emperor's counsel.

Daraku (dare-ah-kew): The dark lord's son.

Darkhawks: Elite group of fighters located to the New World.

Dawning gale: A mysterious songbird with camouflaging feathers. The bird is known to be heard singing in the Mountains at dawn, but because of its spectral feathers it is rarely ever seen. It's considered by many as a bad omen to see a Dawning Gale.

Day of Light: The New Year begins on the first day of summer, and the longest day of the year. It is the most celebrated holy day in the Empire.

Dire, the: A small grouping of islands in the Brovic Ocean, seven leagues off the Coast of Rodaire, beyond which no one dares travel. It marks a point of no return in the Brovic Ocean. All who have sailed beyond it have died or never returned.

Dragon Ring: A ring used by Luminaries to train and protect apprentices

Dragon's Well: A large underground structure on the island of Denmee used by the Court of Dragons. Housing meeting room, study chambers and a Library. The Well has an expansive open circular center full of arching openings where the winding stone steps descend from the surface.

Dreamer's smoke: An alchemist's dry potion that produces a cloud of white mist and renders all who inhale it asleep.

Drizar: Large reptiles that live in the deadlands.

Drooping pine bark: A common tree in Tovillore, its bark is used in fires and wards off the Sagean's beasts. It burns blue.

Dust Room: A sacred room inside the Tregorean Palace containing a magical dust that is attracted to the spirit of things; blood, objects, substances, and people.

Efferial-rock salt: Alchemists salt, used in healing spells and potions

Egregore mind: An ability of the One people of Wanvilaska to share each other's thoughts.

Elegan Language: An ancient undecipherable language of the Eckwyn Age. Its use predates the Territhian language instituted by the Sagean Empire.

Elum Blade: A sacred sword of the Shadowyn. With a short thin blade, it is holstered upside down and is only 2 and half feet long, including the long hilt. The technique and material used to make the blade are unknown.

Encumbrance, the: People's term for the Coalition of Nations. Referring to both the corruption and game of politics.

Emberbroth: A spicy burning alcoholic drink, served both hot and cold.

Eruptor: A power charged rifle, that fires electrical bolts. It is nearly three times stronger than a pulsator.

Firespark: A thick red liquid, an alchemist's potion created during the Great War. It explodes in a burst of fire once in contact with air.

Furies: A term used by alchemists to describe the known and unknown forces of nature.

Gas discharge lamps: Sealed airless glass tubes, with a local capacitor, producing an electrical current that charges a chemical inside, producing light. Oxygen is white, sodium vapor is bright yellow, or orange and krypton is blueish white or green when low.

Genesis Chamber: The main chamber inside the Temple of Ama where the Sintering Fountain resides.

Goreadoom Ant: Giant yellow stripped ants that burrow in the Jungles of Nahadon at the base of trees. Their bit is known to be so painful their victims pass out.

Great War, the: The Great War spanned for 990 days. It began on the 1st of Emberheart in the 15th year of the 23rd epoch and ended on the 1st of Jovost year 18 of the 23rd epoch.

Greencoats: The organized policing force of protectors and law enforcement throughout the world. Also known as peacekeepers.

Green Leopard: A fierce predator found in the Jungles of Nahadon that hunts by body heat and breath, It lives in trees and hunts at night.

Guardian amulets: The amulets said to be constructed by the ancient Luminaries to protect the world. The number of amulets made, and their individual powers are unknown.

Guardians of Illumination, the: A book written by Orin Ioka. It is the oldest account of the Luminaries in existence.

Hammer blast rifle: A powder ignited projectile gun for long range accuracy. Discontinued manufacture and use following the Great War and the invention of charged ammunition.

Hellfiend: A mutation of the bear family. This beast is very rare, seen only once during the Great War. Tracks have been found in both the Sun Mountains and the Soaring Mountains.

Horse types:

Cold blooded horse: a larger horse used to pull carts. These horses are harder to scare and used by military forces.
Hot blooded horse: a fast and slim horse used for speed. They are known to scare easily.
Light horse: a racing breed
Warm blood: a mix of cold and hot blooded horses. They are athletic and strong and the most commonly used for travel.
Nyrogen: a rare breed of horse from the southern regions of Rodaire. They are temperamental, but considered the fastest horse in the world.

Illumination surge: The moment a luminary's powers are truly born inside them. It is the point when the luminary's ability to store energy that they've unconsciously gathered is released. This may occur at any time, but the later in life it takes to occur, the stronger and deeper the luminaries well for energy will be.

Imperial Road: A white stone road arrayed throughout Tovillore, connecting the major cities. The stone road has four grooved tracks to allow wagon wheels to stay in position. Most major settlements and cities are along the track. Also known as the stone track.

The Jaws: The road between the Howling Forest and the Leaving Forrest. Both known to be home to wolveracks and Bonelarks.

Joulestone: *See crystals.*

Joybird: A performer in a showman's traveling circus.

Kihan: What the Tregoreans call themselves.

Lark of the Dead: The act of dueling or gunfighting between two people.

Legion of Light: A group of zealots and believers in the teachings of the Sagean faith. Disbanded after the Great War and the fall of the Sagean Empire.

Linage Book: A book on the Accounts of Talents of Sagean Luminaries.

Lionized, the: Contemporary zealots of the Sagean faith. A radical organization rising up with fall of the Coalition and the appointment of the Prime Commander. They long for the return of a Sagean Emperor.

Longneck Cawacons: A large herbivore with towering necks and wide base bodies that are low to the ground. A rare but gentle animal often seen in the circus menagerie.

Luminaries: A special race of humans with the ability to sense, control, and manipulate energy. This process is referred to as binding. The flows of energies they sense are referred to as the tempests. Once, they were common and collectively ruled the world under separate factions. The separate factions were divided based on their world views, and beliefs. Each faction — its own religion. For reasons lost to history, the Sagean faction took control in the 6th epoch. Most of the other factions were killed or died off. During the reign of the Sagean Empire, their own numbers of luminaries also dwindled.

Luminance Squad: A squad appointed by the Prime Commander to hunt down and capture Qudin Lightweaver.

Magnetometer: A device that measures magnetism—the direction, strength, or relative change of a magnetic field at a particular location.

Magnotype: A typewriter machine with intricate gears and an ink well. It uses magnetic displacements of a needles and gears they are used to communicate messages across the world.

Manus Zabel: The master showman, illusionist and show runner for the *Show of the Magnificent.* A traveling circus throughout the Mainland of Tovillore and Rodaire that Ellaria traveled with as a teenager.

Melodicure machine: A gem powered machine of unknown origin and construction, in use by the Whisper Chain. It aids the Chain in finding people throughout the world.

Menodarians: A race of beings that once existed mostly in Merinde. They are known for their slender, tall forms and their intellect. They have flat faces and were known to be closely guarded and distrustful of other races.

Meiyoma blade: The common sword in Rodaire. Characterized by its long gentle arching blade with two hand length handles. Handles range from plain wood to decorated jade. The hilt is commonly in the shape of a crescent moon.

Miner's Collective: The headquarters for the Moonstalkers, the Bounty Hunters Guild in Amera.

Mirthless: A tall monstrous humanoid being with a face structure that looks like exposed bone. And thin skin pulled tight over muscles that the creature looks almost bloodless.

Monarch trees: Extremely large trees that grew to incredible heights. Only known grove exists on the island of Hazon.

Moonstalkers: A guild of organized bounty hunters.

Moonstone dust: An alchemist's dry potion. A fine powder that protects against evil spirits.

Moorlon: The high plateaus and farming plateaus of the Tregoreans.

Mudfoot: A slang term or derogatory reference to river folk who live along the banks of the Uhanni River. They are known to attack or rob small ships and vessels.

Mystcat: A special breed of cat that is unusually attracted to the gifted. They search out and bond to luminaries and other gifted beings. They are quizzical, sneaky, and very loyal. They love heights and their fur is usually white and gray, all gray, or black. With black being the most rare. Their eyes can be green, blue & yellow and they produce a low harmonic purr. They also bend their ears in patterns of anthropomorphic communication. Additional powers remain unknown.

Ovardyn (O-var-din): The lord of darkness and ruler of The Nothing and the realm of Evil Spirits.

Nil Wasp: Giant poisonous wasps that nest in the Jungles of Nahadon

Nothing, the: The domain of Evil Spirits. It is the realm where the demon Ovardyn dwells.

Nowarin Basilisk: Large sand snakes in the Nowarin dessert. They can grow to be the size of whales, but are mostly unseen, as the desserts are uninhabited.

Paravin Schools: Small schools of higher learning in some of the cities. An alternative to the larger Guild run universities. With the aim to teach trade crafts.

Peace King: The Free Cities of The New World were instrumental in the Resistance's success in the Great War. Lead by Arno Danehin, the fourteen-year-old son of Bara Danehin who was killed in the battle of Axern. Arno Danehin railed the troops to win the battle and for the rest of the war assumed the leadership of the armies of the New World. After the war, he was named the Peace King of the Free New World.

Phifer cloth: A cloth of scientifically engineered material that is microscopically fused metal with alchemic symbols sometimes engraved into the weaving. It is impact resistant, highly conductive and so light of weight that it floats on water or even would fail to crush a dandelion. The lithium mesh coat is typically worn by soldiers. Gold colored or black, depending on the rank. Its nickel phosphorus alloy lattice acts as a thermal insulator, acoustic and vibration dampening.

Prolaten: A government official in Kotalla that is the voice of the people.

Protagen force: An eternal fury of bound elements more powerful than the opposite pulls of magnetic energy.

Pulsator: A handheld, charged gun or projectile weapon that fires charged tungsten rounds or bolts. It replaced the less powerful and inaccurate powder firing guns. They are notoriously expensive, and the many components are sought after for various modifications and customizations.

Quandinium: A metal found in abundance across the world. It is most often used in building construction for its strength and lack of conductivity. Other characteristics include: corrosion resistant, a high melting point, ferromagnetic.

Quarter Day Festivals: There are four festivals at the quarter marks of the year. One in each season; Brighden (spring), Alustra (summer), Harven (fall), and Solstar (winter).

Ravenhawk: The nickname of war hero Ellaria Moonstone. A general of the Resistance in the Great War. The name was derived from her service as both a general and a spy during the war.

Raven's breath: An alchemist's potion, truth serum.

Ravinors: The most feared of all the Sagean's beasts. These rare monsters retreated mostly to the south swamps of Tovillore and into the jungles of Nahadon after the war. They are the most intelligent and dangerous of all the beasts. They are lizard like humanoids, walk on two legs and have long snouts with exposed sharp teeth. Sharp claws on their hands and short spiked tails. They are presumed to be reptilian but have many anthropomorphic traits and social behaviors.

Reckoner: A card game played in the major cities. The deck of cards is housed in an action turner that counts down the individual turn meter. Starting after the third turn the reckoning can appear on the turner — ending the game. Anywhere from 2 to 8 people can play, but rules vary. The cards have individual strengths and weaknesses, represented by figures and objects throughout Territhmina history. The object is to field the strongest set of cards to defeat your opponent. The game evolved from the Eckwyn

Age and was outlawed for eighteen hundred years until the Empire issued a new and revised deck of cards featuring Sagean Lords. As a way to quell the prominent families forming an uprising in the 19th epoch. A reprint of the original pre-Empire deck was made during the Great War, but an actual fully intact set of original cards has never been found.

Red Spear (aka The Red Dune): A massive rock spire of red clay in the Echo Canyons, used as a prison by the Sagean Empire. The prison was discovered during the Great War and shut down.

Rendered: Automaton beings or machine hunters built by the Sagean.

Religions of Territhmina:
The Sagelight Faith: The great One, The Light,
The Faith of the Fates: The Entwiner
The Great Creator Amazuie: Hazon
The Great Diviner: Harrinari

Rhuskero Bull: a large grey skinned bull with a single horn. The bull is famous in Adavan and was once used for sport.

Risen World, the: The realm of souls ascended to a plane of existence of pure energy. Where they reside in peace and harmony until they are called upon for a new life.

Rune Book of the Sintering Fountain aka The Dragons Awakening: An ancient book on the sintering fountain and the Scepter used to activate the machine.

Sagean (Saw-Gee-in): The luminary leader of the Sagean faith and Emperor. According to believers of the faith, the Sagean is the living manifestation of the God of Light. The Sagean Empire ruled the world uncontested from the 6th epoch until the 23rd epoch, when the empire was overthrown during the Great War. The last Sagean Emperor, Mayock Kovall, the ninth line of the Sagean progression was defeated by Qudin Lightweaver in the battle of Dragon Spine. The Sagean luminaries can control energy, and were known to manipulate the minds of others, control animals, and alter their appearance.

Sagean's Consortium, the: The name for the remaining army that continued to wage war for the Emperor after the Sagean's death at the Battle of Dragon's Spine. The Consortium waged war and continued to cause conflicts until they were defeated, almost three years later, at the Black Spire of the Citadel.

Sagean Testament: A book guarded by the Sagean ruler passed down to each in line. Its contents are unknown to anyone outside of the lineage of Sageans and their closest acolytes.

Sagelight, the: Can refer to the Sagean faith or the sacred religious text itself.

Sagemitter gauntlet: A glove. It is light as a feather, and only partially covers the fingers. Made of phifer cloth, it allows a luminary who wears it to easily harness and form the energy they sense and bind it into solidified objects.

Scepter of Corinsure: A large black scepter with a dragon wrapping around the staff and engraved alchemist's sigils. The top houses a brilliant blue gem. Named after the 2nd Sagean Empress.

Scholar's Guild, the: An organization entrusted with control over education, curation of history, all publications and select institutes of higher knowledge. Including supervision over alchemists, machine patents, inventions, civil planning and architecture.

Scree: People who were abducted by the Sagean and his agents and whose soul were taken for the Soul Gem to power the Sintering Fountain. There are many names for people suffering from this affliction throughout the Mainland.

Shadow dust: A fine powder that blooms into a cloud of black mist. Created by alchemists during the Great War.

The Shadow Field: A forbidden are of the jungle south of the Tregorean Province beyond the Wall of Nagari.

Shadowyn, the: A small province hidden in the mountains. They train a group of elite warriors for protection from the outside world. Known for their stealth and ability with swords.

Shodders: A common term for cheats, cheaters, grifters, halfwits and anyone who tries to swindle someone with faulty goods, false claims or bad products.

Silver six gun: An old powder fired handgun. The predecessor to the pulsator. These, like all powder powered guns, were discontinued after the Great War.

Sintering: The pressing, molding or binding of elements together.

Sintering Fountain: An ancient machine found in the Temple of Ama. The machine rests inside the Genesis Chamber. Powered by a large crystal of trapped human souls, the fountain is said to have been created to transform humans into Luminaries.

Spotted Shadow Cat: A large feline native to Harrnika, the wasteland savanna of The New World. It is usually dark red fir and spotted. They are slim and extremely fast.

Soul Gem or Soul Crystal: A large crystal ball used to contain deposited souls. Protected by metal bands.

Stonebank, the: The affluent section of the city of Aquom.

Sualden: The name for the heart of the Tregorean Province. A massive city carved into the mountains facing Lake Azeerall.

Tazrus Shroud: During the luminary wars, the ancient luminary Tazrus produced a spell so powerful it concealed the great advancements of the Eckwyn Age from all who lived. Including the wave gates.

Tempest Stone: An ancient artifact said to contain the collective knowledge of the ancients.

Temple of Ama: Also called the Temple of Souls, the ancient structure is a complex of jagged spires and ruins in the jungles south of the Tregorean Province in a forbidden are known as the Shadow Field. The towering center spire contains the main temple and the Genesis chamber.

Territh: The name for the land or below the surface of the ground. Interchangeable with soil, dirt or ground.

Territhamy: Scientific study of the land.

Territhian language: The common language throughout Territhmina. Instituted by the Sagean Empire in the 9th epoch. It is the universal language.

Territhmina: The name of the world. The origins of the name predate the Age of Eckwyn.

Territh Driver: Pyramid constructed ground hammer or pile driver used to excavate the ground.

Tinkersmith: A skilled technician with small machine parts, gears, gadgets and workings.

Trancing sand or Ghost sand: Alchemist powder used in sigil spells.

The Traveling Show of Wonders: The current traveling circus of the Mainland of Tovillore and Rodaire, run by Archibald Zabel. It Includes a Menagerie tent for animals and attractions, a Mystics tents for magic shows and elixirs, and fortune tellers, and seance rituals, The Joybirds tent contains the spirits bar and a stage for live local acts, & the Grand Spectacles tent for jugglers, acrobats and large stage shows.

Tregoreans: A race of beings who are known to live in the mountains and jungles of Nahadon, a providence they have lived in untouched throughout the Sagean Empire. They are recognized by their pointed ears and pristine facial appearances. They have been reported to commonly wear tight clothing that camouflages into the surrounding forests and jungles. Very little is known about them, as they do not let outsiders in and are very protective of their lands. It is believed that they live twice the length of time of humans.

Trinity Guard: An ancient order of three bonded specially empowered people to protect the world; consisting of a Luminary, a Nimbus Warrior, and a Fusion Mage.

Torakuma: A mythical large mammal that once lived in the northern snow filled regions Sharing a classification origin of both felines and bears, the large tiger like animal, has thick white fir with black stripes at its face. The females have twisted dark grey antlers that angle backward. Also called an Ice Panther or Tigerbear.

Tune of the Redeamer: A famous song.

Tungsten Carbide: Metal used in military weapons due to its extremely high melting point.

Turquoise Flats: A cavernous expanse blanketed by a bright colored lichen. The lichen softens in the sun and hardens at night.

Ultrarians: An elite special forces unit established by Kovan Rainer, the war hero, near the end of the Great War. This force tracked and defeated the final remnants of the Sagean supporters called the Consortium.

Underdeath: A slang term meaning worse than death. Meaning something as horrible or revolting as a corpse.

United Coalition of Nations: The collective governing body of Territhmina. Established, following the Great War, a pact for peace, unity, law and order was signed by all the nations of the known world. While every nation signed the treaty, only a select number of ambassador seats were granted for inclusion on the Coalition Council based on population and land size. At the time the New World was given only one chair represented by their King.

Varium Crystal: A small, hollow, delicate crystalline glass jewel that can be filled with an alchemist's concoction, like firespark.

Vazey: Aloof or evasive.

Viper Lords: The five coastal cities of Nahadon are controlled by individual rulers.

Wall of Nagari: A ancient stone wall bordering the Shadow Field jungle.

Warbird: Small mechanical hummingbird used by the Sagean and his Court to send messages.

Wave Gate or Acuber magnetic wave gate: Ancient stone and metal gates, constructed with gemstone stars. They were once used by the luminaries to travel instantaneously around the world. Their locations are unknown. Texts suggest they utilize special matter to warp space, allowing objects to pass at speeds faster than light on a gravitational wave to another gate through a unique magnetic connection.

Wavelifers: Term used to describe people who make their living sailing the Anamic Ocean or Zulu Sea.

Way of the Wind: The Rodairean style of sword fighting.

The Western Wall: A Tregorean battlement wall that snakes along the eastern slope of the Shade Mountains in Nahadon, overlooking the Dry Coast. The Wall extends eight hundred leagues from north to south and protects the Tregorean Lands from invaders from the West.

Winddrifter: A smaller airship typically built from a modified sailboat. It uses a steam powered engine and a large air balloon along with large sails to navigate the skies. Sizes, styles and colors vary.

Whisper Chain, the: An organization for the delivery of secret messages, started during the Great War as a secret courier service. They have since expanded their organization to every major city. Their offices are often indistinguishable and hard to locate. Access to the organization and their services is exclusive to its members.

Wolveracks: A beast from the great war once controlled by the Sagean. They are a solitary animal with the size and features of a very large wolf. They have pointed ears and long fang-like teeth. Their upper mane is very full and wiry, but their hind legs are muscular and short-haired. They have a tough hide and strong tails that grow up to five feet in length. Their eyes can glow yellow when they are aggressive. They don't live in packs, but sometimes hunt in them. Considered very dangerous and aggressive, they become ravenous by the smell of blood.

Wraith or The Night Wraith: A mystical spirit believed to be the hand of death and the messenger and guide to the Nothing.

Wrythen, the: A dark spirit entity that appeared to Qudin on the Dragon's Spine just before he vanquished the Sagean Lord. It seems to be drawn to luminary powers.

Xand Zosmos: The author of the greatest book of alchemy that the Scholar's Guild owns. It surfaced sometime before the Great War.

Zacaren language: A thick dialect spoken throughout Nahadon, but mostly in Zawarin. The language includes a lot of words considered non-territhian.

Zenoch: A race of beings in the northern mountains of the New World. They are recognized by their blue skin. They are very secretive and considered extremely dangerous. The government of the New

World has not tried to expand into their lands. Instead choosing to section off various points as border stops to prevent people from wondering too far.

Zenithal: The summer season is commonly referred to as the zenithal season. In reference to the sun.

About the Author

Steven Rudy is an emerging author of Fantasy and Science Fiction. He studied architecture and creative writing at the University of Colorado at Boulder. Currently he lives with his wife and three children in Colorado and works as an architectural designer.

This is Steven's second book.

You can find him at https://stevenrudybooks.com/
or on social media...

facebook.com/EpicFantasySeries

twitter.com/MysticPeddler

instagram.com/stevenrudyauthor

CPSIA information can be obtained
at www.ICGtesting.com
Printed in the USA
LVHW030836140122
707968LV00005B/24

9 781737 065234